COMPUNCTION

EHMBEE WAY

For information about this title or to order other books and/or electronic media, contact the author:

Ehmbee Way
www.ehmbeeway.com
ehmbeeway@gmail.com

ISBN Paperback: 979-8-9872721-8-3
ISBN eBook: 979-8-9872721-9-0

Names: Ehmbee Way, author.
Title: Compunction / Ehmbee Way.
Description: [Canton, Ohio] : Ehmbee Way, [2023]
Identifiers: ISBN: 979-8-9872721-8-3 (Print) | 979-8-9872721-9-0 (eBook)
Subjects: LCSH: Identity (Psychology)--Fiction. | Neurasthenia--Fiction. | Perception--Fiction. | Reality--Fiction. | Spirits--Fiction. | Enemies--Fiction. | Suicide--Fiction. | Mental health-- Fiction. | Metaphysics--Fiction. | Curiosities and wonders--Fiction. | Dreams--Fiction. | Philosophy of mind--Fiction. | Stream of consciousness fiction. | LCGFT: Psychological fiction. | Experimental fiction.
Classification: LCC: PS3605.H534 C66 2023 | DDC: 813/.6--dc23

Cover and Interior Design: Creative Publishing Book Design
Cover Art: Bogdan Maksimovic

COMPUNCTION

For those who are lost

"I put my heart and soul into my work and have lost my mind in the process."
—Vincent Van Gogh

PART I

CHAPTER ONE

As I abruptly slid back into what should have been a more manageable state of consciousness, I found that the first thoughts stampeding into my head were centered, in no small part, on my immediate surroundings. I needn't guess where I was nor strain to remember the circumstances that led to me lying here either. Though I could scarcely believe it, I had to admit then and there that awakening here, inside of my bathtub, had finally become as depressingly commonplace as the sore necks, bruised legs and interminable exhaustion that so often accompanied my daily resurgence.

Hoping to delay that resurgence as much as possible, I fought against the compulsion to open my eyes and saturate them with more evidence of a reality I could not bear. Though I wished otherwise, I knew that life would not permit me to remain in that groggy, transitional state—where my mind would fastidiously flush away all the alluring components of my dreams before resetting itself for the burgeoning day. The cosmos was beckoning me away from that fleeting, enigmatic space between dreams and the world that accepts us once we abandon them and so I tried, to no avail, to propel my consciousness back whence it had come.

Just then, my bruised, jean-covered legs forgot their confinement and jutted up against the unforgiving porcelain surrounding them. Annoyed, I shifted my position, but not too much—not enough to expedite the process of wholly waking from my slumber. I attempted to convince myself that small, low-effort movements might be enough to get me back to sleep but I knew it was futile.

It was as if my skull was full of water that was only microseconds away from boiling. I was, therefore, not surprised, or even particularly grateful, when the neurological dominos, which invariably lead to human sentience, began to fall within that heated skull of mine. Unable to halt, or even contain, that biological process, I was forced to submit to it and, in doing so, I reluctantly allowed my mind to spill out into the universe.

As my consciousness grew more powerful and I inadvertently transferred my thoughts toward the chaos surrounding my life, I adjusted myself once more and, in doing so, felt the gun greet my foot through my black, high-top shoe. I can still vividly remember the first time I brought the weapon in there with me…

It was six months ago, on the night of my last run-in with the police. At that point, I had already taken to ingesting pharmaceutical-grade sleep aids on a nightly basis. I did so in spite of a growing suspicion that I was developing an addiction to them, which was curious because, if anything, these pills actually exacerbated my fatigue.

I assert as much because, while the medication successfully put my physical body to rest, it elicited quite the opposite effect on my unconscious self—inspiring flurries of subconscious manifestations that did little to quell my mental exhaustion. More often than not, when under the influence of these particular pills, I would wander the walls of my trailer, in a fugue-like trance, wherein logic itself seemed to abandon me. Still, I knew no way of subsisting without those drugs so, on that night six months ago—just like any other night—I took my medication, hoping it would grant me the sleep I so desperately wanted.

Shortly after swallowing one of those unusually large pills, I crawled onto my mattress, got under the sheets and waited. Sleep, however, continued to elude me. My impromptu encounter with the authorities several hours earlier had electrified my mind, making sleep impossible. After hours of failing to attain that calm, elusive and somewhat dormant state of mind that always precedes any worthwhile sleep, I rose from my bed, grabbed a handful of additional pills and put myself well beyond the recommended dosage.

It was still difficult to get to sleep that night but, eventually, with the aid of my medicine, I must have been able to do so because, as I recall, I awoke, from a sleep-like daze, to a soft but persistent clicking sound that seemed to be emanating from the trailer's only bathroom. The bathroom was, by way of a white doorframe, attached to my bedroom so it wasn't uncommon for drippy faucets or leaky pipes to disturb me from time to time. This particular noise, however, seemed much more deliberate and far less random than any faucet or pipe. I tried to ignore it at first—hoping it would either subside or that my desire for sleep would overcome it—but, when I could take it no more, I sat up in my bed to investigate.

The noise ceased as soon as I opened my eyes, making it difficult for me to find its point of origin. At first, my ocular scan produced nothing out of the ordinary: my sleeping dog across the room (who seemed oblivious to any foreign sounds), some rickety, old furniture and several unopened moving boxes—all of which had been caked with a thin layer of dust. It did little to obscure the "James Singer – Bedroom" labels I'd written on the tops of them though. Credit for that went to the natural darkness surrounding me. I basked in it for a moment but I heard no more clicking—just the soft breathing of Blue, my bullmastiff companion.

Satisfied then that the auditory intrusion had abated, I lay back down, on my back, and closed my eyes. Again, I heard that soft clicking but this time it was coming from the floor at the foot of the bed. Immediately (and with quite a bit more concern this time), I shot back up into a seated position and gazed out into the darkness. Once more, the noise died off as soon as I arose.

Moving in the same way a frightened child might, I crawled forward, on my hands and knees, to the foot of the bed, and peered over the edge. From my vantage point, I found only dirty carpeting and two rectangular moving boxes—the larger of which stood about three feet high. With a growing distrust, I stared at them both and began to wonder if my mind was playing tricks on me again.

That's when a pure black arm exploded out of the larger moving box and reached for me! Instinct alone caused me to recoil but, within an instant of doing so, the creature inside the box had somehow catapulted itself into the air and, before I could react, it landed on top of me, forcing my back against the mattress. If I hadn't been so utterly terrified at that moment, I would have probably marveled at its strange form.

It had a head, a torso and two fully functional arms but it possessed neither legs, nor any discernible facial features whatsoever. It was, in truth, more of a silhouette of a man—the blackest black I have ever seen. It was so black, in fact, that its entire body was clearly visible ("pronounced" even), against the already light-starved room.

From what I could tell, it achieved this darkened state not from the color of its skin but from the sticky, black smoke that was billowing out of its body and clinging to me like a displaced spider web. Every individual pore on the creature's body oozed the strange substance, without any indication of ever drying up. Worse yet: it stunk of dead animal and ethanol, which stung not only my nose but my eyes as well.

I tried to scream but, with inhuman speed, its left hand shot forward and closed in around my neck, cutting off any chance for sound to escape. I've had an adversary's hand around my throat before but this was different. In this encounter, the legless wraith seemed more interested with keeping me still than he did with actually choking me. The fact that he had no lower half didn't impede on his ability to achieve this goal either. His strength was otherworldly and it felt as though not one but several men were holding me down.

He was determined to keep me on my back but I resisted nonetheless. I grasped his undulating, gaseous arm with both hands and began to try and peel his grip away from my neck but his hand didn't budge an inch. What's more: his unwavering body felt like four hundred pounds of bricks, stacked on top of my chest.

As I struggled in vain to wriggle free, he then brought his right hand close to my face and extended his pointer finger so that it was hovering inches from my sweat-drenched forehead. For a moment, I thought he had assumed this pose to mock me—to point at his helpless victim in a humiliating manner—but, as it turns out, the creature's intentions were far worse.

Before I could react, he plunged his finger directly into the center of my forehead and began slowly pushing down, through my skin, and into my very skull! Once the initial shock of my predicament had dissipated, I quickly released my left hand from around his wrist and began to try and pry away the black, evil finger that was drilling into my head. My efforts, however (desperate as they were), did little to dissuade the wretched phantasm and so he continued driving his finger into me with very little resistance.

My skull felt like it was ready to blow apart, into hundreds of fragmented pieces, but the devil continued to drill further and further into my head. As he did so, I could hear the unmistakable crunching of bone in my ear canals. It sounded like the oral surgeon who (several years prior) had been gripping, ripping and cutting wisdom teeth out of my head, with the aid of some sweet-smelling gas that had failed to put me completely under. I didn't have much time to ponder that experience, though, because it was at this point that the creature began tightening his grip around my neck.

As I wildly gasped for air I couldn't find, I noticed something slithering underneath my attacker's smoky, hollow face. Underneath the billowing surface of the wraith's expressionless visage, it appeared as though an abnormally large slug was moving in such a way that would suggest it was an entirely separate, parasitic entity, living inside of the ghastly wraith. Unable to break free, I was forced to watch as it made its way from the wraith's face, down his neck and toward his outstretched arm. Somehow I knew that this slug-like abomination was en route for my head. That thought caused my adrenaline to surge but even still, it wasn't enough for me to shake free.

Within a few seconds, the insect-like organism underneath the black smoke of its host found its way into my attacker's hand, where it continued on, toward his extended finger. After it reached the tip of his finger, it disappeared from view and began burrowing into my own head. I could feel it thrashing and wriggling about in there and that, along with my oxygen-deficient lungs, caused the room to start to spin. I was growing faint and I was close to surrendering my life to the pair of extra-dimensional intruders until I suddenly remembered my gun.

In the dresser, next to my bed, was a .357 Magnum. The funny thing is: I didn't have to actually grab hold of the weapon for the homicidal apparition to disappear, right before my eyes. He did that the moment I simply reached out to acquire the weapon. My dog noticed none of this and continued lightly snoring, in the corner of the room.

With the firearm in hand, I waved it madly about the room before realizing the object into which I had poured my hope was empty. After a few more panicked seconds, I called out to Blue but he, in some inexplicable way, didn't seem to hear me. With the gun still raised, I then ran my hand over my forehead, only to find it was smooth—a bit wet, to be sure, but smooth. Both terrified and equally perplexed, I leapt out of bed and began frantically searching my nightstand for ammunition.

In the dark, as my eyes scanned the entirety of the room as though my life depended on it, I searched with my hands. In my haste, I knocked over my alarm clock and even my lamp but I found nothing. Eventually, it dawned on me that the bullets I sought were likely inside one of the unopened moving boxes scattered about my trailer. I had packed the ammunition separately from the sidearm for safety reasons.

Recklessly, I dashed toward the smaller, undisturbed box, tore it open and began searching for the six elusive armor-piercing rounds. Tossing the scattered contents about, inside of the box, didn't prove helpful so, with great trepidation, I looked inside of the larger box, where my attacker had recently been hiding. It too proved useless so I cursed my luck and abandoned any hope I had of finding what I sought in the stifling darkness.

I then tried to shake Blue awake but, to my disgruntlement, the dog proved completely unresponsive to all of my well-intentioned prodding. He just continued to lightly snore, as though he had been drugged. He was not, however, exhibiting any signs of distress, which was at least somewhat comforting—enough so that I was able to readjust my focus, without any accompanying guilt.

With my heart both racing and sinking at the same time, I changed tactics and cautiously slipped a pair of tattered jeans over my boxer shorts and then clumsily forced my feet into a pair of black sneakers, at the side of the bed—looking over my shoulder as I did so—afraid I might have to run, should this horrific incarnation make itself known once more. I did all of this while maintaining a death grip on the empty pistol. In its current form, the weapon was more of an inert memento—a physical keepsake from a patriarch long since buried—but, as a blunt object, it could still crack a man's skull. I wondered: could it also repel a wraith?

I didn't see its "form" but, at this juncture, the entire bedroom began to fill with black—true black. It started to gather at the ceiling and then began descending downward. It came out of the wall, behind Blue, and enveloped him without him protesting as much as a whimper. I ran out into the hallway but it was there too; it was closing in on me.

Only the bathroom, between my bedroom and the end of the hallway, for some reason, was immune to this converging darkness. Desperate and terrified, I retreated inside and locked the two doors, which led either to the hallway or into the master bedroom. Despite the powerful sleep agent still working to overpower my system, I alertly cowered in the tub, waiting, in silence, for hours. Eventually, though, both the pills and the emotional toll I had endured caught up with me and I lost consciousness.

***

When I awoke the next day, I exited the tub and checked my completely normal-looking forehead for scars that were conspicuously absent. As I did so, I could hear Blue scratching at the door, indicating he wanted to join me in whatever I was doing. Eventually, I left the mirror into which I had been staring and tended to my now fully-responsive dog. Next, I tore open all the remaining unopened boxes that, up until now, I'd been too lazy to unpack. The two labeled "James Singer – Kitchen" produced no ammunition and neither did any of the similarly labeled boxes in any of the other rooms of my dilapidated, single-wide trailer.

I concluded, then, that the ammunition I hoped would protect me had been lost in the move and I resolved to purchase more from the local gun range, the outdoor hunting store or anywhere else I could find the resource. Much to my dismay, however, my desire to acquire bullets came at a time when the world was experiencing a global pandemic and resources were scarce: toiletries, bread, even ammo—especially ammo.

After returning home empty-handed and feeling as hollow as my useless gun, I considered reporting the previous night's incident. Who on Earth would have believed me though? I wasn't sure, at that point, if I even believed myself. In all likelihood my psychiatrist probably already suspected that I was on the brink of psychosis. If he learned of this incident, I was sure he'd have no choice but to institutionalize me. With that in mind, I began to try and convince myself that I had experienced some sort of sleepwalking nightmare—even though I knew, deep down, that I hadn't.

The proof came that evening when the wraith appeared again—this time from a perched position, on the ceiling above my bed. His back, his hands and his newly-formed set of fully-functional legs were sticking to it and keeping him in place up there. When I opened my eyes and noticed him, he dropped down, on top of me, and used those legs to straddle me, while his left arm held me down by my throat once more.

This time, however, he lowered the side of his head—the part where his ear should have been—and positioned it just above the place where his pet slug had tunneled into my head. His distinctive odor was the same as the night before and I was gagging on it. He ignored my convulsions, though, and held himself still for several seconds, as if he was straining to hear something from underneath my forehead.

In his distracted state, I was able to get my fingers wrapped around the handle of my gun and, when I did, like last time, he disappeared. With a bit more urgency this time, I leapt out of bed and began trying to wake Blue. Somehow, I knew that yelling at him and shaking him wouldn't work but I attempted both actions regardless. That's when the darkness poured out of the wall behind him and completely absorbed him, just as it had done before.

I tried to run but it corralled me back into the bathroom just as it had done the previous night. Once I was there, with the doors locked, I heard that bipedal monstrosity howling and thrashing about my trailer. It sounded like an entire mob of derelict teenagers overturning furniture and slamming themselves against my walls.

I knew my empty sidearm wouldn't protect me should the demon find its way inside of my bathroom but I was still clutching it fiercely nonetheless. In desperation, I tried to dial Emergency Services on the phone I had swiped from my nightstand but the device wouldn't work and I was sure the creature was somehow behind its malfunctioning state.

After a few more minutes of unabashed wailing, accompanied by equally loud and malicious ransacking, I averted my eyes toward the floor and tried telling my trembling self that it would all be over soon. That's when I caught sight of the outfit lying between the toilet and the tub—the same one I had been wearing the night before, when the thing just beyond my door first attacked me. The black, high-top sneakers, slightly ripped, black, V-neck T-shirt and the pair of dark jeans, which had already begun to marginally wear through at the knee, were all there, where I must have carelessly discarded them.

Both this night and the one before it had been particularly hot, which I had tried to combat by sleeping in nothing but my boxer shorts. Unlike last night, however, when the phantasm appeared this time, it didn't leave me time to clothe myself before I escaped into the bathroom. I couldn't deny that my near-nakedness was making me feel even less secure and so, in the midst of the chaos outside my door, I made an effort to bolster my confidence by adorning myself with the outfit before me.

Once every piece was in place and I pulled that last shoelace into a bow, the trailer became eerily silent. I dared not open the door; I dared not even breathe, though I was grateful for the sudden silence. Just as I had done the night before, I waited there, in the bathtub, until my medicine overtook me and I finally fell asleep.

* * *

The next day, as before, Blue greeted me as though nothing unusual had happened. My home told a similar story, for there was no evidence of the carnage I heard from behind my shower curtain. The trailer was relatively clean, save for the individual messes of my own creation. I decided, at that moment, that, at least for now, I would resolve to keep these paranormal experiences to myself—at least until I had some understanding over what was happening to me.

When night returned once more, I abandoned my bed and took up residency inside the tub, in an effort to circumvent the wraith's murderous tantrums. I also made sure I was wearing that same outfit as well. Through trial and error, in the weeks that followed, I came to learn that the strange creature was apparently willing to give me free reign of my home so long as I committed all of my nighttime sleeping to the tub—clothed in that same outfit, which had, without my approval, become my unalterable, de facto sleepwear.

While admittedly strange at first, I eventually accepted the situation and even learned to find a peculiar sort of comfort within the familiarity of my garments. Every day, I would awaken, remove them, wash them and then put them back on, before eventually retreating to the bathroom in order to avoid the wrath of that malicious specter. It became such a habit that I would often awaken without any memory of even switching into them.

The gun was always inside the tub too. Sometimes it would be under my pillow; other times it'd be closer to my feet and sometimes I would find it hidden somewhere beneath me. There were instances where I'd even awaken to find it resting in my hand. On those days, I was glad the instrument was empty.

For the next six months, as summer gave way to fall and eventually winter, I was able to avoid that shadowy figure—in a corporeal sense, that is—but I could still feel his presence. I could feel the slug he left inside my head as well. I suspected the little blighter was somehow feeding off of my dreams and replacing them with the nihilistic musings of its master. Unable to deter it, it continued to nest inside of my brain and poison my thoughts.

In some sense or another, I could always feel the slug's master—almost as though it was watching me... ubiquitously stalking me, from a veiled but closely intertwined reality that was just beyond my comprehension. I tried not to dwell on it, though, for if I did, an inescapable feeling of dread would often overtake me. The fiend planted that dread deep inside my head, where it was festering and spreading throughout my essence, like a psychological plague.

Its now somewhat insidious presence, for whatever reason, always seemed more pronounced at night and a bit more muted during the day but, in some fashion, it was always there. I assert as much because, as the changing seasons grew darker, my mental condition continued to deteriorate to the point that my notion of reality had begun to fuse with what I used to be able to clearly define as my unconscious dreams.

The more often this coalescence occurred, the less confident my befuddled mind could recognize which dangers were real and imminent and which ones were merely perceived and spurious. Mentally, physically, spiritually... nearly every second of life was exhausting. I longed to dig that mollusk out of my head. I longed to get my life back but I had no idea how to do so. So I continued on, with my prescribed medications, despite the fact that they only made my situation slightly more bearable.

My psychiatrist had been helping me too. He knew of my insomnia, my paranoia and my depression but I had purposely omitted telling him about both the smaller creature in my head and the larger one who put it there. He knew I was keeping something from him, though, and he'd been trying to draw it out of me for some time. Oftentimes, he would try and compel me, in one way or another, to take an intrinsic accounting of myself, journal my findings and then present them to him so that we might discuss what I had written.

Much to his chagrin, however, I'd always resisted his wishes. I felt I had no choice, for I was afraid that if I opened up a metaphorical doorway through which he could truly see me, the tattered threads that held my soul together would quickly unravel. I'd personally seen what a lifetime in and out of mental institutions looked like and, as a result, I had always elected to keep the intricate particulars of my own condition private—from my doctor and from everyone else as well.

All of that was about to change though. I'd had enough of sleeping in the bathtub so, after six months of doing precisely that, I finally decided to acquiesce to my doctor and draft a note detailing everything I had experienced since the night that faceless evil first appeared to me. Despite having experienced his torture firsthand, however, I knew that others would never be able to accept my accounting of the situation; more specifically, I knew that once I admitted all of this to my psychiatrist, my life—what little of it I had left—would be over. Upon learning the true state of my mind, I couldn't imagine any scenario that didn't end with my imprisonment, into one of those foreboding, state-funded facilities.

I didn't care though. I couldn't take any more. So, after I stepped out of the tub and prepared Blue and myself for another day, I entered my drafty office, pushed aside some of the accumulated clutter, sat down on my squeaky, slightly-torn chair, opened a notebook and began preparing to outline a confession for my psychiatrist. Before I took to filling those blank pages with admissions of my compromised mental state, however, I titled the document "Doomsday," for I knew that when I read it to my doctor on Monday, my life would be over.

CHAPTER TWO
(Six Months Earlier)

It had been unusually arid on that fateful day six months ago—even for mid-June. For that reason, I had committed to barreling down the steamy Ohio interstate with no protective gear other than some fingerless gloves, a pair of black leather boots and my trusty three-quarter helmet. Under normal circumstances, I would have preferred to don a riding jacket as well—especially on the highway—but, with the oppressive temperature being what it was, I was willing to risk the forty-five-minute ride in a violently flapping T-shirt instead.

The wind breaking around my body had my shirt behaving as if it were having a seizure but I didn't care because it was also making my ride much more tolerable; that ceased when I merged onto the off ramp and came to a stop behind a large semi-truck. The loss of air flow, as I waited there for the light to turn green, had me sweating almost instantly. Until that moment, I had been enjoying my ride to Diane's. In the sudden absence of the helpful wind, however—with the heat and the fumes from the truck accosting me—I quickly grew thankful that her house wasn't much further.

A few minutes later, I was dismounting in Diane's driveway. Once I had secured my helmet to the forks and locked them, I strode toward her front door, where I was treated to some melodious reggae tracks pouring out of her living room speaker. I liked that about Diane. She had a creative mind, which often manifested itself in the music she chose. I wasn't sure if she'd hear her doorbell, with the circumstances being what they were, so I made a fist and pounded it against the frame of her door.

"C'mon in," I heard her yell, in a friendly tone, from behind the obscured walls of her tiny home.

As soon as I crossed the threshold of her doorway and entered the living room, I fondly recognized an intoxicating, skunky stink wafting through the air. She had been smoking the devil's lettuce and my nose was reveling in it. "Thanks for waiting for me," I chided her.

"What?" she called back, in a mildly offended tone, from behind what I could now tell was the bathroom door.

"It smells good in here," I answered.

"Oh. Yeah. Sorry. I left some for you on the coffee table, if you're interested. Help yourself. I'll be out in a few minutes. Sorry! Girl stuff!"

"Take your time," I said, while simultaneously collapsing into her couch, as though I owned it myself. "The AC feels good."

"Yeah; can you believe this heat?!?" she remarked. "Are you sure you still want to walk?"

"Eh… I'm kind of wishing I wasn't wearing jeans but yeah. I think I *would* still like to walk. It's only, like, a mile and a half, right?" I had asked the question while frowning at a napkin, on the coffee table in front of me. On it were several orange slices, along with a discarded peel. When Diane answered in the affirmative, I carefully slid it all away from me—toward the edge of the table—and then picked up a clear plastic bag that had about ten nickel-sized, sticky, green buds lying at the bottom.

As I lifted the bag closer to my face to inspect its contents a little more carefully, I could see the greenery inside was covered in thin red hairs and microscopic, white, glistening crystals. "This stuff looks pretty good," I called out, in a voice slightly louder than the music filling the room.

"It is. Try it."

"I don't know if I should. I've got the bike..."

"Well," she began, "by the time we walk there, wait for a table, eat and walk back, it'll be at least three hours. Plus, I'm gonna have some margaritas... If..." she hesitated, "that is... if it won't bother you, I mean."

"No; I'm fine," I responded, as I pinched some of the shake from the bottom of the bag and packed it into the pipe-like apparatus that had been placed on the coffee table. Soon after, I brought it up to my lips and, with one flick of the lighter, I ignited the plant and began sucking its fumes into my lungs. I held the smoke there for a few moments, until it became uncomfortable, and then released it into the air, thereby adding to the smell I had noticed when I first walked in. I then slunk back into the couch and told Diane, "You know, you should really just get a license for this stuff."

"I know."

"It's not hard to get one."

"Yeah. I know." With that, I heard the distinctive-sounding motor of a hair dryer kick in, which signaled the end of the conversation—or at least her temporary disengagement from it. Before she activated the device, I had been primed to tell her all about the economic, medicinal and ethical benefits that come with a legalized approach but she had already heard me pontificate on all of that several times over.

Instead, I waited there on the couch, in silence, trying my best to ignore the hair dryer and focus on the music permeating the strangely decorated room. Diane had a flair for the macabre, which was evident in all the dead insects she had placed in glass cases and hung on her walls. In the middle of all of them, however, there was also a large black and white framed picture of her on stage, playing her violin; I remember thinking that it seemed out of place amongst all the creepy-crawlies everywhere—or maybe it was they who were out of place. I always thought my cousin should have been a musician but I couldn't deny that she seemed content as an entomologist too.

As I waited for the THC to take effect, I stared, from the couch, at a thin white lab coat she had draped over a chair—until some bizarre sort of praying mantis-thing I'd never noticed before caught my attention. It had been encased in amber and looking at it made me wonder what the world was like back when it roamed free.

Eventually, I grew impatient and convinced myself that I would need to metabolize a bit more smoke in order to feel its effects so I hit her bowl two more times before setting it back down on the coffee table, where I had found it. Just as I finished exhaling, the blow-dryer stopped and the bathroom door opened.

As Diane walked into the cloud hanging in the air she warned, "Be careful, man. This stuff is probably a lot stronger than what you're used to."

"Honestly, I don't feel anything but thanks for the warning. You look nice, by the way," I said with a smile.

Diane was a few years younger than me (not quite middle-aged but not that far from it either). She typically dressed her age but it wasn't out of necessity. If she had wanted, she could have passed for someone in her late twenties. On this particular day, she had chosen a long, flowing, orange-colored summer dress that went all the way down to her pasty shins. It stood out against her long, brown hair that she had been fastidiously grooming only moments ago.

"I just gotta grab a pair of flip-flops and I'm ready," she then told me. I nodded and smiled at her, as she stood there in the hallway. Then, as if she had just thought of it, she asked, "Are you sure you're still okay with Hector's? I completely understand if you want to go somewhere else."

"No. It's okay. I... I actually think it would be... sort of 'therapeutic,' you know?"

"Have you been there since...?" but she left her question hanging indefinitely.

"No."

"I didn't think so. You sure you're not gonna freak out?" she asked with concern.

"I want to see it," I said calmly. "I've been thinking: that view from the patio there—that's probably the last thing she ever saw." With her head hung low, Diane told me the same thought had crossed her own mind, as well. She almost seemed ashamed to admit as much.

"I guess I must have told you this before," I then stated, "but one of the girls they interviewed said Beth had already passed out before she even got into the car. She said her friends basically carried her there. Said they were all stumbling around, laughing and half-carrying, half-dragging Beth, toward the car."

"I'm so sorry, James. I know you loved her very much."

"I *did*," I admitted before tapering off for a moment. I left that last word hanging and Diane was waiting for an explanation so I decided to give it to her. "She was my entire world, Diane, but things... things were not great."

"I know. You told me."

"Yeah; I'm sorry. I don't mean to harp on it; I just... I haven't told many people. You're one of the only ones who knows everything."

"Don't apologize!" she interjected. "It's fine. I don't mind at all."

"Thanks. I just... I know I said this before but I often feel like I'm dishonoring her if I'm honest about the state of our relationship. The night that she... Almost no one knows this," I admitted, "but she actually left me earlier that night. She packed a bag and just...

left. I knew it was over but I didn't know I'd never see her again! People at the funeral—they kept talking about how much she loved me and… and I knew it wasn't true. I had to just nod my head and keep silent though."

"James, I don't… That's just so awful."

"I know. And I'm sorry. I realize I can tend to drone on about it with you. I just don't have many people I can talk to about it."

"Oh my God! It's fine! Really!"

I thanked her as she walked toward a pair of partially disintegrated, black flip-flops that appeared to have been placed, in a designated spot, beside her front door. With her leg extended and her toes pointed in the direction of the flimsy footwear, she addressed me: "You know, if you ever want to tr—" but she was cut short by the ringing of her phone, in her purse, on the table in front of me. "Crap. Hold on," she instructed, while walking over to retrieve the item. "Do you mind waiting outside, while I take this?" she then asked, while staring at the device.

"Not at all."

"Thanks. It's my mom. I just need a little privacy. I'll be quick."

"Say no more," I stated, whilst rising from the couch and venturing back toward her front door. She thanked me, as I was turning the knob, and, before I shut the door behind me, she had already connected the call and greeted her mother.

Once I was outside, I slowly shuffled back to my bike and leaned up against it, as I waited for Diane to conclude the call. It was at that moment that the psychoactive component of the controversial plant I had inhaled began to really make its presence felt. Diane was right. This particular strain was, indeed, quite a bit stronger than the low-dose, sleep-inducing variety to which I was accustomed. "Creeper." That's what we used to call buds like these. It took a little while for their effects to "creep" up on a person.

As my muscles loosened and the stresses of my life somehow became far less important, I looked across the street with a mixture of both contentment and mild paranoia. In the neighbor's yard, a solitary goose was wading in a three-foot-deep pond that may or may not have been intended for him. After what seemed like hours of staring at the bird, Diane finally emerged from her house and asked, "Ready to go?" She was already locking the door behind her, as she anticipated my answer, but I waited until she had moved closer to me before indulging her with one.

"I'm actually pretty high," I responded, as I straightened up off my bike and fished a pair of sunglasses out of my saddlebags. "I think I accidently overdid it."

"I warned you!" she exclaimed. "Did you want to stay in and just order something instead?"

"No. I'm okay. I actually prefer to be outside—even in the heat," I admitted, while slipping the dark lenses up, over my nose. "It's nice."

"Yeah; I'd like to walk too," she agreed, as I zipped the storage compartment shut.

"As long as you don't mind my stupid commentary. You know I'm talkative when I'm high."

We had already begun our journey when she laughed and said, "No. It's fine. Talk away. I feel like I haven't seen you since Grandpa Singer's funeral!"

"Yeah. That was… a while ago," I said slowly, with what she must have perceived was a struggle to gather my thoughts.

"What do your AA buddies say about you smoking weed?" she then inquired with a smirk.

"I don't really advertise the fact that I use it. I'm not ashamed of it, mind you. I just don't feel like trying to explain it to people who can't grasp it."

"Can't grasp what?"

"For me, it's all about a person's intent," I said with conviction. "My intention with cannabis, unlike alcohol, isn't to party—not now, at this point in my life, anyway. My PTSD got me my prescription but the truth of the matter is that it's more of a cheap form of meditation, ya know?"

Diane absent-mindedly nodded her head so I continued: "I think I accidently overdid it back there but, under normal circumstances, it's a way to help me wrangle my mind and keep it from ruminating on the past… or shooting ahead to the future. It helps me to concentrate on what I'm doing, or should be doing, right now, in the moment. For that reason, it keeps me focused, which by default, also makes me more a bit more creative. That's sort of what meditation's supposed to do too, right? This is just a faster and cheaper way to achieve it, don't you think?"

"Huh?"

"Sorry," I laughed. "I'm rambling again."

"No; *I'm* sorry," she countered. My mind was somewhere… else. Please. What were you saying again?"

"It wasn't important," I stoically asserted, while purposefully falling behind my walking companion, in order to avoid a child's tricycle that had been carelessly abandoned on the sidewalk, directly in front of my path. After we passed the tiny machine, in a single-file line, she waited for me to catch back up and take my place beside her. When I did, I asked, "So what did your mom have to say?"

Diane then confided in me that her father's condition was much worse than what we had all believed. Alzheimer's. The doctor's most recent prognosis—the one she had just discussed with her mother—wasn't very inspiring either. "I was wondering," she then admitted, "if I should try and tell him the truth, during one of his more lucid moments—you know, so he can get in order whatever he needs to get in order. So he can 'make his peace.' Then again," she argued with glassy eyes, "maybe it's better to not say anything."

For a few seconds I stayed reticent and let the singing birds, in the trees above us, break the silence surrounding us. Using them as my muse, I then told her the following: "The day before my dad died—when it was obvious he was at the end—everyone knew it. The doctors knew it. My family knew it. I knew it. I heard him ask my mom, at one point, 'Is this it? Is this the end?' She told him it wasn't and, well, he died in his sleep, later that night."

Staring at the sidewalk cracks consistently appearing and disappearing below my brown-laced black, leather boots (a poor choice for both fashion and a hot Ohio afternoon), I added that, "I always wondered: did he go to bed thinking he was going to awaken the next day—that he still had time to say something he hadn't yet said? Or did he know? I just remember thinking: if he had asked me that same question—if he asked whether or not this was the end—what would I have said to him? Would I have told him the truth? Would I have urged him to make his peace or would I have lied to him and tried to put his mind at ease with false hope? To be honest, I don't know what the right answer is—for you or for me—and, uh, I'm glad he didn't ask me. Because… Because I honestly don't know how I would have answered him and I think—no matter which way I chose—I would have always second-guessed and regretted my answer."

Diane looked upset. I could tell she was deep in thought—no doubt questioning her own situation—when she sniffed loudly and asked, in a slightly broken voice, "What's happening to our family, James? It's like, one by one, we're all falling apart."

Although I didn't verbalize an answer, I made sure she saw the forced, half-smile I offered, before dropping my head low to stare at the unending sidewalk.

"I assume you heard about Aunt Angie." she said with a detached callousness.

"Yeah…"

"My mom told me the other day," she explained. "I told myself I wasn't going to mention it but..."

"She tell you what she did this time?" I asked, as my eyebrow crested over the ridgeline of my shades.

"She... no. All she said was that it had something to do with a talk show or something."

"Apparently, she thought the host of one of them was sending her secret messages, through the broadcast, that only she could decode. Devin found all of her scribblings about it, in one of her notorious notebooks—page after page of 'translated' messages from the TV."

"Oh." Diane said, while unconsciously slowing her pace a bit.

I could tell she was having trouble finding the right words so I tried to provide some humor to our conversation by adding, "Hey, at least she's not dismantling everything she owns, looking for government listening devices this time."

"Yeah," Diane uncomfortably chuckled.

"Or getting caught trying to climb onto the roof of a random office building because the Secretary of Defense is sending a helicopter there to pick her up, for a top-secret mission." Another uncomfortable laugh. For a moment we walked in an awkward silence until I broke it with, "It's okay, Diane. You know the cycle by now."

"I know."

"Crazy Aunt Angie. She has an episode; she's admitted somewhere; they regulate her medication; they release her; she stops taking it because she thinks she's cured and, shortly after that, the delusions start again. Rinse and repeat. She's been that way since long before you or I were ever born."

"I know," she started. "And my mom said the same thing. I just never know how to comfort her about it. She's... She loves her sister. *Both* of her sisters—obviously—but... It's just a lot for her right now. I just don't know how you stay so calm through all of it."

"You know how these things go, Diane. In three months, she'll be out."

"Yeah…"

"And then, after another eight or so, it'll happen again," I added, as I quickly knelt down to retie my boot.

Diane silently chewed on her lip, as she patiently waited for me to loop my generic, non-matched, grocery store laces together. Once I finished and we had begun walking beside each other again, she persisted: "You know, she told me once how no one ever believes her… about anything. Can you imagine how awful that would be—to just keep everything to yourself? Writing your crazy thoughts in notebooks because anytime you say anything even remotely strange, everyone assumes you need reevaluated or re-medicated?"

I could tell that reminiscing over our aunt's schizophrenic escapades wasn't bringing Diane the levity I had hoped it would and so, as I casually stepped over a pothole in the side walk, I asked if she'd rather change the subject of our conversation. When she responded in the affirmative, I inquired about her love life. After a bit of prodding, we spoke of discarded boyfriends, for several minutes, until I eventually asked, "So who's this new guy I keep hearing about?" I lightly nudged her with my elbow, as I asked my question.

"We're just friends," she said with an overdramatic, watery eye roll. I then lowered my glasses and shot one of my own back at her (for comedic effect) to which she grinned and added, "I mean, I've thought about it, sure, but it's not really a big deal. Right now, we're just friends and that's fine."

"Why the smile then?" I asked with another nudge, as we slowly traversed the narrow sidewalk wrapping around the very old, forgotten neighborhood.

"Well," she sighed, "last night, we were texting back and forth and he wished me good night. He's never done that before."

"So why do you sound bummed about it?" I confusedly asked. "Isn't that a good thing?"

"I don't know if it was a good night—like, indicating some feelings, possibly—or if it was a dismissive, 'Leave me alone,' good night, as in 'Good night. Please stop bugging me now.'"

"The ol' preemptive good night," I mused, while swatting away a pesky gnat attracted to my sweat.

"It just came out of nowhere. He texted something. Neither of us responded. The conversation seemed to have arrived at a natural stopping point and then, eight minutes later, I got the 'I'm heading off to bed; good night' text. So was that a 'Good night. I wish I could talk to you more' or a 'Good night. You're pestering me; please stop' text?"

"Eight minutes, huh?"

"Yeah. What do you think?"

"What do I think?" I echoed while squinting up at the sun, from behind my shaded eyes. "I think he... what was his name again?"

"Kevin."

"Kevin," I repeated aloud. "I think it's unlikely that Kevin knows the exact number of minutes that transpired between texts and that he probably isn't obsessing over any minor details like that either. Having said that, though, I can appreciate what you're saying. I'd probably be doing the same thing that you are."

"Thank you for your wise words, O Love Guru," she playfully scoffed. "Tell me: how's Fisky? Are you currently dating or not dating? It's so hard to keep it straight."

"She can't commit to any longevity with me," I said emotionlessly. "Just the same as I can't commit to saying 'no' every time she wants to try again. This time, though... It feels different this time. I really don't think she's coming back."

"That really sucks. Are you okay?"

"She just feels like my last chance, you know? In all these years since Beth's death, she's the only girl I've been able to care about and I don't think I have it in me to start over again with someone else."

"There are other girls out there, James. I might even know a few I can introduce you to."

"It's okay. At least I still have Chris," I joked.

At this, Diane broke out into a full-blown guffaw. "The dude who did your mom's cabinets?"

"Yup."

"He's *still* calling you?"

"He never stopped."

"Just think," she started, as we passed under the shade of a massive oak tree in the front yard of a quaint, offbeat, yellow, colonial home, "If your mom hadn't had to go and meet my mom that day—if she hadn't asked you to come over and stay there while he installed her cabinets—"

"Then he would have never been able to chew my ear off and coerce me into giving him my phone number," I interrupted.

"I can't believe he's *still* trying to hang out with you," she laughed.

"Me neither. I know he has plenty of friends. What's so special about me?"

"Do the voice!" she teased. I shook my head in defiance, which forced her to beg. "C'mon! I love the way you do his accent. It's so funny!"

"I'm not in the mood," I grumpily replied.

"Is he still trying to get you to work with him?" she asked somewhat dejectedly.

"Yeah but that's not gonna happen."

"Well, you need to do *something*. My mom told me you walked out of your last job without having any prospects lined up at all! Are you crazy or what?"

I could feel my body's temperature rising, as we continued our stroll through her neighborhood—to the restaurant that was just across the street from one of the allotment's back entrances. The sweat from my armpits began to drip down and form small, moist pools where the hem of my sleeve and the body of my shirt connected. While trying to reposition my clothing, in a failing effort to displace the soggy fabric under my arm, I ventured, "That was the worst job I've ever had and I'm including my teenage, fast-food days in that statement."

"Why?!?" she laughed.

"I could barely convince myself to pull into the parking lot every morning. Every inch of my soul told me to keep driving. Everything this company did conflicted with who I was. Down to my core, it felt wrong and I had to lie to myself every moment of every day, just to keep from walking out the door and never coming back."

"I get that but still," she argued, "I don't know if I could just up and leave a job—even if it was a crummy job."

"I didn't *want* to up and leave. I wanted an earnest conversation with my boss, where I could explain myself to her. I wanted to tell her how I was feeling but something unexpected happened before I could. My third week there—when I was already sick of lying to myself and was looking for an exit strategy—she accidently walked in on her husband and found him cheating on her. That started a really nasty separation. She became distant and unapproachable. She took to locking herself away in her office for hours on end—talking to lawyers and screaming at her husband. Sometimes she'd completely disappear for days. She was a mess and I felt bad for her. I hated the job but I had sympathy for her. I wanted to stick it out—until she could get her head back on straight, at least."

"So why didn't you?"

"Her son took over during all of this and he was... 'difficult' to work with. He was the icing on the excrement-flavored cake.

Eventually, I reached a point where I couldn't take it anymore—when I knew, without a doubt, that I couldn't stand even one more day in the place.

"I had planned on talking to the boss after work that day but she disappeared, while I was on the phone. So I just left her a resignation letter on her desk. I always regretted leaving without a face-to-face conversation. I guess I just figured that she had enough on her mind and if she actually cared enough to discuss it with me, she could always call me. She never did, though, so I guess that probably means it's been bothering me a lot more than it has her."

Diane looked uncomfortable listening to my diatribe. It wasn't surprising, then, that when she had the opportunity to speak once more, she tried to steer the conversation elsewhere by asking, "Have you ever thought about going back to teaching again?"

"My old man would be turning over in his grave if he heard you say that," I quickly chortled.

"*Your* dad too?!? What's with our family and teachers anyway?!?" she asked with annoyance.

As I kicked an acorn and sent it skipping across the street, I said, "You know, for the longest time, I thought that. Now, I just think that my old man knew I wasn't being honest with myself."

"What do you mean?"

"I didn't want to *teach* art, Diane. Not really. I wanted to *create* it! I think he figured that out well before I ever did and he was just waiting for me to get there on my own."

"Well," she said, scratching her chin, "you still could, ya know."

"Nah. That ship sailed a long time ago."

* * *

Diane and I continued to discuss our lives as we walked and, before I knew it, we were exiting her neighborhood and crossing a busy, four-lane road in order to get to the restaurant across the street.

I hadn't eaten all day and my growling stomach was telling everyone within earshot that I was famished. It made me feel self-conscious, while waiting in the line that had formed outside the front door. That feeling soon changed to remorse, however, as I scanned the patio tables, to my right, and tried to guess which seats Beth and her friends selected four years ago.

The line was moving terribly slowly, which afforded us some extra time to breathe freely. By the time we'd reached the lobby just inside the double doors, however, we had already strapped on our state-required, surgical masks. The hostess was wearing one too. She was a friendly young woman with green highlights in her otherwise auburn hair, and a small, golden hoop in her left nostril. I caught a glimpse of it when she addressed us and her mask lazily slid down over her nose. After a brief exchange, she gave us a circular pager and explained that it would light up when a table was ready.

The restaurant parking lot was crowded (as expected for a Friday night) but good fortune shined upon us and, without too much difficulty, we found an empty bench outside. The overhanging roof above it provided some shade and neither of us needed much coaxing before walking toward it and seating ourselves. Most other people, it seemed, preferred to wait inside of their air-conditioned vehicles.

For the most part, it was just another typical Friday night. Then, all of a sudden, something within me changed. It was though I had just intercepted a scheme for an impending attack against my own, already-beleaguered mind but there wasn't enough time to properly thwart it.

Four feet above me, several blank, gray, rectangular panels that only I could see began to surround my head. Each one of them was the physical manifestation of some negative thought: "You're not smart enough." "No one loves you." "You're a failure." "You're going to die alone." "We're coming to get you," etc. They were overwhelming—to the point that I couldn't concentrate on anything else! From experience, I knew, at this point, that in about thirty seconds, they would start inching closer toward me and, when that happened, I would lose control.

As they came closer and closer, they began growing in size. They became more ominous; more threatening; more commanding. Closer. Closer. I knew I couldn't escape. They were bombarding me. I couldn't stop them. The timer had been engaged—the thirty seconds of impending dread before I was completely overwhelmed was already counting down. That helplessness—the inevitability of it all and that utter inability to escape it—was terrifying.

I remember turning toward Diane and telling her, "I feel like I'm about to have a panic attack." She asked me if it would help to walk around a little. I said "yes" and that's the last thing I remember.

PART II

THURSDAY

CHAPTER THREE

After I'd finished the initial draft of my so-called doomsday letter, I held its many pages in my hand and studied them as if they were a noose I had just tied for myself. Per my doctor's repeated requests, I had finally composed a note that detailed unseen dimensions, homicidal phantoms, parasitic slugs, a deep-seated paranoia and my nightly banishment to the tub. I imagined my impending imprisonment, as I read it over one last time, folded it and then stuffed it into my pocket, before exiting my tiny office and planting myself on my couch, for the next several hours.

In my living room, across from that couch, where I'd taken up residence, there was a dormant TV, which I had no desire to awaken. Instead, the cluttered wall behind it had captured my attention. There, amongst all the dusty paintings and sketches hanging everywhere, was a small, inconspicuous document that I had displayed inside of an eight-by-six picture frame.

This was the first time I'd looked at that frame in quite a while. I was sitting too far away to accurately read what was inside of it but I knew what it said nonetheless. Officially, it was my long since expired license to teach art, in the state of Ohio. Unofficially, it served as a defunct relic, reminding me of a life I'd long since abandoned.

I abandoned a confrontational sophomore whose unprovoked, profanity-laced castigations against me and everyone else around her would have made even the obscenest sailor blush. I abandoned juniors audacious enough to answer their phones during class and I even abandoned a lazy senior whose refusal to do any of his school work eventually led to the redaction of his full-ride offer to play basketball for one of the most prestigious universities in the country.

I abandoned all of those pubescent vampires—sucking the life from my very being—but I also abandoned my only creative outlet too. With delusions of grandeur in mind, I left the field of education and, in doing so, cut art out of my professional life. As my priorities shifted, it wasn't long before that creative neglect spread to my personal life as well. Now, I was too far out of practice to attempt reviving it and, should I have tried, I was sure I would have only embarrassed myself.

Contemplating my choices thusly caused me to resent that electronic, rectangular black hole in front of me and so, in defiance, I pushed the remote out of my reach and cast my gaze on a blank section of wall. For a long time, I captivatedly stared at that simple, gray-colored drywall and I grieved. I grieved the loss of my passion and I longed for my obscured purpose to somehow reveal itself to me. It had to be more grand than just watching TV until I died, didn't it?

I sometimes felt the only reason I watched television, read books, played video games, rode motorcycles, walked my dog or did literally anything non-biologically-driven was so that I would be able to simply preoccupy myself with something (anything) that precluded me from sitting in silence, as I was at that moment. When I meditated in silence—whether purposefully or indirectly—I would be forced to realize all those other hobbies were more or less meaningless. I could admit that they were *fun* distractions but that's all they were: distractions. It's when I sat in silence, however, that my mind would constantly bombard me with thoughts of leaving my futile and altogether pointless existence behind.

Those thoughts had been utterly consuming me and it was only when my brain was distracted with some sort of task or activity that I was able to stave them off. The second my mind gained the freedom to wander, nihilism was automatically the first place it would go and it stayed there until I forced it elsewhere with yet another distraction. That's all life was to me: a collection of distractions that kept my mind off of ending it all.

I didn't want to share these thoughts with anyone—even my doctor. In part, I didn't want to admit that I had lost control of my mind but I was equally frightened of hearing him, or anyone else, say, "So what? Everyone feels like that."

I had, after all, always told myself that my philosophy wasn't a unique one—that everyone felt this way—which, of course, was either true or it wasn't. If it was true and everyone was constantly trying to distract themselves in order to avoid focusing on the meaninglessness of their lives, then reality was absolutely mortifying and it was no wonder I avoided confronting it; after all, what does it really say about human beings if the only time our minds are unencumbered and free, the first place they go is toward the inevitability that life is pointless and nothing we do matters?

On the other hand, if this speculation was *not* true and this symptom was not as widespread as I'd convinced myself it was, then it was simply *me* who was defective and that made me feel even more isolated and irredeemably flawed. In either case, it was almost too much to bear. That's why I usually drowned myself in life's little distractions. Some days, however—some days like today, for example—I couldn't help but see those distractions for the momentary, fleeting reprieves they truly were.

I knew that eventually the book would run out of pages, the video game would run out of obstacles and the walk would run out of road.

When that happened, I also knew that I'd be forced to recognize that nothing surrounding my situation had changed except for the fact that I now had less time to try and find a way out of this perpetual cycle than I did before I began that book, game or walk.

Unfortunately, as was so often the case, my thoughts had made me rife with procrastination—so much so that I unknowingly spent hours deep in existential thoughts and six-month-old memories of that day with Diane, while I mindlessly watched shadows slowly dance across my wall, until they eventually disappeared completely. It was only when I casually noticed their absence that I came to realize that, during my musings, the sun has already sneakily set and the geese who frequently gathered just outside of my trailer had stopped honking. Perhaps they finally flew south, for warmer weather.

Those birds astounded me, for they had the ability of flight, as well as the intuition to perceive this place was dying, yet, for reasons I could not explain, they stayed. Then again, I too had access to air travel and enough instincts to recognize the desolation before me but I remained stuck here as well. As I began to examine why that was, I couldn't deny the fact that I'd wasted yet another day, lost in the confines of my own mental prison.

Between the insomnia, panic attacks, depression and all the medications I was taking to combat those conditions, my mental state was deteriorating rapidly. More than anything, though, I was scared—scared of that pernicious phantom who had some unknown designs on my life. It had been months since he physically assaulted me but the psychosis he left in his wake allowed a constant barrage of paranoia to infiltrate and influence every facet of my life.

Even though I hid the whole truth from him, my psychiatrist, through counseling, was at least helping me to somewhat cope. He was a longtime friend of my father's and I used that against him—telling him things that weren't completely true because I knew that, when he heard them, he would acquiesce and give me the medication I wanted.

I got the feeling he didn't want to give it to me—that he might have suspected it was actually doing me harm—but I always put on a good show when I needed to convince him I needed it. It was hard to admit it but the truth of the matter was that my desire for those drugs outweighed the muzzled cries for honesty, coming from deep within my soul.

Still, he loved my dad and, by charging me nothing but the time it took me to confide in him, he showed it every time we spoke. In return, I repaid him with half-truths and fantasies about a life where I didn't need him. I should have told him I was grateful that he'd chosen to help me but I never did. Eventually, he'd have this doomsday note, though, and, at that point, he'd have the truth and my life would be over.

As I considered all of this, I finally mustered the energy to slide onto the floor, next to my dog, Blue. Big Blue, my cowardly bullmastiff companion, was afraid of nearly everything: the other dogs outside, the squeaky football he refused to touch—even something as innocuous as my recycling bins had, for him, been a constant source of terror. From the day my then-wife Beth and I were first acquainted with him until now—all these years later—he would literally run out of the room and hide every time he heard the infrequent crackling of any discarded plastic inside of those bins.

I could tell my languid disposition was making him uneasy so I decided to spoon him for a little bit. "A little bit," as it turned out, was about thirty seconds because that's how long it took for one of the bottles in the recycling bins to pop, down the hall, in the kitchen. It might as well be a starting pistol because he was off, to bury his head, under my bed, the second he heard it.

After the dog retreated, I gave up on trying to interact with living things and committed myself to preparing for a nighttime jog instead. The endorphins that jogging managed to release usually helped to calm me down and I was hoping that tonight would be no different.

After coaxing Blue out, from underneath my bed, I tended to all of his biological needs. Once I was satisfied he'd taken enough energy in and let enough waste out, into the yard, I laced up my running shoes and began to stretch. While doing so, I thought about life and all the recent sieges against my mind—sieges which that faceless ghost was surely orchestrating, with the help of that parasitic slug living inside my skull.

Cardio, however, helped. It was good not only for the body but also for the mind; and so, while I used to run to stay in shape, I now ran in hopes of avoiding my nemesis. With that in mind, I locked the door behind me and set out, into the darkness.

* * *

In my experience, it was usually more productive for me to run in the morning but my particular neighborhood made night-running a viable option too. This community was small—I'm guessing about 120 trailers, stretched over a half mile; what's more, the streets were wide; the sidewalks were paved and traffic was sparse. It was quaint and quite a step down from the house I had recently lost but it was also somehow less stressful as well.

My allotment wasn't far from the city but it was secluded enough to offer an attractive level of privacy that I found comforting. That's because my neighborhood was a closed community so, other than the residents who lived there (and the geese who were too stubborn to leave), there wasn't usually much to obstruct my run.

I thought about the seclusion of my neighborhood as I ran. Just me, trekking though the endless darkness. I was alone; I was running and there was nothing else. Just this. As I followed the sidewalk, through the final cul-de-sac, it looped around and redirected back toward whence I came. That's one lap, I told myself. Three more to go.

It had begun snowing much heavier, since I first left my home. With nothing to watch but my own breath and the white flakes melting on my clothing, I decided to keep my head down. Doing so better kept me on the shoveled path and made it easier to watch for icy spots and debris along the way.

The bitter wind snapped at my face. I was wearing long johns under my sweats, gloves over my hands and a stocking cap atop my head. Over that, my hoodie was pulled forward, in an attempt to better shield me from the elements. None of it, though—not even my elevated heart rate—was enough to keep me warm.

The silence was surreal but also slightly uncomfortable so I decided to temporarily stop and open up the music app on my phone, in order to kill the imposing hush surrounding this cold Thursday night. As I adeptly scrolled through familiar menus, I popped in my earbuds and selected a workout-inspired playlist the app thought I would enjoy. Suddenly, there was music. Well… "dance" music, that is.

I wouldn't call the electronic pulses pouring into my head "music" but they did, at least, help me to run. While the overproduced, formulaic and altogether uninspired beat pushed me forward, I could quickly recognize that this hastily-constructed anthem idolizing material possessions, dancing prowess and physical attraction wasn't a particularly thought-provoking piece of art. These sounds were the neatly-packaged, short-lived commercialization of art, masquerading as music. They were the antithesis of art.

Still, when I was running… that beat… that commonplace, non-innovative, familiar beat—it kept me moving. For that, I could appreciate the sounds my earbuds produced and I could feel good about the fact that I'd found a way to harness something so otherwise unappealing to me. Suddenly, the glass seemed half full and so I took a sip and turned the volume higher (evidence that my hypocrisy knew no bounds).

I ran and so too did the music app on my phone. The algorithm embedded within it had chosen a particularly terrible playlist to accompany me on my run—one that the app had aptly named "Workout Fuel." I mused that perhaps I was tricking my brain into believing that if I ran fast enough and far enough, I might actually escape the sounds being pumped into my ear canals.

As the singer rhymed "baby" and "maybe," I rolled my eyes at the disembodied snowman head near my feet. Good for her, though, right? In truth, I wished I had the nerve to follow my own dreams the way that singer had likely followed hers and, at least for that, I admired her—whomever she was.

As I reached what I considered to be the optimum speed, I could see, from my peripheral, the various trailers in my neighborhood appear and then quickly vanish back into the darkness. Mostly, though, I saw only my breath and my Skechers pounding the street in front of me. The snow from last night had been piled into tight, man-made, miniature hills, encroaching over the sidewalk and into the street. Still, the threat of traffic was virtually nonexistent and the road was plenty big.

Then, without warning, the volume level I had set decreased dramatically. As was always the case, this dip indicated that my phone had just received some sort of notification. This, of course, piqued my interest and I wanted to investigate but, for some reason, I kept my head pointed toward the ground and it was at that moment that I realized something had changed.

I was confused at first, as to what it was that was out of kilter. It was as though time itself had slowed down and I was both stuck in it, as an active participant, but also observing it from afar, at the same time. Paradoxically, I was somehow able to leisurely examine my situation from afar, while simultaneously experiencing it firsthand, in real time.

The first oddity, on which I began to focus my attention, in a strangely calm manner, was the absence of vision I had somehow only casually noticed. While before, my environment was mostly dark, it had suddenly become exclusively so. Gone were the distant trailers and trees, yes, but gone too were the immediate ones, along with the sidewalk, the snow, my shoes, my breath… everything. Nothing but a dark void lingered. My eyes were open but sight completely eluded them.

I wanted to touch my face, to confirm what I already knew—that my eyes were indeed open and were searching for anything onto which to lock—but my body wasn't responsive. It and everything around it was proceeding in slow motion, while my mind continued to function at the correct speed. I had become a conscious, sightless pinball that was uncontrollably bouncing all throughout the darkness: up, down, twisting about, slowly banging against this and then that and then a sudden, halting thud.

Then nothing. There was no pain, only confusion. What just happened? Where am I? What's going on?

Slowly, some unknown source began to generate various, blurry images throughout the void and my vision commenced to recalibrating itself. Groggily, my focus began to improve and, while not functioning optimally, I was able to gather that I was lying on my back and looking up at the dark sky. My left arm was resting palm up, over my head, and my right was palm down, limp and positioned underneath a parked car above me.

Pieces of glass, broken reflector and handwritten pages, marked in blue pen, were strewn all about me, in a disheveled mess. Above me, a crowd had gathered, forming an imposing circle I could not escape. I must have been out for at least a couple minutes, I speculated.

Through the auditory fog, I discerned the words "know" and "name" with an inflection and then a pause. I tried to answer "James Singer" but the garbled mush that came out of my mouth was unintelligible. My pantomime efforts to make my identity known by reaching for the ID card that was in my pants was cut short by a large woman mumbling something about staying still. I didn't hear exactly what she said but I got the gist that I should lie prostrate.

It wasn't until that exchange that my brain began to catch up the situation in which I now found myself. Without hesitation, it reminded me that I was still human and could definitely still feel discomfort. Right on cue, a pain in my left leg began to course through my body. Suddenly, I felt compelled to test my leg's limits. Attempting to move it proved excruciating and only confirmed that I should try and remain still.

Grimacing as I did so, I raised my left hand to cover my face. It was cold. Where was my glove? Had someone stolen it? No. Was it knocked clean off my hand? As I pondered this mystery, I realized that my feet were cold too. Still able to move my right leg, I adjusted it to feel my socked foot make contact with the rear passenger tire of the parked car overtop of me. No shoes either. How strange!

Pain began to overtake me and I feared I was going to pass out again. That's when the flashing lights began to strobe above my head. I heard a car door open; then another. An officer of the law began to clear out bystanders and I heard him ask someone in the crowd if I was okay. I think I answered for myself and said "yes" but I can't be sure.

It's my vague recollection that he told someone to make sure I remained still—that help was on the way. Something like that. I don't remember exactly but that was the core of it.

Just then, a warm tongue touched my cheek. I knew that sensation. Somebody's dog had gotten too close. I wasn't upset though. Besieged by this traumatic event, I welcomed the unexpected companionship.

As I strained to turn my head and see, I noticed the tactical vest he was wearing and I realized he was the officer's dog. I wondered if the officer had left him there to keep the crowd away from me. "Don't worry, buddy," the mongrel then suddenly muttered, snapping me out of my trance. "We're going to get you through this."

CHAPTER FOUR

I knew I hadn't misheard the guttural, almost smoker-like, voice that emanated from my new canine companion. Nonetheless, I stared at him, in awe, unable to dismiss the improbability of my presently unfolding encounter with him—no matter how much I yearned to do precisely just that. Dumbfounded, I stared at him and he back at me.

When it was clear that he was waiting for me to react, I addressed him, nervously and with a twinge of fear in my voice, asking simply, "What… What on Earth is happening right now?"

The dog then incredulously turned his head to the side, as dogs are wont to do, and so I continued my increasingly frantic inquiries: "Who are you? Where am I? What's going on?!?"

I can understand how a person might think the more prudent or even more obvious verbal reaction would have been to reaffirm what I claimed to have heard—to softly and inconspicuously ask the dog, in a voice near to a whisper, when I was sure no one else was looking, if that dog had indeed just spoken clear intelligible English. Having experienced the situation myself, though, I can report that I never faltered in my faith that he had addressed me, in spoken word.

Yes: I tried to remain inconspicuous to the crowd but I didn't require affirmation about what had just occurred. I knew unequivocally that this dog had spoken to me. There was a bit of desperation in my voice, which I'm sure he must have noted, but that was due to the fact that I found my predicament to be credible and true—not because I had any doubts in it!

It took him an unnerving amount of time to respond and that made me increasingly anxious. To me, it seemed like eons, though I imagine it was only seconds. Perhaps he was expecting a question centered around validating his ability to speak. Perhaps he was disappointed that I hadn't, as of yet, asked it. Did he prep for this moment? Did he rehearse a scene where I was a bit more bewildered? Did he want that? Had my acceptance of the situation confused or unhinged him? Was he just messing with me?

"I heard one of the witnesses say he didn't have his lights on," he finally began. "Lives here in the park, I think. Probably just pulled out of his driveway and hadn't realized it yet."

"What?" I gasped, scanning the crowd out of concern someone would see me talking to this dog. No one seemed to notice me at all though. The two women I could see, without straining myself, were both busy chattering amongst themselves; besides, all they would have observed—should they have decided to look my way—was me talking to a very normal-looking, middle-aged, male German shepherd, in a seated position. His mouth never moved—not in a way that was consistent with forming words, that is—but I heard his voice nonetheless.

"It makes sense: black car, no lights, nighttime, earbuds. I saw one on the ground, on my way over here, by the way." He paused as I reached my hand to my ear, as if to confirm what he had said. He was right; he nonchalantly noted my realization and then continued: "Your hoodie is up and I can see glass stuck to the back of it. I'm assuming you had it pulled down, over your face?"

"Uh, yeah," I stammered.

"That's what I figured. Kind of a perfect storm." With that, he suddenly stood up on all fours and exclaimed, "Oh yeah! The storm too! Who the heck jogs at night, in the snow, with their head down and earbuds in, by the way?"

"I… uh…" My trailing thoughts began to prevent a well-thought-out answer to his question. Slowly, my eyes started to survey the carnage around me. The glass stuck to the back of my hoodie—I had been thinking that it was gravel poking into the back of my head but yes: glass made more sense. It fit in with the broken pieces of reflector, blood (mine, I had assumed), and the car underneath which the right half of my body now lay. I also heard voices but, as I strained my neck, to see in multiple directions, my vision betrayed me, displaying only blurry outlines of people encircled around me.

"They've called an ambulance," he told me. "Don't worry. I think he's just collecting statements from everyone right now."

Giving up and letting gravity slowly return my head to the pavement, I confusedly asked, "Who?"

"Who, what?" he fired back.

I was annoyed at how quickly he retorted—almost as if he had already read the script of our conversation and he was jumping ahead of his lines, without letting the words sink in, as the rookie actors from my local theatre often did. "Who's collecting statements?" I asked, trying to curtail the irritation in my voice.

"Oh. Sorry. Officer Walcott. My partner."

"Oh." I was trying to let everything sink in but, after a few seconds, he interrupted my puzzled thoughts.

Impatiently, he asked, "You don't recognize me, do you?"

I struggled for a moment to study his face but the ludicrousness of the situation overtook me. As I pondered his question, I saw the beast return to a sitting position. He almost seemed pleased that he had stumped me.

Is he seriously asking me if I recognize him—as compared to other German shepherds? It was too much for me and, as my mind deliberated over all of this, I got the sense that my new acquaintance took an odd satisfaction in my failure to place him.

Sanctimoniously, he then cut into my timid silence: "Typical human. My name is Cinnamon."

"Cinnamon," I repeated, as if I had never heard the word before. In that moment, my brain began to formulate a joke about cinnamon and "Spice"—an exotic dancer who was a friend of mine—but I thought better of it. Too esoteric, I told myself. Instead, I simply remained quiet and tried to let his name sink in.

"Do you even recognize Officer Walcott?"

"I don't think I'm supposed to sit up to look. I tried a moment ago and it didn't go so well." He started to interject but, talking over him, I added, "Things farther away are kind of blurry too."

"That's not important anymore," he retorted.

"What's not important anymore?" I queried.

"Just sit up and look. No one's going to stop you."

With a more-than-subtle amount of pain coursing through my leg, head and neck, I managed to erect my torso, in a somewhat reclined position, by resting my forearms against the cold, snowy concrete below. My vision was beginning to correct itself, which allowed me to gaze upon the countenance of the police officer I had been instructed to examine. He was speaking quite intently to a man who was waving his arms all around, and pointing toward a vacant spot, in the street, as he answered the officer's questions. This officer *did* seem somewhat familiar but my mind struggled to place him.

As I probed the depths of my brain for the comfort that comes with identifying a strangely familiar face, I let my focus stray and began to take note of the other bystanders talking amongst themselves and to their own electronic devices. It was almost as if they were willfully ignoring me. Observing their various placements, in the circle they had haphazardly formed around me, I began to fear that they would all at once descend upon me, rushing toward my helpless form at any moment, as they murmured amongst themselves, driven by their frantic attempts to divine meaning from all of this.

In all their devotion to each other, however, they had seemingly failed to notice that the source for all their inquires was now alert and stirring. They spoke readily amongst themselves and shouted unintelligible statements at Officer Walcott but seemed almost oblivious to the fact that I was there at all. I wondered if they even saw me and, in truth, I actually hoped that they didn't. Even the woman who had already addressed me once before seemed unaware of me now.

Despite little evidence to the contrary, I couldn't help but feel as though my anonymity would, at any moment, give way to the crowd's urge to assert itself into my life. That made my inconspicuous status fragile—more fragile than I would have liked—and so I kept a cautious eye on the crowd.

Hampered by my insecurities, I watched them and, as the rapport between Cinnamon and myself began to thrive, so too did my overwhelming concern for how the mob would perceive me, should they suddenly come to realize that I had been conversing with a dog. "All these people..." I started to say.

"Neighbors," he answered, before I could even formulate my question. "People who heard the screeching tires and the impact of metal on meat. Ignore them. My partner and I have them under control. They won't bother you."

His phrasing left something to be desired but perhaps he was right. Peering more closely at everyone around me, my outlook began to change and I found myself inclined to believe my new friend. With that in mind, I chose to try and avoid thinking about everyone else and turned my attention back to Cinnamon.

I reflected on his question about whether or not I recognized his partner for a few short seconds. I then wiped some of the falling snow from my face and responded to my inquisitor: "Your partner—he does look kind of familiar."

"All of this should seem familiar to you, really."

Pondering Cinnamon's words, I realized that this was, indeed, all eerily reminiscent of another run of mine. Was this conversational dog somehow in my head or had I displayed that look—the one we all get when we suddenly recall something that someone else has asked us to remember? I either displayed that look or Cinnamon was psychic because, before I could respond verbally, he triumphantly belted out, "Yeeeeeeah. Nooooooow you remember."

"I... I don't know what you're talking about," I lied.

"You, on the ground. Squad cars all around you," he prompted. Turning my head to toward the car underneath which half of my body had been cast, I stayed silent, hoping my lack of cooperation would encourage him to stop harassing me. Instead, he said, "We have to stop meeting like this."

* * *

I continued to ignore Cinnamon for several moments, until he bit down into my arm—not hard enough to draw blood but hard enough to get my attention. "Hey!" I cried out, snapping my head back toward him.

"I'm talking to you! Pay attention," he then demanded.

"I *am* paying attention!" I defiantly hissed, in an elevated whisper I hoped wouldn't attract any unwanted attention.

"Admit it then," he pressed. "I know you remember us."

"Fine. Yeah. I remember you."

"You remember *both* of us," he insisted.

"Yeah," I bitterly conceded. "I remember *both* of you."

With a bit of smugness, he then said, "Never thought I'd run into *you* again."

"Me neither."

"Figured you'd be dead or in jail by now," he indifferently told the ground.

"Why would you say something like that?" I asked cautiously, while simultaneously trying to mask the offense I took to his statement.

"You just didn't seem… 'right.' What was going on with you anyway?"

I thought for a second and then asked, "And what makes you think I'm 'right' now? I'm having a conversation with a dog, after all, aren't I?"

"There was something up with you that day," he prodded. "You know it's true."

"Why are you so interested?"

"Humor me."

After a somewhat awkward silence, I finally relented and told him, "That was the night that I…" But I stopped. I was scared to continue—to admit what I knew to be true. He waited silently for me to continue and so I let the night sky above me reacquire my gaze and then said, "Everything changed that night."

"Changed how?" Cinnamon wanted to know.

Without any foreseeable escape from his line of questioning, I admitted, "I've been… I've been reliving that night in my head, over and over, for some time now." I could tell he wanted more but I didn't give it to him. Eventually, in an effort to change the subject, I added, "Your partner was actually pretty decent to me. He could have made things a lot worse on me, if he wanted to."

Puffing up his chest, Cinnamon concurred with me: "I've known him my whole life. He's no pushover. Above all else, though, he *does* truly want to help." As he spoke the last part of that sentence, I noticed his proud tone softened a bit.

I could tell he was enamored with his partner and I wanted to commiserate and tell him I too appreciated my own personal experience with Officer Walcott so I did. I furthermore told him that I always felt guilty that I didn't have a chance to properly thank him for the way he handled my previous encounter with him.

The dog seemed to consider this, for a moment, before he responded: "He has to keep working crowd control and, after the ambulance arrives, he'll have to hang back to finish his investigation. It's unlikely you'll get much of a chance, honestly."

As I reflected on the dog's words, I looked back toward Walcott's direction. He was talking to an older man now. The younger, more animated man, with whom he was speaking earlier, was now pacing nervously, off to the side. He, like everyone else in the crowd, seemed to be waiting to talk to Walcott again.

"That's too bad," I asserted, as I continued to observe him.

"You know, you could talk to *me* about it," the dog offered.

"Talk to you?"

"Why not? I'm his partner, after all."

As I evaluated his proposal, Cinnamon began to shift his head around, to better bite at his backside. Not content to simply stop there, he raised his left hind leg a few inches off the ground, to better make room for his head, which he placed there to more easily lick his most private of areas.

I didn't know what to say and so I looked back toward the sky and said nothing. Before long, he noticed the uncomfortable silence and said, "I don't know why you all get so bent out of shape about this."

"I'm sorry. This is all just… really, really strange, isn't it?"

"Only as strange as you make it."

"What does that mean?" My teeth had begun to chatter, as I voiced my question. I imagine the initial shock of the situation was wearing off and reality was starting to creep back in. Unfortunately, on this night, reality was cold and I was underdressed.

Cinnamon ignored my chattering and I was actually glad for it. "Look, I'll help you get started here. I'll tell you what I remember of that night, okay?"

Without considerable hesitation, I agreed, eager for a momentary reprieve in his line of questioning. Talking to Cinnamon made me feel… "unprepared" and being unprepared made me feel like a moron. Because of that, I was happy for the opportunity to recalibrate my brain to the situation at hand.

"So," he began, "we had just finished up with a domestic violence call. Real piece of work, this guy. When we pulled up, they were both on the lawn, screaming at each other—boyfriend and girlfriend, I think. I don't think they were married." He paused for a moment to think. "No… no; I don't think so but… I guess don't really know. Anyway, this guy had a look in his eye, like he was going to kill this chick. Seriously. I think it might have been a homicide call, had we arrived any later."

"You could tell all that from the car?"

"Absolutely! Body language, the look in his eye, the shouting! Besides all that, humans have a sort of… 'aura,' I guess—for lack of a better word. We can pick up on it—see things that you don't think we can see. Things you're trying hide, even."

"An aura?"

"Yeah. We have an amazing ability to sense things that you don't. I could try to explain it but that ambulance will be here soon so I'll just leave it at this: we sense things that humans don't."

As Cinnamon continued his story, I began to wonder how far away the ambulance actually was and why no one was checking on me. I was growing colder by the second. I held my fear in check, though, and tried to keep my chattering jaw still, while I observed the animal.

My wandering mind had caused me to miss some of what he was saying but, as I became invested in the conversation once more, I remember him saying, "And Walcott kept telling the guy to be quiet and to sit on the ground—ya know, in order to deescalate the situation." I nodded, hoping he wouldn't need any further affirmations that I was listening to him. He didn't. "The guy just kept screaming, though, as if he didn't even see us. He heard Walcott threaten to let me out of the car, though, and that suddenly calmed him down."

"I bet."

"Humans can't understand us—well, ones who aren't like you anyway—so, to the suspect, I was just barking nonsense but what I was actually saying was, 'Let me out of here, Walcott! It's go time!' I couldn't wait to neutralize this guy. That's not what he heard, mind you, but he definitely understood."

"What do you mean, 'humans who aren't like me?'" I interrupted once he had taken a moment to catch his breath.

"You know: in your 'situation.'"

"What do yo—"

"Listen. Your transgression with us—it wasn't a big deal. I mean, I remember it, of course, but we deal with crazy stuff like that almost every day. You understand?"

"I do but I—"

"Just listen then," he said, cutting me off once more. Next, he took a long, deep breath, which I took as evidence that he wasn't willing to entertain any more of my existential questioning. Since he was, thus far, my only source of information and because I was slightly intimidated by him, I decided to give him his wish and relent a bit, at least for the moment.

When he seemed to be satisfied that I had decoded all of his nonverbal admonishments, he continued, in a slightly annoyed (but also somehow softer) temperament: "Anyway, as is unfortunately so often the case, this particular woman decided not press any charges."

"Really?"

"Yeah."

"That's normal?" I asked.

"I don't know if I'd say 'normal' but it's common."

"Oh."

"Apparently, she just wanted him off her property so, once Walcott was satisfied that our suspect had calmed down, he allowed him to dive off to stay the night with his friend. Literally, about thirty seconds after we had finished up and driven away, we got a call that some guy had OD'd at Hector's."

"I can understand why people thought that," I said, swallowing my shame as I spoke. Gathering additional courage, I decided to add, "That's not what happened though."

"So what did happen then?"

After I took a deep breath of my own, I told him about my night with Diane, six months ago. I spared no detail and the conversation flowed freely until I reached the point in the story where I was about to lose consciousness on the bench, outside the restaurant. "As we were sitting there, on the bench," I mumbled, "I started to feel a panic attack coming on. I don't know if… do dogs get panic attacks?"

"We get anxious," he explained. "Yeah. Some more so than others. We get headaches; we get cancer. We get almost everything that you do."

I felt like telling him there's anxiousness and then there's a panic attack—just like there are headaches and then there are migraines. And if a migraine is the embodiment of physical pain then a panic attack is its psychological equivalent.

Instead, I just said, "Well, I started to feel a panic attack coming on and—"

Just then, our conversation was cut short by the sound of snow crunching under an approaching boot. Having noticed the audible disturbance, I cast my line of sight toward its direction and saw the aforementioned Officer Walcott. As our eyes met, he took a kneeling position, hovering just above me and spoke: "Hey, buddy. Cinnamon, you keeping him company?"

CHAPTER FIVE

Officer Walcott was noticeably younger than I. If I had to guess, I'd say that he was in his early thirties. He was clean-shaven, with blue eyes and thick, black eyebrows. On his head, he wore a gray stocking cap, with "Police" printed prominently on front. It hid his short, black, militaristic-fashioned hair but I still remembered it from our previous encounter.

When he asked if Cinnamon was keeping me company, he asked it in an indirect kind of way. He had moved his eyes off of me and seemed to be staring at something behind me, off into the distance, when the words left his lips. Such was his posture and tone that I wasn't actually sure if he was speaking to me, to Cinnamon, to both or to neither of us.

Chiming in before I could answer for myself, Cinnamon claimed, "Yes I am."

I was paying acute attention to the interaction between the officer and his dog and, in doing so, I hesitated to say anything myself. Walcott seemed to pay his companion no mind. Was he ignoring him or did he just not hear him and, more importantly, I wondered: how was it that I found myself in a situation where I was even asking this question?

For the first time that night, I suddenly began to wonder if some part of my brain had been damaged in the accident, causing me to hallucinate or, if that wasn't the case, if I was perhaps unconscious in a hospital bed somewhere, drowning in the delirium of my own mental coma. Was I actually there at all—physically present there in that moment? How could I be sure? Then again, how can anyone ever be sure of that, at any point in life?

Was this a dream perhaps? At the time they are occurring, dreams seem very real. In most cases, it isn't until we awaken that we begin to pick apart certain elements that seem absurd to our waking minds. While we're held captive by the dream, as it unfolds around us, it doesn't seem absurd at all.

I was noticing the ludicrousness of my situation at it was unfolding in real time though. Did that mean I'd achieved some sort of lucidity within my dream or did my apparent cognizance of everything—my ability to recognize the absurd, that is—point to the fact that I was actually awake?

And who's to say our minds are functioning more precisely once we're awake anyway? Maybe the dreaming mind is the one that's operating correctly, or at full capacity, and the woke one is simply the side effect—the less powerful alternative we're forced to endure, while the subconscious mind recharges itself in preparation for the next time we sleep.

The dreamworld was certainly more interesting than the insipid one that had imprisoned me for the last forty-one years. With that in mind, perhaps the more pertinent and pragmatic question should have been: Do I even *want* to wake up, if I'm dreaming? What if the reality to which I would awaken was actually much worse than this current Hell I've created for myself?

Up until now, I had accepted Cinnamon for what he was but seeing how another human being reacted around him caused my curious mind to race. Walcott seemed unconcerned with any of this. As I pondered my situation, his gaze left the space behind me and met mine directly. Once he acquired it, he maintained his eye contact on me and waited patiently for an answer.

I thought about asking him if his dog could talk, which reminded me of that joke I very much liked. Taking a metaphorical step back, I decided against such an inquiry. I didn't want them putting me in some kind of a psych ward—not before my doctor got the chance to do it himself on Monday, that is.

I also thought better of telling Walcott that I recognized him. Ultimately, I decided Cinnamon was probably right. It wasn't the right time to try and chitchat with the officer. And so, teeth chattering, I simply responded to the question that Cinnamon had already taken the liberty of answering for me: "Yes, sir. He's keeping me company. Thank you."

At that moment, Walcott started to present me with a blanket he had been holding under his arm, when his radio belched out a garbled message from dispatch. The ambulance had been derailed from its mission, for some reason that was unclear, but a new one was now en route.

"Copy, Dispatch," he affirmed, pressing the button on the intercom that rested just below the front side of his shoulder. As he did so, the blanket fell from under his arm and landed within my reach. He didn't seem to notice.

While he spoke, I sat up, determined to utilize the garment to alleviate the cold as best I could—especially on my feet. My left leg felt broken and the severity of the throbbing pain it had been forcing me to endure was beginning to escalate. In a slow and careful manner, I relocated my right foot, from underneath the car, and brought it toward my left foot, until my right and left feet were touching each other. At that point, I tucked the blanket under them, like some sort of modern-day mummy.

"Suspect is in my car," I heard Officer Walcott explain, with his head turned toward the device on his shoulder, as I worked on my new wrappings. Oblivious to my struggles below, he and the mysterious voice on the other end of his communicator continued to exchange information for a short time. Toward the end of their dialogue, I heard him say that he would continue to "gather additional evidence" while we waited on the ambulance. The muffled dispatcher then acknowledged him and faded silent once more.

"Keep him company," he then instructed Cinnamon. "An ambulance will be here soon. I've got another patrol car coming too." Then he flashed a warm smile and said, "Holler if you need me. I'll be right over there."

"The sooner, the better," I grunted, in as upbeat a manner as I could muster. "My leg is killing me." I had a growing fear that the damage was worse than I had been allowing myself to believe and it was becoming harder to hide the truth from myself.

At almost the same time I gave my response, Cinnamon bellowed (nearly talking over me, as he did so) a very simple, "I got this, Walcott."

"It won't be long," Walcott said and, with that, he disappeared into the crowd once more.

Walcott wasn't quite as I remembered him. He still seemed to be logical and in control of the situation—he still seemed "professional"—but he was lacking the compassion I remembered. I assumed he was simply overwhelmed by all of the moving parts of our crime scene; regardless, I was glad that he was the one in charge. I didn't need him to be my friend, after all. I needed him to be a good cop.

I didn't let the officer's odd behavior concern me too greatly; in fact, talking to another real human being had elevated my mood quite considerably. I was cold and my body felt broken but, in him, I had just found new hope that my mind might still be intact!

"If it makes you feel any better, I can tell you that he wouldn't walk away from you if he thought your life was in any real danger," said the talking dog next to me. Hearing his voice put an immediate damper on my newly-acquired optimistic outlook.

"Oh. Okay."

"I mean, your leg is meeeessed up," he went on, "but I don't think you're going to get any worse than you already are."

"Thanks." That joke—the one from before, about a talking dog—suddenly found its way back into my head again and I felt compelled to try and use it to lighten the mood a bit. "Hey, you wanna hear a joke?"

"I don't like jokes," he grunted, with a bit of derision in his voice. I imagined, if he might have been human, that he would have raised one of his eyebrows, as he said it.

He actually made no faces that were uncharacteristic to a dog at all. With his mouth remaining still, I was forced to consider the possibility he was communicating telepathically. I speculated over asking him to explain this for only a moment, before ultimately deciding that the explanation would only confuse things more and waste more time.

"Sooo, you and Diane. Six months ago. Panic attack, on the restaurant's bench…" he said, in an attempt to entice me to finish my story.

I realized that talking to Cinnamon about everything, though difficult, was, in a way, therapeutic. I tried to let that notion guide my words and so, with a positive frame of mind, I attempted to delve back into describing the traumatic evening that, for some reason, had caught his interest.

"Right," I began. "So anyway, I felt it coming on. I KNEW it was coming, as we were sitting on that bench. I remember telling Diane, 'I feel like I'm about to have a panic attack.' She asked me if it would help to walk around a little. I said 'yes' and that's the last thing I remember."

"So you blacked out?"

"Diane told me that she remembered me putting my head on her shoulder. She told me later that she thought I was just trying to be funny so she moved her shoulder away and that's when my entire body just collapsed into her lap. I don't know. I'm not really sure how I fell. This is her recollection, mind you. I wasn't conscious for any of this."

"That must have been when we got the 911 call." Almost on cue, the sound of the nearing ambulance seemed to rise an octave or two.

I accepted Cinnamon's prompting and continued. "She said my breathing was shallow and the people in the crowd were all worried."

"And that was from a panic attack?" he asked in a way that was both skeptical but also affirming.

"Here's how I rationalize it: think of a computer—an older computer actually. That'd be an even better analogy, I think. Let's say you're on this computer and you're runni—"

Another interruption: "Computers are those little rectangular screens that humans stare at all day—like the one Walcott has in his car, right?

For a moment, I had almost forgotten I had been speaking to a dog. In this perceived distortion of reality, I recognized that I wasn't sure what presuppositions I should employ with him. Deciding it would take far too much time to describe the nature of computers, I simply replied, "They are," and then, "You might not understand all of this but please just bear with me."

Though he seemed to be trying to fight it, I then saw Cinnamon's tail wag, which was comforting, but the maddening sirens were forcing me to raise my voice to the point where they dismantled most of that comfort. They were close. Probably within the scope of my vision, had I been standing.

Pushing past their wails, I went on: "So you've got this older computer and, while working on creating a sales report, you're also messaging friends, listening to music, uploading pictures and you've got an article pulled up in your internet browser that you were reading from earlier in the day.

"Then, all of a sudden, the screen just goes blank." For dramatic effect, I paused here. I don't think it produced, in him, the outcome I had intended and so I picked back up slightly dejected. "There was too much data to process and it overloaded," I explained. "Well, that's what happened to my brain. Too many foreboding and negative tiles coming toward me. Dying alone, guilt, purposelessness, failure, unresolved conflicts, an inability to change… These thoughts and many more were all represented in these rectangular tiles, circling my head and they were all descending upon me—all at once. It was too much to process. Not enough computing power to handle it all. My brain just shut down and had to reboot itself, like an old computer."

That last sentence—it seemed as though I had spoken the first part of it at a much higher decibel than the second half for, in the middle of vocalizing it, the sirens had gone silent. I listened for a moment and then heard a door slam shut. They were here.

* * *

I left Cinnamon in silence, to digest my commentary, while a young man in hospital garb approached us. He had mid-length, well-kempt, reddish-brown hair and a beard to match. I placed him somewhere in his late twenties, although it was my assertion that he was trying to deceive others into believing him older, with the addition of the aforementioned beard. If that was indeed his goal, I can clearly attest that, with me at least, he did not achieve it.

Kneeling down beside me, as Officer Walcott had done, the young emergency worker began a dialogue with me, assuming, like Walcott and Cinnamon did, that I went by "Buddy." I supposed that there were worse colloquialisms they could have chosen and so I accepted the greeting without insult. "Hey, buddy. You doing okay?" he asked.

"I'm cold." It seemed the most relevant and pressing ailment so—odd as it may seem—I had no trouble prioritizing it over my throbbing leg and head.

"I bet," he said, in a reassuring tone. "We're going to get you loaded up and out of here, as soon as we can, but first I'm going to need to brace your head and neck. I want to make sure they're not going to be bouncing around when we move you, okay?"

"I would nod but that would seem counterintuitive."

This caused a laugh and not just a polite one. I could tell he actually found it humorous. That's good, I thought. Get him in my corner early. "I've actually been moving it quite a bit already," I then admitted.

"Well, don't move it any more, for now. I want to do a quick check first. Can you tell me what your name is?" he asked while performing a visual scan of my head and neck area.

"James Singer."

"Nice to meet you, James. I'm Jeff."

I gave him an obligatory smile—the kind I would give when I knew I was *supposed* to smile but I didn't really want to do so. I had to be careful not to display too much enthusiasm; I know it's asinine but I feared that offering too much positivity would somehow signal my consent for him to abandon his duty of tending to me.

It struck me then, at that moment, that, since regaining the ability to speak clearly, this was the first time anyone had bothered to ask me for my name. "My name," I mumbled to myself, as my brain began to flood with additional content from the night Cinnamon and I were describing. "That was the first thing those people in the crowd asked me too."

"What's that?" Jeff asked, as he meticulously and over-cautiously turned my head slightly to the left so that I was facing Cinnamon and the sobering truth that our postponed conversation might have reached its conclusion.

"Nothing. Sorry." I knew Cinnamon must have heard me too. We stared at each other in silence but I could somehow tell.

Pushing down around my neck, Jeff inquired as to my tolerance to his intrusions: "Can you feel this, James?"

"Yes." I continued to stare at Cinnamon.

"Any discomfort? Any pain?"

"Not really."

"Can you feel right here?" Jeff pressed.

"Yes; I can feel that."

"Good." Mirroring his delicate assault, on the other side of my neck, he asked, "Do you remember what happened?"

I was sure my answer wouldn't be helpful and that any explanation I gave would only postpone me from getting into the warm ambulance waiting behind me but I answered diligently, nonetheless: "Not really. I was jogging around the neighborhood, like I normally would, and then, all of a sudden, everything went black.

"I was awake but… but I couldn't see anything, ya know? At the same time, I felt my body bouncing all around, like a pinball. It didn't hurt though; it was really more confusing than anything. I just kept thinking: what the heck is going on? And then," I offered, "when I could see again, I woke up under this car."

"Okay, well, I'm sorry to say it, Bud," (he had forgotten my name already), "but it looks like you were hit by this car that you're lying under right here." I wanted to tell him sardonically that my elite powers of detection had already deduced this but I let my chattering teeth bite my preverbal tongue instead. "Can you wiggle your fingers and toes?" he then asked with concern.

I affirmed that I could and then I did it, thinking he might ask me to prove it.

"Good. Now, I know you're cold but are you in any pain right now?"

"Yeah; my leg. It hurts, if I try to move it."

I assumed, as that old joke suggests, that he would recommend I don't move it but he didn't take the bait, much to my relief. I bet he'd heard that one a million times anyway.

Looking over my left knee, with much dismay on his face, he explained, "Well, I'm not an investigator or anything but I'd say your knee here was probably the impact point. Try to keep it still, okay?"

"Okay."

Apparently done with his initial assessment, he finally began to offer a little more insight. "All right, well, the good news is that I think your head and your neck are probably okay, which is actually pretty remarkable. We'll need to get you some X-rays and have a doctor look at you to be sure, of course, but the initial indicators look promising—at least to the point that I'm not too worried about moving you onto the stretcher. Still, we're going to brace your neck just in case."

"So, you think it hit my knee?" I asked that question, to which I already knew the answer, in hopes that it would prompt Jeff into offering some additional information. Luckily, it did.

"Again, I can't say for sure but, looking at the windshield, it looks like the back of your head and your right elbow actually went through, before you rolled off, over the top of the car." He then paused for a moment and yelled out instructions to someone by the name of Tammy: "Tammy, let's get the stretcher and a neck brace out here!" Turning back to me he said, in a much softer voice, "You just try to relax. We're going to get you onto the stretcher and in the back of the ambulance in just a minute."

"Please hurry," I implored. "I'm freaking freezing. My teeth are starting to chatter."

"I can hear 'em. I think even the neighbors can hear 'em. Just hold on; we're almost there." At that moment, as Jeff's footsteps trailed off behind me, I decided I liked the young emergency worker. He had a good bedside manner to him.

As I turned my head back toward Cinnamon, I began to assume that, through various distractions, I had squandered my opportunity to speak with him. "Well," I began to tell my furry friend, "I think that's going to have to be the end of our conversation."

No sooner did those words exit my mouth than I noticed the increased output of the strobing police and ambulance lights, which surrounded the only background my prostrate body could see. Each passing second, they seemed to grow noticeably brighter. Up until this point, they had been more of a minor, muted sort of ambiance, but one to which I had seemingly grown accustomed—like a flickering light in an office building that's just out of reach.

"What's going on with the lights?" I asked Cinnamon.

The snorty sneeze, with which he replied, didn't do much to comfort me and, before I could follow up with another inquiry, I had to involuntarily shield my eyes with my arm. That's because, in almost no time at all, the lights had become almost unbearably bright!

Although I could do nothing other than cover my eyes and wince, I heard a conversation erupting between Cinnamon and another masculine voice, outside the range of my vision. The masculine voice boomed but I could not ascertain the language it was speaking. It wasn't like any spoken language I had heard before.

Curious to put a face to this new character—especially since he and Cinnamon could apparently understand one another—I moved my arm a bit and allowed my head to turn his way. Squinting, I was surprised to see that he himself was the source of the pulsing blue and red light; it wasn't coming from a siren at all. He was carrying it, over his shoulder, contained in what looked like some sort of light-emitting ball.

It was a large sphere—much larger than his blurry head—and looking directly at it caused me to continue to have to squint. After a minute or so, however, my vision slowly became more accustomed to the glow.

When I was finally able to behold the character I had been straining to see, I was absolutely dumbstruck at what I observed: a roughly ten-foot-tall, bald… "thing," clothed in nothing more than a pair of gray boxer shorts—spattered in tiny, conspicuously-placed red hearts—and an open lab coat (complemented by an unusually large stethoscope, which hung from around his neck and contrasted greatly against his otherwise bare chest).

His strange attire, however, was little more than a descriptive footnote, when compared to his third, blinking, working eye—larger than his other two and protruding right out of the middle of his bald forehead. Over his shoulder, he carried that pulsating ball of light and kept his two, smaller, human-like eyes fixed on Cinnamon—while investigating me with his larger, remaining eye.

Mouth gaping, I stared, without even the slightest idea what to do or say. Jeff and a large woman dressed similarly to him, who I could only assume was Tammy, walked right in front of this lumbering behemoth and knelt down beside me. One of them must have had a stretcher because I could feel my body being adjusted onto a cold plastic slab underneath me but I didn't actually see it. That's because I couldn't look away from the strange creature I've been describing. My mind was able to focus only him—this three-eyed, hulking anomaly of humanity.

CHAPTER SIX

As the two paramedics worked to secure my body to the gurney and my neck inside a Velcro-laden, cloth brace, Cinnamon and the creature continued their conversation. The giant spoke words I couldn't comprehend and Cinnamon replied with those that I could: "Yes, Albert. No, Albert. Yes. Yes, now. Do it now!" the dog insisted.

Upon hearing this, the creature, who was apparently named "Albert," produced a large orange and yellow pill, from inside one of the front pockets of his white lab coat. Having now furnished the object, Albert held it out, away from its body, in a pose that suggested the creature was either studying the pill or presenting it to the world that surrounded him.

For several moments, nothing happened. The strange being simply held the medicine between his thumb and index finger, basking in the glory of his discovery. That feat alone was impressive, for the pill was so large that I would have needed all five fingers to grip it myself.

For a panicked second or two, I imagined Albert was going to try and coerce me into attempting to swallow that unswallowable pill. I was, therefore, relieved when he closed his fist around the pill, causing it to explode and expel glittering dust, of nearly every imaginable color, into the night air.

Instantly, the dark night that had surrounded us initiated a meta-morphosis I had previously thought impossible. I gawked, in disbelief, as it generated seemingly random, swirling patterns that quickly evolved into new shapes and molds of their own, filling my peripheral with wonder. What was once simply "the sky" began to pulsate, almost as if it was not only conscious but also no longer devoid of shape! In rapid succession, I saw different sections of it begin to bear color as well.

Gone was the uniform and perpetual, lifeless void of black night that I had come to accept, like all my ancestors before me. I watched, beguiled, as, in its place, patterns of pinks, yellows and oranges began to emerge and permeate the empty space around us.

At this juncture, the paramedics, who seemed unaware that any of this was happening, had finished with my neck brace. Due to its constraining nature, my head was now partially immobilized, which forced me to look upward—not that it would have mattered. Nothing on Earth could have kept me from staring anywhere but upward, at the place where the sky used to be.

Enveloping nearly everything around me, the night had ceased to behave as it always had throughout all space and time; I was now bearing witness to a new kind of reality, where all of the empty space around me began to swirl and clash with itself, not unlike a much more pastel version of Van Gogh's *The Starry Night*.

As I continued to stare it, I couldn't help but liken the way it behaved to cells and/or bacteria interacting, under a microscope. Mesmerized, my eyes patrolled this new sky—this collection of beautiful, ever-changing and (I postulated) "living" organisms. Some repelled each other, while others seemed to absorb their brethren upon their slow and deliberate collisions. All of this formed wonderful and completely unique patterns, shapes, colors and sizes. Some grew, some shrank but they all shared the same slow pace and they all bedazzled the imagination.

Suffice to say, different and clearly-defined sections of the sky were now full of color, moving and bending all about in such a way that I lack the necessary skills to describe.

Retaining their shapes and their place in existence were this Albert fellow, Cinnamon, myself and the two paramedics: Tammy and Jeff. Though my neck's mobility was limited, I still had enough range to make them out.

In order to avoid something in their path, the two emergency workers abruptly turned, which allowed me to catch a glimpse of the ambulance toward which I was being carried. The back door and the inside were vaguely translucent, but still somewhat visible, while the front half of the contraption seemed to dissipate and even merge with the swirling background around us. Cinnamon was following beside us but Albert was not and, as we moved further away from him, the giant slowly disappeared back into the haze he had seemingly concocted.

Now hoisted into the back, Jeff and Tammy worked to secure my makeshift bed, as Cinnamon jumped in, seemingly unconcerned about any possibility of colliding with them. He was out of my line of sight, somewhere on the floor, but I was too preoccupied with everything to care.

Jeff then murmured something about being ready and Tammy responded by walking mere inches away from where I assumed Cinnamon was probably sitting. Once there, she made the motion of closing the vehicle's back doors. I state that she "made the motion" because I felt the wind of the door shutting; I heard the slamming of the latching mechanism locking into place and I even saw a mild outline of the doors themselves shutting but, if I strained against my brace just right, I could still clearly see right through those doors.

The entire ambulance was like this, actually. There was the table onto which I was strapped, the paramedics, the walls of our motorized transport and some equipment but most of it just faded into the background. I heard the engine start and I felt the motion of our advance but the ever-changing, fluid background surrounding me made it hard to tell if we were actually moving or not.

Trying to will myself into a completely upright position, so that I could look down and find Cinnamon seemed futile but I attempted it anyway. Betwixt the physics of the reality where I had always existed and this new and decidedly unfamiliar one, where my soul now lingered, I half expected my body to pass right through those straps, like some ethereal specter, or perhaps in the way that sunlight penetrates water. Alas, this restraint from the old world proved constant here too.

"Hold on!" I heard Cinnamon exclaim, from somewhere below me. I gathered he must have watched my failed attempt at righting myself.

Still able to sit up a few inches and tilt my head forward slightly, I did so—just in time to catch sight of a spectacle that would have left me flabbergasted only thirty minutes before. Now, however, the spectacular—the disruption of everything I had once thought infallible—seemed almost commonplace. Having spent the amount of time that I had in this dimension, I was awarded with a sort of curious bravery that I hadn't actually earned and, as such, I suddenly had more interest in documenting strange events like this than I had in fleeing from them.

It began oddly but still innocently enough. So that I could better see it, the beast's neck seemed to stretch itself forward, past where the limitations of reality should have permitted. I could have handled that but it showed no signs of stopping and the longer it grew, the more my unearned confidence waned. Despite my growing discomfort, his neck continued to elongate itself, thereby closing the gap between us, and that's when I truly lost my nerve.

I saw his neck alter its direct path toward me and begin heading, instead, toward the see-through ceiling. For a moment, I thought it had completely deviated from its course but I soon learned it was simply creating a loop—the kind one would see on a roller coaster's tracks. Upon finishing the loop, his head started back toward me once more but, as it did so, it began to rotate, in a circular motion.

What had started as a sense of brave curiosity quickly devolved into bewilderment and then outright terror, as I watched his head spinning, like a slow-moving top, attached to a neck that was already forming a second loop, on its path toward me. Involuntarily, I began to scream but it did me no good.

Eventually, he finished his second loop and, with that, his face aligned itself to mine. It was as if his neck and head had been following a predetermined, mathematical course that placed his face a few feet above mine, at the exact moment his neck stopped growing and his head ceased spinning.

* * *

"Oh, don't scream," Cinnamon's head annoyingly pleaded, from the end of his elongated neck. "I'm just trying to get a better look at you."

The familiarity of his voice was still somewhat reassuring but his grotesque presence no longer was. I felt like I was going to start hyperventilating at any moment. "What in the... What is going on?!?" I screamed out. I had hoped to sound authoritative but, upon hearing my voice crack, as the words left my mouth, I knew I had lost that intended effect.

I was tense and I was pulling, in vain, against the straps that held my body to the gurney, still not convinced they might not simply let me slip through somehow. Cinnamon must have felt my unease. "Look, I really didn't want to scare you," he tried to explain. Gnashing my teeth, I continued to stare, unsure of what to say and so he continued without any interruption: "I can go back to just being a normal dog. Well, one that talks, that is. Would you like that?"

Several times, I slowly and deliberately used my shoulders to lift my head a few inches off the table, letting it then fall back down, each time. I imagine that strained and compromising motion would have been unintentionally comical for anyone who could have observed it but the neck brace didn't make it possible for a more typical sort of nod.

Cinnamon stared for a second and then quickly retracted his neck and head out of my line of sight. I was now unable to see him, without uncomfortably stretching my bonds to their limits, but I assumed he had returned to his previous physical form.

Not sure what to say or do, I allowed my head to lie against the padded stretcher and tightly closed my eyes. I was hoping that this was a dream and that I could force myself to awaken, if I concentrated hard enough. When that didn't come to fruition, I reopened my eyes and bellowed, "What the heck was that?!?"

"I went too far. I know. I'm sorry. I'm going to keep my form," he said calmly and assertively. Tammy and Jeff were calm too. They didn't seem to notice me at all, in fact. I could hear them casually whispering amongst themselves, as they rummaged for something in the cabinets to my left.

"What *are* you?!?" I roared back at Cinnamon, not satisfied with his attempt to downplay his spinning head performance.

"Interested. That's what I am. Interested in hearing the rest of your story."

"What is this?!?" I cried. "Where am I? Who are you? Who was that... that thin—"

"Ah!" he suddenly exclaimed, cutting me off. "That was just Albert. He just... Well, he just gave us some extra time here, I suppose."

"Who's Alb—"

But he didn't let me finish. "It's best not to focus on that," he warned.

"Well, what… I… Am I? How are we even… Am I actually even here, in this ambulance right now?"

More succinctly than I would have preferred, he answered, simply, "Yes."

"These paramedics…" As best I could, I strained my shoulders to twist my gaze in their direction. Upon doing so, I learned that they had apparently found the coveted item they were seeking; in fact, from what I could tell, they were so enamored by it that they didn't even seem to notice the warped reality which had imprisoned us all.

Bothered by their apparent lack of perception, I watched as they removed what looked like a couple toothpicks, from a jar they found in one of the cabinets. "Hello?" I condescendingly yelled at them. Can you even hear me?!?"

Cinnamon spoke: "They're, uh, well, I guess…" He paused and then said, "They're kind of 'with me' now."

"And what does *that* mean?"

"Well, they're kind of here and… not here. They can hear you if they need to hear you, I guess, is the best way to explain it."

Unprepared for what was about to happen next, Jeff approached me and then used his thumb and his index finger to pry open my eye. Before I could ask what he was doing, he said, in a sympathetic but also exegetical manner, "You have very small fragments of glass in your eyes so I'm propping them open, to mitigate the risk of you blinking and rubbing it in worse."

I must have given a panicked look because he then said, "I know it's uncomfortable but don't worry. This is more of a precaution than anything else. We need to get that glass out but we don't want to try picking it out of your eye, while we're driving down the street. Too risky with hitting a bump or something like that. There is a doctor that is going to be waiting for you, when we arrive. He'll get the glass out and then you'll be able to blink again. Until then, just try not to think about it, okay?"

I couldn't see, feel or otherwise sense any of the glass fragments Jeff mentioned but I believed he was telling the truth about them so I submitted simply with, "Yeah." After doing so, Jeff inserted a small, wooden, beam-like device between my cheekbone and the space under my eyebrow, where he pinned my eyelid—effectively keeping me from shutting it.

As Jeff worked to pry open my second eye, I turned the focus of my thoughts back to Cinnamon. "This is so freakin' crazy!" I said to him. "I mean, I don't even know what—"

"Albert gave us some extra time but it won't last indefinitely," he quickly interjected. "So your story… You said you blacked out, right?"

"I'm sorry; this is just so freaking weird."

"I know," he said, a bit more sympathetically than I would have expected a dog with a rotating head could be. "Don't worry about that now. You were at the restaurant. You had a panic attack. You passed out and you were just starting to wake up," he prompted again.

And so, with my terror now somewhat quelled but my hunt for incoming, dangerous oddities ever-vigilant, I tried to get back into my previous state of mind and continue my story. I began slowly: "Yeah, well… So, I woke up."

* * *

I told Cinnamon that when I first awoke, on that bench six months ago, I found myself in a confused but somewhat euphoric state. The first thing I remember, as that feeling began to dissipate and I slowly reestablished my connection to the real world, was a man bent over me, trying, in vain, to communicate some sort of message. I got the sense he was growing frustrated from having been trying to do so for some time.

Specifically, I recall the man's light blue eyes. It wasn't the color that made them memorable though. I remember them because he was trying, unsuccessfully, to camouflage them. For what I presume was intended for my benefit, I got the sense he desired to hide the concern and, more importantly, the fear that was present within them.

Even with the mask he was wearing—one of those pandemic masks that were, at that time, a prerequisite for interaction with the physical world—I could tell he was unsure of himself. That look in his eyes betrayed him and told me he had never come across anything like this before. I took that to mean he was still very young.

When he asked me my name, I had just then, at that very moment, become cognizant of the fact that, up until that point, sound itself had been imperceptible to me. Then, all at once, it came rushing back, manifesting itself in the form of his question. Suddenly, I became aware of the chirping birds, the gentle hum of traffic and the murmur of the blurry crowd I couldn't quite see—as if I was staring at them through a pair of dripping wet sunglasses.

I thought I answered "James Singer" but, at the time, all I was capable of producing was incoherent babble. To my own detriment, though, I hadn't yet come to realize my new disability. I thought I was speaking clearly. For that reason, I found it extremely strange when the man asked me my name for a second time. It wasn't until later that night that Diane explained to me that my attempt of communicating my name was actually nothing more than slurred nonsense.

At about that point, my hitherto myopic vision started to come back into focus and, with it, I could see that the unmistakable concern in his eyes was also present in the eyes of his masked friends. There were three of them in total—all standing over me and staring, only a few feet from my flaccid body. One continued to ask me my name, while another spoke, on the phone, to what I had to assume was a 911 operator. He was talking about me and he was panicked—frantic almost—which only intensified my own consternation.

As my awareness grew, a larger crowd of onlookers began to reveal itself to me. Three young girls, who were wearing masks of their own, were off to my inquisitor's right. All of them had their phones pointed toward me, as if to suggest they were recording me.

Staring at them sparked the realization that I had suffered an episode so intense that it actually shut my brain off and caused me to collapse. Now, as I began to regain consciousness, I found myself surrounded by strangers, asking me repeat questions, talking about me on their phones and filming me, as they did so. All of this, along with the THC that was still present in my system, only exacerbated the situation and sent my paranoia into overdrive.

As soon as I became aware of everything that had happened—of everything that was continuing to happen—the almost calm and serene state in which I initially awoke came crashing down and my panic attack reestablished itself in full effect.

I had to escape the advancing sirens in the background. I had to escape the ambulance I couldn't afford, the cops I didn't trust, the strangers asking me questions I couldn't answer and the girls who were recording me on phones I couldn't avoid.

As if my freedom depended on it, I boosted my head off of Diane's lap, rose off of the bench that had been supporting us and took a step toward the street; however, one of the three guys in masks put his hand out, in an effort to stop me. I didn't care though. I brazenly charged toward him, undeterred and ready to do whatever it would take to get by him.

My natural response is almost always flight over fight but, if I'm cornered, history has proven that I will definitely fight. I think the masked guy who put his arm out to stop me from fleeing the scene must have seen that in my eye and, when he did, he backed away.

That "would-be altercation," in and of itself, stood out to me because of how uncharacteristic an interaction like that was for me.

Seeing a man back up and clearly submit to me like that was so rare, in fact, that I can't think of a single time, other than that, that it's ever happened. Ever! The dominance I asserted didn't make me feel any better though—quite the opposite, actually. It reinforced the fact that something was really off.

I was, nevertheless, relieved that my path was now clear. With the man out of my way, I charged forward, toward the busy street, in the hopes that getting across it would help me avoid any further third-party entanglements. Diane kept pleading for me to stop but I wouldn't listen. My brain wasn't working; it's almost as though it was collapsing in on itself and my entire body was only moments away from imploding.

Finally, after she accepted the inevitability that she'd get nowhere arguing with me, she acquiesced and grabbed hold of my arm to help me across the road. She could see I was still woozy and expressed concern that I was going to faint again. I too felt like I might but I didn't care. I had to get out of there—away from those people, those phones, those looming sirens.

After Diane navigated us across the main street, we made our way into the back of her residential neighborhood. I was still more than a mile away from her house and I didn't have to cross any more main roads to get there but I was unable to let loose and truly run, with Diane floundering behind me, trying to keep up. She was slowing me down but I nonetheless felt indebted to her because she hadn't abandoned me.

The walls and the sirens were closing in, time was running out and the fact that it wasn't yet completely dark meant that hiding would have been impossible. For a second, I thought about taking off in an all-out sprint but, after vacillating over it for a few seconds, I ultimately decided I'd rather be caught with Diane than to escape without her. Everything in my life, at that moment, other than her, had gone berserk and I didn't want to leave her.

Escape was impossible. Apprehension was a foregone conclusion and my anxiety was at its apex. I started to feel as though I might pass out again. My overwhelmed, malfunctioning brain searched for an answer but was unable to find one. Like George Bailey, I lamented over ever having been born and I began to vividly fantasize about simply ending it all, with the first opportunity I'd get.

I just kept thinking: four short years ago, I was happily married, wearing expensive suits, traveling the country and making well over six figures. Fast forward a bit and I'm in the throes of yet another mental breakdown, running through an unfamiliar neighborhood, frantically trying to elude paramedics and police officers, sweat running down my face, heart beating through my widower's chest, barely scraping by and romanticizing my own demise.

Suddenly my thoughts were interrupted by the hairs on the back of my neck. Intuition told me they were standing up because someone or something was behind me, watching me. As casually as I could, under the tumultuous circumstances of the moment, I turned my head to see something that's always haunted me.

A massive, gloomy and foreboding cloud—one that stretched across the horizon and from the ground, up into space—had left the restaurant, on a path toward me, while covering everything it touched in grayish shades of black and white. The buildings it had already consumed were silent, dark and nothing in or around them moved. I watched as it passed over the busy road we had just crossed, while transforming the vehicles it touched. Cars, motorcycles and trucks alike all came to abrupt stops and shut down the instant they made contact with the barometric anomaly.

With a panicked look on my face, I screamed out, "Don't you see that?!?"

Spinning her head around so that she had a similar line of sight to my own, Diane desperately asked, "See what?" She spoke the words with such a sincere concern that I could tell she herself was on the verge of tears.

As my quaking legs turned to rubber, I knew the unescapable cloud would overtake us both in seconds. With no hope of avoiding my fate, I wanted to spend my last few seconds of freedom removing my wet, sticky, clingy shirt. I was on the brink of overheating and I hoped that doing so would cool my core temperature during my impending imprisonment.

I didn't get the chance, though, for it was at that exact moment that a K-9 unit pulled onto the street I was occupying. When I was in clear sight of it, the car stopped and the officer who I would later come to know as "Walcott" got out.

* * *

When I got to this point of my story, the ambulance transporting Cinnamon and me hit a large bump, which brought me out of my reverie and caused me to temporarily pause. The sudden jolt was actually reassuring, however, because I took it to mean we were still moving. The fluid, colorful background, merging with walls that should have defined the boundaries of our vehicle, made our progress hard to detect—so much so that not even the windows offered any clues that indicated movement of any kind.

Upon noting this, I heard Tammy giggle at something Jeff had muttered. That's how their language seemed to function now; unless directed specifically toward me, I heard only low murmurs. Looking her way (again, as best I could), I saw that the two of them were fully engaged in what appeared to be an important, albeit quiet, conversation.

Neither she nor Jeff—despite his close proximity to her—seemed to notice the freshly-formed hole around her left eye socket, where her eye should have been. I didn't know what had happened to it, in the time I had taken to relay my story, but her eye was simply… gone.

When she bent over me to ask if I was doing all right, I mumbled that I was, though I hadn't actually given her question much thought; I was transfixed on not only her newly hollowed-out eye socket, but with the rest of her face as well. It was covered with boils of various sizes. One of the larger ones, on her cheek, seemed ready to burst and, before she stood back up, a few droplets of some sort of pus-like fluid fell from it and landed on my shirt.

Not wanting to offend her, I pretended I didn't notice and looked Jeff's way, to see how he was doing. His blindingly white teeth had begun to melt and drip back into his mouth, filling whatever statement he made to Tammy with a mild gargling sound. I gathered that all of this was evidence that this world was becoming unstable. I didn't much mind though. I wasn't scared. For some reason, I just wanted to finish my story.

In that moment, in the same unnatural manner as before, the "dog" stretched his neck back up and positioned his head above mine, as he had done before. Oddly, I didn't much care this time and—even more oddly—he seemed to have known I wouldn't. I wasn't able to shut my eyes but I wouldn't have done so anyway. Solemnly, the dog then stated, "When we came around that corner—that's when we saw you. Even from the car, you looked pretty crazy. It was… what? Lewis Avenue, right?"

I wasn't sure and I admitted as much. I told him all I really remembered was how Officer Walcott was calm and understanding. I didn't tell him about the strange cloud that vanished once he pulled up because it wasn't necessary. When he learned about my panic attack—that I didn't have medical insurance for the ambulance that had been dispatched to my location and that I awoke, in a drugged and confused state, to strange people in masks, surrounding and filming me, he seemed to begin to sympathize with my situation.

"After hearing all that," I explained to Cinnamon, "Walcott told me he understood my aversion to the cops and the ambulance. After the paramedics checked my blood and I refused any additional medical involvement, he allowed me to walk back to Diane's.

"To this day," I softly admitted, "I still can't believe he didn't try and charge me with disorderly conduct, fleeing the scene or who knows what else. The dog started to muster a reply but I cut him off and declared, "It's hard to admit it but that night—it forced me to really look at myself and, when I did, I realized I couldn't go on living, as I had been. I assumed I'd been losing my grip for a long time but that night proved it in spades."

* * *

After I finished speaking, Cinnamon took the form of a "normal" dog once more and shrunk back down, effectively disappearing from my line of sight. From somewhere below my confining ambulance bed, where I couldn't see, it sounded like he was violently shaking his head back and forth, whipping his cheeks with his ears, as dogs are wont to do.

For a moment, I was tempted to admit my shame for wasting everyone's time—paramedics and police officers who I'm sure had better things to do—but I wasn't able. Before I could formulate even one more sentence, the misshapen, blob-like, boil-covered globs that were once Tammy and Jeff had hoisted me into the air, signaling to me that we had reached our destination and were ready to depart.

They didn't look even remotely humanoid at that point so I couldn't be sure but I think Tammy was in front of me and Jeff was behind. They were pushing me toward the vehicle's doors—toward where I assumed Cinnamon was sitting.

I heard the lock release and felt the frigid night air pass over my body as soon as the doors opened. I'm sure Cinnamon did too. Taking a cue from Tammy and Jeff, he then jumped down, out of our mechanical transport.

I knew this to be true because, as soon as the doors opened, I heard his nails scratch the pavement of the parking lot below us. Soon after, they were frantically scampering across it, before finally trailing off into the unknown. So, with the emotionless courtesy one might expect from a cop concluding his interrogation, the curious dog creature with whom I had been speaking scurried back into oblivion.

Tammy and Jeff then managed to get a pair of wheels to extend out of the bottom of my bed and placed them on the same pavement that had just come into contact with Cinnamon's paws. As we progressed through the parking lot, patches of concrete, cars and certain areas within the sky began to appear sporadically against the new faux reality Albert had introduced into the environment. I watched as the invisible edges of the world underneath Albert's hallucinatory blanket undulated, as if they were trying to reestablish themselves as the dominant reality.

Eventually, our trio passed through some automatic doors and, as we progressed forward, they, like everything else, disappeared behind us—consumed by the unstable, yet strangely beautiful void. The next discernible shape to appear was something that resembled a front desk. My gelatinous compatriots engaged the blurry figure behind it, as two normal-looking aids took me and began wheeling my mobile bed down the hall.

We were moving at a good pace and I wanted to close my eyes to enjoy the slight breeze the speedy cart was providing. Instead, air passed over my irritated, pried-open, arid eyes and caused them to itch, while I thought about the strange dog-creature who had just abandoned me.

It wasn't long before we reached our destination and the two aids left me alone, inside a very normal-looking hospital room. This quiet room didn't seem to be phasing in and out of reality, like everything else. For the first time since Albert crushed that gigantic pill, my surroundings seemed "normal," which I should have found comforting but something still felt off. Though I tried to convince myself otherwise, I had an eerie feeling in my gut that something insidious was approaching.

My worrying was abruptly halted when a doctor barged into the room, exhibiting a commanding presence not uncommon in his profession. He was in his early sixties, I guessed, with a white ring of hair surrounding the back of his head. He seemed nice enough. He was asking me questions about what happened, how I was feeling, who he should call, etc. I answered without much emotion and he soon after retreated to the back of the room, where I could hear him rummaging around for something.

With my neck still in a brace, I fought against the compulsion to try and look behind me, in the doctor's direction, and chose instead to wait patiently. After a moment, he returned—apparently successful in his quest to obtain what appeared to be a tiny pair of tweezers.

As if he was playing that popular board game that shocks players for failing to tweeze small plastic pieces without touching the metal sides surrounding them, he went to work on my eyes. Slowly and deliberately, he picked small fragments of glass out of them. I remember being surprised that they didn't send someone younger but I can't deny his hand was steady and his technique was flawless. After a few moments of observing his competence, I stopped worrying about the procedure.

This glass-picking practice went on for a minute or two and, when he had finished, he abruptly walked away, without saying a word. My eyes were still propped open with sticks and my body was still strapped to the table so I panicked slightly, when some unseen force began wheeling me forward. Before I knew what was happening, my head entered into a cubby hole, which had been cut into the side of a small metal box. Once there, my neck was locked into position, as if it were being held captive by a set of medieval stockades.

Above me, four glass walls disappeared into a metal ceiling, about four feet from where my head was stuck. From the top of that ceiling, there hung a small metal claw. I cried for help but none was forthcoming. Instead, I was overcome, all at once, with the stench of ethanol and rotting flesh. I knew then that I was in the presence of the shadowy figure who attacked me half a year ago—hours after my original encounter with Walcott and Cinnamon.

Seconds later, he approached the glass, while toxic smoke rolled off of his body. He seemed strangely calm and he said nothing. Instead, he took control of the machine and (immobilized as I was) forced me to watch, as the claw slowly dropped closer toward my forehead.

That's when I felt the parasitic slug inside my forehead erupt out from within me and reach for the claw above us. With blood streaming down from the new opening in my head, I saw the little bugger reflected back to me through the glass and so I roared, "What do you want from me?!?" My inquisitor, however, offered no response, choosing instead to stay fixated on the slowly-descending claw he was controlling. When the claw reached the strange, insect-like creature hanging halfway out of my head, it captured it, lifted it, removed it and dropped it into what I imagine was an opening at the bottom of the contraption that had immobilized me.

Afterwards, the demon lifted his hand high and held the bug there, as though it were a precious egg that he wanted me to observe. He then placed his other hand above the creature and, through some unexplainable devilry, used it to draw a very bright light from within the insect.

Surprisingly enough, the light had a sweet odor to it. If introduced to that smell under different circumstances, I probably would have even enjoyed it. On this particular instance, however, once the mysterious phantasm had absorbed the light that entered its hand—like smoke pulled into a fan—the insect, like its master, began to stink of rotting flesh.

I noticed, also, that this strange ritual had left the strawberry-sized creature as translucent as the ambulance doors that brought me here. What's more, this was the first time I clearly saw its head and how it came to an unnaturally sharp point, which I assumed aided it in burrowing into its victims.

With the insect now hollow once more, the wraith controlling it deposited it back into the machine and forced me to helplessly watch, as it slowly made its way back, across my immobilized neck, over my cheek and toward my forehead. Just as it pierced my skin, with its sharp-tipped head, I heard a dog bark and was instantly transported to safety.

PART III

FRIDAY

CHAPTER SEVEN

Without even opening my eyes, I knew I was back in my tub. I knew that being there meant I'd only moved from one shrouded reality to another and, as if that fact wasn't bad enough on its own, I knew, too, that my grasp on existence itself was beginning to deteriorate, at a rapidly increasing rate.

My head still hurt but not like it did yesterday—not nearly as badly as the throbbing in my knee. I had slept with it pressed against the tub in such a way that most of the weight of my body was behind it, driving it into the porcelain wall. As I rolled onto my back, to alleviate that throbbing, I came to realize that I had no memory of taking my pills nor did I remember wandering into the bathtub last night.

A medically-induced lapse in memory wouldn't have been anything new. The severity of this particular incident, however, was alarming even to me. I could no longer ignore the fact that my dreams were getting more frequent, more aggressive and, as evident from last night's escapade, more vivid—so much so that even when I woke I was having difficulty distinguishing what was real and what wasn't.

My snowy jog... My time with Cinnamon, Albert, Tammy, Jeff and Walcott... Even the bystanders gathered around me and the car—they all seemed so real. They *still* seemed so real. My encounter with all of them felt exactly like a legitimate memory and nothing like a distant dream.

That thing—that ethereal, faceless, shadow-wraith thing that has been stalking me—he felt real too and he was getting stronger (or perhaps more desperate). For the last six months, he'd been tormenting me from afar, twisting my mind from the safety of some imperceptible dimension but now... Now he was getting more brazen and better at blurring my understanding of reality itself.

Panic attacks, sleepwalking and recurrent nightmares were all conditions that, up until then, I'd been able to somewhat predict; however, as I stared at the warped ceiling above me, I had to accept the fact that I was losing that ability. How could I ever hope to find the comfort that often accompanies predictability in a world as capricious as this one? How could I ever find a routine in *anything* when I was growing as suspicious of the waking world as I was of the unconscious one?

Yes: I could admit my psychological degradations to myself but, even in my tortured mental state, I was reluctant to admit them to anyone else. While thumbing the folded doomsday note in my back pocket, I began to wonder if I shouldn't reconsider my plan to give it to my doctor.

What other choice do I really have though? Insanity—it's doing the same thing over and over and expecting a different result, isn't it? That seemed to be the most popular definition that people constantly quoted at me. If they were right, then I needed to try something different, to prove I was still sane. It was an interesting paradox: admit my insanity in order to prove I'm sane.

Regardless, I knew that sleep was no longer a viable option so I lethargically schlepped myself out of the tub and into a standing position, on the bathroom floor. My eyelids felt like they had tiny anchors attached to them, as I unzipped my pants and inspected my aching knee. It was obvious that a bruise had already begun to form and I was sure, as the day went on, that it would only grow in size. As I sighed and re-zipped my pants, my phone called out to me, with its familiar song.

Abandoning my sloth, I reached into my pocket and retrieved it, in order to terminate its incessant demands for my attention. It offered little resistance and a quick swipe of my index finger put an end to its caterwauling. I didn't even look to see who was on the other end. I needed more time to gather my thoughts first.

Closing my eyes, I let the triviality of the new day resonate inside of me and it didn't take long before it began to numb me. After several long, self-reflective seconds, when I finally opened my eyes again, I stared at the phone and wondered if I'd still have it after carrying out my plan for Monday. After a bit more contemplation, I engaged the fingerprint reader, on the back of the device, to open it up for use. When the phone sprang to life, I saw I had several notifications awaiting my perusal.

I skipped the "Missed Calls" and "Memories" notifications and headed straight for "New Text Messages." There were two: an automated text, from my doctor's office, confirming my appointment on Monday and another from a former colleague of mine named Tina. It said, "Did you get that e-mail I sent you last week?"

Tina and I used to work together and she, like me, wanted out. She'd been talking about leaving for quite a while and I had promised to help her, by way of reviewing her resume. With my insecurity around my own lack of employment, however, I couldn't bring myself to get started and so I'd been ignoring the poor girl. I felt properly selfish for doing so; regardless, I continued my pattern of avoidance by closing her text and opening my newest "Memories" notification.

Every so often, through some technological programming I didn't fully understand, my phone would find old photos I had taken and then resend them to me, as "memories." I'd taken this particular series of images exactly one year ago. They were all of me alongside Fisky—my on-again, off-again girlfriend. She'd been "off-again" for over six months—by far our longest separated stint.

The photos themselves showed us laughing and smiling, while ice-skating around a small, snowy island in the middle of a frozen lake. One of those images—the one I stared at the longest—had us both posing for a selfie, underneath a tree where I had carved "Fisky & James" inside of a heart.

Below the photo, my phone, which had recognized Fisky's face, displayed all of her information, including her name, number, e-mail address and "Last Text Message." She had sent it more than six months ago and it said simply, "We need to talk." I had called her right after I'd received it—a piece of information also archived for me by my phone—and I hadn't spoken to her since.

I knew, deep down, at the base of my soul, that a long-term romantic relationship would never work between Fisky and me. There was, however, an unmistakable chemistry between us so, on multiple occasions, we tried a platonic friendship but that never worked either. Despite the lies I told myself at the outset of such attempts, I knew that I would always want more than a friendship from her.

She then would either reject that sentiment (which, of course, would crush me) or she'd acquiesce to it, only to change her mind several months later (which, of course, would crush me). That was our cyclical pattern. It was inevitable. I couldn't be her lover because it would always end in heartbreak and I couldn't be her friend because I'd always end up yearning to be her lover. I knew, in other words, that she was a doomed prospect but, even with that knowledge, I still loved her nonetheless.

That's a terrible place to be—to know irrefutably that the outcome of a relationship will always end in one's own destruction but to still want that person anyway. The only solution I could find was to try and avoid her altogether but doing so, as I had been, just made me feel guilty. I was afraid she perceived my deliberate disengagement from her as a slight—a feeble attempt to punish her for hurting me. She didn't deserve that. She wasn't, after all, approaching me with malicious intent; quite to the contrary, I believe she actually wanted to make it work every time she committed to trying. I, therefore, felt guilty when I ignored her and helpless when I engaged with her. It was a catastrophe. It was Hell.

For the moment, however, I tried not to dwell on Fisky and focus, instead, on the automated message from my doctor. I scrolled back up and read it again. Monday. That was only four days away. Knowing that I'd be able to force a conclusion by then was frightening but it was also ironically empowering. As I thought about that momentous day, I ran my fingers through my matted hair and considered the future. Was I really ready for this? Though I couldn't honestly know for sure, I supposed that I would find out soon enough.

* * *

With my thoughts still on Monday, I reluctantly decided to examine my missed calls. My mother had called once (the call I just ignored) and there were multiple "missed" calls from Chris as well. He had apparently tried me several times last night. He called so often, in fact, that I programmed my phone to silence his calls altogether—to not even alert me when they were happening, in real time. I felt guilty for doing so but short of completely blocking him, which I knew was also wrong (but somehow worse), I didn't know how else to avoid him.

I'd met Chris several years back, at my mother's house. She had hired him to install some cabinets but, when the installation day came, an emergency arose requiring her presence. Not wanting to leave a stranger in her home unattended, she asked me to sit in, while he completed the work and I agreed.

For the majority of the day, Chris talked ad nauseam—as if it was his only goal in life. As he did so, he seemed completely unaware of my attempts to politely drown him out with anything I could grasp: books, the TV remote, my phone. Nothing worked. He just seemed so thrilled to talk to me that I eventually gave in and chatted with him, while he completed his task.

He told me about a new business venture he wanted to start, as a life coach, but mostly he wanted to know more about me. I remember thinking what a rare trait that was. After he'd heard enough of my stories, he told me I should give him my number, "so we could hang out sometime." I had no intention of befriending him but I didn't want to hurt his feelings so I gave it to him. I had never physically met him out anywhere; nevertheless, he continued to call and to treat me like I was some sort of VIP. It was flattering, of course, but annoying as well.

Seeing his name, along with Tina's and my mother's, reminded me of the quandary I'd create if I continued to leave all of those people unanswered. Chris, without a doubt, would just continue to call until I answered him. My mother... who could say? Once, when I was sick and passed out upstairs, in my own home, sleeping with my phone turned off, so as not to be disturbed by it, she sent my brother over to confront me because the only logical reason for not getting back to her within the hour was that I must have been dead or, at the very least, taken hostage by Islamic terrorists. To be sure, Chris was a little less extreme in his reasoning but I knew his incessant calls, like those of the telemarketers I ignored, wouldn't stop until I finally answered one of them.

Don't get me wrong: on some level, I liked Chris and I didn't want to ignore his calls—especially since he always seemed to be coming from a place of genuine concern—but he was a talker and I didn't much feel like talking. Of course, I loved my mother too but I just wanted to be left alone, with my thoughts.

So, at the bottom of my mother's chat log, in the "Reply" section, I constructed a "Saw I missed you. Can't talk now but everything cool?" text message, which I also sent to Chris. Not writing them each their own personalized messages made me feel like a schmuck. Still, I left the phrase copied to my clipboard just in case I would need to use it on someone else.

Ashamed but also satisfied, I propelled myself into the bedroom, plopped down onto my bed and removed the doomsday note from my pocket. Because of what it represented, I was considering throwing it in the trash, when my phone began to ring once more. My Caller ID proclaimed the call was from my psychiatrist's office, which was odd because they'd never called at an unscheduled time before. For a moment, I deliberated on whether or not to answer but my curiosity eventually got the better of me. So, with a lack of vigor and a hint of concern, I used one hand to place the note back into my pocket and, with the other, I connected the call and answered, "Hello?"

I could tell the receptionist on the other end hated her life; I could hear it in her voice. She seemed annoyed by the very fact she needed to call me at all. The feeling was mutual. I almost told her as much because I thought it might endear me to her. Ultimately, though, I decided that I didn't really care what she thought of me. If we both hated ourselves, why should we have to try and like each other?

Up until this point, all of my sessions with my psychiatrist had been done through the phone but now the receptionist was calling to tell me that, if I wanted it, I'd be able to meet with the doctor in person. As peoples' concern over the pandemic began to taper off, businesses were starting to get laxer with their isolation-based policies. Apparently this business was no different.

So, without giving it much thought, I agreed to this new format and thanked the woman on the other end for mentioning it to me. "Sure," she quietly replied, while loudly clicking her mouse and aggressively pecking away at her keyboard. Through her labored breathing and her abuse toward the inanimate objects occupying her desk, I could tell she'd rather be elsewhere.

For several long seconds, she produced the only sounds between us. I wasn't sure if she expected me to speak so an awkward silence began to grow, as her key clicking continued. As I paced back and forth, between the bedroom and the bathroom, I wondered: should I tell her about the three-eyed, giant doctor, the talking dog, the translucent slug, my otherworldly stalker or the deteriorating space-time continuum? Finally, after what seemed like centuries, she asked if I needed the office's physical address.

After I affirmed that I did, I could then hear her ruffling through some papers, while she herself searched for it. This told me she was likely new. Once she had found the paper for which she had been searching, she then relayed the address to me and I stopped, in front of the bathroom mirror, to type the location into the scheduling app on my phone, while the receptionist waited.

Only then, as my time with the office worker drew to its end and we bade each other a good day, could I hear even the faintest murmur of joy in her voice. It actually made me feel bad, knowing that, in mere moments, she'd likely have to make another phone call and reignite her misery all over again.

I found myself yearning for sleep, as I terminated the call and deposited my phone onto the cluttered bathroom counter. Even if it had to be done in the bathtub, I always preferred sleeping in the daylight's warmth. Through the blinds and the closed window, I could feel the sun calling to me. It reminded me of how it used to hold me and comfort me in its warmth, while I slept. If only it would do so now.

The sun seemed to freely lend its radiating tranquility, while the moon worked feverishly, throughout the night, to fill my head with incessant babble—to unhinge me and to pose questions that could not be answered! Its lunar pull blurred reality and penetrated my skull, skewering my sanity and forcing me awake to struggle endlessly, as I concocted indecisive and maddening schemes that led altogether nowhere and, at the same time, everywhere.

It was in the light where I was most comfortable—where it would make the most sense to let my guard down and sleep—but it's in the dark that I most often closed my eyes and left myself vulnerable.

While lamenting my diurnal biology, I was suddenly overcome with despair. I felt an unfillable emptiness inside of me and so I began to sob—not uncontrollably though. These were just a few leftover tears, from a well that had dried up long ago. I casually wiped them away, as I hunched over the counter and inspected the open bottle of sleeping pills there before me.

"Zero Refills Remaining," according to the sticker prominently displayed on the front of the bottle. That didn't really matter though. I had enough to last me until Monday. After that... well, I doubted it would matter.

Placing my left hand on my cheek, I pushed down, in a circular motion, against all the skin around my face. I hoped that doing so would somehow rejuvenate me. It didn't.

Then, as I scrutinized the much tinier, virtually unreadable directions on the back of the bottle, I saw one line that stood out. In bold and enlarged print, the warning stated: "Do not take more than one pill every 24 hours." I'd had enough of the world's constant warnings, though, and I wanted sleep above anything else.

Suddenly, every object in the room (including myself) assumed its own individual muted shade of gray—everything except the floor, that is. There, a shin-high, black, smoky tar arose from beneath the flooring and attached itself to my legs. Like a mouse caught in a glue trap, I tried to yank them free but quickly found that I lacked the necessary strength. My eyes then started darting about the colorless room, as I searched for any explanation for these bizarre circumstances. Eventually they landed on the bathroom mirror, which, in some inexplicable way, failed to cast my reflection back to me!

With disbelieving and tightly-squinted eyes, I leaned forward, until my face was only inches from the mirror. It was casting back the darkened room behind me but my own reflection was still conspicuously absent. Flummoxed by this strange development, I continued to search for myself until a jet-black fist, from the other side of the mirror, suddenly slammed into the glass.

The loud crash of the fist against the glass would have caused me to fall over, had my legs not been held still by the smoke below. Even with my legs in a stationary state, I leaned back, as much as possible, only to watch, in horror and astonishment, as my nemesis—that shadowy maniac from before—appeared behind the glass and began a violent, fist-smashing barrage against it.

Before I could give the situation much thought, though, I found myself grimacing and clutching my head in pain. I did so because I could feel the animal living inside of my skull thrashing about and wrecking the insides of my head. Then, when the pain became near unbearable, it addressed me in spoken form!

"Do it," the disembodied voice commanded with as much menacing conviction as I had ever heard. It sounded both distorted and forceful at the same time. Writhing in a standing position, I ignored it for as long as I could but it wasn't long before it repeated the demand in a much louder tone: "Do it now! Take them!"

"Leave me alone," I shouted back, out of frustration.

"DO IT! DO IT! DO IT!" it demanded with an even harsher emphasis than before. Just then, the creature behind the mirror landed a blow that caused the fragile instrument to crack. Concentrating his efforts on that crack, he then began pounding on that weakened area over and over again, without showing any noticeable signs of fatigue.

"Get out of my head!" I retaliated, in a voice I had tried to elevate, in order to match that of the petulant insect inside of me. Despite putting all of my energy into that attempt, I noticed that the louder its voice grew, the feebler my own became. After a few more similar exchanges between us, while the wraith continued chipping away at the fractured mirror, the creature inside my head kept increasing the volume of its voice at an exponential rate. It almost sounded like it was being amplified through a stadium-sized speaker while mine sank to little more than a whisper. The reverberations caused by its howling were so intense, in fact, that I could actually feel the air around me begin to shake.

"DO IT! DO IT! DO IT!"

I desperately covered my ears and shut my eyes, in an attempt to drown it all out. All at once, the room then became quiet and, when I opened my eyes, the smoke, the slug and the wraith were all gone. The bathroom mirror was back to normal too but the room itself was still gray. In order to try and remedy that, I planned on raising the window's blinds but found that my body would no longer obey my commands.

I fought to regain control over myself but it was useless. Exhausted, I eventually ceased struggling and allowed whatever was controlling me to reach for that bottle of pills on the counter.

CHAPTER EIGHT

Now, with a mouthful of medicine, the being controlling my body reached out for a well-hidden, long since discarded bottle of water. To the untrained eye, the tepid bottle of liquid would have appeared camouflaged amongst the disheveled wreck of various toiletries scattered across my bathroom counter; however, this being and I—we shared the same mind and he knew exactly where to look.

In his haste to acquire the item, in a body he was still learning to control, he accidentally knocked over a capped aspirin container, causing it to tumble into the sink below. Without much consideration for the fallen bottle of headache pills, he then grabbed hold of the water, while allowing the container of aspirin to roll back and forth, at the bottom of the sink, until the drain plug finally held it in place.

As if he was taking a shot of something much stronger, he then threw the water down my throat and forced me to swallow. Pausing only for a moment, he took another mouthful of sleeping pills and repeated the process. He then did it again. Another mouthful of pills, another shot of water. And again. And again.

I don't remember exactly how many times he repeated this process but I know we voided the contents of the container. Upon ingesting the final dose, he arrogantly chucked the weightless bottle to the side. It's strange but, at that moment, I actually felt emancipated—as though I had instantaneously shed all the encumbering worries, trepidations and anxieties that weighed down my poisoned soul. I felt so good, in fact, that I didn't even mind it when he opened up that aspirin bottle, at the bottom of the sink, and started the process all over again.

Although I myself controlled nothing, the level of freedom I began to feel was intoxicating and I was actually glad I had submitted to whatever was happening to me. I didn't want that liberating sensation to end and therein was the irony, which, even as I continued to choke down pills, was not lost on me. I knew what prolonging this escapade would likely mean for my future (or lack thereof) but I didn't care.

A strange calm was washing over me, as he polished off that bottle of aspirin and tossed it aside, like he had just done with the empty bottle of sleeping pills. I was convinced that this would be the story of my death, which, whether I liked it or not, would be forever tied to the story of my life. I imagined various people in my life relaying the details to others and discussing it amongst themselves. It wasn't the story I wanted to leave behind but I, like so many others, had no control over that. I simply accepted it.

Throwing open the medicine cabinet door, he then began looking for our next consumable. He found a few remaining allergy pills so down they went. He found a small leftover amount of cold medicine too and decided to take that as well.

With the water bottle now empty, he carelessly dropped it, placed both of my hands on the counter and leaned forward, until, once again, my face was only a few inches from the medicine cabinet mirror. He then forced me to peer into it, as if he expected some sort of revelation that never manifested.

I always hated the mirror; it was an irrefutable reminder of time lost. The young, handsome, twenty-something man I fooled myself into believing I still was, had been snuffed out long ago and here was the evidence, staring right back at me. I hoped it wouldn't be the last thing I ever saw. I would have preferred just about anything else but he kept me standing there for several minutes, until my body began to metabolize the chemicals in my stomach, making me woozy in the process.

Suddenly, the proper amount of light and color returned to the room and I regained control over my body. After a few random movements to confirm I was once again in charge of myself, I extended my pointer finger and began raising it toward my open mouth. I stopped before I inserted it, though, and froze.

I don't know why I ultimately decided to drop my arm back to my side but I did. I could try and rationalize that I didn't know how to make myself throw up or that I knew it was already too late but there was something more to my decision—something I can't explain. I just didn't feel like struggling anymore. I had accepted my fate and trying to undo it seemed pointless and counterintuitive.

As I stood there contemplating my life, my thoughts swiftly turned to Blue and I was overcome with shame. He was standing in the doorway, staring at me. His tail was between his legs, which I took to mean he was frightened from hearing me chuck empty pill bottles across the room. Even in his timid posture, however, the dog displayed an unmistakable speck of optimism on his face.

"Who's gonna take care of you?" I asked him, half expecting him to respond, as Cinnamon would have. Determined to leave my friend in a situation where he could survive without me, I walked briskly toward the kitchen, with Blue in tow, eagerly following, only inches behind me. On my way there, as I neared the front door, I passed my jogging shoes and the small puddle of water that had formed beneath them. With my hands on my hips, I stopped and stared in disbelief at the physical confirmation that those shoes had clearly been in the snow last night.

As I spun around to think, I noticed that a pile of mail I didn't remember retrieving had been placed on my coffee table as well. Thumbing through the stack of personalized envelopes and ambiguously-addressed advertisements, with the hope that doing so would jog my memory, I saw nothing else that lent me any clues as how this pile of papers came to rest on my coffee table.

I came across flyers for stores I didn't want to visit and bills from companies I didn't want to pay but it did me no good. I just stood there frozen, holding that stack of papers, which claimed to prove my existence. For several seconds I stood like that—until Blue's well-intentioned growl reminded me he was in the kitchen waiting for me.

Eventually, I dropped the stack back onto the coffee table and entered the kitchen, empty-handed. Once I did, I slid open the back door just enough to accommodate the dog's need to come in and out as he pleased. Apparently satisfied with this development, Blue barreled past me, into the world beyond my door.

Next, I filled not one but two oversized dog bowls full of water and placed them on the floor. Finally, I filled his food bowl and left the bag sealed but out in the open, where he would get to it. Blue was a good dog and I knew he wouldn't tear the bag open unless of course he was starving and I was too… well, "dead" to feed him.

About the time I finished arranging everything for my dog, I started to slip into an even drowsier state. Apparently, pills take effect much quicker when one consumes an entire smorgasbord of them.

With unconsciousness on the imminent horizon, I decided I had better trudge back down the hall and into the bathroom, where my pillow was crumpled up, in the corner of the tub. Laboring quite a bit more than I expected to, in so short a time, I reached the door and made my way inside. Standing there, I noticed that I had started to perspire.

I turned the cold faucet handle as far as it would go and, upon doing so, cool water began to flow out of the nozzle. Using my cupped hands, I then brought a handful of the cool liquid to my face, to try and make myself more comfortable. After I removed my hands from my face, however, I noticed they were stained red.

Horrified, I saw that a thick red liquid was now pouring out of the faucet. By all accounts, it appeared to be blood so I shut the sink off, grabbed a towel and hurriedly wiped the red from my hands and face. That's when I heard a concerned feminine voice broadcast itself from somewhere within my phone. "James," it happily exclaimed, "I'm so glad I found you!"

Still holding the bloodstained towel in my hand, I paused and turned my head toward the voice, coming from the phone on my counter. Bewildered over the whole situation, I began to ask myself how or when I had even dialed a number. Unsure of where to start, I simply stammered, "Whaa? Um… Hello?"

"Hello, yes. Do you not hear me?" it quickly retorted.

At this juncture, I had all but forgotten about the towel. Like a zombie who had just turned and, in the process, lost the majority of his motor functions, I dropped it onto the floor and just stared the phone, propped up against the wall. I stood motionless, still unsure of what was happening. After a moment of silence, my inquisitive nature got the better of me and I cautiously stepped toward the counter, onto which the device had been left—in its familiar, stationary position.

Towering over it now, I inspected it from above. Other than the voice that had only moments ago echoed through its cold, glassy surface, it elicited every indication of dormancy. This seemingly innocuous gadget, however, gave me an eerie feeling and I sensed a clandestine purpose emanating from somewhere within it.

* * *

I spent most of my adult life skeptical of ghosts and spirts but, since first meeting that homicidal wraith and then taking a romp through the psychotropic bedevilment of last evening, I no longer knew what to believe. I therefore utilized a bit more caution than I normally would have, as I slowly extended my left arm, with the intent of seizing that easily recognizable instrument of communication, to inspect it more closely.

Without warning, I watched, in disbelief, as this hitherto jejune amalgamation of metal, glass and plastic began to transmute itself from that familiar, six-ounce rectangular-shaped tool that fit so snugly in my pocket, into something else altogether. I stood paralyzed, gawking as it sprouted what would soon become four fully-functional appendages out of both its right- and left-hand sides. In less than a second's time, it willed a total of eight green, plasticky legs to burst out from within itself, creating loud, cracking pops, as they erupted into the room.

My hand alarmingly shot back and covered my gaping mouth, while I instinctively backed into the wall. My eyes were transfixed on the eight new, twelve-inch protuberances that were slowly flailing about, in the air. Before I could make a decision on what to do next, these new limbs began to crack once again—all in quick succession—as they bent and formed what seemed to be knees.

The phone then flipped itself over and, on each side of its body, its stem-like legs cracked and bent in two distinct directions. The four legs that were closest to me fractured in the middle, and bent toward me, while the other four legs—the "back" legs—bent the opposite way, toward the wall behind the sink. The feet followed next; at the bottom of each leg, where the plastic touched the counter and the back wall respectively, eight nubby feet appeared after more shrill-sounding cracking and popping.

I shuddered at what happened next. Those eight nubs planted themselves firmly onto the closest surface (wall or counter) and, with the assistance of each leg's bending knees, lifted the phone into the air, thus giving it an arachnid-like appearance. Literal chills shot through me and I even gasped in horror, as it adeptly utilized its new legs to quickly retreat several inches up the wall, just as a silverfish would do, once it realized a potential predator had spotted it.

Without forming any discernible words, I cried out in dismay.

"I'm really sorry!" my phone belted out, from against the wall to which it was sticking.

Not knowing what to say next, I tried to think of a way to quickly and succinctly articulate my dismay, my frustration, my fear and my overwhelmed and beguiled mind. I didn't even know where to start so, instead, I just shouted some particularly nasty obscenities into the ether.

"This form—is it… Does it frighten you?" the creature asked. Just then, as I heard those words, did I begin to take notice of the calm and strangely soothing female voice that spoke them. Something about that voice… It was understanding somehow. It was instructional yet patient and empathetic—the kind of voice I would expect from a teacher or counselor of sorts.

For a moment, that voice disarmed me. With my angst temporarily halted, my brain began to gradually function once more, allowing me to better examine the situation; however, I was far from achieving a true sense of relaxed comfortability. Even so, I was grateful that the voice addressing me was able to somewhat soothe my mind, even if ever so slightly.

My knees and elbows were slightly bent but locked in place. My entire body was as stiff as a rusted door hinge and, until now, I hadn't dared to move it for fear it might break. That voice though—that voice made me think I should try.

It took deliberate focus but I was eventually able to cautiously unlock my left arm and hold it out, toward my phone, pantomiming that same "stop" posture I had seen cops and crossing guards give so many times before. I assumed this stance, as a meager and ineffectual means of protecting myself, should this creature decide to lunge at me. With my arm now mostly extended, and my mind still transfixed on that voice, I began to crack open my mouth to speak.

I don't remember what I intended to say but whatever it was abruptly rushed out of my head, creating a vacancy for everything except fear. Instead of engaging in discourse, I howled, as this cellular anomaly scuttled further up the wall, away from my outstretched arm.

I could feel it: the panic attack. The thirty-second warning bell had gone off. I knew that, in a matter of mere moments, I would either be psychologically overwhelmed or passed out completely. I had to get out of that room! I didn't know how far I'd get before my affliction overcame me but I didn't care.

In an apologetic tone that failed to settle me this time, the plastic monstrosity before me bleated out, "I really am sorry and I was hoping we wouldn't have to go through all of this again. I kind of sens—"

And with that, I pivoted around, into an explosive, crouched stance—not unlike the one I had adopted when I need to change directions, while running back and forth sprints, as a kid. This abrupt action would have given a split-second indication, to the creature across from me, that I intended on running out of the room so I moved as quickly as I could, in order to preemptively circumvent the abnormality on my wall from trying to stop me.

Out of my periphery, as I initiated a purposeful stride I had hoped would carry me to safety, I saw the creature scamper off the wall and onto the sink, where it reached out, with a few of its legs, and yelled "Waaait," in a worried tone. I was in no mood to listen though. Driven by instinct, I plunged through the doorway with equal parts desperation and determination.

* * *

My left leg was the first part of my body to pass through the archway that separated the bathroom from the hallway. I was mid-stride, several inches off the ground, as I waited expectantly for my shoe to touch the cheap laminate floor in the hallway outside. That never happened, though, and I was both as confused as I was terrified when it continued down, well beyond where I had expected the floor to be. As my leg continued downward, through the floor, so too did the rest of my body, as if I had just blindly run off the edge of a cliff.

I passed through the floor, which seemed to be nothing more than a hologram. First my shoe, then my leg and finally my entire body fell through that mirage, creating the kind of ripples one would expect to see in a lake or a pond and, as I fell into the blackness below me, my body twisted so that I was facing the doorway from whence I had entered this world.

After falling for what I surmised was only a few feet, my descent slowed considerably and I began to feel like I was hovering weightlessly in the space below my floor. The reverberations caused by the ripples of my plunge were now moving violently through the floor, wall and ceiling of the trailer above me. Eventually, they became so extreme that the building itself seemed to melt completely away. Only the archway of the door remained now—its white, glowing trim juxtaposed against the otherwise black and empty void where I now floated aimlessly.

Coming from the doorway, I could see the light from the bathroom cutting into the otherwise all-encompassing darkness. I could also hear a garbled voice, calling for me. It seemed worried. It sounded like the creature who had possessed my phone but the voice was being drowned out by static—the kind I used to hear when I would turn on an old tube TV to a station it couldn't receive. "White snow," we used to call it.

The utter absurdity of the situation had caused a temporary delay in the countdown to my impending panic attack. Such was the intensity of what had just transpired that my mind had completely glossed over the feelings of dread that had nearly overtaken me, just moments ago. I was, therefore, confused but somehow comforted as well.

The voice that would have been calming to me, had it been attached to a different body, was now indiscernible amongst the distortion that surrounded it and so, while floating in a world that—by all accounts—seemed to be deficient in gravity, I somehow managed to twist my body away from that doorway, toward the perpetual darkness below me.

In that direction, darkness shrouded everything. The lost city of Atlantis, in all its grandeur, could have been only a few feet from where I was floating but I wouldn't have been able to see any of it. When looking downward, as I currently was, I couldn't even see my own hand in front of my face.

At that moment, I remembered the miniature flashlight attached to my key chain. Given the far superior flashlight function on my phone, that three-inch, light-generating tube was a gift I thought I'd never need but, to be fair, I hadn't anticipated fleeing from my shape-shifting, sentient phone and falling through my floor, into the abyss, either.

Anxiously, I reached into my front pocket, acquired the device and then twisted the tip of it into the "on" position. Though it did provide a miniscule amount of illumination, it told me nothing about the size of the space I was inhabiting, for it was only able to pierce a few feet into the darkness, before its light ultimately tapered off into nothing.

I've read stories about cave divers and how, after they swim down and reach certain cave floors, they'll sometimes discover small openings—openings barely large enough for humans to pass through—which they somehow manage to squeeze by, in an effort to delve further into the cave's hidden chambers. Many times, I've heard divers describe those areas below the cave's first floor as being filled with utter darkness. They'll say that their flashlights provide the only light, in any direction, and that, when they're in those secret chambers, they get the sense that they're almost floating in infinite space. Finally, I had some semblance of what they meant.

Still, this was not "total" darkness. I at least had my little key chain flashlight, as well as the light source above me. It was coming from the doorway through which I had just passed.

That inauspicious archway above me—it now existed as the only remnant of my otherwise dissolved trailer, where my possessed, spider-like phone was waiting for me. The light spilling out of that doorway was faint but consistent. It seemed to stretch on, traveling in a tight, mathematically-straight line that evenly decreased in size, until it came to a focal point and formed a small rectangular shape, which seemed to be just in front of me.

From where I floated, I had presumed that small rectangle—the only other discernible shape in any direction—was only a few inches tall; however, when I reached out to grab it, I realized the singular light source, in an otherwise lightless universe, had compromised my depth perception and that this small rectangular light was actually much further across from the place where I was levitating freely. Through logical deduction, I postulated that it was likely much larger too.

Subsisting within the darkness, there was only the doorway above me, the beam of light spilling out of it and the path it illuminated, toward the mysterious rectangular object far off in the distance. Determined to reach it, I began to emulate the motions of a swimming frog and grew alarmed when my efforts didn't propel me forward. Instead, I thrashed about, in a stationary position.

It was then that I inexplicably began slowly and uncontrollably drifting back toward the doorway above me, as if I had been caught in some sort of invisible tractor beam. As I ascended, my body was slowly pulled—feet first—into the light the doorway was casting. When I was fully immersed in the light and I was close enough that it seemed I was only moments away from being pulled back through the portal disguising itself as my bathroom doorframe, however, I made my move.

Without much effort, I positioned my leg so that my shoe was on a collision course with the outside of the doorframe. Seconds later, when it made contact, I bent my knee and kicked off against that white wooden frame, like an untethered astronaut kicking away from the outside of his ship, as if he was on a suicide mission. Having thus jettisoned myself away from that door, I found I was drifting toward the distant, illuminated, rectangular object, which I hoped would offer me salvation.

I was now traveling toward my destination, in the middle of an illuminated pathway that existed between where I had been and where I was heading. Though it was through the deliberate efforts of my one-legged lunge that I was currently propelling myself forward, along that pathway, I couldn't help but feel like I was somehow escaping, or possibly even altering, my destiny. It was both enthralling and worrisome, at the same time.

Once again, the auditory distortion returned and I could hear an obscured voice behind me, yelling a warning about something; however, the further I progressed, the less audible it became until, finally, I heard nothing at all. When the voice finally cut out completely, it left me in total silence. At that point, I tuned back, to look upon the archway once more, but, to my amazement, there was now a giant, snug-fitting mirror inside of it. It fit so well, in fact, that it was almost as though it had been fashioned for the specific purpose of filling up the white doorway.

While the old doorway had been *generating* the light, it seemed that the mirror, which took its place, was simply reflecting it. As I came to realize that, my determination to reach the mysterious object, at the other end of the light tunnel, only increased.

While I helplessly drifted toward that tiny white rectangle, I could see it gradually beginning to take shape. Slowly but surely, it began to resemble yet another mirror, inside of another white, human-sized archway. Eventually, when I got close enough that there could be no doubt that I had correctly identified the peculiar mirror, I was able to see my own reflection advancing toward itself.

Somehow, my body came to an unexpected halt when I was just inches away from my reflection, inside the eight-foot-tall mirror, which, for all intents and purposes, seemed to be an identical clone of the one from which I had just pushed away. It made no logical sense but somehow these two mirrors—the new one in front of me and the old one behind me—were reflecting a trail of light between themselves, with no discernible source to be found.

For a moment, I stared at myself, floating in the silent and slightly chilly nothingness that surrounded me. Then, although it should have been far behind me, where I left it, I watched the mirror I had escaped suddenly materialize only twenty yards behind me, thus granting me the ability to stare at my reflection's reflection.

These two mirrors pointing at each other had somehow captured not only my own reflection but also the only light in the otherwise pitch-black abyss. I tried to imagine how this could be possible, while they cast my corporeal form back onto itself in perpetuity—creating an infinite loop of identical dimensions whose existence all depended on the survival of my own.

Unable to look away, I kept my gaze focused on the mirror in front of me. Without warning, I watched it crack and splinter in such a way that caused it to form a pattern resembling a spider web—the kind one might expect to see when someone's head slams into a windshield from inside a car. It stayed that way for a couple seconds only and then flashed a much brighter light that momentarily blinded me.

A few seconds later, when I could see again, I found myself hovering outside the doorway to my bathroom—though, when I somewhat timidly peered inside and transfixed my gaze toward the sink, I could tell this version of the room was slightly different than the one I had just escaped. There sat my seemingly inert phone, propped up against the wall, amongst some soap, my toothbrush and a gaggle of other insignificant toiletries. Below all of that, there was a curious pile of disheveled and discarded pages strewn about the floor. Blue ink covered all of the pages that weren't turned upside down but, from my vantage point, I wasn't able to read any of them.

Other than the pages and the lifeless phone on the counter, the room looked much like the one I had just left. Unsure of what to do next, as I floated there, amongst the nothingness, I continued to stare at the scene that had been laid out before me, until my heart unexpectedly sank into my stomach. It did so to warn me I wasn't alone.

Just then, some undetectable, covert force ripped my shower curtain clean off of its rungs and that's when I saw my extradimensional stalker—standing there inside the tub. Luckily, however, from what I could tell, he did not seem to see me. It appeared as though he had previously entered into some sort of dormant state and, for that, I was extremely thankful.

He didn't move. He simply stood there, with toxic black smoke billowing off of his lowered head, while it filled up the room, in the process. In truth, he didn't seem to be aware of anything at all and, as I floated there, I hoped his meditative state would continue. With nowhere else to go, I had to simply hope that he wouldn't sense my presence and suddenly awaken.

After hovering there for a minute or so, without any noticeable changes in his condition, I grew a bit more emboldened. I waved my left hand at him but I thankfully received no response at all. In my mind, his inaction seemed to insinuate stability in his latency and that allowed my muscles to relax and my constitution to loosen. That was a mistake.

The moment I let my guard down, blood began to drip upward from the specter's head. It didn't simply fall out of view though; instead, it trickled upward, to the top of the doorway separating me and that room, and it began to gather there. Fearing his hibernation was coming to an end, I tried to turn myself away to escape but, for reasons I can't explain, I just flailed about, unable to turn my body and retreat.

I was, however, able to at least spin my head around and, when I did, I saw that the mirror behind me had been steadily moving forward. I knew this must have been true because now, it was almost close enough to touch. "Almost," but not quite.

Through the reflection of the mirror behind me, I could see steady drips of blood were still collecting on the ceiling, inside of the doorway in front of me. Then, as if a dam had broken, that slow dribble of life-sustaining fluid suddenly cascaded into a violent and gushing deluge and, before long, there was a river of red flowing from the creature's head. Flowing upside down, it took no time at all before it began to envelop the doorway from the top down.

In a panic, I abandoned the mirror behind me and spun my head forward just in time to see a black, smoky tentacle reach for me, through a waterfall of blood. I was sure it was going to pull me through the blood-soaked archway, toward my death. At that moment, the slug in my head began to break through my skin but I covered him with my left hand and tried to force him back into my head. Just before that tentacle reached me, a green, plastic-like leg shot out from behind me, grabbed hold of my shirt collar and yanked me back, through the mirror behind me.

CHAPTER NINE

As I hurled through the gateway, I realized, along the way, toward my impending collision with the inside of my bathtub, that I had been dragged through my bathroom mirror. Before I could fully process the implications of this apparent truth, however, I thudded hard against the tiled wall, just above my tub, before carelessly rolling downward and landing awkwardly inside of it.

Trying to stand and collect myself (and experiencing much pain in doing so), I heard that calming feminine voice address me once more: "I'm sorry to have pulled so hard but I didn't have a choice." Clutching my side in pain, I used the wall behind me to leverage myself into a standing position so that I could face what I postulated was either my captor or my rescuer. I wasn't sure which.

Before me, just below the mirror, which housed my various medications, was the eight-legged, electronic nightmare from which I had originally attempted to escape. Not unlike a centipede, it perched itself in between the wall and the counter below, with each surface containing half of its many appendages. Resting in this position, the screen of my former phone, which seemed to constitute both the insect's body and also its head, was strategically positioned to face me directly.

Flabbergasted and utterly drained of energy, I gave up any attempt to appear imposing; rather, I decided to slump into the stability of the wall above the tub to support myself. I'm sure I looked defeated, propped up against that wall, but I didn't much care anymore. "What the… Who…" I blathered but, after uttering those words, I cut myself short. I didn't even attempt to articulate anything further. My brain was straining to catch up and I had given up trying to pretend otherwise. Instead, I simply breathed heavily and waited for whatever was to come next.

Before it answered me, the creature generated an image of my tub, on what had become the screen or central point of its body. Quizzically, I turned my head (probably not unlike Cinnamon had done) and my mouth opened as if to speak, yet no words fell out.

"Maybe you had better sit down," the phone offered, extending one of its arms forward, in a gesture not unlike one that a human would make, when offering a seat to someone. Witnessing the objectionable movement of its plastic appendage involuntarily caused me to recoil, as much as the wall behind me allowed, but the physics of the room, coupled with the shear exhaustion I felt, helped to mitigate the severity of that cowardly movement.

"I'm sorry," the voice said, noticing my distress and apologizing once more. Slowly and deliberately, it brought its limb back to rest upon the counter, as it uttered those words.

"I don't care any…" I stopped and sighed. I didn't mean to have so blatantly retreated but the action had just squirmed its way out of me. It made me feel cheap and I wished I could have taken it back. "Look, it's fine. Just… Just what the heck is going on?!?"

"Well, before you ran off, I was about to ask you abo—"

"And what was that?" I blurted out before it could answer my original question.

"What was wha—?"

"That place! Is that going to happen every time I try to leave this room?!?"

"Well… it—"

"And did you, like, 'save' me or something?!? I assume that was your 'arm' or 'leg' or… Whatever! That it was you pulling me through that… that doorway and back in here again."

The creature paused for a moment and seemed to collect its thoughts before answering. "You… you weren't supposed to see that. That's… you're not ready for that. You really shouldn't have run off like that but… We're fine. For the moment, just stay in this room and talk to me. You'll be fine in a little bit." Although it had no face, I imagined it to be smiling, in a genuine sense, when it said this to me.

Despite the fact that I wanted to let its soothing tone pacify my angst, it wasn't to be. The insanity of the entire situation began to sink in and, without warning, I began to feel the inevitability of a panic attack once more. "Not again!" I desperately cried out, while simultaneously cupping my hands over my face, in hopeless submission.

"What's wrong?" it cooed.

"I'm going to have another panic attack. I can feel it coming on," I said, dejectedly. I was convinced, as I had been in the past, that once again the familiar, dread-soaked and uncompromisingly cruel terror, to which I had become accustomed, was on its way to ravage me once more. No different than any other time, I was helpless to escape it. "Not this again," I began to stammer.

"Look, it's jus—"

But I cut its words short, with an angry and dismissive wave of my hand. I was hoping my silent tirade would somehow end my imminent suffering, or at the very least, give me a second or two of reprieve before it overtook me. I then removed my face from my other hand and clasped them both over the back of my neck, before sliding back down, into a somewhat kneeling position, to await my punishment.

That effeminate voice, which my now sentient phone transmitted, through the electronic delivery systems embedded within its core, was encouraging. It became a sort of auditory sedative being administered through my ears: "Just relax. Please. Sit back on your butt. Breathe. It'll be easier," it told me.

Tentatively, I began to acquiesce and breathed deeply. Though frantic, I allowed my rear end to drop a bit further until it came to rest, at the bottom of the tub. There, in a sitting position that had raised my knees up around my chin, I waited. In some way, it was helping but it wasn't enough. Nearly in tears, I murmured in dismay, "Can you please just tell me what is going on?"

"Yes," it replied, with an almost magical clarity. "Listen… Wow. I'm really sorry. I was hoping we wouldn't have to go through all of this again." My trembling was dwindling but it had not subsided completely. With my head lowered, I continued to shake and quietly listen. It paused a moment, as if to give me the chance for another outburst. Once it was sure there were no more forthcoming, it continued. "As I was starting to say, I kind of sensed something about you—a 'shared energy,' I guess you could call it. We're on the same wavelength, you and I. Really."

My response was to grab a chunk full of my hair and slightly turn my bloodshot eyes toward what had up until recently been my phone. "I'm not here to hurt you," it suggested, "so please try and calm down and center yourself. I think it will help."

Feeling a bit better, I closed my salty eyes and felt the sting that always follows when doing so. I continued to take deep breaths and, in doing so, I started to feel the captivating force of the panic attack begin to dwindle. I had, of course, tried this method before but this was the first time it had ever netted any positive results. In the background, I could hear the voice cheer me on, with encouraging words, as I continued the technique.

After a bit, when I felt confident that I had avoided another meltdown, I opened my eyes and gazed upon the strange creature before me. It sat in the same position (halfway up the wall and halfway on the countertop) and its screen was presenting a slideshow of serene landscapes—much like a screensaver would do: ocean, forest, desert, mountaintop and more. They were all there.

"That's better, no?" it asked, without really asking. It already knew the answer. My shaking, at this point, had become intermittent at best. It hadn't completely abated but I think we both sensed that it soon would. "Yes," it confirmed, as if it had read my mind. "I can sense that you're more centered now. You know," it said, "I also sensed your energy, from all the way across the cosmos. That's how I found you."

"What do you mean?" I incredulously asked.

"I was actually really hoping I'd be th—" But it stopped short upon witnessing a violent spasm shoot through my body.

Without warning, my anxiety began to increase once more. Promptly and peacefully, my new ally then corrected my distraught mind's trajectory before it had the opportunity to become unmanageable.

"Calm down," it said once more and, as it did so, it began to change the physical makeup of the room we occupied. Somehow, my arachnid-shaped companion had begun to comingle the image on its screen—a natural, crisp-looking spring, surrounded by a lush green forest—with the dingy bathroom, where we currently sat. Astonished at the scene unfolding before me, I watched as, in matter of seconds, the space behind me changed in such a way that it matched the image the phone was displaying.

The cold, firm porcelain, on which I sat, suddenly elevated itself several feet off the ground, while simultaneously morphing its composition to exist, now, as warm, soft and inviting grass. Behind me, a field began to stretch out for several hundred yards, until it disappeared into the tree line that had formed a natural border for whatever was beyond them. To my left, a picturesque spring begged to be explored, as it glistened majestically from the sun, shining down above it. Birds chirped above my head, as they traveled to and fro.

In front of me, everything stayed the same: the doorway, the vanity, the mirror and the phone. On the ground was a disheveled mess, containing various items from around the house. I opted not to focus on the unchanged, however, and instead twisted my body to gaze in amazement at what was behind me. I was so distracted by all this beauty around me, I had completely forgotten all about my panic attack.

I felt I needed to say something but, once again, I didn't know where to start—a recurring theme, I was beginning to notice. My attempt, as per usual, was anything but eloquent: "Where… how are you…" I managed to spit out.

"Just keep breathing. Slowly. That's it. Close your eyes. Breathe," it instructed. I obeyed, basking in the warmth of the sun. I kept my eyes shut and felt the anxiety drain out of me, through my pores. The voice had become silent, allowing me to acclimate to this augmented state of mind, which it had helped to foster.

Eventually, I opened my eyes. As I sat forward again, the mirror's reflection showed me the natural landscape behind me. It was comforting. The phone hadn't moved but it was showing a new slideshow now. Famous art seemed to be the theme. Every five seconds or so, it would display renowned paintings, famous sculptures, busts of historical composers and even pictures of well-known playwrights I had come to appreciate, throughout the years. All this, intermingled with the forest it had created, was extremely soothing.

* * *

Sensing my newly acquired feeling of Zen, as the strange, phone-like creature surely must have, it finally spoke once again. "I find this pocket of space-time calming. Does this help?"

Looking around at the beautiful world this pocket sized being had created, I was almost forced to admit I felt better and to thank my benefactor for helping to calm my mind, with the veritable utopia behind me.

"Listen," it began, "I'm actually really glad I was able to locate you. I can feel your qi. I can sense that it's aligned with mine—that we were destined to encounter one another. It's as if our spirits are on a parallel course!"

"Do I... Do I know you?" I was almost forced to ask.

"I suppose in a way you do."

"How? None of this makes any sense!"

"The universe is... expansive. The limited understanding we have of it..." It paused for a moment and recalibrated: "Just because you might not be able to understand how it's working doesn't mean it isn't."

Still unsure of what I perceived as cryptic babbling, I persisted: "So, what does that *mean*? Do you know what's happening to me?"

"I know that in one reality—in at least one version of it—your essence and mine are closely connected. And I don't know how to explain it, other than to say that this connection transcends certain 'perceived' limitations of space, but it does. So believe me when I tell you that I recently felt a pull toward your energy. When I felt it, I just knew I had to find you. Does that make sense?"

It didn't. This new age talk—I wasn't sure how those gangly old nuns from my childhood would have felt about it. Still, I didn't want to engage in a debate with a being as powerful as this and so I kept my spoken skepticism in check and answered, "I guess."

"Don't you feel the pull?" it probed, likely sensing my discomfort.

"I don't know *what* I feel. I don't know what's going on. I don't know where I am. I don't know who... or even *what* you are."

"The tru—"

"And I definitely don't know what the heck that was out there, beyond that door," I interrupted, motioning toward the doorway, as I did so.

"Yes, well, you're not ready for that. If you can't understand the pull that is temporarily aligning our universes, then you'd never understand that so, for now, let's shift our focus and talk about something else."

"Why?"

"To be frank, our time is limited and there are more pressing matters at hand," the phone explained, in a regretful tone.

"Like what?" I asked, slightly agitated. As I took a glance back toward the trees behind me, I was beginning to feel more and more dubious as to the merits of the being across from me. Still, under my present circumstances, I'd concluded that talking through my situation was probably the only way to escape it.

"I'm not completely sure but it's why I was drawn to you—why I was able to temporarily connect our realms," it continued.

"I don't know about any of this spirituality stuff but I ca—" But I didn't get to finish.

"It doesn't matter if you know about it. I do. Trust me when I say that I was drawn to your light. I was drawn to it because it's similar to mine. But others will be drawn to it too. Others who aren't as… 'agreeable' as me. They'll try to snuff it out. You're now a beacon for both evil and good, alike. It's part of the reason I was able to find you. We're emitting similar frequencies."

"So, are you like Cinnamon somehow?"

"Well…" the voice said, chuckling slightly. "I guess you could call me a like-minded confidante from somewhere beyond your imagination."

"I don't know about all this stuff," I retorted, unable to hold my tongue any longer. I had hoped my declaration wouldn't be perceived as contentious; however, the need to say it finally outweighed my desire for peaceful discourse. "I think I might be having some sort of a mental breakdown. Or maybe all of these manifestations I'm experiencing are just the last gasps of my dying brain."

"Maybe you're right. I'm not sure. And it doesn't matter what you believe or what your reality is. Our conscious minds can still connect over a cosmic chasm of differences that can both contradict each other's realities, while still being paradoxically true."

Though I didn't completely understand, I was somewhat encouraged by the creature's morbid transparency and I tried to convey that feeling by furrowing my brow and raising my left hand to my chin.

"The truth of the matter," the creature continued, "is that right now you and I are here together and we are talking. It is reality. It might exist within another reality altogether but that doesn't make this particular interaction untrue. You are a part of this moment, here in this place, at this time."

"Okay. Okay. So... what do I call you then? Do you have a name?"

"Assign me whatever name you like. What comes to mind?" it asked.

What *did* come to mind, I wondered. I wasn't sure. As the creature patiently waited for a response, I closed my eyes and emptied my head, determined to name this entity after the first thing my mind conjured up. "I see the color purple," I truthfully exclaimed.

"And so it is."

Satisfied with the interaction, I began anew. "Okay... 'Purple.' So you're here to talk to me but you don't know why?"

"It would appear so."

"Well, until you figure it out, maybe you could try again to explain that abyss under my floor. If you could just tr—"

"I thought we had already established that you don't possess the capacity to comprehend that world yet," she interjected before I could finish. She was respectful and nice but firm too. "Wouldn't it be better to focus on that which you can affect instead of chasing that which is beyond your control?"

Dumbfounded by the sudden bluntness of her statement, I stammered while my brain tried to process her observation: "I don't... What do you mean?"

"You do it all the time. You stare at this screen and you ignore the things you could improve so that you can fuss over the things you can't."

After Purple's blunt assessment, I was suddenly flooded with a particular indignant regret I had long since buried, within the recesses of my mind. Out of nowhere, she then asked, "What just popped into your head?"

"Why?"

"Your light—it just flickered," she excitedly explained.

"What do you mean by that?" I asked dubiously.

"Just indulge me please."

"Well," I started, "I just... something you said reminded me of a conversation I had once with this girl I used to work with. Tina was her name."

"It flickered again!" she shouted enthusiastically. "Tell me about Tina."

CHAPTER TEN

As Purple prodded me to pontificate on my relationship with Tina, I couldn't help but wonder about her motives. Over the last few minutes, she had begun to earn my trust but now I found myself skeptical once more, wondering if I had been bamboozled by some kind of tarot card-reading charlatan, playing off of my emotions, in order to scam me.

I was probably an easy mark, I posited. Much like the sobbing drunk girl, meandering along Bourbon Street is an easy target for a palm reader, I too was clearly out of my element and impressionable here in this world I now inhabited. The difference, I suppose, is the drunk girl, while inebriated, still has the option of walking past the encouraging and invitational wave of the New Orleans con artist. I, however, was, at, least for the time being, captive in this place and so I reasoned my trepidation moot; regardless of her motives, I really had no choice but to discuss whatever topic Purple wanted.

"Right. Tina…" I started, my voice unable to camouflage my suspicion of Purple's over-exuberance. Luckily, she didn't seem to notice my less than enthusiastic tone—that, or she simply paid it no heed.

"Yes. We should talk about Tina," she confidently concluded, much like I imagined that tarot card reader in the bayou would have, after consulting the moon, or whatever the heck it was those people did.

"She's actually been asking me for help with her resume," I reluctantly admitted.

"Did you give it to her?" she asked, as though she had no knowledge of the information stored within her memory banks.

"No," I admitted, as I tilted my head back, to stare at the bright blue sky above me.

"Why not? She wanted your help, no?"

"I don't know," I replied, with my head still tilted upward. "I just... Well... You know how you... I don't... I just..." Then I stared straight ahead, ran my fingers through my hair and said, "I just have a lot going on right now."

"That's not what it looks like to me," she instantly shot back, in a joyous, childlike outpour that often accompanies a child catching an adult in a lie.

In that moment, Purple reminded me of my friend's daughter and how I used to try and tease her—telling her I forgot her birthday or that we ordered her the spicy chili instead of the plain chicken nuggets she wanted, or something to that effect; specifically, it reminded me how, despite my insistence to the contrary, she would continue to rebuke my false assertions and, as she did so, her confidence would only grow, making her more emboldened in her quest to assess and then dismiss the harmless lies I attempted to feed her.

It occurred to me that, whether genuine or faked, Purple's voice displayed a similar tone. When I allowed myself to assume her motivations were pure—when I compared her state of mind to that of my friend's child—I felt a bit more at ease, for children aren't hard to read. Whether their words are pure or shrouded in deception, it isn't difficult to ascertain which. To me, they were no subtler in their incessant hints for greasy fast food and cheap plastic toys (packaged together for $4.99) than Blue was when he locked his eyes on me and drooled, as I munched on a sandwich, from the comfort of my couch.

To be clear, I wasn't suggesting Purple was immature. After all, this grossly-deformed demigod had somehow learned to manipulate space and time. It's just that, in my mind, her inquisitive exuberance matched that of a child's. Maybe this was simply a strategy she was employing—to encourage me to let my guard down—but, at that moment, I had decided not to try and expose it. Her zest for life was helping me to better cope with my situation and to prove that the exterior shell of her terrifying appearance did not match what she was on the inside.

Satisfied with this adjusted attitude I now harbored, I abandoned my contemplations and agreeably concurred that, "I suppose you're right; I *don't* have a lot going on right now. I have nothing else going on, besides what is here with me in this room, right now." This I said with a smile, just before turning my head to bask in the warmth of the sun behind me, just above the tree line.

"So what then?" she eagerly asked.

"Well, I didn't… I mean, I don't know what I could really do to help her." I turned back to face Purple once more. "*Me*, help with *her* resume? I'm not even employed anywhere myself."

"Do you know what I think?" she asked rhetorically. I didn't but I suddenly really wished I did. "I think you're just worrying more about yourself. Your own problems. Your own needs."

"It's not that. I mean, yes. It's probably partially that, if I'm being honest," I admitted, "but no. It's only a small part. I just… does she really need my help on this? I mean, she sees, what—a hundred resumes a day? Why would she need me to give her advice on hers? She should be giving *me* advice."

"Why don't you want to give her your advice?" she calmly inquired. "She's clearly asking for it."

"I don't…" But I stopped and thought carefully about what I wanted to say next. The truth of the matter was that, whether Tina realized it or not, I had, in my own estimations, failed her once before by offering poor counsel and, in doing so, I felt I had discredited myself to her. I had, therefore, stripped myself of the right to give any additional guidance. Up until now, however, I committed to keeping all of those feelings hidden because admitting them to anyone, other than myself, would have exposed me as a fraud and I didn't want to face that fact just yet.

Eventually, I said, "I don't know if I'm ready to get into all of that. I don't know if this is the right place for it."

"On the contrary, you're in the perfect place for it."

I had a strong suspicion she was probably right. No one else here knew me. No one else would hear. Still, I played dumb, for some reason, and asked, "How do you mean?"

"You'll just have to trust me. Go ahead. Say what you need to say."

Ignoring her for a moment, I turned my head toward the crisp-looking spring and wished I could get up, walk over to it and take a sip. Eventually, after several seconds of silence, I relented and said, "Okay. Fine. I'll answer your questions, if it'll get me the heck out of here."

With that, I paused and looked down at a blue ballpoint pen, sitting on the lip of the tub, next to me, just between the place where the grass of Purple's distorted reality ended and the dreary yet familiar reality of my bathroom began. That blue pen—had it been sitting there this whole time? Had I just now noticed it? I couldn't deny that it seemed out of place there but so too did everything else.

As I continued to stare at it, I gathered my thoughts and then spoke: "Um, I guess I would say that I've been avoiding Tina's e-mail because simply responding to it would make me feel… 'superficial,' I guess."

"Why so?"

"Well," I responded, "on the surface, yeah; I could maybe help with that—with her resume, I mean. I could write her a nice reference too. I think that's what she *actually* wants. But I could help her much more if..." Then I stopped, recalibrated and said, "It's not even that I *could* help her, actually. It's more that I feel *obligated* to help her but in a different, more meaningful way."

"What do you mean?" she asked.

"I mean helping her with her resume isn't really helping her in the way she needs to be helped. I can't say for sure but I have a growing suspicion that helping her in *that way* would actually be hurting her. I'm just now realizing it, as I talk it out with you, but I guess that puts me at an impasse. If I help her with her resume, I'm actually hurting her and if I tell her why that's the case, it would require me to admit my own stupidity and my own glaring deficiencies."

Again, I paused before finally admitting, "I'm just reluctant to 'truly' help because doing so kind of inadvertently forces me to admit certain flaws within myself that, well, I know are true. I can admit that to myself but it's hard to admit it to her. Admitting it to her... That makes it real. That makes me vulnerable."

"Admitting what to her?"

"I can't say for sure," I said, "but I think... I think I probably failed her and, as such, I don't really deserve to be in a position to help her now."

"So you feel you owe her an apology then?"

"Yeah. I guess so."

"Apologies almost always make us vulnerable. The sincere ones do anyway." As Purple tried to explain this to me, the image on her screen changed from a bust of Ernest Hemingway to Leonardo da Vinci's famous painting, *The Last Supper*; however, I chose to avert my eyes to the bathroom mirror, in order to take in the reflection of the gentle spring behind me, while still facing forward, toward

Purple. "The very nature of an apology," she asserted, "is to admit your shortcomings, while asking the aggrieved party to acknowledge and forgive them."

"True…" I had momentarily thought about contributing more to her tangent but stopped when I realized I hadn't anything to add just yet.

She noticed. "So why is this any different?" she challenged.

"Because I've been thinking that I might have really messed up with her."

"Did you hurt her?"

"Not physically," I quickly asserted. Then, after a second or two, I continued: "Maybe not even mentally either. I… I think I accidentally told her something that probably wasn't true. I didn't do it on purpose, though. At the time, I thought it was true. I thought I was really helping her but now… Now, I'm starting to think I gave her terrible advice."

"I think I know where you're going with this," she declared, in an even more cheerful voice. "If she got advice from an inauthentic you, it only stands to reason that the advice, too, would be warped, right?"

"Yeah; I th—" But I wasn't able to finish.

Jubilant, now, as her screen changed to Vincent van Gogh's *The Starry Night*, she exclaimed, "I get it! I *definitely* get it!" Then she abruptly self-censored her own enthusiasm, in an attempt to regather herself, and said, "Sorry," in a deliberately diminished tone. "Go ahead. Take me through it, exactly as it happened, okay?"

"Yeah. Sure. Good. Okay. So… I used to work with Tina. We shared a small office together. This company where we worked—it was quite a step down from where I worked before. Actually," I said, staring up at the line where the sky ended and the ceiling began, "I don't know if a 'step' is even the right metaphor. It was more like a free fall, off the side of a mountain."

At this, Purple chuckled and, in doing so, actually caused her body to vibrate a bit. For a moment, I thought of how bizarre that was but I ultimately decided to put it out of my mind and return to my lecture: "Anyway, in short, I went from being the guy with the corner office, the unlimited expense account, the frequent-flyer miles, the exorbitant paychecks, the connections, the skilled team working underneath him and a million other perks it would take me an hour to describe. I went from that to this forgettable, nameless, entry-level sales schlep who had no faith in the service he was selling. Still, I needed to do something so, for a short time, that's where I ended up."

"Money can be a powerful motivator," Purple said, in a dejected tone.

"So can desperation and, more than anything, that's what I was feeling. I had been knocked off my pedestal and I was desperately trying to get back onto another one, as quickly as possible."

After that, the strangely familiar creature on my wall asked, "So, working there you got to know Tina then, yes? You became close with her?"

"That's just it," I said despondently. Lowering my head, I admitted to Purple, "I really didn't get that close with her at all—at least not in a way that sufficiently stroked my ego."

"That's an interesting way to phrase it. What do you mean exactly?"

"I guess I should start by saying I was very different then. I certainly didn't realize it; in fact, I would have strongly argued against it, but, in retrospect, I know now that I was very concerned with money and prestige—with getting back into a position where I had both of those things, that is."

"The pursuit of money and prestige," Purple explained, "can compromise us very quickly, if we're not careful. Its allure can be intoxicating—especially to someone who's lost it and is trying to regain it."

"You're not wrong," I conceded. Then, I brought my gaze directly toward where I believed Purple's eyes likely were, hidden beneath all that glass and plastic somewhere. When I was satisfied she saw me, I plainly said, "But I didn't realize any of that then. Allowing some time to pass showed me how bitter and full of vitriol I was back then but that's not me now. Not even close.

"I certainly have my own myriad of problems but pride, greed and insecurity about my place in the business world are no longer among them. Before I go on, I just think it's important that I make that distinction. I realize, in other words, what a tool I was. The company's issues were the company's issues but no one was forcing me to work there. I chose that environment, at least in some part, because I thought it would help catapult me back to the top and that's on me."

"So, would you say your pride, at that point in your life at least, was making you dissatisfied, or maybe even 'ashamed' of your position there?"

"Kind of. Really, though, I think it was more of the illusion I allowed myself to be a part of."

"What do you mean?"

I'm sure Purple was picking up on the frustration in my voice but I allowed it to escalate, unchecked, nonetheless: "It's just... It's all a scam. And I'm not just talking about this particular company. I'm talking about corporate America, in general. I was so desperate to regain my station within it, though, that I purposefully pretended not to see how awful working at that company would be for me. I knew it from the first interview but I didn't allow myself to accept it.

"Despite knowing deep down that it was untrue, I kept telling myself it was a good company and that I could get ahead if I just kept plugging away. I told myself that because I wanted to believe it but it simply wasn't true. The truth of the matter is that their ideals, standards and ethical code didn't mix with mine and it put me in constant conflict with myself, without even realizing it."

"Well, it sounds to me anyway like you were very proud. Probably a little jaded too."

"I was." There was no use in arguing with her. I knew she was right. "Eventually, I smartened up and put my energy elsewhere but, at the time, all I wanted was for management to see my value and promote me to a better paying, more prestigious position—like the one I had lost.

"Funny thing is: I don't even know why I wanted a more prestigious position. Why would I want to be an integral part of a company to which I was ethically opposed? 'Pride and love for the material world.' That's the only answer that makes sense to me. I can clearly see the folly in following that path now but, at the time, I was blind to it. So just keep that in mind, when I tell you what I'm about to tell you."

"Okay. That makes sense. So what happened?"

"Well, like I said before, Tina liked me but not in a way that I wanted her to like me." As if answering her question before she could ask it, I concluded my statement by asserting, "No; not in a romantic way either. It wasn't anything like that."

"Yeah. Didn't stroke your ego or something like that…"

"Right." Purple was a good listener and it was making my confession easier. "Anyway," I continued, "now that some time has passed and I've gained some perspective, I think I can accurately note things like 'she didn't stroke my ego,' whereas, back then, I would have likely taken offense to such an accusation."

"Self-improvement is a process—in this and every realm where sentient creatures dwell."

More of her cryptic nonsense. I decided to ignore that last part and carry on before getting sidetracked: "Right. Well, you see, before I became this successful businessman, I was this mellow, empathetic, artistic individual—an art *teacher*, even—and, even though all of that had changed over the years, I guess I still felt that deep down I was this misunderstood bohemian who was just wearing a business disguise.

"Tina, I viewed as a kindred soul. She wasn't shy about her art and her passion for it. She revered art but, at the same time, she sat there, making next to nothing, at her day job there with me. They treated her horribly; they paid her far less than she was worth and she continued on—admittedly miserable—thinking that her only recourse was another menial job that would probably treat her just as badly.

"At her core, though, she was, and is, an artist. More importantly, she was a *practicing* artist. She was living her dream and she was doing it every day! She would bring in poems she wrote or paintings she painted. She was the real deal and I—*I* was the fake.

"I saw myself as an artist wearing a businessman's disguise and I just assumed she saw the same thing, when she looked at me. But she didn't. The truth of the matter is she *did* see the real me—this broken-down, self-deluded sales guy who had compromised his dream, chasing prestige at this questionable little company that didn't even care about him.

"At the time, I had completely lost myself. The disguise was no longer a disguise at all; it was reality and she saw it clearly! And of course that's what she saw! How could I have expected her to see anything to the contrary?!? It bothered me that she viewed me as this middle-aged sales guy, ready to sell his soul to the highest bidder but, as it turns out, that's exactly what I was. She saw what I had become, with no knowledge of what I used to be, and it bothered me."

I hadn't been looking at Purple, as I spoke those words; I stared off in her direction but I was looking through her. Upon finishing, however, I shifted my gaze back toward her screen. Her slideshow had continued on throughout my rant.

A picture of Wolfgang Amadeus Mozart stared back at me from behind the glass screen. I understood, then, how she had employed the help of these artists in order to coax this confession out of me. I wasn't upset about how she potentially manipulated me with these great artists though. I was more distraught over the realization that she apparently thought my vanity was elevated to such a level that it dared to suggest I had something in common with these historical icons.

Did my pretension know no bounds at all? Was I *still* just pretending?

"So why did it bother you so much?" my philosophical phone asked, snapping me out of my daydream. "Who cares how she saw you?"

Refocusing myself, I answered, "Because it was a sobering fact that I didn't want to face. I wanted to believe I wasn't really a salesman but that's *exactly* what I was. She shattered the illusion I had talked myself into believing."

That answer didn't seem to suffice, however, as it elicited a barrage of additional questions from Purple: "Why? How? Did she say something to you? What exactly do mean?"

"No. She didn't really say anything. I could just tell. The way she looked at me, the way she responded to me. She treated me the way you might treat a stranger sitting next to you on an airplane. She was polite and she pretended to be interested in our conversations but there was a lot of uncertainty and distance there. It never, ever dissipated either."

"I guess I can understand how that would be frustrating," Purple responded, in that radiant voice of hers. Purple, a formerly inanimate object that I would shove into my pocket, didn't seem to have any discernible facial features, as she perched herself there against the wall and the counter space, so I deeply appreciated her soothing voice. It let me know there was something more to this hideous spider-like creature before me. I was grateful that such a wonderful voice belonged to her.

Feeling a bit more at ease, as these revelations of the self continued to ooze out of me, I continued: "I just always wanted her to feel like

I was on her side—because I thought I was—but I got quite the opposite feeling. Talking to Tina meant looking into the mirror and seeing the real me."

While speaking, I crawled out of the tub and stood directly in front of my mirror—using it as a prop, in my own didactic message. Standing there put me in closer proximity to Purple and so I lowered my voice, sighed and continued: "At the time, I didn't realize that's what was happening but that's what was happening. I think that's why I wanted her to change the way she saw me so badly. I was just like her, wasn't I? Why couldn't she see that? She couldn't see it because it was no longer true and I just hadn't realized it yet. She did though. She realized it."

"And so, you just recentl—"

I didn't let Purple finish her thought. I wanted to keep going. "She didn't fall for any of my sales guy schmooze. The worst part is, I myself didn't even realize it *was* schmooze. I didn't even realize how fake I was."

With that revelation now voiced, I turned to resume my position in the grass, just beyond the lip of the tub. As I lifted my leg over that lip, I inadvertently kicked the pen that had been resting there and sent it plunging toward the bathroom floor. For a moment, I considered picking it back up but I ultimately decided against it and returned to my seat in the paradise Purple had created for me.

When I was comfortable once more, I continued: "I couldn't figure out why she didn't like me. Everyone liked me. For Pete's sake, it was my literal job to have people like me and almost everyone did! Not Tina though. And she never said one thing negative about me either. I could just tell. I could sense it. She was nice and she was pleasant but there was a huge invisible wall there and I just couldn't get through it."

I felt like I had been talking for eons. I was hoping Purple would take over and was relieved when she did. "I know you must already realize this," she began, "but awareness is the first necessary step toward change. I went through a similar ordeal myself." This caught my attention and I wondered what kind of issues my phone might have been dealing with, from within the depths of my pocket.

"Art—specifically, music—is my life," she asserted, seemingly unaware of my Attention Deficit Disorder. "Music is my essence. For a time, however, I ignored music and I pursued other avenues for various reasons that would take too long to explain. The point is, the path I was traversing was sucking my soul dry and, when I finally realized it and changed course, I felt better almost immediately. That's not to say it was easy, though, because, while I felt better for making the change, I also felt remorse for having wasted so much time figuring out that I needed to."

"Yeah. I guess I feel similarly," I said, while my brain was still formulating its response. "It's through philosophy and art that I most easily connect with people but instead of using those skills for good—in a way that could help people—I allowed my greed to twist me and, in the process, I weaponized that gift. I… I 'cheapened' it, all in an effort just to get sales. And the worst part is that I didn't even realize I was doing it. I didn't even realize what I was becoming—how this reduced shell of a person I had become was so much less than what I could be."

"I told you: we're connected," she calmly informed me, once again. "We're of similar mindsets."

Shrugging my shoulders—the way that always annoyed Fisky—I replied "I guess," and waited to see what she'd say next.

She must have sensed my skepticism. I wondered if she hated that shrug too. "It's okay," she told me. "You don't have to believe me for it to be true."

"I suppose so, if truth is relative."

With that, Purple began to laugh, telling me, "That's a whole 'nother conversation."

"I suppose it is."

"So then Tina—she was right about you? Is that what you're reluctant to admit to her? Is that what's causing the barrier?"

I noticed, at this point, that a bird had flown out from behind me and landed on the tub, inches away from where I was sitting. Extending my index finger out straight, I cautiously moved my hand toward the animal, hoping it would hop onto my outstretched finger. I got too close, though, and it flew away. I turned my head and watched it fly off into the forest behind me. Keeping my head turned away from Purple, I commenced to answering her question about what, specifically, happened between Tina and me.

"So, we were talking one day. It was kind of end of the day chitchat. Just she and I shooting the breeze, while closing the office down. Anyway, we somehow got on the topic of her art. Earlier, in a separate conversation, we were talking about her financial troubles and, in my mind, I connected the two things and I decided to give her some unsolicited advice. 'Unsolicited'—that's a nice way of saying advice she didn't ask for."

At this Purple chuckled—that beautiful voice of hers made all the more intoxicating when surrounded by the assurance in her laugh. "Yeah. That kind of advice is very rarely well-received," she said.

"Yeah. And this time was no different. So anyway, I don't know if I was saying this in order to ingratiate myself with her as a former artist—like I said, I desperately wanted her recognition as such—or if I wanted to help her achieve her financial goals or…" I thought for a second and then continued: "Actually, I supposed it was probably a mixture of both but what I told her was this: I said, 'When I was younger, I was very artistic. I sketched all the time and I wrote all the time too: journals, short stories, poetry, whatever. I loved it. It was who I was. It even led me toward a short career in art. I realized, though, at some point, that I would never be able to make the kind of money I wanted to make doing any of that. Even *teaching* art, which I thought was the one exception, didn't bring me enough money to actually satisfy myself.

"Imagine an art teacher who is more concerned with money than art. Is it any wonder I left that world for the corporate one? I explained to Tina that I had to leave, when I finally realized that to be successful in art, it wasn't about talent; it was about who you knew. I told her writers and artists were a dime a dozen because I honestly believed it. I told myself those same things. I told myself things like that because it gave me an excuse not to succeed. It put the onus on some nebulous injustice that I had no way of fighting. It made me a victim. It gave me an excuse to fail."

"We are so alike!" Purple merrily chimed in. So enamored was I with her voice that I put my head on my fist, much like *The Thinker*, and looked at her with almost a sort of reverence. I half expected to see that sculpture appear on her screen; however, without even acknowledging the gesture, she continued on with her statement: "That is *exactly* what I went through. Until I finally decided that I was going to do what I was meant to do."

"Anyway," I said, rudely ignoring Purple's contribution to the conversation, "I told her that I essentially had to grow up and actually change myself—to change who I was at my core—in order to make money. I said it in a much nicer way, of course, but the underlying message was still there: sell out. Give up on wasting your time writing and painting and setting up personal exhibits at local art shows. Give up on your dreams and change who you are so you can make more money.

"I probably said that because it was the path I myself followed but, in the end, it didn't help me much. Yes: I've earned money and accolades but the world is 'literally' crumbling around me." As I said the word "literally," I waved my hand toward the doorway through which I had passed earlier.

"Well," Purple answered, "if it makes you feel any better, I'm sure you weren't the first person to give a message like that to another person."

"It doesn't. It doesn't because I actually meant it and, at the time, it was actually coming from a place of sincerity. I truly, honestly, desperately wanted to help her. The advice I was giving her, though—it was awful."

"Did she end up tak—"

"She was just so talented, ya know?" I quickly interjected, before Purple could start a new line of questioning. "But here she was, working a job that was meaningless to her—a job that was deflating her soul and providing her with just enough money to make her ends meet."

"People have to do what they have to do to make ends meet."

"Yes but it was eating away at her," I argued. "I could see it. It was so apparent. And my advice? My advice was to double down on that misery. 'Find a career that pays more and follow it blindly, casting aside all of your character traits that would in any way hinder your advancement toward that goal. Find that artist inside you and kill it—or, at the very least, put it to sleep.' Again, I wasn't anywhere near that harsh. I don't remember exactly what I said but that was certainly the gist of it."

"Did she end up taking your advice?"

"I don't know." I hadn't intended for my voice to sound concerned, as I said that, but it did. I took note of it and continued, making an effort to be a bit more even-keeled: "I took my own advice, though, and, left shortly after that, to continue my search for the almighty dollar."

Upon finishing my recollection to Purple, she began to walk forward so that she was completely flat-footed on the counter and not halfway up the wall. Once there, she bent her green knees, creating several cracking sounds until the phone part of her body was lying back on the counter, close to where I had originally left it. Her legs then slowly retracted themselves back into the body of the phone and, as this happened, she spoke: "Go ahead and shut your eyes," she commanded.

I saw, through the reflection of the mirror, that the grove behind me was beginning to dissipate. Chunks of reality began to wither before me, causing ripples throughout whatever unknown fabric held this place together. Much too frightened to do anything but obey, I shut my eyes, hoping it would all be over when I next opened them.

"Remember: your flame is burning brightly now," she said in a different, unrecognizable, almost robotic voice. "There are multitudes who would try and extinguish it. Beware and good luck."

It was the last thing I heard her say. Under my eyelids, I could see an orange and yellowish hue, suggesting the room had been illuminated in splendor. After a moment, however, in the same way that water fills an empty fish tank, my eyes began to fill with purple, until purple was all I could perceive.

PART IV

FRIDAY EVENING

CHAPTER ELEVEN

The alarm had been triggered. From a weathered but still very potent speaker, its shrill and unmistakable wailing filled the air. Just above the obnoxious, sun-faded speaker, behind a wiry cage that someone had embedded into the mortar, a red strobe light was continuing on its repetitive, circular path, effortlessly dismantling any sense of security that I'd been able to cultivate.

As the warning persisted, violent, rolling rapids of conscious thought began their daily assault against the dam that separates the curiosities of the dreamworld and the more sinister, structured thought patterns permeating what I perceived to be the "real" one.

The first leak that sprung forth was crisp, vibrant and colored purple. It was one of many, threatening to destroy the barrier that was keeping me in limbo. I knew it was only a matter of time before everything collapsed completely but I didn't give in, as the alarm suggested I should, and tried, instead, to savor the waning moments within the crumbling integrity of my placid reality.

Before I even opened my eyes, I could somehow feel her absence—in a physical sense, that is. Purple's haunting yet undeniably therapeutic encounter had caused more stress than I cared to absorb in my mentally fragile state and, despite actually having helped me, I had to admit that I was briefly relieved in her physical vacancy from this place.

As the dam threatened to break and I began to stir once more, however, I knew, without any doubt, that her strangely sanguine voice would forever endure as a vestige within my mind; it had been permanently branded against my brain, with a hot iron, and the freshly seared flesh that bore the touch of that red-hot instrument was still sizzling. Soon it would cool and reveal a scar that would stay with me for the rest of my life.

It was at this point, while the purple blister was forming on my brain, that the dam reached a critical state. While the alarm continued to bellow forth its unmissable warning, I wondered if perhaps Purple also left some similar scar or trace of herself deep within the electrical innards of the phone that had just played host to her spirit.

While my groggy mind lazily speculated on that possibility, I was pulled dangerously closer to consciousness by a familiar tune emanating from that empty shell. That electronic encumbrance of mine was rudely alerting me, as it so often does, that someone, somewhere, wished to speak with me. I didn't care, though, and so, as best I could, I tried to ignore it.

Recent events had stained and muddled my grasp on reality, leaving behind the residue of confusion, apathy and hopelessness. I could not, however, avoid thinking about those events forever. I knew that I would soon have to initiate yet another Hellish day but I preferred to do so slowly, rather than springing forward and answering my irritatingly persistent phone, all while simultaneously being bombarded with the relentless interrogations of my own mind.

With concerned reluctance, I cautiously agreed to yield my opposition to reality and thus commence to abdicating my languid state of being. In what I hoped would operate in a slow and orderly fashion, I permitted the examination of the pestering, unending and utterly pointless existential questions I knew I had to ask myself.

Still, I remained silent and motionless, in the hopes of lending my brain some extra time to recalibrate itself, as the phone continued its auditory onslaught. As I defiantly held my eyes shut, I was forced to confront the fact that I'd been encased inside of cramped and unyielding walls, which had constrained and twisted my body into a fetal-like position.

That sudden awareness indicated that I'd likely discover additional bruises today, should I search for them. I thought I might, once my overwhelming desire for physical comfort finally triumphed over my misguided attempts to calm my mind, by remaining immobile within the walls of my porcelain tomb.

In addition to the formation of new bruises, I had also found there was an ache in my stomach that I couldn't quite place; it's wasn't hunger, nor was it the type of pain I would expect from overexerting my core in any way. Still, it nagged at me and caused me to superfluously cover it, with my hand—as though that simple motion would do anything to alleviate my discomfort. Regardless, I did it anyway and then... silence.

The phone's all but deafening siege on my brain had finally ended and, with it, its demanding cries for attention. Still clutching at my distressed midsection, I uncoiled my right knee, inching it toward the back of the tub. Not yet willing to open my eyes, I searched, with my leg and my foot, to examine whether my gun was still there. Even with a black, generic high-top shoe sheathing my foot, I could tell I'd made contact with the instrument of death.

Locating the sidearm seemed to be the last piece of evidence my brain required before convincing me the dam had completely burst—that I was now fully awake. I, therefore, relented from my stubborn, utterly pointless protest and opened my eyes. As I'd already deduced, I was lying curled up in the tub and staring straight ahead at its dirty walls.

My experience—like that of the one I shared with Cinnamon—was too vivid to have been a dream. It had to be… "real." So, still grabbing at my stomach, I lumbered out of the tub to investigate the merits of my hunch.

As I rose, I noticed, first, the capped bottle of sleeping pills, sitting neatly on the counter, next to a forgotten water bottle. Upon examining it further, I was inclined to believe that all the pills were there. I hadn't counted but it looked to be roughly filled with the same number of pills that were there when the being controlling me first opened it.

While I pondered this, I turned behind me and adjusted my gaze toward the ground. No pill bottles scattered about; no blue pen; no mess; no nothing. The floor housed only an old tattered bath mat, an electronic scale, tucked away in the corner, and a trashcan containing some discarded tissues. Feverishly, I picked through them, looking for pill bottles but I found none. Retracing my steps led me back to the medicine cabinet behind the mirror, where I found the rest of the pills I thought I had consumed were intact, unspoiled and untouched.

Although hesitant, I knew I must face my phone next. Sitting there on the counter, it waited for me to pick it up and examine it. As I lifted it from its resting place, the screen flashed the date and time, signaling to me that it was early in the evening, on Friday.

Incredulously, I used my fingerprint to unlock the phone so that I might continue to study it. Three more missed calls. That's the first piece of information it gave me. Chris every time. The thought of confronting his persistence overwhelmed me and I set the phone back down in dismay.

It was then that I realized my phone shouldn't have awoken me by ringing for him at all. Did the "silent" setting I adopted specifically for muting his calls somehow reset itself? Was it killed by some automatic update? A quick check showed me that the phone did update itself, during the time I lost. That seemed like an unlikely answer but I supposed it was, at least, feasible.

And what about the wall behind the tub? From where I stood, it looked like a professionally tiled, slightly moldy bathroom wall but I couldn't be sure there wasn't a forest, a field and a glistening spring behind it. I wouldn't be satisfied until I knew for sure so I cautiously stepped back into the bathtub and placed my hands on the wall behind it.

It was solid. I applied a small amount of pressure to be sure. Still nothing. The next time, I pushed much harder. Nothing. I threw my shoulder into it, a bit more brazenly, at this point, but it still wasn't budging.

Satisfied with the wall's integrity, I apprehensively looked toward the open door, leading out into the hallway. As I approached it, I was gripped with the fear that it might be a gateway to somewhere else—to that dimension where I encountered my nemesis.

I could feel my heartrate begin to rise, as I contemplated sticking my arm through the doorway. Finally, after gathering enough nerve, I slowly began to extend it out, toward the unknown. Hearing the scraping of Blue's paws across the hallway floor, however, caused me to recoil. He must have heard me rummaging around in the bathroom. Seeing him prance toward me—tail wagging profusely—brought some much-needed levity to my situation. I would have expected him to approach nervously, with all the noise I had been making.

With a complete and utter disregard for the doorway's potential hidden power, the dog shot right through and accosted me with an invasion of nuzzling love and seemingly forced sneezes. Bending down slightly, I greeted my companion with mutual adoration and hugged him, with my eyes still glued to the doorway through which he had just passed. Fixated on it, I couldn't help but dwell on my last encounter with it and, while I considered the potential impact of that encounter, I continued to absentmindedly pet the dog—less enthusiastically with each stroke, until I eventually stopped altogether.

It only took a moment, after ceasing my petting, for Blue to become disinterested and, before long, he about-faced and strolled out of the bathroom, back through the same doorway he used to enter. As he initially started to leave, I nearly reached out to grab him and stop him but I selfishly withdrew my arm, in order to watch the dog navigate between the rectangular space once more.

After having done so, he seemed fine. And so, with a curious mixture of both confidence and also trepidation, I followed the dog and walked through the doorway and out into the hallway myself.

From what I could tell, everything was as it should be. Breathing heavily, through my nose, I exhaled in relief, closed my eyes and braced my hand against the wall in front of me. Reveling in the moment for a bit, I finally reopened my eyes—half expecting to be somewhere else completely but being pleasantly surprised to learn I wasn't.

It was at this point that I remembered purposefully leaving the sliding patio door open for Blue. I needed to check and see if that actually happened or not so I set my intention and started toward the kitchen.

I was not even able to take two full steps, however, before the phone summoned me with its familiar ring once more. Irritated, I stormed back into the bathroom to inspect it. Chris. Again! I knew he wasn't going to stop and so I allowed obvious frustration to seep into my voice when I answered and blurted out an agitated "Hello?"

* * *

From what might as well have been another world altogether, Chris greeted me, with the assistance of my phone. "Hey, brother! It's me Chris," he announced, as though he assumed I didn't already know.

"How's it going? You doing okay?" he asked, in a tone that was both cheerful but also laced with a bit of concern, which I found irritating.

His accent was very slight—almost unnoticeable—but I'm good with voices and I would have recognized it, even without Caller ID. Though he was more than ten years my junior, he always, somehow, sounded older. I wondered: was that perception of mine, in some way, related to the cultural differences in our upbringings?

He told me once that he had moved here, when he was twelve, from somewhere in the Middle East. I didn't remember which country, though, and, with all the time that has passed between us, I always felt too ashamed to ask him to tell me again.

"Hey, Chris," I responded out of forced politeness. "Yeah; I'm okay." Clearly, I was not but I was vehemently opposed to discussing the particulars of my situation with him and so I decided to keep my responses curt, in order to end this conversation promptly. "How have you been?" I obligatorily asked, as I stared back at myself, in the bathroom mirror.

"Oh, you know, brother. Just living the dream." In what I assume was an effort to seem more amicable, I noticed him dialing back the level of concern in his voice. It was still there but I appreciated him at least downplaying it, to better match my own emotionless mood.

"Cool, cool, man. How's the life coach business going?" I politely asked although, I didn't really care. "You still moving forward?"

"Oh, yes. Absolutely. Thank you for asking, bro! I have a new client that is just amazing. Amazing. You should see her. She runs a real estate business—you know, to help people?" he asked rhetorically. "And she has three branches in Ohio and two just south of here, in Kentucky. It's amazing."

"Oh. Wow. Cool." I didn't have it in me to be outwardly rude to Chris. I did like him and I appreciated his thoughtfulness but he just wasn't a priority. How could he be, after what I had just experienced… twice now?!?

"Yeah; she's good people," he told me.

"That's great." Suddenly, my mind shifted back to Blue. Did I leave that big bag of food out for him? Did I actually leave the sliding door open, at the back of the trailer? Determined to find out, I abandoned my reflection and headed toward the kitchen to investigate.

"Yeah; I just thought she really jelled with my own mission, ya know? Community, faith, connecting everyone together, helping each other? It's what I've always wanted. I feel it in my bones, bro. It's amazing, you know?"

"Yeah, Chris. You've definitely said it many times before. I'm glad you're chasing your dream." I purposely left emotion and excitement out of my voice when telling him this but I really was happy for him. He was making his own path and rallying other, like-minded individuals to his cause. I had a lot of respect for that.

"Well, at least for now, I still do cabinets, obviously."

"I was going to ask you about that," I lied.

As I entered the kitchen, I stopped first to inspect the closed door. Blue was already there waiting for me, tail wagging ecstatically. Simply by looking at the position of the lock, I could tell the door was sealed but I gave it an unenthusiastic tug just to be sure. It didn't budge. Blue, however, seemed as though he'd been expecting the door to move and, despite his wagging tail, I assumed he must have been disappointed. His pacing, as he switched his weight between his two front paws, told me I had better let him out so I slid the door open and watched him dart off into the yard, losing sight of him as he turned the corner of the trailer.

"Yeah; I know we've talked about it before," Chris continued, "but it's hard to completely abandon my other job. I mean, my dad—well, not my *real* dad but my dad over here—he still needs a lot of help. I think I already told you about that."

"Yeah." Longing to escape my situation, I stared off, behind the trailer, waiting for Blue to pop his head around the corner.

"Right. Yeah. We talked about that. Well, anyway, the family business has been good. I can't really complain about it, right?"

"No; I guess not," I affirmed, in a monotone voice.

"It's provided me with everything I need to survive. I just… I feel the calling and I know I'm meant for something more, bro. God is amazing, though, and I know He'll put me on the right path, when it's time."

"Well, I'm happy for you, Chris." Again, I really was. I just didn't want to prolong our conference.

"Hey, brother, I know you said you're okay but you sound a little off. Are you sure everything is all right?" There it was. That concern in his voice had returned.

For better or for worse (I would say "for worse," probably), I have always had an issue with dishonesty. That's not to say that I don't lie, of course. I lied only moments ago, after all, telling Chris I was going to ask about his cabinets. I understand that life would be nearly impossible without taking part in some minor deceptions but that doesn't mean I enjoy doing it, or that it doesn't bother me. So when Chris asked me if everything was all right, I didn't know how to respond right away. If I told him what happened, he'd think me crazy; maybe he'd even call someone to intercede on my behalf.

"I just…" I started, as my mind stalled for a more amenable way out of his question concerning my mood. That's when I remembered Blue. "My dog just ran off, around the trailer. Sorry. I'm kind of waiting for him to return, while I'm talking to you." Technically that statement was true and, more importantly, it had the potential to derail our conversation. In order to further push that agenda, I then asked, "Do you have any dogs, Chris?"

"I love dogs!" he proclaimed enthusiastically, "but no; I don't have any." Then, before I could utter any follow-up, he hastily mentioned that he'd love to meet mine sometime.

"Yeah. Maybe," I reluctantly responded.

Then, after a brief pause, he asked, "Are you sure everything's okay, bro?"

My brain was failing me. It was lagging behind like a struggling internet connection, while I waited for it to display the answer to my conundrum: how do I quickly end this conversation without lying or hurting Chris's feelings? Just then, as I spied Blue cheerfully prance around the corner, back toward the sliding door, I called out his name, so that both he and Chris could hear it.

"Sorry," I offered next. "My mind is still sort of on my dog. All this snow has turned my yard into a muddy mess. Just gotta make sure I clean his paws before he muddies up my entire trailer." As I knelt down to do so, I hoped that the interruption would take the conversation elsewhere. Not wanting to leave anything to chance, though, I once more tried to guide it there myself. With my head pinning the phone to my shoulder, I asked, "Say, did you ever end up taking that trip of yours?"

"The wilderness retreat?"

"Yeah." As I closed the sliding door behind me, Blue sauntered on his newly-cleaned paws, over to the pantry where I kept his treats, and plopped down on his haunches. While he waited there expectantly, I couldn't help but smile slightly. I then realized, as I was reaching for those treats, that his gigantic bag of dog food was in there as well.

After a short lull, Chris pulled me back into the conversation, when he affirmed that, yes, he did take his retreat. As I handed Blue one of his treats, which I had to fish out from the bottom of the box, I could almost hear Chris's mind deliberating against itself. Despite the fact that humans typically love talking about themselves and despite the obvious social cues indicating that I didn't want to be interrogated, he abandoned any attempt to regale me with tales of his expeditions and instead declared that he'd love to tell me about it "sometime"—i.e., not now.

"Oh!" I exclaimed. "I just thoug—"

"I'm worried about you, brother," he then said quite plainly.

Dejected, I sighed through my nose and faced his inquiry head-on: "Honestly, Chris, things are a little fuc…" I paused for a moment and tried again. "Things are pretty… 'unusual' right now. I've got a lot I'm trying to deal with." There. I could admit the problem but not get into details. If he didn't move on, I was going to start to actually get angry, which is an emotion that almost never took hold of me.

"You worried about money still?" he asked, fishing for a response, the same way a police detective might—the one who's pretending to be on the suspect's side, that is—the "good" cop, as it were.

"No. I mean, yeah but no. That's not it," I attested dismissively. Why did he keep persisting when I clearly didn't want to talk to him? What was with this guy?

"Is everything with your family okay? Did you ever end up fi—"

Finally, I could take no more and I vocalized (rather rudely, I'm ashamed to admit) what I had been trying to convey this whole time: "Honestly, Chris, I'd kind of rather not talk about it right now." As I mouthed the words, I caught a bit of sting to my voice and I instantly regretted my tone. Blue was annoyingly perceptive and, when he picked up on my rapidly degrading mood, he abandoned my side and scampered off toward the bedroom.

"Okay. Okay," he calmly responded. "You know you're a bro to me, man."

"I know."

"Ever since that first time we met at your mom's."

"Yup."

"I was like, 'This guy—this guy is a bro.' That's why I called you 'bro,' remember?"

"I definitely do."

"I just knew!" Chris then paused and I took that to mean he was regathering his thoughts. "Wow. So you can talk to me, man, if you want to. What's going on?"

Rolling my eyes, as I placed my hand over my head, I walked into the living room and responded, "I just... I'd rather not."

"Okay. Okay. Cool. Cool. Hey, I know it's been a while since we talked," only it actually hadn't, "and I know you said you have a lot on your plate right now but, when you free up some time, I'd still love to find a way to partner up with you. Maybe we can help each other. I've got so many ideas, in my head, of where this business could go. I was wondering if you might be able to meet for lunch later this week. What's your schedule look like?"

I recognized the old and outdated sales close he was attempting. Part of me wanted to call him out on it but he was too nice a guy. The strategy goes something like this: ask the customer for something—to confirm an appointment, to answer a specific question, to agree to a contract—and then be quiet. Wait. "Whoever speaks first, loses."

Various times throughout my professional career, I had heard that phrase excreted from one self-affirmed "sales guru" or another. I always thought it was such a crock. Still, like all the other drones allowing our souls to be drained for a paycheck and whatever additional meager perks we convinced ourselves were worthy of trading more than a third of our lives for, I too sat and listened to those gurus, all the while knowing they would never sell me any product—even one that I wanted—if they employed any of those outdated and insulting strategies on me.

Eventually, I told myself that if I already knew Chris's technique wouldn't work on me, I might as well be the first one to speak. By remaining silent, all I was actually doing was extending my own suffering, wasn't I?

Besides, who's to say Chris was actually attempting the closing technique my mind was accusing him of attempting? Was that really what he was trying to do? Had I become so warped and twisted that any time someone tried to help me, I automatically went on the defensive?

Exhausted from his badgering, as well as my own postulations regarding his intent and his methods, I plopped down on the couch to provide my answer: "I appreciate the offer to partner up, Chris, but nothing's really changed on my end."

"If you change your mind, let me know," he countered. "I'm meeting with a lot of good people and helping them with just about everything under the sun."

"I'm glad. Stick with it, Chris. Follow your dream." The world needs people like Chris. His unescapable tenacity could be motivating when people allowed him an audience. I knew it was wrong to shut him out; I felt it from within me but I was dug in at this point and my hubris had taken hold of me.

"Yeah," he persisted, ignoring my rude indifference. "There are a lot of life coaches out there, bro. A LOT."

"Oh, I know."

"And most of them aren't really helping their clients. Faith and community—that's where it's at, brother. We need to help each other. It's what God wants."

"Definitely."

"People trust me. They trust me so I treat them right," he added.

I wasn't sure how to even respond to that and so I simply said, "Sounds like things are really starting to pick up."

"They are. They are. That's why I was going to say I'd still be open to finding a way to bring you on board. I meet a lot of people who are looking for artistic help in their businesses. You're good at that, right? You're good at talking to people too and you believe in faith and community—treating people right. I know God put us in front of each other for a reason."

I didn't know that he did though. It was possible, I supposed, but it was also possible that all of this was just random chaos that Chris was viewing through a spiritual lens, in order to assign it meaning so that he could attain some misguided sense of control over the ambiguity of our existence. That's a conversation I didn't want to have, though, so I simply told him, "If you meet someone interested in my services, yeah. Let me know. And don't worry. I'll definitely give you a cut, for your trouble."

"Oh, I'm not worried about that at all, brother! No commission necessary. Just do the same for me and spread the word about me, okay?" That sounded fair and I genuinely wanted Chris to succeed so I agreed. "Excellent," he then declared, after I had done so. "I just thought, with all my connections, I might be able to get some money in your pocket, in case that was stressing you out still."

And there it was. All of this—just a backdoor attempt to pry into my life. It was as flattering as it was annoying. "Thanks for thinking of me," I responded, as stoically as I could.

"Oh, absolutely. Hey, I met this guy—he's got a great background in web design and he's going to help me get a website out there so I can better market myself and reach more people. I want to reach *everyone*, bro!" he excitedly exclaimed. "Anyway, he understands faith and community, ya know? Good dude. Good dude."

"Cool. Good luck." After stating as much, I moved my phone from my ear and held it out in front of my face, in order to see the time. When I looked, it reminded me of how much of my life I'd been wasting.

As Chris prattled on—completely content and with no regard for time—I felt every excruciating second, like a nail being slowly pushed into my skin. I wanted to throw my phone across the room and examine my thoughts alone but I knew I'd have to finish this call or he'd just initiate another one later today and force me to go through all of this again.

"Hey, are you still moving out West soon?" he cheerfully asked.

"No; I'm still here. I had to stay for my brother's wedding a while back. Now, I'm just kind of waiting to see what happens with everything." Unaware of how I began the process, I noticed, at that point, that I had begun pacing around my living room.

"I feel your pain, brother. I'd really love to discuss it with you sometime soon. You still think you're going to be free at the end of the month?"

"I'm not sure, Chris. Some things have changed on my end…"

"Yeah; a lot has changed, amigo."

He was fishing again and I was half tempted to grab the line, pull him under and drown him. Instead I conjured up a monosyllabic "Yup."

"You don't really sound like yourself."

"I'm… Yeah; I'm fine, Chris. I just have a lot going on right now," I reaffirmed to him. "Sorry I haven't had a chance to call you back. I'm just really busy." Why was I apologizing to him? I always did that. Shouldn't he have been apologizing to me for reaching out as often as he did, without any indication from me that I, in any way, welcomed his attempts to connect? Still, I knew that it wasn't fair for me to want him in my life only when it was convenient for me and I felt guilty for trying to make the relationship one-sided, in that way.

"I get it, Jim. I get it." Instead of telling him that I went by James, I stayed purposefully silent. "Glad you're okay and I understand busy. I get busy too. Trust me: *super*-busy," he retorted.

"Well, I certainly don't want to keep you," I said, in a thinly-veiled attempt to steer the conversation toward its conclusion.

"You can't keep me!" he laughed flamboyantly. "I'm always here if you need me. You know that to me you're a—"

I couldn't stand to hear him call me a "bro" one more time so I cut him off before he could. "Well," I quickly interjected, "I don't want to keep you at this hour; besides, I've got to get back to it myself."

"First of all, my friend, you're a bro." Ahhhh! "As for our conversation, we can always talk later. No worries on my end. I just want to make sure you know, though, that you can literally call any time—day or night."

"Thanks, Chris. Maybe I'll try you again in a couple months, when I get a little more time."

"Okay. Maybe I'll reach out before that. Things can change quickly around here."

My pacing had drawn me back into the hallway and, as I moved past the bathroom, on my way to my bedroom, I caught, out of the corner of my eye, several pages, with blue handwritten ink, scattered about the bathroom floor. I was certain they were not there before.

From the hallway, I stopped in my tracks and stared at the disheveled pages, strewn about the floor. It was almost as though I could sense some sort of mystical energy coming off of them. Without even realizing it, they'd drawn me close to them. Bending down, I picked one of them up and realized it was part of the doomsday note that was supposed to be in my back pocket. Instinctively, I patted that pocket and could tell it was empty.

"Cool?" Chris asked, taking me out of my stupor.

Absentmindedly, I answered: "All right, Chris. I appreciate it. Really, I do and I hate to be rude but I've gotta get back to it, yeah?"

He told me something about reaching back out soon and that he'd be praying for me but I wasn't really listening. Once I heard his voice stop, I responded, barely intelligibly, with a "bye," hung up the phone and began collecting my psychological confession, in order to return it to my pocket.

CHAPTER TWELVE

While I gathered, perused and collated the various pages of my doomsday proclamation, from off the hallway floor, Blue strolled up behind me pulled me from my reverie with a commanding bark. "What, Blue?" I asked without even trying to hide the annoyance in my voice. The dog didn't seem to mind though; he just arched his back and began wagging his tail. "Not now," I impatiently scolded, as I stuffed the freshly-folded pages back into my pocket.

Unsure of what to do next, I paused and looked down at my best friend. He noticed and it caused him to wag his tail brazenly, as though he believed we were playing some sort of game. I, however, was in no mood so I despondently walked into the bathroom and took a seat on the ledge of the tub. Blue, for some reason, took that as a cue that I wanted to pet him so he high-stepped into the room, after me. I thwarted his attempt at burying his face inside of my crotch but conceded to half-heartedly pet him at a respectable distance, while I pondered recent events.

Staring ahead, at the cabinet doors underneath the vanity, I tried to make sense of my life, while Blue basked in the attention I was giving him. While I ruminated on my seemingly hopeless condition, I noticed that one of the two cabinet doors was slightly ajar. Out of curious boredom, I stuck my finger in the crack and, with a disinterested flick, flung the door completely open. With a trivial indifference to life itself, I casually scanned the contents of the cabinet until my gaze landed on a bottle of drain cleaner. After studying it for a bit, I was hit with a powerful but terrifying thought, which I then voiced aloud, to both my dog and myself: "I don't think I can die."

I'd already survived an overdose and even a head-on collision with an oncoming car, hadn't I? With those events in mind, I rose off of my seat and grabbed hold of the deadly chemical that had caught my attention. As I held it and considered my theory, my mind recalled a memory it hadn't accessed in ages.

There was this kid in my school—Lucy, I think her name was—and her tale went something like this: Lucy had been getting wasted all night—booze, benzos, coke, even PCP. She was ingesting all of these substances at her boyfriend Jack's house and, as the night wore on, more and more people started arriving. I don't know the exact details but, apparently, at some point, some unknown girl from another school showed up and Lucy, in her confused state, found her to be a little too flirtatious with Jack.

Later, during a scuffle between the two them—where Lucy tried to beat the other girl to death with a chair—people intervened, pushed Lucy aside and then turned their collective attention to the injured girl. During the time that elapsed while they removed Lucy from the situation and began assisting the girl she assaulted, Lucy stormed into the bathroom, locked the door and started screaming that she was a god. This went on for a couple minutes, until her somewhat discernible screams were replaced with bloodcurdling and completely inane ones.

When her boyfriend kicked open the door, he found an open bottle of bleach, still spilling out of the bottle and onto the floor, along with Lucy, on all fours, retching in the corner and screaming in pain. One of the kids who was there told me the smell was overwhelming and not just because of the stink of bleach either. He told me a cloud of burning flesh—the kind that comes from second-degree chemical burns—was seeping into the air, from out of her mouth, and mixing with the chemicals on the floor, to create the putrid aroma.

Lucy didn't die right away either. The chemicals had burned the inside of her throat and the lining of her stomach so horribly that she suffered for days, in the hospital, before finally meeting her end. She had apparently downed a shot glass full of the deadly agent, in an effort to prove she was immortal. At least she was high on PCP when she did it though. I was, at that very moment, considering doing the same thing, for the same reason, and I was as straight as a yardstick.

While evaluating all of this, I unloosed the bottle's cap and took a whiff. The toxic fumes that wafted into my nostrils caused me to involuntarily snap my head back and stretch my arm forward, to create distance between the bottle and myself. After that, I decided my plan was foolish—that the risk of being wrong was too great—and so I twisted the cap back into place.

I had bent forward, to return the bottle to the cabinet under my sink, when the cap started spinning backwards, at a high rate of speed, before shooting off and crashing into the ceiling. The moment it made contact, however, it stuck there and the entire room once again faded into a collection of muted grays. As before, my clothes and I were no exception.

Assuming that another attack was imminent, I turned to run out of the room but, when I did, I saw that black smoke was beginning to gather in the hallway, in the bedroom and (I assumed) in the rest of the trailer as well. Instantly, my mind went into survival mode and I slammed both of the bathroom doors shut. Doing so meant I had kept the smoke at bay but I had also trapped myself in the bathroom with the slug who was growing increasingly active inside my head. I could feel his tail whipping about and smacking the inside of my skull, like a frenzied animal trying to escape its cage.

I was grimacing and holding the left half of my face in my hand when the bottle cap above suddenly fell to the floor, leaving a circular hole in the ceiling where it had been. With one eye covered and the other squinting upward in pain, I stared, in disbelief, at that hole above, when something from the other side spoke to me. "DO IT!" that same confrontational voice from before aggressively bellowed.

"Get out of my head!" I screamed back at it with as much anger as I could muster. Again it repeated the same demand but this time, it was so loud that the walls themselves shook and pieces of plaster began to fall from the ceiling. I tried to yell back but my voice was barely audible. I was a mouse trying to squeak over the roar of a lion.

"DO IT! DO IT! DO IT!" the voice commanded again, as the gray walls and floor began to crumble. With my hands over my head, I squatted down and prayed for it all to end but that only emboldened the voice, which began yelling louder and more frequently. "DO IT! DO IT! DO IT! DO IT! DO IT!" It simply wouldn't stop. As I helplessly cowered there, on the floor, a piece of the ceiling fell and landed next to my foot and, at that point, I gave up trying to resist.

Upon my silent submission, the voice stopped yelling and the gray room stopped shaking. Slowly and timidly, I removed my hands from the top of my head and began to look around. The room was strangely calm but I was unable to relax in it. Without warning, I had lost control of my body, just as before.

I tried to resist the force controlling my body but doing so was both excruciating and exhausting. That said, my rebellion didn't last long. Too tired to keep fighting, I relinquished control and watched helplessly as my hand, with no corresponding instructions from me, removed a small cup from within the medicine cabinet. It had been used, up until then, to house Fisky's toothbrush. Unable to stop myself from doing so, I dumped it out, onto the counter, and filled the cup with a shot glass worth of drain cleaner, before capping the bottle and setting it down, on the floor.

I then took two quick breaths, grabbed the container of unnatural liquid and threw it back, as if it were a shot of tequila. As my head flew back, I catapulted the chemical concoction down my throat, like I had done so many times before, at a multitude of bars and parties alike.

* * *

The bitter, stinging taste of lye dismantled my taste buds, as the poison invaded my mouth. I didn't have the luxury of time, to further dwell on its flavor though. My mind—concerned, as it was, with more pressing matters—quickly catalogued the odd sensation and then turned its full attention to the rupturing flesh inside my throat.

The lingering chemical mixture—now coating the lining of my esophagus, in the wake of its downward trajectory into my stomach—had begun to blister and burn away at that fundamental pathway to life. Losing all control, my body began to malfunction, seizing up like a car whose transmission had just failed. I fell to knees and released a guttural scream that was partially an agonizing wail and partly my body's unsuccessful heaving attempt at expelling the deadly liquid from within me.

Lurching forward, stricken with unimaginable pain, I propelled my chest over the lip of the outer bathtub wall, wondering if it wouldn't be better to keep the poison inside my stomach—fearing the additional damage it might cause, should my body's defenses force it up and back out through my throat once more. As each excruciating second ticked away, I felt more and more convinced that I had misjudged the limits of my own mortality and that I was going to die because of it. Another dry heave. Another tortured scream.

Dizzy with pain and able to take no more, I somehow garnered the strength to stand—though not completely erectly—turn around and wildly stagger back to the vanity counter space. Being hunched over, in a doubled-up state, kept my head level with the counter—making it convenient to rest it there, while my eyes darted frantically about, in an attempt to locate anything that could lead to my salvation.

There was, however, no such salvation to be found. I didn't, after all, even know for what I was searching. Unable to fathom my impending demise, my dismay escalated rapidly and I neared the verge of sobbing. After a moment, my mind abruptly whipped me out of my self-loathing and flashed the unmistakable warning that I was slipping uncontrollably into unconsciousness. At the same time, something explosive was brewing in my guts. I didn't know which would happen first but I could tell both fainting and retching were inevitable.

My insides were ready to erupt, as the foreign agents I had introduced churned together with the legitimate bile of my stomach—poisoning it and causing violent spasms that conjured forth waves of unnatural fluids, crashing against the internal walls of my stomach. The last thing I recalled, before the real madness began, was feeling like a powerless passenger, in my own body. I was there but I had no control over anything. The plane was plummeting; the pilot was dead and no one else on board knew how to fly.

Everything went black and I couldn't even raise my arms to brace myself, as my body fell forward, on a collision course that I judged would leave the top half of my carcass hanging, half inside the tub. It was at that moment that I felt my very consciousness being sucked backward, out of my head and down through my throat.

As my disembodied consciousness passed by my dilapidated innards, it felt as if I was viewing my insides from behind my driver's side window, as I lazily sped down the highway. During this trip, however, there was no comforting music to drown out the sound of my own sizzling flesh, as I whizzed by, along a path that surely led to the inside of my stomach.

Like a rock thrown from a ship, I splashed down into my own juices, helpless to escape my predicament. Was I going to drown or maybe even dissolve in there? Did I even need to breathe at all? I had no arms, no legs, no torso and no head. I could neither speak nor move but I was somehow subsisting there, within the churning, acidic oceans of my own stomach.

Before I could even begin to make sense of the situation, however, I found myself racing back up through the esophagus, surrounded by a yellowy, pasty slime, until I, along with it, was jettisoned out of the mouth, where I found myself rocketing toward the bathtub floor, only to splatter there, with unmistakably brutal force. After the rest of the contents of my stomach had found the bathtub floor and gathered around me, I found myself looking up at my previously inhabited lifeless body. Warm drool still hung from its lip and cascaded down into the tub below, where I now found myself.

I learned, at this point, that I was finally able to struggle a bit. As I strained to bend what seemed to be my newly acquired neck forward, I saw that some upchucked goo was miraculously adhering to me, forming what mildly resembled a human outline. Hastily taking inventory of my new body, I noticed that I apparently now had one grotesquely enlarged, bulbous left leg and another, much smaller right one—probably a quarter of the size of its counterpart. It didn't appear as though I had feet of any kind.

My midsection had a hole through the center of it but still seemed to be functional, as far as I could tell. Raising my arms to inspect my hands, I was dismayed to find that I didn't have any. My left arm disappeared and continued to drip away at the point where I would have expected my elbow to have been. My right arm was at full length but a watery, dripping stump was located where I would have expected to have a hand.

I struggled to stand but it was in vain. What's worse: gravity had begun to tug at the gelatinous stomach fluids that surrounded me, pulling me, against my will, from the tub basin, down toward the drain, at the back of the tub.

From what I could tell, my body was mostly comprised of half-digested, gelatinous extracts, tiny bits of carrots and a brownish/yellowish bile that was both bonding me together and, at the same time, dripping off of my extremities. What I did not seem to possess, however, was a spine and that is perhaps why I couldn't raise myself fully, to better fight against the slow descent into the drain.

Desperately trying to prevent my lagging progression and save myself, I attempted to dig my misshapen arms and legs into the porcelain beneath me; however, much to my chagrin, they wouldn't stick to the dirty floor. Along with the rest of the contents of my stomach, they simply slid lazily along the floor, toward my impending doom.

Without any hope to thwart the advance of the milky substance propelling me forward, I began to panic about the unknown terrors deep within my drain. As I began to contemplate what I postulated would become my unfortunate resting place, a voice snapped me from my dread.

"I'll keep us from moving past the elbow joint," it arrogantly said, almost scoffing at my apparent concern, as it did so. Straining my neck, as much as I was able to do so, I lifted my head forward to try and locate the voice but I saw nothing that offered me any insights.

Ahead of me, I saw only the slow-moving river of vomit, leisurely making its way down the slope of the tub. Various chunks of food meandered through the viscous slop, like logs headed toward the edge of a waterfall. Most of them had lost their original coloring and had faded, instead, into a sort of bland, tannish hue.

As my speed increased, hurling me toward my descent, I lay back, accepted my fate and took one final look at my body above. It was massive! I wished I had more time to try and determine whether it was breathing or not.

Just then, as I felt my new legs go over the edge of the drain, my right arm—the "normal" one—inadvertently wrapped around one of the larger pieces of food that was just a touch bigger than the opening of the drain. Although it had very little color, I could tell, from the texture, that it used to be part of an orange. Holding on tightly, as the river continued to pass over us, I felt relieved for a brief moment. That is, until it spoke.

"If I fall in, it's because I want to!" I heard it exclaim, in a tone that would suggest it was engaging in something tremendously strenuous.

"What?!? Who?" I started but I was cut short. This partially digested piece of sentient fruit that was keeping me from plummeting down the drain then released a victorious groan—the kind one might expect to hear from a weight lifter, as he dropped his barbell, after a triumphant lift. As he did so, I watched as his form buckled inward, pushing us under the top lip of the drain stopper and leaving nothing between the putrid sludge that was behind us and the deep chasm in front of us.

No longer able to resist the will of the mudslide of stomach bile that surrounded us, we were helplessly claimed by its gravitational-like pull. With my arm still locked around that piece of talking fruit, we both screamed, as we were pushed forward, over the edge, into a free fall, down into the bleak, lightless pit.

CHAPTER THIRTEEN

It didn't take long before the orange and I landed at the bottom of the drain. Making contact with the elbow joint there, at the bottom, wasn't, by any means, pleasant but it didn't really hurt either. For the moment, at least, the threat of being washed further down the pipe had subsided.

The light from above provided only the most meager of illuminations inside the pipe. Everything was black and, in every direction other than up, I could just barely make out only a few inches of space in front of me. Looking up, on the other hand, was so bright that it blinded me so I kept my eyes looking forward, into the black, eerie emptiness that engulfed me.

Bracing myself against the side of the pipe, I was able to rise into an awkward but stable position—one where my enlarged and elongated left leg held me erect, while my smaller, nubby right leg dangled in the air. Coaxing my new body into this position caused me to rethink my somewhat hasty hypothesis about not having a spine but, even so, my newly-discovered mobility brought me little encouragement. Leaning against the back of the pipe, there in the dark, I felt isolated and abandoned.

After a moment of silence, I heard a loud, exasperated gurgle from above, followed by a brief but concerning lull. A few seconds later, chunk-heavy liquid fell onto my head and shoulders, as it plopped down, from the pipe above me. Despite the ferocity of the bodily noises that produced the substance, however, I was relieved to learn it was only a minuscule amount—especially when compared to the volume I had just experienced. After it passed over my slouched body, it began to flow forward again, breaking around the contours of my monstrous ankle and meandering harmlessly around me, on its journey further down the pipe.

I supposed I must have been heavy enough to avoid its pull and remain somewhat stuck in the tar-like sludge that surrounded me; however, had the combination of the muck and my one-legged foothold not been enough to keep me from being swept away once more, that expelled piece of orange probably would have. To at least some degree, it seemed to be blocking the path in front of me, although it was hard to tell for sure, due to the absence of light in that place.

From what I could gather, though, it sounded more than confident in its ability to fight against the liquid that was flowing past it; I heard it making loud, karate-like grunts, in front of me, as if it believed those battle cries—and not its size and placement—were what was keeping us from prolonging our belly-up ride, down the dark, slimy slide.

I knew for sure that the danger of falling further into the darkness had ceased, at least momentarily so, when no more liquid trailed down the pipe and pushed past my bulbous ankle. At that point, I wanted to speak but the orange beat me to it.

"You're welcome," his masculine voice smugly exclaimed, from somewhere out of blackness, in front of me. I could just barely make out the outline of a shape that I assumed was him but it was too dark to be able to know for sure.

"Um, thanks," I told him and then quickly added, "I think."

"Not a problem at all." He seemed like he both expected and needed the validation of my praise; I heard it in his voice. If I could have seen his face—if he even had a face, for that matter—I was sure it would have been smiling arrogantly, as if he had just overcome some monumental feat.

"Were you just… were you just doing karate?" I asked, somewhat accusatorily.

"Psshh. Karate!" he belted out. "Try mixed martial arts! Why just stick with karate when I've mastered so many other disciplines as well?"

I was struggling to understand how that was even possible. "Okay but, I mean, you're a part of an orange, right? How are you even… I mean, do you even have arms and legs and whatnot?"

"I am *not* just an orange!" he seethed.

"I didn't mean any offense," I told him earnestly. I'm just trying to understand how yo—"

"You'll never understand anything if you simply rely on your eyes to tell you everything," he quickly retorted, before I could finish my statement. "Master Yoda looked like a decrepit old hobgoblin but he turned out to be a Jedi master, now didn't he?"

Using a bit of snark to combat his aggressive nature, I responded by asking, "Was that the original trilogy or one of the new ones where he was making karate noises in the dark? I can't remember."

"'Mixed martial arts,'" he angrily corrected, "and even though it's imperceptible to your eyes, you should probably be grateful because I used it to save you from being washed down the drain.

"Right. Well, I *did* thank you and also, we're *in* the drain soo…"

I don't think he liked the way I left the last part of my statement hanging but I didn't care. I wanted him to know how asinine he sounded. Already, this piece of regurgitated, citrusy slop was starting to annoy me with his brazen arrogance. "We're in the elbow, dummy," he corrected. "If I hadn't helped you up there, you would have fallen even further in."

I supposed he was right. He had helped postpone my fall and, although I couldn't see for sure, he did also appear to be partially blocking the path further into the drain, up ahead of me. "Okay. Yeah. Okay. Thanks. Thank you," I told him with much more sincerity.

"No need to thank me; I'm just doing my job," he proudly asserted.

"But I thought you said you wanted me to than—"

"Is this really what you want to be talking about right now?!?" I could hear the annoyance in his voice. I wanted to tell him it was mutual but decided against it.

"Uh, no. No, I suppose not."

"So? What then?" he questioned.

"Okay, well, for starters, how do we get out of here?"

Indignantly, he then asked, "Don't you want to know my name?"

I did. In that moment, I felt bad for not having asked for it yet. The comfort I was experiencing, in what should have been a much more alarming situation, should have concerned me more but it didn't. The fact that this was now the third phenomenon I had experienced in two days made it easier to jump right into a conversation, yes, but it didn't give me the right to be rude and so I told him, "Yes. I'm sorry. Yes. Who are you?"

"You can call me..." And then he paused for a moment—presumably, to be sure I was listening intently—and, in a noticeably lower voice, he proceeded in giving me the name, "'Night Blade.'"

As he spoke the name, a very small flame ignited near the pipe wall just behind him, illuminating the upper part of his body, where I assume his face would have been. It reminded me of children with flashlights, telling scary stories around a campfire. Luckily, the flash provided enough light that I could see back toward the end of the pipe, before it began to slope down again, behind him. I couldn't observe the scenery for very long, though, because, after only a second, the minuscule flame he generated had already begun to recede back into nothing.

"Woah!"

"Pretty cool name, right?" he asked.

"No!" I cried out, irked by his obliviousness. "It's a terrible name. Night Blade?!? C'mon, man! The fire! The fire is why I 'woahed.' *That* was actually helpful. How did you do that?"

"A magician never reveals his tricks," he retorted, snubbing me, as the flame disappeared completely, leaving us in darkness once more. "Also, Night Blade is an awesome name."

"Can you make another one?" I enthusiastically begged. "I can barely see."

"Maybe I don't feel like making any more right now." His voice was more definitive than it was teasing. Somehow, that was even more infuriating. I wondered if he modeled himself that way or if he was just that naturally annoying.

"Because I don't think your name is cool?" I mocked.

"No! And it *is* cool, regardless of what you think!"

"Because you can't then," I scoffed, hoping he would try and prove me wrong.

"I can, if I ca—" He then stopped himself from whatever he was about to say and took a moment to gather his thoughts instead. "Fine," he eventually told me, when he was ready to begin again. "I'll tell you. It's not like you could ever do it yourself anyway."

He made sure I heard the condescending and blatantly forced chuckle from under his breath before he continued. "There are these little miniature methane clouds down here. If you know how—and no: you can't learn how. If you learn how, you can light them, as they pass by. They only burn for a few seconds but they can apparently help wussies, like you, who are afraid of the dark. If you want, I can light more, as they pass by."

Methane? Could it really be methane? That didn't sound right to me and so I told him: "This isn't really sewage though. How do you explain the methane and aren't you worried you'll blow us all to H—"

"Oh! Look who knows everything all of a sudden!" he sneered. "What else can you tell me about the situation, O Wise One?"

"Right. Okay. Sorry." I knew he was right but his attitude that was making it difficult for me to listen to him.

No sooner had I finished apologizing than another flame—this one closer to the sludge-laden floor, somewhere in between Night Blade and myself—ignited and quickly burned itself out. I wasn't sure if Night Blade was actually inflaming the gas himself or if he was simply present as it was happening. Ultimately, it didn't really matter; I was just grateful for some light.

For the duration of our conversation, this would continue to happen sporadically: a bit of gas somewhere in our makeshift room would ignite, provide visibility for a couple seconds, and then disappear again. Although there wasn't much to see, I was, as I said, grateful to be able to see anything—even if it was through the fleeting nature of a fickle flame I had not the wherewithal to harness.

"Apology accepted," he told me, in a tone devoid of any discernible emotion. "Just remember who the boss is here."

But my curiosity had gotten the better of me and I had to ask: "Did you… Did you wait until there was a cloud of methane close to your face so you could light it just before revealing your ridiculous name—you know: for dramatic effect?"

"My name is not ridiculous!" he screamed back at me, from across the darkness.

"Night Blade, right?"

"Yes."

"And you don't think that's ridiculous?"

"I think it's awesome!" he yelled out, like someone who could no longer control his frustrations would. "I think lighting methane on fire is awesome! I think *I* am awesome and that *you* are jealous! What do you think about that?" If he had arms, or a chest for that matter, I imagined he would have been beating them together, like an ape, trying to establish his dominance.

"I don't think," but then I stopped midsentence and asked, "Is Night Blade even your real name?"

"Irrelevant."

"Because it sort of seems like you just christened yourself with it right now," I persisted.

"James Singer. Yes; I know who you are," he mocked. "Only someone as pretentious as you, James Singer, would be haggling over my name, at a time like this. You're literal puke and your old body is up above you—above a smelly, slimy drain pipe you can't even climb. But yeah. Let's argue over my name."

"Okay, okay. Yeah. You're right. It's just… crazy things like this have been happening kind of… a lot recently and I just… It's insane, yes, but I don't even… I mean, how do you even… I don't want to say I'm 'used' to it because I'm certainly not. I just—"

"Oh, for Pete's sake!" he interrupted. "You want to ask if you're dead or not. You want to ask if you're going to get back into your body or not. You want to know what you're doing, stuck down here, at the bottom of a drain, talking to NIGHT BLADE." I could tell that, in his mind, over-emphasizing his name would somehow legitimize it.

"Uhh, yeah!" I vigorously exclaimed. "Yes. Yes to all of that. Can you help me with that?"

"Unfortunately, no," he blandly responded. "I'm not sure myself. This is a bit weird for me too."

Frustrated, I plainly asked, "Well, what *can* you tell me?"

"I can tell you that the diet soda you drink is pointless. It still has caffeine in it so what's the point?"

"What?!?

"You drink a lot of it and I don't really know why. Also," he seamlessly continued, "I can tell you that, despite what you may have heard, honey badgers are not even one of the world's top ten most menacing life forces. There is a fungus, in remote parts of the world, that attaches itself to an ant's brain and causes it to crawl to the top of a tree branch and wait there, for a bird to come down and eat it, thereby infecting the bird with the virus, as well. After that, the bir—"

"I don't care about birds and infected ant brains!" I interjected loudly, no longer able to contain my exasperation.

"Well, excuse me for trying to prepare you for th—"

"What I care about are those other questions you raised."

"Yes, well, as I said, I'm not able to answer those at this moment." In this line of questioning, at least, he appeared to be almost grateful for his lack of insight—as if the frustration it caused in me was a secret source of joy for him. He was trying to mask it but I could tell nonetheless.

"If you can't answer those questions, then why bring them up?!?" I barked.

"Why do *you* think I brought them up?" he fired back.

"I don't... I don't know!" And I didn't. I didn't care either. I just wanted answers.

"Typical," he said, chastising me, as he did so.

"All right, 'Night Blade'—by the way, I'm not calling you 'Night Blade,'" I added. "What's your real name?"

"If you want me to answer you... you will call me 'Night Blade,'" he said, scolding me, as he continued his harangue.

* * *

Like it or not, I was stuck there and, from what I could tell, this strange being was more or less my only guide. After recomposing myself, I started to tell him, in a more defeated tone, "I don't know what I'm doing down here." Then, in order to better verbalize my surrender: "I don't know what I'm doing down here, '*Night Blade*,' in this muddy, sludge-filled hole, while I'm literally covered in puke." Before he could respond, however, I found myself chuckling at what I had just said.

"What's so funny, Singer?" he asked, in the antagonizing manner to which I was growing accustomed.

"Nothing; it's just… All of this. It kind of reminds me of something at my wedding. That's all."

"A slimy drain pipe reminds you of your wedding?" he snidely interrupted. "That's nice."

"Not that. No," I said to him, in a reassuring tone. "There was this girl there—Penelope was her name, I think…" After pausing for a moment and attempting, in vain, to confirm her name with myself, I eventually gave up and said, "Anyway, she'd eaten a bunch of oranges earlier in the day. Then she got super drunk at the wedding and let's just say she 'deposited' them into a bush during the father-daughter dance." Smiling to myself, I then told Night Blade that, when she went home, she left her expensive designer shoes there in the mud, next to the bush. "I always wondered," I finally said, "if she ever went back and tried to retrieve them."

"I don't really understand the concept of weddings," Night Blade jeered. "Where I come from, the male is bound to the female in a quite literal sense so there really isn't any need for any legal documentation or ostentatious ceremonies. It's apparent, as soon as you see their combined form."

Night Blade then fell silent and I looked down, into the darkness, where I couldn't quite see the sludge that had surrounded my own misshapen leg. "Can you just tell me what's going on?" I asked as earnestly as I could. "Please. Is any of this even real?"

At that point, the pipe began to shake violently, which was not uncommon during Ohio winters. As was typically the case, I was relieved when it stopped, after only a few seconds—though it was for different reasons this time. Up until now, a burst pipe would have meant a repair bill and a minor inconvenience. Down here, however, I got the sense that it could lead to far worse.

Once the pipe settled back into place and the loud groaning that accompanied its sudden spasms had faded away, Night Blade began to speak again, as though he had been completely unfazed by the incident. "Always assume that whatever situation you're in is real—because it is. Otherwise you'll be tentative and unable to react. You'll be unable to truly commit to anything and, in battle, that could mean death."

I thought for another second or two and then asked, "Well, what about if I'm having paranoid delusions that, if acted upon, could *also* result in injury or even death?"

"If you have the wherewithal to recognize and diagnose yourself as 'delusional'—or even if you're starting to think you *might* be delusional—then the reality of the situation is that you already know, or at least suspect, that something is wrong. If that's the case, you need to accept your reality and take action to change your situation."

I liked the philosophical side that had just emerged in the stranger across from me. In an effort to try and keep him more amenable, I then admitted, "I guess you're right. In some capacity, this *is* reality. I *am* here. Without the insight of the future, there's no use in questioning the authenticity of my existence, right?"

"I think your pea-sized brain is finally starting to get it," he taunted. "Humans—especially slow-witted ones like you—don't have the clarity of the future when they're in the present so why worry about it? Focus on the moment and do your best—even if it means accepting that you're stuck somewhere you don't want to be. It doesn't matter what you'll think of this situation later—whether you perceived it all correctly or not. Right now, it's the only reality you know so try and treat it as such."

"That's... kind of heavy," I admitted. "Maybe I should have had *you* give the speech at my wedding. I'm sure everyone would have loved you!"

There was no flaming gas, when I spoke my words. Those intermittent flashes of clarity—while at first I welcomed them, they eventually began to haunt me; after all, they were illuminating my situation (both figuratively and literally). The darkness, while cold and mysterious, provided me with endless possibilities; on the other hand, the light from those momentary fires only served to remind me that I was stuck down here, with this strange creature from whom I could not escape.

Before he could respond, however, my dog's deafening bark crashed down, like thunder, from up above, as it reverberated through the pipe, back down to Night Blade and me. I tried to look back up, toward the source of the animal's cry, but the light was still too bright and I had to shield my face, with one short, drippy left arm. After I had done so, I turned away, back toward the darkness in the pipe.

I wondered, at that moment, if the dog's barking was his panicked reaction to discovering my previously-inhabited body draped over the side of the tub. Deflated, I stared out into the bleak nothingness around me, waiting for another fiery flash. After a few seconds, though, I grew tired of waiting and addressed Night Blade once more: "The reality of *this* situation is that I am just completely stuck down here, aren't I?"

"It would appear so," he calmly answered.

"I don't want to be down here, man." I didn't actually know if he was a man but I thought that calling him an orange might set him off on another tangent and I certainly didn't want to call him Night Blade again. "I don't want to be stuck down here, in this forsaken cesspool of world I've found." As a new light flashed and quickly burned itself out, I paused. "But I don't want to be in that one up there either."

* * *

The strange being across from me didn't strike me as the best confidant so I was, at least to some extent, consciously censoring the information I presented him. If, on the other hand, I had felt any inclination to be more forthcoming—and subsequently more vulnerable—I probably would have told him that a large portion of my unease hinged on the fact that I really had nowhere that I actually wanted to be. Ever.

It didn't matter where I was or what I was doing; I always wanted to be somewhere else—until I got there and realized I didn't belong there either. It was a perpetual and cyclical dilemma; it made me feel like no matter what I was doing or where I was located, it was the wrong activity and the wrong place.

As I contemplated this inescapable and never-ending cycle of displacement and detachment, I began to better accept my current situation. Of course, arriving at that realization didn't change the hopelessness of my situation but it did at least allow me to view it with some measure of familiarity and that, thankfully, strengthened my demeanor.

"So are you going to just sit there and sulk?" the half-eaten orange calling himself Night Blade called out, from within the darkness.

"No," I told him. "No I'm not." I knew I just needed to push through all of this, as I had done with Cinnamon and Purple already, and so I asked, "So, what do we do?"

"For someone as daft as you obviously are, I've already shared far too much," he defiantly retorted.

"If I ever get out of here," I began, to say, from against the pipe which was still supporting me, "I think you should consider allowing me to manage you, as a motivational speaker."

"Not interested."

"You haven't heard the pitch yet: 'Hawk-Talks': self-defense, philosophy and... uh... Oh! Scorn!"

"It's never going to happen," he calmly asserted, as yet another cloud of gas caught fire and then promptly burned itself out.

"My, well, Beth—she had a background in P.R. I'm betting she could have helped too."

"Beth?"

"Yeah. My... She was my wife," I explained calmly.

"You've mentioned your marriage multiple times now. Why did you split up? Did you pester her the same way you're pestering me?"

At this I laughed and said, "If she would have acted like you, I suppose I probably would have but no. That's not why we... I mean, it doesn't really matter at this point, does it?"

"No but I've got nothing else to talk about down here—unless you want me to tell you about the three-mouthed mating ritual of the nor—"

"Stop! Pass. Pass on that."

"Are you sure?" he asked, with a creepy sort of sincerity.

"The truth of the matter is that, for whatever reason, Beth just sort of fell out of love with me. Well, 'romantic' love anyway. We were friends for more than a decade before we ever even went on our first date and I think she just wanted to go back to that reality. Maybe she just liked who she *thought* I was. Maybe it took getting to know me, on a much more intimate level, over the course of several years, before she finally decided that I wasn't the person she wanted to spend the rest of her life with."

"And now what? You want vengeance?"

"Of course not. I mean, she's not actually... I... I just I feel bad. If I had been a better person, maybe she wouldn't have left that night. Maybe she'd at least..." I then paused for an uncomfortable amount of time before admitting, "It's my fault. I shouldn't have built my life around my marriage. I shouldn't have put that much pressure on her. I should have... I just should have been better."

"That's pathetic. Go on."

"I don't know if it's 'pathetic.' It's just... 'misguided.'"

"No," he corrected. "It's pathetic."

"Well, regardless, it wasn't fair to her. I just keep thinking: how horrible of a person am I that she just wanted to get away from me? My actions—they indirectly caused... They..." I then took a deep breath and said, "I just wish I could have held onto her for just one more night.

"Instead, the world watched as I was forced to grieve a woman I didn't actually know at all. The woman in the casket looked like Beth but the Beth I knew had died before she ever got into that car. And that's always been a reality I've had to hide from almost everyone."

"You know, if you really thi—" but my partially-absorbed compatriot was cut short. Above us, we heard my previously-inhabited body garble forth that excruciating sound we both recognized as a signal that more of my old stomach's contents were forthcoming.

"Can you hold off another wave?" I fearfully asked, although I felt I already knew the answer.

No sooner than I had finished my brief question, did we hear the steamy hot liquid crash into the tub floor, above us. It sounded like a freight train slamming into a porcelain wall. After a second or two, a new liquidy nightmare began cascading down the pipe, on its way toward us, with unrelenting force.

My knee began to buckle, as it made contact and pushed past me, on its way toward the orange at the end of the pipe. This wasn't the thick, viscous sludge from before. This was hot, free-flowing liquid and, unlike the last batch, this river was able to gush forward, without restraint, at a much greater speed.

Night Blade started to shout, over the roar of the rushing tide, "I'm not afraid of a litt—" but then I heard him grunt and I knew he was gone. From much further down the pipe, which he was previously blocking, I heard him yelling something I couldn't quite decipher, before the liquidy grave consumed him, washing away any trace that he had ever existed at all.

* * *

The quick-moving, regurgitated bile that carried Night Blade away would have done the same to me, had I not found the strength to withstand it—strength I was sure I didn't have but somehow found nonetheless. Still, I was thankful I didn't have to fight its influence for long. In a matter of seconds, that explosion of burning hot repugnance moved past me and disappeared into the pipe, further down below. Though it wasn't able to carry me with it, it might as well have, for it had left me with nothing and no one.

I was now surrounded by total darkness as well. Something must have been blocking the opening above, for no more light was descending down through it. Gone too were the methane bursts that illuminated my conversation with Night Blade. Feeling utterly alone and full of despair I called out into the blackness but heard no response, other than my own slight echo, as it bounced off the pipes below me.

I was completely lost and, for the first time, the reality that I might actually be stuck here indefinitely began to creep into my mind. Even my own body was starting to melt away. It had begun to slide down the pipe I was using to prop myself up. I knew it was serious when my right leg suddenly made contact with the ground on which I stood. It confirmed the feeling that I was shrinking—in my left leg, at least.

It was *not* just my left leg, however. It took less than a minute before my entire body was nothing more than stagnating slush. No longer could I control any appendages. I couldn't even tell if I still had appendages or even which way was up. I tried to scream but found I had no voice.

Just as I felt myself on the verge of succumbing to another panic attack, a beam of light shone down from above and stuck me with encouragement. Whatever was blocking my path had been removed and I now saw clearly that the only way out of this misery was up through the shaft above me. Somehow, I suddenly knew that I needed to climb—and that doing so was going to be a momentous and arduous task—but even in the knowledge that tremendous difficulties awaited me, I was relieved to at least know where I needed to go.

As I contemplated this, my determination grew exponentially and, through what I could only assume was some sort of divine intervention, I began to will myself back into a human shape, once more. First, I used a newly formed pair of arms to push my torso upward and, soon after that, I grew a pair of legs that helped me to stand. I never looked down at them, though, because, while all of this was happening, I kept my eyes fixed on the light above me.

I remember reaching my arm upward, toward the light, and placing my slimy yellow fingers on the pipe, in front of me. I was ecstatic to learn I had hands and fingers now! As they searched the contours of the pipe, they came to land on a bit of old food that had hardened to the pipe, forming a handhold, of sorts.

It was then that I began to notice a multitude of similar handholds, scattered throughout the slimy cylinder. All along, these were here! Had I but noticed them, I wouldn't have had to sit down here, with that annoying orange!

Determined to reach the next one, I began to lift myself up off the ground, as everything slowly faded to white.

PART V

SATURDAY MORNING

CHAPTER FOURTEEN

I awoke to a sore throat—not because it was riddled with second- and third-degree chemical burns though. This felt more like the irritation and drainage of a typical Ohio winter. Whatever the cause, I coughed loudly and brought up some disgusting phlegm that I lethargically, yet violently, spat out of my mouth. I didn't even bother opening my eyes or moving my head, as the gob of mucus slapped against the tub wall, where I was sure it had stuck.

The rational side of my brain wanted to examine my encounter with Night Blade but I was afraid that scrutinizing that event might inadvertently conjure another panic attack. My mental state was weak enough as it was. No need to further accelerate its decline with unanswerable questions from beyond my scope of perception.

With a desire to distract myself, I decided to drown my constitution with a faux sense of vigor. Once I convinced myself I had manufactured it, I carelessly and expeditiously sprung from my sleeping chamber. Doing so, however, caused me to accidentally kick the .357 Magnum at the bottom of the tub. It didn't hurt though. In truth, I was actually more annoyed and embarrassed than I was injured.

To my shadow, I let loose a frustrated expletive, which my dog incorrectly assumed was meant for him. That much was obvious when he backed out of the room, with his head held low. Though I felt shame for having upset him, I considered his timid retreat a welcome diversion because it gave my mind somewhere else to focus itself.

"Hey, boy," I said aloud, while addressing my friend with legitimate compassion. I had hoped that doing so would coax him back into the room with me. His tail began to bashfully wag and I took that to mean he was happy to see me. He'd probably be happier if I let him out. He'd probably be happiest if I fed and let him out.

I then turned my attention to my phone, in order to check the time. Without any effort at all, the device quickly displayed both the time and the date but I didn't notice either of them. All I saw was that I had three text messages awaiting me. They were all from Chris. All three of them!

I didn't even want to read them so I set the phone down, just as I realized the whole reason I engaged it in the first place was to learn the time. I muttered something under my breath about how scatterbrained I was and then looked at the phone once more—this time with a bit more focus. By employing a bit more concentration this time, I quickly learned that I'd awoken in the twilight hours, between the birth of one day and the death of another—where my insomnia so frequently ran rampant.

"I'm sorry, boy," I told the dog, who didn't seem to be overly concerned. "I should have fed you a long time ago. Come on. Let's go out and you can have your dinner after you come back in, okay?" The dog apparently agreed. I could have asked him nearly anything in that voice, though, and he would have consented. "Want me to shoot you? Yeah? Yeah? Want me to shoot you? Do ya? Do ya, boy?" He wouldn't have cared. In a way, I envied that about him.

As I prepared to leave the room, I happily noted that everything within my field of vision had returned to its previous state. Cabinet doors were shut; the ceiling was intact; toothbrushes and cups were where I left them and the only grays in the room were the ones that were supposed to be there. After checking to make sure the bottle of household cleaner was tucked away where it belonged, I walked down the hallway and into the kitchen, with Blue happily following closely behind.

Sliding open my door, along its familiar track, I created an opening for the dog to exit into the outside world. It wasn't even open all the way, before he scooted past me, as if he was avoiding a game-ending tackle. Once beyond me, he leapt off of my deck and ran, full bore, around the side of my trailer and out of my line of sight.

Lamenting his impetuousness, I shook my head and slid the door back into a closed position, effectively barring any additional snowflakes from entering. They must have begun to fall again, while I was asleep. It wasn't a "heavy" snow but there was enough of it that several pieces found their way inside, only to crash and deteriorate almost instantly, onto the warm floor that greeted them.

Almost as if I was automated to do so, I robotically shuffled toward the pantry, where I kept the dog's food. Using the cup inside of the bag, I scooped it full and walked toward Blue's bowl, where I intended to deposit the contents of the cup. Before I could do so, however, something lying across the top of his bowl stopped me in my tracks.

Upon examination, I quickly learned that the mysterious object in the dog's dish was a missing page from the doomsday letter I planned on presenting to my doctor on Monday. "What on Earth?" I said aloud, as I instinctively knelt down to check the page I already recognized from a standing position. Distracted by my discovery, I dumped Blue's food into his dish, returned the cup to the bag and then placed the newly-discovered third page of my note in between the second and fourth pages that I already possessed. Once I was sure the note was in the correct order and that no more pages were missing, I folded them all and returned them to my back pocket.

Standing with one hand on my chin and the other on my hip, I tried to rationalize how the page got into the dog's bowl. When no suitable answers presented themselves, however, I stamped my foot and loudly cursed my inability to make sense of the situation. Blue was trying to figure everything out too. Out of the corner of my eye, I spied him cowering at the door. His body language suggested he was ready to run back into the yard, for a fear of what I might do to him.

I've never hit that dog—not even once. I doubt I've ever even yelled at him, really. Why was he such a coward? Forced to apologize but not really meaning it, I tried to comfort him and dissuade him from following his instincts and running back into the yard, as I shuffled, head down, toward the door. "It's okay, boy. Come on. I'm sorry," I implored.

The doughy and extremely delicate beast kept his distance but seemed to be a bit relieved at my relaxed demeanor, as I slid the door open. He then decided to run inside, effectively avoiding the paw-wiping ritual on which I had always insisted. "Blue!" I cried out, in frustration. He didn't care. He ran right by his food and into the bedroom to hide.

Shaking my head, as I slid the door shut and locked it, I was forced, once more, to confront the reality that my dog was yellow and no amount of conditioning would change his nature. I had bigger concerns than my overtly timid dog though. With everything that had happened to me over the last twenty-four hours, I knew I should try and force myself to sleep but I was too anxious and jittery.

I wished I could have just laid my head down and slipped off but I was far too energized for that. Considering my recent escapades, I told myself that sleeping pills probably weren't the best road to travel, on my quest for sleep, so I searched for alternative measures to employ.

I started by taking Blue for a stroll around the neighborhood but that did little to tire me out. Upon returning, I tried switching on the television and watching that same old familiar show I loved so much. It was my hope that doing so would calm my weary mind with a sense of familiarity that would eventually lead to a more placid disposition.

And so, from my chair, like a king on his throne, I watched my TV and let it distract my mind, as if it were my own personal court jester. I knew all the characters' lines before they even spoke them. I'd seen that expertly-written show so many times that it was almost like the characters were my actual friends. That, at least, comforted me a bit.

Several hours later, my eyes became heavy enough to suggest I might be in luck so I let Blue out one final time before we headed our separate ways—him toward my bedroom and me in the bathroom. My spare pillow was at the bottom of the grimy tub, waiting for me, which was both comforting and disheartening at the same time.

Before long, as I restlessly fidgeted in the tub, my mind was whittling away at any misconceptions I had about falling asleep, choosing instead to recount all the evidence behind my crumbling reality: Cinnamon, Purple, Night Blade and, of course, my spiritual stalker and his estranged head-worm.

I'd gone over my experiences with them so many times that I wanted to scream! "Why won't you let me sleep?!?" I asked the creature in my head, as I pounded my fist against my forehead. I figured, if I couldn't sleep, neither would it.

I tried counting sheep, meditating, reading under a dull light, praying and even sink-showering—where I would lather myself in the sink, with only the most minimalized amounts of water and soap. Nothing. My mind was a full-bore steam train and it would not be derailed. At 6:00 a.m., I decided to concede. Blue, for one, was happy because he correctly assumed he'd get his breakfast a bit early.

* * *

After tending to Blue, I decided that an early morning drive was my best chance for decompressing my brain. It was winter in Ohio so the sun had been missing for nearly thirteen hours. That bleak absence of light, along with the soon-to-be warm, toasty insides of my truck, accompanied by the rhythmic undulations of the road, was not only my best chance for sleep; it was probably my only chance for sleep, lest I give into the pills once more.

Determined to embark, I plopped down onto my worn-out but still comfortable chair. My black sneakers weren't going to provide much warmth in the tundra beyond my door so I left them behind for an old, beat-up pair of Doc Martens boots that had been with me for over twenty years. Fisky hated them but I appreciated their durability and so, despite her pleas, I refused to get rid of them.

As I was lacing them up, I located a half-consumed bottle of water on the coffee table, in front of me. In only a few gulps, I finished the whole thing, before capping it and setting it back down. It was at that moment that I realized I should have been hungry. I *should* have been hungry but I wasn't. Perhaps this satiated stomach of mine was the effect of the poisonous household chemicals I might have ingested.

After I'd finished with my water, I stepped into the cold morning air, hurried to lock the deadbolt on my front door and then briskly slid into my manual-transmission pickup truck. Once there, I anxiously compressed the clutch pedal and turned the key but, for some reason, the engine didn't turn over. Sometimes the truck would falter like this if I wasn't pushing the pedal in far enough so I waited a few chilly seconds, tried again, and felt a slight—but also somewhat expected—sense of relief when the vehicle finally sputtered to life.

Seconds later, I found myself bouncing down the road. On most occasions, I'd play music or podcasts through my phone but not on this day. On this day, I needed the quiet hum of the road to ponder my situation; besides, the thought of removing my gloves, in order to manipulate the music app on my phone, didn't seem worth it. I also knew that engaging my phone would bring to life the unread text messages from Chris that were still awaiting my perusal. Sorry, Chris, but procrastination is still the best policy for me.

Should I have felt bad for that? Should I have felt bad for the fuel I was burning—just for the sake of being somewhere other than my trailer? And what about my window? My broken, driver's side window was permanently cracked open, at the top, which I always addressed by running my heater at full blast. Should I have felt bad about that too? To a small degree I did, but not enough to change what I was doing. I just had to be somewhere else. Anywhere, really.

Aimlessly driving down the cold, barren highway brought me a bit of relief—like I had temporarily escaped some sort of punishment. It was early and the old road was devoid of other motorists; they must have had better places to be—must have had loved ones to comfort them at home. Even with that in mind, it was encouraging to put distance between myself and my trailer. Unfortunately, though, I knew it wouldn't last. Eventually, one way or another, I'd be forced to return to the Hell that was my life. Still, I was grateful for the momentary distraction, even if the excursion included a fast-approaching expiration stamp.

As I traveled down the dark, lifeless road, I decided it was finally time to confront my trepidation and read my text messages from Chris. This reckless act wasn't something I'd do in a big city, or somewhere with heavy traffic (I tried to rationalize to myself) but it was acceptable here, on this deserted road.

Message one (shortly after our last phone conversation ended): "Didn't like the way that ended, bro. I know you don't like talking on the phone but I'm here if you need me."

Message two (a little over an hour later): "By the way, my new client who I told you about is getting breakfast with me next week. He's a big motorcycle guy so I thought you might want to join us. He's a pretty cool guy. I think you'd get a kick out of him. LMK."

Message three (two hours after that): "Just want to make sure you're okay. Shoot me a quick text and let me know you're good, okay, bro? I'm worried about ya."

What I text back: "I'm fine, Chris. Breakfast's gonna be a no-go for me. Thanks for asking though."

Disgusted with the whole situation, I attempted to toss my phone onto the passenger seat but my low-effort, half-hearted fling caused it to bounce off the front of the seat and land onto the floor below. Embittered, I verbalized something that sounded like "Errrrrgh!" to the windshield in front of me. Despite knowing better, I took my eyes off the road and reached over, to the passenger side floor, to try and retrieve the gateway to my electronic identity, as I barreled forth into the nothingness that surrounded my truck.

I was growing more and more annoyed, as I toiled to find it. This trip, short as it may have been, was presenting absolutely no chance for me to attain tranquility or introspection. "Relaxation?" I felt like a fool to have considered that concept as anything more than a pipe dream. My phone was causing me both mental and physical strain, as I struggled to secure it and, as if that wasn't enough, my aversion to Chris's persistence was festering inside of me and slowly driving me into a frenzy.

As I quietly seethed over Chris's messages, I tried and convince myself that I'd rather throw my life away completely than give it to people like him. I would have rather been controlled by chaos than polite acquiescence because I believed that I could at least fight the former under my own terms. I could feel my phone, just outside my grasp, at the tip of my fingers, as I crafted these thoughts.

Although I'd located the all-important device, I couldn't quite pull it in. Sitting up straight again, I checked the road. Still empty. I had veered a little off course, in my struggling, but the road was deserted so it didn't seem to matter. Knowing exactly where the phone was now, I shifted over, toward the edge of my seat, as far as my seatbelt would allow, and lunged back toward the device, with my arm fully extended in its direction. Still, even as I did this, I could not keep my thoughts off of the fire that Chris's text message had ignited within me.

As I stewed over it, I finally got a firm hold on the object whose momentary absence had plagued me so. Smiling, as if I had just been named "Artist of the Year," I began to quickly right myself back into my seated position, straining my oblique muscles, as I did so. At the very moment, with a triumphant smile on my face, I returned to the proper seated position—the one the manufacturer intended, when building my truck—where my enthusiasm quickly dissolved into terror.

I couldn't see the details of the vehicle about to slam into me, in a head-on collision. All I could see was the bright, all-encompassing flash of its headlights.

CHAPTER FIFTEEN

Instinctively, I swerved back to my side of the road, narrowly avoiding what would have been catastrophic damage and probable death. Behind me, I heard the horn of the vehicle I narrowly missed blare out into the darkness, piercing my ears, as I struggled to keep myself on the road.

It had been salted earlier but the new snow, minor as it was, was enough to cause my tires to lose their traction and swerve toward the ditch, after my sudden jerk of the wheel. With intuition leading my actions, I pumped my brakes and laid into the fishtail I had inadvertently initiated (just enough to keep from losing complete control). Thankfully, it worked. Within a second or two, I was back in command of my truck.

Shaken from the near miss, my entire body began to tremble, while I watched the white snow outside lose its color and turn to a bland shade of gray. Seconds later, my head began to throb as the thing inside of it sprang to life. I could feel it flipping about inside of my head, like a fish out of water. While wincing in pain and pushing the palm of my hand against the outer walls of my head, my stereo suddenly switched itself on and began broadcasting that same menacing voice from before.

As before, it's only command was that I "DO IT," which it repeated over and over, at 20 percent of the speakers' maximum volume. While struggling to maintain control of the truck, I let go of my head, threw the transmission into neutral and pushed the brake pedal all the way to the floor.

Despite my efforts, the truck continued on its course, like a mounted horse who had been given the freedom to wander where it pleased. I tried yanking the steering wheel and even engaging the emergency brake but nothing worked. The brake click-click-clicked and the wheel spun freely but neither affected the truck's mobility in any way. I even tried opening the driver's side door to jump out but the handle wouldn't disengage the lock.

The truck just kept casually rolling along until it gradually slowed its pace, in order to enter the turn lane to my right. Ahead of that approaching turn, I could see an abandoned auto mechanic's garage, which looked like it used to be a gas station before that. Now, it was simply an old, dilapidated building. As I progressed toward the empty parking lot, my entire body moved from a concerning tremble to all-out, violent convulsions.

Nearly overwhelmed, the ghost truck charged forward, pulled into the vacant bay and then stopped abruptly—the way in which one might expect a student driver to stop. Again, I yanked on the door handle but it didn't yield the result for which I had hoped. During all of this, the volume on my radio had been steadily growing so that the voice yelling for me to "DO IT" was now at an overpowering 65 percent!

Out of sheer panic and desperation, I began driving my bare fist into the radio screen, in an effort to disable it. At the same time, my right was glued to my head. I had moved it there in order to thwart the creature underneath my skin from resurfacing but now it was filling up with warm blood.

The volume reached 80 percent when it began to seep through the gaps between my fingers and drip down my right hand. My left was a ferocious battering ram but the stereo's volume continued to increase as I repeatedly pounded my bloody knuckles against the tiny screen that was recessed into my dashboard. Each time I pulled my fist away, there were more traces of blood on it but I still persisted, undeterred, like a veritable madman.

By the time the volume reached 90 percent, my ears felt like they were about to start bleeding as well! The voice was driving me mad with its "DO IT! DO IT! DO IT!" Do what? What on Earth did it want this time?!?!

My knuckles hurt; I was near the point of hyperventilating and my brain felt like it wanted to jump out of my skull. My bloodshot eyes were hopelessly searching for salvation. When they landed on the rearview mirror, however, they showed me the *last* thing I wanted to see. On the other side of the mirror was my faceless stalker and once I noticed him, his arm broke through the glass and his hand wrapped around my mouth.

Something must have been in his palm because I suddenly felt a candy-sized, hard object on my tongue. I tried, of course, to spit it out, but his hand would not budge, despite the fact that I had postponed my assault and let go of my head in order to remove his hand from my face. I might as well have been a toddler trying to overpower the heavyweight champion of the world. His hand wouldn't budge. Instead, he started jerking my head backward and then forward again.

After the third time, the foreign object inside my mouth fell to my throat and I involuntarily swallowed it whole. At that moment, the slug burst out, from within my head, and the arm that was coming through my rearview mirror released me and grabbed hold of it.

Saddled with an exhaustion I had never felt before, I slumped back into my seat and caught a whiff of that sweet fragrance I'd hoped I'd never smell again. It was the smell I had noted from before, when the wraith was draining the slug of its essence. As the demon's outstretched hand continued to visibly drain the insect of some multicolored light housed within its innards, I slowly, cautiously and with as little movement as possible, rolled my already-cracked window down a bit further, so as to keep from alerting either creature to what I was doing.

Once I had enough clearance, I then sprung forward in my seat, ripped the mirror off of the windshield and tossed it out the window. Instantly the stereo volume plummeted from 99 percent to zero and the worm inside my head let out a feeble scream before retreating back into my head. I was completely drained of life but I was still breathing.

With the truck still running, I spilled out, into the abandoned garage. In a fetal-like position, where I was breathing heavily and trying to gather myself, I saw some discarded fast-food wrappers and some discoloration on the floor, indicating something large and heavy had once sat there. The floor was greasy and dirty but the room was otherwise empty—likely picked clean by petty criminals long ago. All at once, as I was examining my surroundings, a cold wind hit me and intensified my seizures.

An unbridled desire to escape the outside world compelled me to try my luck at pulling shut the metal garage door through which I had just passed. My body fought against me, as I took hold of the old cord hanging above me and yanked. As the rusted metal wheels ground against the old, steadily degrading track that held them captive (screeching as they went along), I noticed a broken lock lying just outside. Apparently, I wasn't the first person to enter this place without permission. It took brute force but I eventually closed the stubborn gate, effectively walling me off from the world outside, for which I was granted a morsel of reprieve.

With my convulsions growing in length and ferocity, I hobbled back to my truck and got inside. I felt physically numb and hoped that the warm air blasting through my vents would reinvigorate me. I hoped that I wouldn't lose too much of it through the slightly cracked window I wasn't able to shut.

Having been in this situation before, I knew the only thing that would calm me down was something that would take my mind off of the track on which it was currently running. Desperate for anything familiar and comfortable, I opened the music app on my phone. I then found my favorite artist and hit "play."

With enormous trepidation, I raised the volume from zero to 10 percent and then wiped the blood from my screen with the sleeve of my coat. I then closed my eyes and tried to focus on the music emanating from my speakers. At first, it had no effect. I continued to shake while my mind was unraveling. After a bit, though, the soothing, euphonious melodies began to put me at ease. The truck grew warmer too and this also helped to relax me. The world was crashing down around me but there, in the cab of that truck, I was suddenly content and so I accepted the tranquility of my situation and allowed the music to distract my brain and drown out my worries.

Eventually, my anxiety subsided and the exhaustion left in its wake caught up to me. Part of me wanted to leave, at that point, but I was too comfortable and slightly drowsy as well. Without opening my heavy eyes, I told myself I could listen to one more song before heading home.

CHAPTER SIXTEEN

It's funny how drastically our emotions can change, in so little time. It wasn't long ago, for example, that I was utterly and inescapably helpless and desperate, in the grip of another anxiety-fueled meltdown. Fast-forward only half an hour and I would find myself experiencing a sensation that quite nearly bordered on euphoria, as I drifted off to sleep, exhausted, slumped over, at the wheel of my gently humming truck. With my eyes shut, my brain became uncommonly peaceful and I happily (and even eagerly) lost consciousness.

Then, as if fate itself decided to intercede, I was, at once, yanked back into reality and stricken with consternation, as my eyes slowly opened to the demonic-looking being standing over me. It was tall—probably close to ten feet, I would guess. That was the first thing I noticed—how it towered over me so.

As I struggled to get my bearings, I found myself lying on the cold, wet cement floor. This, of course, was odd—especially since I supposed I had drifted off to sleep in my truck. Still, I was not alarmed by my whereabouts; more than anything else, I was extraordinarily confused as to how I ended up in this new place—much as I was when I woke up under that stranger's car the other night.

Slowly, I began to reacquire my senses, which, unfortunately for me, meant the forced inspection of the creature before me. It had two bulbous yellow eyes that jutted out the sides of its head, rather than in the center, where one would expect to find a human's. To the sides of its greenish mouth were two jagged mandibles, which gave it a likeness akin to some sort of giant insect— either a locust or a praying mantis, to be more precise.

I attest that it was "like" a mantis because it wasn't quite as simple a categorization as that. While it did have the greenish, skeletal-esque upper body one might expect to see on an insect, it was also sporadically covered in brown and white fur. I would later find out that the fur concealed the creature's entire back but, at that moment, I could clearly ascertain only that it covered the top of its head, the middle of its bare chest, the center of its biceps and its equally odd legs—on which I will delve a little deeper momentarily. Past the bicep, however, the arms looked more like narrow, green, jagged machetes, ready to cleave me in twain. Underneath those two massive, blade-like arms, it also had four smaller arms. Each of them contained two green fingers and one green thumb, without which it wouldn't have been able to grip and lift much. Still, even with those extra arms, I got the sense that its proficiency in lifting and carrying would be extremely limited—probably bordering on a disability.

I made this assumption because those four arms were not only scrawny—especially when compared to its dominant blade-like set above—but they were also deficient in length too. Stretched out fully, I couldn't see them traveling outward more than a couple feet. Staring at them, then and there, they kind of reminded me of arms that might belong to a T. rex.

Where what I could only describe as its thorax ended, it wore a pair of black polyester shorts, with a white stripe down the side of each leg. Its legs are where it truly boggled the mind though. Instead of the insect-like appendages one might be given to expect, it had two brown, furry, meaty, mammalian legs—the kind that made it seem like it was descended from the kangaroo family.

Though I was completely perplexed by the twisted form before me, I had little time to study it. Slowly, I became cognizant of the fact that, since awakening, this thing had been intermittently slapping me all about (not violently but persistently), with the blunt side of its hatchet-like forearms. After a momentary lull in its aggressive behavior, while it halted to observe me slowly regaining consciousness, it suddenly and without warning renewed its efforts, causing me to bury my head and face in my arms.

As I continued to protect myself, my ears struggled to clarify the exact words that rained down on me from above. I could, however, ascertain that they sounded raspy, aged and decidedly female. Were it not for the dire situation I have been describing, I would have thought the voice belonged to a kind, old grandmother. In this moment, however, she sounded like a barely audible but emphatically crazed old lunatic yelling at me to awaken.

"Stop! I'm awake!" I finally yelled out, wishing the assertion would quell her incessant battering of my face, buried inside my arms. I had hoped that, by shouting that statement, from the fetal position I had unconsciously adopted, she would be able to denote my obvious surrender. Thankfully, she must have understood because she stopped hitting me after I finished my plea.

My ears hadn't fully adjusted yet—that, or they were being drowned out by some unknown and likely nefarious variable. I could tell the creature in front of me was yelling but her agitated, grandmotherly-like voice was now barely discernible. It was as if a white noise bomb had just exploded, right next to my head.

From her difficult to distinguish, raspy barbs and her frantic motioning toward the open garage door, through which I had recently driven, I was able to determine she desperately wanted me to exit the building. Despite her grotesque form, I felt compelled to oblige her, for it seemed almost as if she was trying to rescue me, in some way I didn't quite comprehend. Without delay, I rose to my feet and half-hobbled and half-ran, while she, alongside me, bounced like a cartoon character, out of the garage and into the snowy night.

Once outside, my faculties seemed to sharpen once more. The crisp early morning air focused my vision almost immediately. My hearing, too, had proved itself more acute. As we ran, it relayed the disturbing thuds of this creature's giant kangaroo paws on the concrete below, until the sound of crunching snow overtook the slapping that's created when paw hits pavement.

Had this happened to me two days ago, I would have kept running, through the field we occupied and into the woods beyond, trying to elude the beast that was accompanying me on my impromptu early morning run. After everything I had been through, however, I knew better. If this thing wanted to kill me, it could have easily done so back in that garage. And so I ran with my new companion until she finally came to an abrupt halt. At that moment, I followed her lead and bent over, to catch my breath.

Once I had it, I began to attempt to formulate a question. I was going to ask what in the world was going on but, before I could string the words together, the entire garage, along with a good portion of the empty farm land behind it, swiftly flashed a brilliant blue light that was so intense it blinded me for a moment. It dissipated quickly, though, and, after I moved my arm from in front of my face, I saw that the building we had just occupied was completely encased in what looked like a sparkling blue crystal. Distraught, I tried to verbally address the situation but, alas, I hadn't the foggiest idea of where to even begin.

* * *

"That woulda been you," the insectoid-mammalian thing told me plainly, as I failed to wrangle my thoughts together, in a cohesive string. "Of course it had to be another crystal," she then said, as I looked back and forth between her and it—the giant blue crystal that had just burst into existence, in a chaotically beautiful fashion.

"Shoulda known it wouldn't have been any different over here." She spoke those words as though she was only mildly surprised at the phenomenon we had just witnessed and that she was more disappointed in herself for not predicting it correctly—kind of like a mechanic who first guesses a defective battery but who, upon a minor inspection, learns the actual problem is in the starter.

"Is that… I mean, did you…" But I couldn't find the right words. My mind was moving faster than my mouth could articulate.

Pointing at me with one of her short, nubby, dinosaur-like arms, she then said, "I take it seeing something like that was a first fer you?" With a simple nod, I let her know that her assumption was correct.

"It's a tricky sort of thing, really," she said, ignoring my inability to formulate a clear and intelligible sentence. "How do I explain it?" She then took a moment before eventually telling me, "The Earth can form different—well, I guess, 'defense mechanisms,' actually, is what I'd call 'em." Upon finishing that sentence, she became quiet and seemed to drift off in her own thoughts.

"Anyway," she continued, after a momentary lull, "the defense mechanisms that get triggered kind of depend on a lot of different things: climate, time of day, where we are in the calendar and a million other things I won't bore you with now. This *particular* defense mechanism, as you can probably see, is some sort of crystal barrier. That's what I call 'em anyway. Everybody calls 'em something different but don't let that fool ya. They're a lot more common than you might think."

"This… is a defense mechanism?" I humbly responded, hoping she'd tell me more about the formation of the geological structure that had quite nearly consumed me.

"Sure is. Don't go trying to get through it neither," she continued. "Hard as a diamond. If I do nothing, it's gonna be there fer weeks, at least." She had a strange but comforting accent that, for some reason, made me want to trust her. I knew that made no logical sense and so I tried to consciously fight against that internal sentiment.

"Weeks?" I meekly repeated.

"Oh yeah. At least. Maybe months even. Stuck in there?" she asked rhetorically, while nodding her giant head toward the even more massive crystal-like structure. "You'd of starved to death fer sure."

"Yeah. I… I suppose I would have," I cautiously agreed, still mostly incredulous of the entire situation.

"You look confused, honey, so I'll clue you in a bit, if I can."

I was, which I admitted, and I thanked her for the offer.

"See," she began, "I was mining over there, in the field area around that garage. I was looking fer Tanzarillium and I found some too. I know a guy who's going to pay me a lot of money fer it."

Luckily, I didn't have to wait long for her to show me what Tanzarillium was. Extending two of her tiny arms to their limit (the set closest to her waist), she reached into her shorts somewhere and rummaged for a second before she lifted out a gray rock, riddled with brown craters. "This," she then exclaimed, allowing me to study it for a short while, before she put it back somewhere inside her shorts, "is Tanzarillium, in case you didn't know. I know a guy who needs this bad. Gonna be a big payday," she then attested. "There's actually a lot of it 'round here. Been finding it all over this area, all morning."

I wasn't sure how to react so I simply smiled, as friendly as I could.

"When I took this last bit out of the ground," she then went on to say, "the Earth sort of… 'reshuffled' itself to try and make up fer the deficit I caused."

"Reshuffled?'" I quizzically asked. "What do you mean? What deficit?"

"It's…" But she struggled to find her words. Finally, she began again: "It's hard to explain without getting too technical but, basically, when you take something from the Earth, the Earth tries to compensate. Think training yourself to become left-handed, if you somehow were to lose yer right."

I nodded that I understood and kept the fact that I was already left-handed to myself.

"So… if it's not able to reconstitute itself correctly—if it simply can't use its left hand yet—you'll get a defense mechanism, like that crystal, that's intended to keep people away until it's back to what the Earth considers 'acceptable' fer this area."

"I guess that makes sense," I admitted.

"I didn't know fer sure it would be a crystal over here too, mind you, but I figured some kind of defense mechanism was coming, when I located and removed my haul here." Then, somewhat apologetically, she added, "And I didn't notice you until after I had already removed it."

"Oh."

"That garage door was down after all but, just as I was about to leave, I noticed tire tracks in the snow, leading inside." She gestured her intimidating, razor-sharp arm toward the quickly fading tire tracks my truck left behind us, as she spoke. "When I stopped to listen, I heard yer truck running so I knew someone was definitely in there and I had to act fast. Had to cut you out of yer dang truck too!"

As she said this, I suddenly noticed gray metal shavings—the same color as the metal of my truck—stuck to the blades that stood in place of her forearms. "I banged on the window but you just wouldn't wake up," she explained. "When I finally cut the door off, you just fell on the floor, like a dead fish. I didn't think you were gonna wake up at all, truth be told. A few more seconds and I would have had to risk trying to pick you up with my trusty slicers. That's always a fifty-fifty kind of thing," she admitted, trying, unsuccessfully, to mask her pride in saving me. "Glad it didn't come to that!"

I was glad too and so I enthusiastically thanked her for saving my life.

"What in tarnation were you doing in there anyway?" she then demanded, with a noticeable decrease in her jovialness.

"I, uh… I guess I just sort of—"

"You're lucky I happened to look that way when I did."

"Yes," I admitted. "I suppose I am."

After a brief, shared silence, she then suspiciously asked, "You ain't from around here, are you?"

"Um, actually, I live not too far down the road. Just a few miles, really." As I spoke, I pointed toward the deserted highway and to the general area of my trailer beyond it.

"Well, that ain't good," she rumbled from somewhere down in her gut.

"What do you mean?"

"I was mining over there too. Back that way—impenetrable barriers for miles. Not exactly like the one here but similar enough. Slightly different set of variables and whatnot. Anyway," she then said, after taking a deep breath, "I'm afraid yer not gonna be going home anytime soon."

"What?" I heard what she said clearly but I simply didn't know how else to respond.

"Weeeell," the creature began, turning her head to where my finger had been and pausing, in contemplation of some kind, "good thing yer wearing boots, I s'pose. If I were you, I'd head in the opposite direction." And, with that, she turned and started hopping away from me, back into the woods whence I assumed she came.

"Woah!" I hollered, causing her to halt and turn her head back toward me. "Hey, I'm sorry but I can't... I mean... I can't just leave my truck there. And my home... And my dog... All those people... How do I... Do you at least know how I can get through that crystal?"

"Nothing gets through crystal. That's the whole point. It's there cuz I took something. If ya want it to go away, you'll need to leave something to make up for what I took. You gotta be careful though; reshuffling the elements ain't as easy as it sounds. The Earth can be quite particular, you see."

"Well, can't you just put that rock, or whatever, back?" I pleaded.

"'Tanzarillium.' And... Maybe. Maybe not though. Who's to say? Putting back exactly what you took doesn't always work; in fact, it rarely does. I s'pose I could try but, as I said, I've got a lot of money riding on this." As she finished her statement, her tiny arms patted the waistline of her black- and white-striped shorts.

To that, I said nothing. In trying to examine my options, I quickly came to the realization that I had none. I must have looked pretty pathetic then and there, for the creature then broke out in a laugh she could no longer contain.

"Oooh," she cheerfully exclaimed, after her chuckle had subsided, "I'm just messin' with ya, honey. I can show ya how to get yer truck—and everything else—out of those crystals. Before I found you, I was about to head back to the office to work out a way to remove more of these things anyway."

To say I was relieved would have been underselling that statement. My shoulders loosened and I audibly exhaled my stress. Feeling more comfortable, I asked this strange being, "So how do we do that? I mean, I'm not doubting you or anything. I'm just curious. This is all very strange to me."

"It's actually not all that complicated, Honey. A little research and some mild infiltration. That's all."

"Infiltration?" I didn't like the implications of that word so I asked, "What do you mean by infiltration? And what about—"

"Honey," she then said, taking back control of the conversation before I could go any further, "there are a lot of details but I'd rather not get into them right now. Why don't ya come with me and lemme show ya what I mean? I promise: it's really not a big deal. You'll just do a small, little bit of work and, after yer done, I'll getcha right back here to yer truck, with the key to get it, yer home and everything else free. I can probably even put that door back on too."

"Um, well," I began, "how long do you thi—"

"Not long. A few hours maybe."

Gravity-defunct mirror worlds, arachnoid monstrosities, disillusionment of reality, out-of-body experiences and now infiltration? I wasn't sure about it so I asked again: "What am I infiltrating? That sounds… Well, it sounds lik—"

"'Reconnaissance' is probably a better word. Trust me: it's easy. You'll never be in any danger whatsoever."

"But what abou—"

"Look, honey. It's now or never. If you want to learn more, just come back to the office with me. I don't mean to be blunt but time is money and I've got mouths to feed, back at home, ya know?"

"Sure." I did understand but only partially—not as the empathizing confidant she wanted. I never had kids—never wanted them—and that fact always made me a little uneasy, when another person would postulate that I somehow shared all of his or her views and/or experiences on child-rearing.

I didn't want to alienate myself to this seemingly friendly being and so, as I sometimes do in these situations, I simply agreed; rather, I simply chose not to engage in anything that might be perceived as controversial. I supposed I did understand the concept of having to provide for one's offspring, after all. I just had no experiences of my own from which to draw and, in this manner, I was able to somewhat justify my one-word answer.

This creature had, at this point, given me no reason not to trust her and I was currently in a bind, with no other feasible options available so why wouldn't I agree to her proposition? Unable to immediately answer that question, I reluctantly agreed to accompany her back to her office. She did, after all, promise the absence of any danger.

"'Course, it'll cost ya a small fee," she slyly added, after I had done so.

"A small fee?" I repeated back. I knew I only had somewhere around fifty-four dollars in my wallet so I was worried about the specifics of this fee—the total amount, of course, but, perhaps more importantly, whether or not credit cards would be acceptable.

I have this habit of patting my pocket to confirm my wallet's presence, when I'm talking or thinking about spending money. I do it subconsciously and am really only made aware that I am doing so when, perchance, I *don't* feel that reassuring bulge that my mundane and haphazard inspection typically grants me. Such was the case now.

So too was I missing my phone and my keys—all inside my truck, I was sure. I wondered then, as I became aware that I had been unknowingly patting myself down: had this bartering giant seen any evidence on my face indicating I had just come to the realization that I was without my wallet?

"Yes, sir," she affirmed. "I think 25 percent is fair, don't you?"

"Twenty-five percent of what?" I asked, somewhat skeptically.

"I'm just messin' with ya, honey," she then admitted, apparently once more amused with herself. "I don't need a fee. By you helping yourself, you're actually helping me too."

"Well, I guess, let's get going then," I said, trying (and failing) to sound optimistic, as I did so. I wasn't sure what she meant about helping her by helping myself but I was anxious to solve my problems so I decided to keep the question to myself—at least for the time being.

"Splendid!" she chirped back.

"So, how do we get to your office?"

I was half expecting, at this point, for the sky to open up and a beam of light to suck us into space, so that we could enter her office, which I further assumed would be orbiting Neptune. Instead, she simply motioned me over and said, "Come with me. I'll show you. I'm Lulenne, by the way."

"Oh! Hi, Lulenne. Nice to meet you." I replied.

"Likewise."

"Thanks again for saving me too," I added, in the most heartfelt tone I could muster.

"Wasn't nothing, honey."

The way she spoke… Listening to her gave me the feeling this kind, old… whatever she was, was going to take me back to her cottage, somewhere within the woods, and offer me cookies and hot chocolate. I began to hope for peanut butter cookies with icing and, as I did so, I introduced myself: "I'm James. James Singer."

"Well, hop on, James. I don't want to be late to work so we've gotta chop-chop, lickety-split, if ya know what I mean." With that, Lulenne bent down and turned from me, in order to present her furry back and the implied invitation for me to climb aboard it.

Not wanting to overstep, I cautiously began to question her proposition: "You want me to—"

"Sure, honey," she affirmed, before I could even complete my question. "Climb on up. It'll be a lot faster."

"Okaaaay…" I reluctantly replied. My gnarled black boots crushed the snow beneath them, as I carefully progressed toward her. Even with her crouching down, in a hunched forward stance, she was still quite a bit taller than me. Not wanting to impose or to hurt her, I placed my hands on the fur around her shoulders, for that was as far as I could reach without jumping. As was the case with the fur on her chest, the fur on her back was brown throughout the center but, around the natural borders it created with her skin—where it stopped growing out of her green insectoid body, close to her sides—it was white, with even more white bits speckled in here and there, throughout the design.

Sensing my trepidation, she encouraged me to jump. "Ya don't need permission, honey. Just jump on up and throw yer arms 'round my neck."

Without giving it any more consideration, I obliged and wrapped my arms around her—the way a child might with its parent. Much in that same vein, she too then rose to her full height and began hopping back toward the crystal we had just escaped.

"Why are we back here?" I asked, when she stopped in front of it. "I thought we were going back to your office." Perched upon her shoulders, I could see through the firm, glass-like exterior of the mysterious geological anomaly. There, encased within its jagged walls, was the object of my desire (minus a front door). Even through the crystal, I could somehow smell its fumes, which told me it was still running.

"Hop on off fer a second, honey," she politely demanded, while stooping forward, to lower herself, as she had done before. Once I was standing on the concrete slab of road, just outside of the crystal's dominion, Lulenne continued by instructing that I don't touch anything and that I "watch out now" so that I don't get hurt.

Much to my thankful surprise, she then began to explain what she was doing: "Well, first things first. Before I head there, I gotta snatch a little fragment, like so…" With that, Lulenne began chopping at the crystal barrier, cleaving at it with her giant, machete-like arm.

The crystal, however, was unfazed and so Lulenne persisted with a continuous and laborious downward assault. The sheer, unbridled power of this monstrous creature was now on full display and I watched, in awe, as she continued her onslaught, chopping so fast that her arm became an indiscernible green blur.

Despite her Herculean efforts, the barrage of swinging attacks yielded nothing but noise, yet she continued to strike it, undeterred. For several minutes, the relentless clanging of her blade rang out so loudly, throughout our little corner of the world, that I began to fear it might attract something less inclined to help and perhaps more resolute to devour us. Just then, as my doubts began to grow, she finally liberated a small shard that flew off of the crystal and came to rest by my feet.

Trying to mask her pride in extricating the shard from the larger whole, she half covered a grin with her deadly sharp arm, by pretending to wipe something away from her mouth. Instinctively, I bent down to reach for the newly-freed crystal fragment but, before I could grasp it, she bleated out, in an oddly panicked tone, "Stop! It's… too hot," she told me. "It'll burn you."

Heeding her warning, I backed away, as she charged forward and collected the piece—placing it inside her shorts. To do so, she had to lie nearly horizontally on the ground so that her tiny hands near her waist could reach it. I could see relief on her face when she returned to her full height. She noticed the puzzled look on my face and then offered, "I'm used to the heat. I've built up a sort of… 'immunity' to it."

I probably should have been concerned but I was convinced I needed her help so I simply responded by asking, "So, this is going to help you figure out how to free my truck and everything else from within these crystals?"

"It should," she said sympathetically. "Gotta analyze it back at the office to be sure, though. Hop back on and I'll take ya there."

CHAPTER SEVENTEEN

Lulenne bent forward once more and, with a little less hesitation this time, I hitched my arms around her giant, hairy shoulders, in preparation for what would essentially become an improbable piggyback ride back to her office. A moment later, we were bouncing through the snow, into the forest, beyond the road and the ominous crystal that had inadvertently apprehended everything I held dear.

Though it was cold, the breeze from Lulenne's bounding stride was unexpectedly relaxing. It reminded me of riding my motorcycle far later into the year than I should, on one of those days that was *just* nice enough that I could manage the trek without regretting it. I loved those days; they made me feel like I was somehow cheating nature out of its plan to deprive me of my favorite pastime.

Dawn was beginning to announce its presence, as we traveled deeper into the forest. Still, the darkness that had claimed the sky wasn't quite ready to abandon its dominion just yet. Maybe another half an hour or so until that came to fruition, I mused.

Lulenne was quiet, as we traveled. She seemed determined to get to where she was going and I didn't want to distract her so I kept silent too, admiring the massive, pristine, snow-covered trees that our

journey provided. The deeper into the forest we traveled, the more
the trees grew—in both height and girth.

Before too long, we found ourselves amongst row after row of
trees far larger than I ever thought possible to grow, in nature or
otherwise. They were so large, in fact, that I couldn't even tell where
they ended—for looking upward only revealed they were using the
dark clouds above to disappear into the sky. Even with Lulenne's high
rate of speed, it took us somewhere between five and ten seconds to
completely pass by one of them. Needless to say, I began to feel very
small, next to these behemoths. It must have been what a chipmunk
feels like, standing on the ground and staring up at a giant redwood.

After what I guessed was around a twenty-minute journey or so,
Lulenne made a sharp left—our first turn of the trip—and took us
back behind one of these colossal trees. There, at the back of the tree,
sat what I can only describe as an enlarged beehive—one gargantuan
enough that fifty or so people could easily fit inside. "Ever seen a hive
like this, honey?" Lulenne proudly asked.

"No. Never seen one this big." Of course I hadn't but instead of
the dismay and trepidation I usually felt in these encounters, I was
mesmerized and wanted to know more. "I've never seen one on the
ground like this either. Aren't they supposed to be up in trees, or on
people's roofs?" I asked.

Lulenne bent forward again, indicating that she wanted me to
let go and drop back to the snowy ground, which I silently did.
"Pretty sweet, huh?" she said aloud, ignoring my question and gazing
at the slightly dilapidated and seemingly discarded fortress. Her
sharp forearms were resting at her sides. "I call it 'The Hive.' It was
abandoned by its previous tenants. It eventually fell out of the tree
but, other than that, there's just a little structural damage here and
there," she insisted, pointing to the spots she was referencing, as she
spoke. "I got a good deal on it, too—was just sitting there unused,

after all—so I made it my own and moved the whole group in just a few weeks ago."

"Oh. Okay. Good. Glad you like it!" And I was too. She seemed very proud and I didn't know enough about her world to think otherwise so I assumed she had made a good decision in choosing this place to conduct her business. I was, however, curious about her "whole group" and was holding out hope that they would be just as friendly as she was.

"Don't worry, honey," she said, as if she had just read my mind. "They're harmless." She then took a moment, which seemed to indicate that she was pondering the best way to tell me something, before finally declaring, "Steel... he's a bit of a hothead sometimes but he won't do ya no harm. Promise."

"Steel?" I questioned.

"Well, 'Pike.' That's his real name but he prefers 'Steel' fer some reason or other. Been calling himself that so long, I sometimes forget what it even says on his official papers. Never did understand it but that's his business, I s'pose."

"Oh," I replied. What else really could I have said? Having come all this way, I had already abandoned any other option I might have had to better improve my situation. To put it more bluntly, I abandoned any option I wasn't keen enough to notice and, in doing so, I now found myself here with Lulenne and that put me at her mercy. There was no reason to pretend otherwise, for I was sure she knew it too.

"Well, c'mon," she said, inviting me to follow behind her, with a wave of her deadly blade-like arm.

As instructed, I followed closely behind, while we walked through a set of automatic doors that had been installed into a clumsily cut hole, in the front of the imposing structure. The mechanical doors looked odd there, jutting up against the organic frame of The Hive.

The juxtaposition of the natural world and the one that Lulenne had created was not lost on me, as I passed through them.

As we walked inside, I noticed the ground level of The Hive looked much like any other office building. Gray carpet covered the floor and gray cubicles were set up along the "bullpen" area, in the middle of the layout. In the exact center, however, one desk remained prominently displayed, with no cubicle padding surrounding it. It stood out and I would later find out why.

Both the right and left-hand walls were lined with offices that I assumed were for employees listed higher up on the internal hierarchy chart. Oddly enough, however, they all appeared vacant, as we walked by them.

Above the cubicles, on the second and third floors: more empty-looking offices. I had to briefly stop, arch my back and strain my neck to see them all. It looked as though someone had crudely dug the space for them out of the yellow, organic-looking walls. That observation signaled to me that the walls must have been much deeper than I had originally supposed they were.

There were also several soft spots where I could easily detect ugly, unintentional holes, which led through the wall, all the way to the early morning air outside. The dirty, old, rickety scaffolding beneath those holes told me that, at least at one point, someone, somewhere probably had plans to repair them.

The scaffolding wasn't strictly reserved for the spaces beneath the tears in the edifice though. It also served as means of filling the spaces where the floor had apparently crumbled away—making a disjointed yet functionally congruent path comprised of both cheap, wooden scaffolding and much more stable walkways that were accented by ornate glass railings, designed to keep people from accidentally plummeting over the side.

Beyond the third floor, however, there were no more offices. There, The Hive looked more the way I would expect the inside of a hive to look. There, what I saw was a hollowed out shell of a hive, with bits of honeycomb sporadically lining the internal walls before me.

Rather than looking as though the place had been renovated, it looked more as though it had been ransacked and looted—presumable for that honeycomb substance. That theory also explained why so much more of it remained at the top of the structure—where it would have been harder to reach. Bits of it could be found all about the place but it was certainly most plentiful up toward the top.

For a moment, I marveled at the pragmatic absurdity of the dwelling but then redoubled my pace to catch back up with Lulenne, who had not stopped to sightsee, as I had.

Positioned behind Lulenne, with a little more space between us now, I stole a quick glance into the open room, at the end of the hallway, toward which we were moving. Inside, I saw several creatures, of various shapes and sizes, which I couldn't quite make out yet. They appeared to be waiting for us.

As I rejoined my guide, I noticed that her imposing frame looked hopelessly awkward, standing fully erect, in front of a doorway, at the back of The Hive, which was clearly too small for her. She had stopped in front of it and, by default, forced me to remain stationary behind her.

While I waited there, behind her, she lowered her head and peeked inside. At that moment, the first of several new voices I would hear that day made itself known: "6:55, Lulenne," the booming but decidedly feminine voice mocked, in a friendly barb. "We almost thought you were going to be late for once."

Upon hearing this, the room full of unfamiliar voices began to expel that uncomfortable laugh that employees often force themselves to manufacture in front of their bosses. I always supposed people who fabricated faux camaraderie like this assumed that laughter and/ or meaningless small talk helped to humanize them and redirect everyone's minds—including their own—away from the clear and imposing imbalance of power in the room. I assumed they thought it had some sort of stabilizing effect, that is. The ironic truth, however, is when the kinship isn't genuine, it only makes the dynamic of that imbalance even more prominent and easily perceptible—at least that's the way I often observed those interactions and this one was no different.

"Yeah, yeah, all right everyone," Lulenne fraudulently chuckled, cementing her leading role in the performance. Taking a couple steps, as she continued to stoop forward, she finally entered the insufficiently short doorway and lifted her head and neck somewhere up beyond my view. All I could see of her was her furry back, black shorts and kangaroo-like legs.

Once she was inside the room, she introduced me to what I could already tell was a room full of her subordinates. "Everyone, this is our newest guest, James. I had to save him this morning from another crystal. That's why we weren't here sooner."

* * *

As she spoke, Lulenne stepped aside and granted me a berth into the room, which contained a small group of creatures who, upon entering, all simultaneously greeted me in what became a mostly unintelligible murmur. Their friendliness seemed legitimate though—much more so than their laughing from a moment ago—and so I adopted an outlook that told me they were genuinely pleased I was there.

The room itself was uninspiring. From what I could tell, it seemed like a large office that they had converted, somewhat poorly, into a small conference room. One long table—complete with a set of chairs—took up the center of the room. Behind the table, there was some sort of graph (of which I could make little sense) that had been crudely drawn onto an old, beat-up, dry-erase board. There was also what I assumed was a closet door to my right and next to that, a stand that contained everything necessary to brew, drink and flavor one's coffee. As banal and unremarkable as the room was, though, the characters who inhabited it were anything but.

"James," Lulenne began, "This is Joy."

The creature who sat directly in front of me, on the other side of the long horizontal table, then introduced herself with a "hello" and, even in that one-word response, I recognized her commanding voice. She was no doubt the individual who first prodded Lulenne about her arrival time.

Like Lulenne, Joy certainly appeared to be descended from somewhere inside the insect family tree; more specifically, she appeared arachnid in nature, though, for some reason (maybe experience) she seemed far less intimidating to me than Purple ever did. Unlike Lulenne, however, there was little about her to suggest she was mixed with any mammalian DNA except, perhaps, for her long, flowing red hair and the rounded, somewhat human-like features of her face. Her frame, too, was round, though it was much shorter than Lulenne's. I guessed she was actually about a foot shorter than me.

As for her coloring, Joy was almost completely black, save for her clothing, her numerous, piercing orange eyes and some beautiful red spots, on her back. I saw them poking out of the back of her low-cut blue dress—made visible through the reflection of the window behind her. Also popping out of that dress, I observed many arms—too many to count, due to the fact that she kept so many of them in motion. They were all completing various tasks like holding and drinking coffee, writing on a tablet, texting on her phone and brushing back her hair.

Pleasantries between Joy and myself now exchanged, Lulenne motioned toward the next figure, seated at the head of the table, directly to my left, and said, "And this is Kidada."

Now, Kidada's appearance was the exact opposite of Joy's. She seemed, from what I could tell, to be fully mammalian, without any trace of insect or arachnid heritage. She was much smaller than Joy too—maybe three and a half feet tall, at best. Despite having an incredibly long beak, not unlike a hummingbird's, the rest of her facial features were pleasant and much more defined. While Joy's features sort of blended into her facial area, Kidada's were pronounced and would be much more familiar to any standard human; in fact, besides my own, hers was the closest to a human face in the room.

Her body, on the other hand, was anything but human. She did have slender arms and I could clearly count five fingers on each of her hands… each of her *four* hands that were connected to her *four* arms, all of which were covered in the same green and purple feathers that also sprouted out from her head. Feathers adorned her chest as well, although they were white. Her wings, I guessed, were mostly purple and white but I could not tell for sure because she was flapping them so fast they were nothing more than a blur.

She was beating them so fast, in fact, that they kept her effortlessly hovering, in place just above the table. At that moment, I wondered if she might be more comfortable in a chair but that's when I realized she had no legs or feet. Seeing the genuine smile on her face, I told myself that this must be a resting position for her.

I barely had time to gaze at her, though, before she began to bombard me with a flurry of questions spoken as though her purpose in life was to be the fastest-talking auctioneer in history: "Oh my God! I'm really excited to meet you. How are you today? Do you need anything? Did Lulenne tell you abo—"

"Hold on there, Kidada!" The gruff and somewhat condescending voice that had interrupted her seemed to have emanated from Lulenne's midsection. As I turned toward her, to investigate the auditory disturbance, I spotted a tiny but extremely muscular arm emerge from just above the waistline of her shorts. Although it was too small, in stature, to match up with any common primate with which I had any familiarity, the elongated hand and hairy arm before me gave that distinct impression of belonging to one nonetheless.

Another brown, thickly-covered arm then followed and, after that, they both immediately grabbed hold of Lulenne's waistband. Now gripping the material, the emerging creature began to pull itself up and out from somewhere within Lulenne. As it did so—as just the top of its tiny head began to crest into the room—it bellowed, in a surprisingly loud voice, "Lulenne, did you just say he's a guest?"

Until now, I hadn't considered that Lulenne might actually be some sort of traditionally-functioning marsupial but there, in that moment, it was quickly becoming evident that I should probably reconsider my presumptions. Observing this scene, as it unfolded before me, made me wonder if she was wearing those shorts to hide her pouch or if she simply preferred them for some other—perhaps stylistic—reason. I would never have a chance to ask, however, because I was too flabbergasted by the materialization of the being before me, making its way into the room.

By far, it was the tiniest creature there. I wouldn't have put it at more than eighteen inches long—at most (though I would later hear it claiming to be twenty-four). With the exception of its arms, it looked, more than anything else, like an insect of some sort. It was predominantly brown, with two dirty beige wings and multiple size-appropriate appendages, which it seemed to be able to utilize as either arms *or* legs. The first set, manifesting just below its shoulders, however—the first set I saw when it began to pull itself out, from within Lulenne—exhibited unmistakable muscular definition in the bicep and forearm areas, making it clear these were solely, without a doubt, its most dominant pair of arms.

It lacked any clothing, other than a pair of dark sunglasses, which, with the assistance of a giant brown mustache, obstructed all of its facial features. Its booming voice, however, did plenty to personify it and demonstrate its incontestable sentience. Although it doesn't do it justice, the most succinct way I can put it is to picture a one-and-a-half-foot gnat, with one set of muscular, ape-like arms.

Once it had fully emerged, it flew to the opposite head of the table, across from Kidada, and landed in front of a miniature coffee cup, for which it causally began to reach. Lulenne then greeted it with a tone that suggested a mixture of both pride and mild adoration. "Good morning, sunshine," she announced, to the newest member of the room.

Turning to face her, the strange little bug retorted with a simple, emotionless "Hey." It then turned to me and, with much more zeal, exclaimed "And hey to you too! I'm Steel, Vice President of this establishment."

Lulenne slowly plopped down in the vacant seat in front of her and sighed. She seemed tired. "James, Steel. Steel, James" she obligatorily commented.

"What's up?" Steel replied in such a way that he was declaring it—not asking it.

"And these fine gentleman across the table," Lulenne continued, "are Mark and Matt." As she introduced them, Lulenne motioned her arm toward them to help me identify which was which.

First was Matt. Like, Lulenne, Matt was covered in brown and white fur but, unlike her, it covered all of his visible body, save for his nose, eyes and mouth. He was a bit taller than me, by maybe a few inches or so, and it would not have been a stretch to assert that he gave off the appearance of an upright, aging basset hound, wearing human clothing—a pink polo shirt, to be more precise. He also sported a pair of beat-up blue jeans that were hidden by his seated position but made visible when he stood to greet me. It was clear, however, that he wasn't completely canine.

His left eye remained somewhat bland, while his right looked like it would have belonged to a giant fly. As I stared across from him, I could vaguely catch a multitude of my repeated reflection, on the kaleidoscope surface of his eye. On top of his head, two antennae protruded outward. Despite these anomalies, his doggish face seemed able to produce the full gamut of known human expressions; already I had seen him smile, laugh and, out of my periphery, I even caught him roll his smaller, human eye in a disrespectful way—a gesture he made shortly after Steel interrupted Kidada, from within Lulenne's pouch.

Mark, on the other hand, bore more semblance to a green tree frog. He was slightly taller than Joy and his face, too, seemed capable of any and all human expressions, though, to this point, I had really only seen a pleasant smile. Underneath it, however, I could tell he was trying to suppress confusion. On the table, in front of him, was a yellow notepad, with several pages folded back, indicating he had been writing heavily in it.

Clearly the best-dressed of the cast, Mark wore a white button-down shirt, a black tie and black dress pants with black shoes. Mark covered most of his body with clothing but, from the parts of his body that were laid bare, I could see no insect-like qualities—only your everyday, run-of-the-mill, well-dressed, green, human-sized, talking tree frog.

"Why don't you go ahead and take a seat next to me?" Lulenne offered, pulling out an empty chair to her left. Not wanting to appear rude, I obliged her, though my confidence in the situation, in which I now found myself, was beginning to quickly ebb away. Until now, my interactions with strange beings like this had been somewhat limited. Here, however, I was surrounded by an entire cast of mutated misfits. Instead of panicking, I reminded myself that, as an outsider, they likely thought me as strange as I did them.

As I contemplated this musing, I took a moment to study the ensemble before me. Straight across from me was Matt, the deformed basset hound. He sat directly between Joy (the spider-woman, with hazily drawn, humanoid characteristics on her face) and Mark (the well-dressed tree frog). Hovering to Joy's right (my left), at one of the heads of the table, was Kidada (the four-armed bird creature with no legs). Across from Kidada, at the other head of the table, Steel (the gnat) perched himself, inspecting his clearly empty, tiny cup of nothing. Finally, to Steel's left was Lulenne and to her left was me. What a group!

* * *

After Lulenne's aforementioned introductions, Steel was the first to speak. "First thing: I'm going to need some friggin' coffee. Kidada!"

"Yeah, Steel?" she confidently responded.

"Where's the coffee?" he asked.

"It's right behind you, Steel," Matt plainly interjected, before Kidada could answer.

"This is the cruddy coffee," Steel began to protest but abruptly stopped himself, as if he suddenly thought better of making a scene over his beverage options. I assumed that was for my benefit, for he seemed to be looking at me when he stopped himself, although I couldn't be sure, due to the sunglasses he was wearing.

"All right," he sighed reluctantly, almost as if it was a warning of some kind. Flying over to the coffee station behind him, he began looking for the correct button to press but he was having a difficult time.

Taking notice of his struggles, Kidada flew across the room, at blazing speed, and located the elusive button on the back and pushed it for him. "There you go!" she cheerfully exclaimed, just before she whizzed back to the other end of the table and resumed hovering in the same place she had been before she opted to assist Steel.

"Great," said Steel. As a tiny stream of coffee, from an equally tiny nozzle, on the side of the unit, began to fill his cup, he then asked, "So, where are you from, James?" Then he flew back to his place at the head of the table and awaited my answer.

"I'm from…" But then I just kind of zoned out. I couldn't concentrate. I couldn't stop staring at him and the pouch whence he came. The quickly diminishing perspective that I was as strange to them as they were to me wasn't holding the weight I had hoped it would.

Everything about the entire situation was just so odd. How did I end up in a board meeting, inside of a giant, dilapidated beehive, surrounded by strange, undocumented/undiscovered life-forms—like this small creature who just crawled out of a kangaroo-like pouch and was now addressing me, at the head of the table?

Afraid of where it might lead, I resolved not to wander the distracting, yet familiar "what if" path that began to bombard my mind: what if I hadn't parked my truck where I did or what if I had just said "no" to Lulenne's offer to come here? I needed a new, more receptive frame of mind.

I reasoned that, while certainly hypocritical, I could "fake it" and pretend this was all normal for me too. After having just sanctimoniously chastised this group to myself, for a lack of genuine emotions, the fact that I was now considering adopting a non-authentic role of my own made me feel sheepish. Despite feeling this way, I reasoned that faking confidence in myself and my ability to handle this situation—doing it consistently and believably, that is—might eventually generate a pure and truthful form of it. Even though I didn't really believe this reasoning to be true, I needed to adjust to the environment before me because, as it was, I wasn't fitting in at all.

Feeling thusly, I spoke with false bravado when I asked, "Do you want to know where I was born or where I live now?" As I posed this question, however, I couldn't help but continue to stare at Lulenne's midsection and Steel must have noticed. He must have noticed my shifty, shy and somewhat lowered eyes and he must have noticed how they didn't match the illegitimate poise I had manufactured for myself.

So, instead of answering, Steel unanticipatedly blurted out, as confrontationally as a gnat could, "What?!?"

"Oh! It's nothing," I quickly replied. "It's just I hadn't heard... I mean... I..." Where was that confidence I had literally just convinced myself I could muster? I had always been terrible at faking anything.

"What?!?" he demanded again.

"Well," I began, "I... Did you... That is, were you... in there this whole time?" As I asked the question, I looked, as harmlessly as I could, toward the black and white shorts that hid Lulenne's marsupium.

"In my office?" Steel responded, in a tone that both sought to define my question and simultaneously confirm it. "Yeah; all twenty-four inches of me. I've been in there for a while now." He then turned toward Lulenne and said, "Sorry about that, by the way. Laaate night last night. You know how it goes."

He spoke his apology to Lulenne the same way a hungover, slightly-humbled alcoholic would speak one to the victim of his previous night's debauchery—one where the newly sobered individual was trying to stifle his grin, while apologizing for transgressions he just then, in that moment, learned he committed; more specifically, his was the kind of recollection that feigned remorse but for which he was, to the keen observers who caught a glimpse of that grin, perceptibly happy. Yes: he was sorry he somehow inconvenienced someone but, more than that, he was secretly happy for the new and interesting anecdote that he had just acquired to undoubtedly tell again, to a new crowd, at a later date. I knew that type of empty apology well, for I had myself given it many times before.

"It's fine, sweetie," Lulenne told him reassuringly—the way a mother might.

"Oh!" I exclaimed, picking up on the intimacy of their banter. "Is, uh, are you her… Is Lulenne your mom?" I asked Steel, as respectfully as I knew how.

For some reason, however, this made him openly contentious and, without any effort to mask it, he quickly shot back, "So what if that's my mom?"

Sensing the tension in the room, Joy looked up from her phone and cautioned Steel, much in the same way one might caution a dog who was giving off the impression that he was about to do something he wasn't permitted to do. "Hey," she said. "C'mon now, Steel."

Lulenne apparently felt the amplification in his temperament as well. "Steel," she said, "just calm down, now. He didn't mean nothin' by it."

And it was true. I didn't. Hoping to defuse the situation before it escalated, I addressed the small creature, somewhat befuddled but fully apologetically: "I don't understand what's… Did I offend you? Really, I didn't mean to sa—"

"I am the VP of this company!" he brazenly interjected. "I'm the VP because I'm the King of Bristles! The friggin' king, baby!" he shouted out, to no one in particular, while standing on his hind two legs and beating his chest, with his two most dominant, ape-like arms.

"Okay." I submissively retorted. I didn't know what he meant by referring to himself as "the King of Bristles" but it didn't seem like the right time to ask.

"Kidada?" Lulenne quietly called out, ignoring Steel's behavior.

"Yeah, Lulenne?" the small, hovering, four-armed bird-girl, to my left, answered. Her voice was soft but it contained just the right amount of confidence. As I would get to know her, in that hive, I would even come to think of her as unflappable, which I realize is an interesting choice of words for a creature that literally didn't seem able to stop flapping its wings.

"Be a doll and go and get my analyzer out of my office, will ya?" Lulenne requested/commanded of her.

"Sure!" Kidada vivaciously cried out, zooming out of the room so quickly that the breeze from her wake further disheveled my already messy hair.

Undeterred from the momentary distraction, Steel wasted no time in reappropriating his captive audience. Speaking as though he hadn't even noticed the drop in conversation, he reestablished pontificating on his merits: "I'm in charge of five friggin' people here and, if you're trying to insinua—"

"Four actually, sorry," Kidada corrected, whooshing back into the room, as quickly as she had left it. Once again, my hair flew even more out of place. As she spoke, she placed a small golden box, not much bigger than my hand, down on the table in front of Lulenne. On the front of it, I could make out an elegantly engraved plate that read: "Nuggets."

"What?!?" Steel shouted at Kidada, not bothering to try and temper his annoyance.

"It's four again, remember?" she asked/explained, while opening up the box for Lulenne. "Zeke's not coming back," she then added.

"I thought he was out, digging for coprolite," Steel questioned in a tone that contained hints of both aggression and confusion.

"He was but he decided not to return, remember?" Joy chimed in, inserting herself into the conversation. "I e-mailed you about it yesterday, after you left. You shot me back a 'thumbs-up' icon."

Clearly frustrated, Steel told Joy, "I need you to remind me of these things!"

"I did," she answered, somewhat befuddled. "In the e-mail. You responded to it."

"Remind me anyway," he scowled.

"So, you don't want an e-mail anymore?"

"Obviously, I want an e-mail but I want you to remind me in person too!" Joy was far less confrontational though. She simply shrugged and started chewing loudly on a piece of gum that she must have acquired while I was distracted with something else.

"Fine," he then somehow muttered and yelled at the same time. "Four. Zeke was worthless anyway." Then, turning toward his mother, he wailed, "Lulenne!"

Lulenne, from what I observed, though, didn't seem quite as concerned with the discussion transpiring before us, in our makeshift conference room. While Steel had been speaking, she motioned Kidada over and whispered that she needed help locating the crystal shard she had gleaned from its larger source not long ago. Trying to be mindful of Steel's tirade, I did my best to ignore them and keep my eyes on Steel, as a show of respect. While I did so, Kidada produced the object, from somewhere within Lulenne and placed it inside her golden box, on the table in front of her. Kidada shut the lid just about the time Steel bellowed his mother's name.

Though she was engrossed in the golden box, Lulenne managed to fumble out an absent-minded, "Huh? What?"

"Were you aware Zeke isn't coming back?" he asked loudly but much more calmly than I had anticipated he would. I assumed he would have been angry at Lulenne and Kidada's seemingly clandestine whisperings, while they fiddled with the analyzer, but he didn't even seem to have noticed.

"Was he the fat one?" Lulenne questioned.

"Yes," Steel quickly answered back to her.

Kidada, however, took it upon herself to correct them both: "Sorry; no," she stated almost begrudgingly. I got the sense, at that moment, that she wasn't fond of correcting one (or both) of them.

Joy, with her eyes in her purse, then responded, as she removed a tube of lipstick from it, and said, "That was Tommy."

"Huh?!?" Steel challenged boldly.

Flying quickly back to the head of the table and hovering in place, where she had been before Lulenne summoned her, Kidada addressed Steel—the rambunctious insect across from her. "Yeah; Zeke was the one doing your digging."

"'*Some*' of my digging," he gruffly corrected.

"'*Most*' of it," I then heard Matt, the fly-eyed dog mutter, from across the table.

Steel apparently didn't hear him though. In a much more somber tone, he spoke once more: "We're going to have to replace him, I guess. Lulenne?"

But Lulenne didn't answer and, in her audible absence, everyone looked toward the giant, hairy, locusty creature, as we awaited her response. Her disengagement from us all caused a brief silence, for she was once again enthralled with the box in front of her. It was quietly dinging and ticking; the top of the box was even slowly and subtly changing colors. Noticing the lull in our banter, she looked up once more.

"Huh? Oh!" she then said, alerting us that her brain had just caught up to the question. "You know, sweetie, I'm not jumping up and down about taking another newbie on just yet." What an interesting colloquialism for a kangaroo to make, I thought. "Besides, James is here now. Lemme think on it and let's talk about it later, okay?"

"Yeah, fine," he told his mother, though he was clearly agitated. Lulenne was already looking back down on the box and didn't seem to notice—that, or she purposely paid no heed to Steel's mood. Steel didn't seem to need her validation, though, because, without even a moment's pause, he addressed the well-dressed tree frog to his immediate right. "Mark!" he cried out. "You're going to have to pick up his slack!"

Intruding on him once more, Kidada looked down on a clipboard she had somehow acquired, without my knowledge, and stated: "Mark and Matt are both super busy. You've already got them doing all of your—"

"They can speak for themselves!" Steel erupted. "Mark, you want to be a team player, right?" It was clear, in the way he asked the question, that there was really only one answer that Steel would accept and, for that reason, I was relieved when Mark gave it to him.

"Uh, sure," he affirmed, though (I posited) not as enthusiastically as Steel would have preferred.

"I'd do it myself," the tiny insect began to explain, "but I have another one of those meetings this afternoon."

"Fooooour!" Matt, the figurative and literal old dog, called out. He seemed almost eager to clarify the details of Steel's sacrifice, for his own benefit, as much as mine.

"First of all," Steel seethed, "it's an indoor driving range—not a golf course—and secondly, a lot of deals get closed there!" Steel retaliated—almost daring Matt to prolong their discourse.

With almost no hesitancy, Matt obliged him by simply uttering, "Apparently so."

At this, Steel slammed his tiny coffee mug on the table, spilling the majority of its contents in the process. At the same time, his wings started beating furiously, though he kept his many legs planted there on the table. "All right," he spat out at Matt. "Now you listen to m—."

"What about this morning, Pike?" Lulenne interjected her monotone, lifeless question, without even raising her head.

Steel then turned toward Lulenne and, in a more somber tone, said, "What?" He seemed taken aback by his mother's use of his birth name.

"What've ya got going on this morning?" Lulenne added. Although she asked her son this question directly, her eyes remained fixed on the pinging, whirling object before her.

"Oh my gosh!" Steel retorted, as though he was recounting something both laborious and also emotionally painful. "I am swamped! Where do I even start? Sooo much stuff! Uh… There's the, um…"

Still not looking over at him, the half-mantis responded: "Maybe when the analyzer finishes telling us what we need to help James, you could assist in showing him what to do."

Although she said "maybe," I got the sense this was more of an edict than a proposal. I believe Steel did too. "Absolutely!" he declared to Lulenne. "Sounds like a great idea," he then added, in confident and emotionless permanence.

After awarding his mother with his acknowledgement, he turned toward me and spoke to me as though I was interviewing him on live TV and had just asked him a fan-generated question about how he got to be where he was today: "Listen to me, James. I got into the Vice President role by hard work, dedication and by knowing everyone in the business. Everyone! I'm the friggin' King of Bristles and I'm here today to dig out the solutions you need." Just as he finished his clearly rehearsed self-promoting answer, to the question I never asked him, he flew off of the table and landed right above the waistband of Lulenne's black track shorts.

"Hey, I really apprec…" I began to tell him but I inadvertently stopped myself when I noticed him rooting around in Lulenne's marsupium. His head and half of his body were inside, while his numerous appendages flailed for a foothold, in the air above. Lulenne seemed slightly annoyed but not enough to comment; instead, she simply repositioned herself to better avoid Steel's kicking legs, while never averting her gaze from the analyzer in front of her. Inside her pouch, I heard him rummaging around, which was actually quite a bit louder than the softly pinging golden box that had captured Lulenne's attention.

After taking all of this in, I slowly started once more, "Uh, that is, I really appreciate that, Steel. And, uh, I didn't mean any offense. I just… I really don't know what's going on here."

"It's okay," he replied, as he reemerged from what he had earlier described as his office. On his tiny head, he had adorned himself with what looked to be a weathered, cheap, plastic crown—the kind a parent might give to a child, in order to satiate its desire to parade around the house, cosplaying as royalty.

In a way that suggested he was joking—but also not really—Steel then delivered his royal decree to Mark. In short, he demanded that Mark copy, with a physical pen and paper, what, from my purview, sounded like quite a bit of information that apparently already existed in their computer system, via this Zeke fellow. Joy then looked up, with her new, bright red "lips," and questioned why he would want Mark to do this and, to that, Steel simply pointed to his crown and said, "Cuz that's the way I want it done." She then shrugged, returned some type of mirror to her purse and began digging in it for something else.

And that's how much of this meeting that I was observing was conducted: Steel demanded copies of various documents, which Kidada always provided, zipping in and out of the room, as she did so; he made demeaning and lascivious comments—one of which was directed at Kidada's backside and he got into several arguments with Matt.

In each of their diatribes, Matt was calm (almost emotionless) and that passive but confident demeanor, for some reason, actually seemed to amplify Steel's instability. At one point, he was nearly screaming about some rare stones that Matt maintained Steel had promised to evaluate, despite the fact that Steel denied ever making such a claim.

Matt then consulted his phone and read aloud an excerpt that pointed to the exact date and time the promise was supposedly made. He even cited the unique circumstances around their exchange. Until Lulenne sided with Matt and told her son to check the stones—all while keeping her eyes affixed on the golden box—I thought the altercation had an actual potential for physical violence.

For as much as Steel clashed with Matt, however, the opposite was true with Mark. Steel would make ridiculous-sounding request after ridiculous-sounding request and Mark (the nervous tree frog) would always agree to carry them out; in fact, every time Steel would speak to him, Mark would frantically scribble everything he said, in his note pad, as if he was taking dictation. Steel really seemed to enjoy this. Several times, throughout the course of the meeting, I could tell he was elongating his allocution simply because he enjoyed the dynamic of a subordinate taking down his lectures.

It just went on and on. Steel and Matt continued to clash, Mark continued to drown in his notes, Joy played with her phone, Lulenne kept her head down (focusing on her box), and Kidada flew all about, bringing various things to the creatures of the room—keeping them on some sort of agenda and checking boxes off of a clipboard, as she did so.

It didn't seem to matter what they requested either. Kidada always had the item or the information and, after giving it, she always made a note of it, on whatever was attached to that clipboard. Though I could only see the back of the board, it seemed like her checks and scribbles were getting closer to the bottom, which gave me hope this would all be over soon.

Although I tried not to, I couldn't help but lament the fact that I was here. I felt indebted to Lulenne for trying to help me when I needed it but the mental toxicity permeating this room made it hard to remain grateful. Did it really matter though? Like it or not, I was stuck there.

CHAPTER EIGHTEEN

Most of the group was, for some reason, laughing about the stupidity of their competitors when the mood finally changed. I had more than partially disconnected so I don't remember the exact details of what they were discussing but it had something to do with the safety measures inherent in teleportation devices—that teleportation should only be attempted in a professional and spacious setting such as ours.

Hearing that perked me up. Teleportation?!? Finally! Something interesting! Too bad they'd only glossed over it, as a sort of passing comment. I was just about to try and inject myself into the conversation, to ask about these devices, but, before I was able, Lulenne—full of sudden exuberance—suspended all other discussions and yelled out, "Got it!"

The golden analyzer box, on the table in front of her, had abruptly given one final declarative ping and, in doing so, flung itself open once more. At the bottom of the box, where Kidada had laid it, sat the same truncated crystal fragment. On the inside top of the box, where, before, there was nothing, there now existed a small screen displaying foreign characters I had never before seen.

These symbols, which appeared more hieroglyphic than phonetic, were slightly obscured by Lulenne's arched body. From what I could tell, no one else in the room had a clear line of sight on them either. Even so, they all seemed just as thrilled as Lulenne. All at once, they cheered and congratulated her in their own individualistic ways.

I was feeling optimistic that I might finally have a means of bypassing the crystal that had displaced me—that I might consequently escape from the lunacy to which I was being subjected—and so I asked, "Does that writing in there mean you figured out how to help me?"

At first, I thought Lulenne had turned her face toward me to say something but I soon realized she did so, so that her eye, on the side of her head, had a better view of that exotic text, on the inside of the lid. "Oh!" she exclaimed, upon further examination. "Wow! This is pretty simple, actually."

At this, I heard the group begin to passionately murmur to itself—everyone but Matt. He raised his eyebrows, in order to play along with everyone else's enthusiasm, though, from what I could tell, he appeared to do so more out of a sense of obligation than wonderment. Witnessing his behavior caused me to question if his lack of conviction pointed to perfunctory indifference on his part, or exaggerated theatrics put on by everyone else.

Reading her findings aloud, Lulenne then addressed the group, thereby silencing their whispers. She then explained to all of us what she learned from the analyzer; more specifically, she told us that only a bloodstone, from the Parallel Embers dig site, in the Ariestian desert, to the south, would satiate the crystal that had disrupted my world. She furthermore told me, in particular, that Steel would show me how to retrieve it and that, for everyone else, it was business as usual.

After the group had finished congratulating her, she addressed her son: "It's been a while since you've done anything like this, Steel!" And then, to Kidada, she turned and playfully teased, "You think he's ready?"

"Yup!" Kidada cheerfully chirped back.

As soon as she did, Steel ordered her to go and get him some coffee. "The good stuff," he then clarified. "The kind in the back—not that tar we have out here."

"Yup!" she responded once more and flew out of the room, behind me.

"Everyone else good on everything?" Lulenne then asked, in a tone that suggested she was about to conclude our meeting. The group then chitchatted for several minutes about topics so foreign to me I couldn't even begin to try and explain them.

Eventually, Kidada returned and presented Steel with another tiny cup, resting on its own saucer. "Your coffee, Your Majesty," she said, as she handed it to him.

At this, Lulenne rose out of her seat, to her full standing height. I hadn't noticed before but it was clear to me now, by the way she carefully avoided it, that she had banged her head on the light fixture above more than once. With the group's attention focused on her, she began to explain, "I'm gonna go back to my office and stu... oohh!" She was interrupted, though, when Steel—coffee mug in hand—flew directly toward her marsupium and forced his way in, without a thought or a care. "Excuse me," she then said, before resuming her speech. "I'll be in my office, for a while, studying this nugget."

From inside Lulenne's shorts, I heard her son address me, in a muffled voice: "James, you can just hang out for a bit. Make yourself comfortable. I'll be with you shortly. Do you want some coffee?" he then asked, in a strangely amenable way.

I actually would have preferred to take him up on the offer, to perhaps ingratiate myself to him a bit more, but, alas, I had quite a disdain for the addictive brown liquid. "Oh, uh, thanks," I started to tell him, "but I don't dri—"

"Kidada!" he barked, before I could finish.

"On it!" she merrily retorted and then flew out of the room, as she had done so many times before.

We were all standing now. As Lulenne turned and stooped under the door, I watched her furry back pass into the larger room. Out of politeness, I tried to hide my relief. Sitting in that room had drained me of what little energy I still possessed and I was desperate to escape.

Finally, Lulenne banked right and cleared an exit path for me but, before I could take it, Kidada quickly blocked it and greeted me with a smile. Hovering at chest level, she extended a human-sized coffee mug toward me with much gusto. "Here you go," she happily said.

* * *

As I walked out of the meeting room and into the larger portion of The Hive's ground floor, everyone scattered to their various corners.

Lulenne crouched down and, utilizing her powerful legs, catapulted herself upward, landing on a rickety wooden walkway two floors above us. With each of her monstrous steps, she freed large clumps of dust, dirt and other nameless crud that had been caked onto the wooden beams beneath her paws. Combined, it formed what looked like a giant brown cloud. Before gravity separated the cloud's various components, making them all harder to see, I watched it lazily disappear, on its way toward the ground, where I stood, looking up at it.

From my new vantage point, I could see, more so than before, that the walls above us were in worse shape than I had previously assessed them to be; that is to say, from where I stood now, I could see the sections of missing wall were more numerous than I had once thought they were. Though I wondered, I had not the heart to ask whether they had naturally disintegrated through time's cruel embrace, or if they had been purposefully removed, by roaming pilferers.

The sun was up now. Because of its presence, through the various voids in the edifice, snowy beams of light shone into the room, illuminating isolated sections of space. That dismal sight, along with the chill that accompanied it, worked in unison to emit an unmistakable sense of desolation from within this strange place.

From down below, I watched Lulenne saunter inside of the closest corner office. From my vantage point, it looked abandoned, though I can't truly attest to the room's furnishings beyond its somewhat misshapen doorway.

Joy scuttled off, toward one of the cubicles in front of me. I remarked, to Kidada, something about it looking tidy over there, as I watched Joy enter through the opening of a cheap, mismatched, three-walled partition.

Kidada smiled and agreed, all while leading me back to that isolated desk I had noticed earlier. It was in a large, open area, in the middle of the room. Before taking my seat, I watched as Mark annexed a station directly to my left, while Matt situated himself at the one to my right.

"I'll be right behind you, if you need me," Kidada explained, motioning toward the empty, Kidada-sized, reception-like desk behind me, close to the sliding glass doors through which I had originally entered the partially-organic building.

Somewhat overwhelmed, I thanked her, watched her departure, set the coffee I didn't want on the desk in front of me and began sinking into the chair that was offered to me. No sooner did my backside come to rest in its pillowy embrace, though, did Kidada recapture my attention once more, zipping past me and snagging the name plaque that had been displayed, on my desk.

"Oops!" she abruptly exclaimed, before the gust of wind that her sudden appearance created had even finished running itself through the back of my hair and neck. "Lemme just get that out of the way for you." I could tell she was hoping I hadn't read the nameplate so, for her sake, I pretended I didn't. Being only four letters, though, even

I was able to decipher it before she snatched it away. Quite simply, it read: "Zeke."

"Thanks," I told Kidada confidently, though, in reality, I wasn't sure for what exactly.

"No problem" she cheerfully retorted. She also told me, before darting away, back to the reception area behind me, to make myself comfortable and that Steel would be down soon. Then, some much-welcomed silence. I knew it was likely fleeting but I happily devoured it nonetheless.

Mildly relieved, if for only a moment, I took the short reprieve from strange questions and daunting arguments to survey my surroundings a little more closely. Right away, I began to dwell on the placement of my desk and how it was different from the others. It existed in the middle of the room, in a fully open space, without any physical barriers surrounding it. I appreciated the fact that I wasn't walled in, as the others were, but, in truth, I might as well have been. I say that because the individual cubicle coverings encircling the others kept me from seeing any of their faces, effectively making even my own spatial freedom nothing more than a mirage.

In front of me, I could see the back of Joy. To the right of me, a velvet wall hid Matt and another one did the same to Mark, on my left. Behind me, I could see Kidada but only if I felt inclined to turn my chair completely around and, at the moment, I didn't.

Due to its unique layout, I presumed this area was intended for some sort of training purposes. It was in the clear center of the room, which was devoid of almost any furnishings—save for my chair, my desk and some odd-looking, metallic contraption that I hadn't noticed before, situated directly in front of me. It was egg-shaped, about three feet tall, with a multitude of vents protruding out from virtually every inch of it. Only in the center was there a smooth, vent-less area. There, multiple blue wires extended out the front, falling to the floor and meandering off in various directions.

Leaning forward in my chair, I focused on one particular wire and followed it back to something that vaguely resembled a phone, prominently displayed right in the middle of my desk. It was rectangular in shape and it sat upright, in a vertical fashion. On the left-hand side, there was a panel of buttons with symbols I had never seen before; on the right, simply a blank screen of some sort. Other than a stack of papers and an empty paper tray, in the corner, this device was the only object occupying space, on my desk.

Listening to everyone go about their routines, as if I wasn't there, made me feel like I was in a waiting room somewhere… perhaps the waiting room of an auto repair shop, or maybe a dentist's office. In either case, as with this one, I was an outsider—an observer only—and I was waiting helplessly for someone on the inside of the organization to resolve my situation. Paradoxically, I always loved and, at the same time, hated being in such positions. I loved that someone was helping to solve my problems but hated the fact that I had no control over their level of concern, engagement, time management or empathy.

Under normal circumstances, I would turn to my cellphone, in order to attempt to disengage from odd and uncomfortable dynamics such as this but, in its absence, I was afforded no such escape here. Instead, I was forced to listen to the constant clicking caused by the incessant pushing of little plastic buttons snapped into the frames of what I had assumed were cheap, commonplace, plastic desk phones, like the one anchored to my own desk.

Hearing just one person repeat that less than euphonious sound would have been demoralizing enough but each of the occupied cubicles had its own passive-aggressive clicker, pounding away at his or her own machine—all but Kidada's that is. Not to be outdone by her comrades, though, she kept busy pecking away at her own, different-sounding plastic keys. Her tapping resembled the sounds dual keyboards would make. God only knew what she was inputting into them.

The clicking all around me was relentless, although no one ever seemed to answer any of it. Click-click-click. Pause. Click-click-click. Pause. Click-click-click-click... Then about sixty seconds of quiet. Finally, a frustrated sigh, a single click and then the cycle repeated again.

Searching for something with which to distract myself, as I waited on Steel, I began rooting through the drawers of my new desk. All of the drawers, however, were empty, save for the top one, which contained several blue ink pens. On the desk itself was an aforementioned stack of papers, all containing three columns of repeated characters, followed by blank spaces.

I was bored so I uncapped my pen and held it a few inches above the paper, awaiting inspiration of some kind. None seemed forthcoming however. Ultimately, I decided to sketch something.

As a former artist, I thought it prudent to try and capture Lulenne's visage so that I might better remember it later. I was, therefore, quickly dismayed when I discovered that the pen betwixt my fingers held no ink. Still, I was mildly determined to sketch because I felt it would help to pass the time. There were two more blue pens in the drawer and, in attempting to carry out my design with each of them, I soon learned that they were both dry as well. I scribbled violently, attempting, in vain, to loosen the flow of ink but it was not to be.

Just then, quite unexpectedly, I heard a loud popping sound, accompanied by a bright flash that had emanated from Joy's area. Naturally, my eyes were drawn to her corner of the room to investigate. To my surprise, however, she was nowhere to be found. I hadn't seen her get up and leave and I couldn't imagine a giant spider-woman, scurrying across the floor, would have been hard to miss. Had that flash and popping noise injured her in some way?

As I pondered these questions, the strange, metallic egg in front of me hissed loudly and emitted a puff of smoke, which shot out from its numerous ventilation ducts and quickly dissipated into the air around it. Concerned for Joy's safety, I spun around and addressed Kidada: "What was that? Where's Joy?"

"Looks like she connected somewhere," she cheerfully responded.

"What do you mean? Connected how?" Just as I finished my question, I heard another pop and saw another flash that both came from Matt's area, to my right. A few seconds later, the machine in front of me vented itself once more.

"Oh!" Kidada exclaimed. "Looks like Matt got one too!"

"It was weird for me at first too," Mark then injected. "Basically, we're teleporting into various dig sites."

"These are... teleportation devices?" I then asked.

But Mark didn't answer. His gloved hands were already clicking away, while he concentrated on trying to find a connection of his own. He had no marsupium to keep him warm, nor did he have feathers or fur of any kind. As I suddenly came to realize this, I began to consider offering him my coat, when Kidada interrupted my thoughts and picked up where the young frog had abandoned the conversation.

Kidada explained how I should think of Lulenne and her team as "archeologists of sorts." She told me how they "visit" dig sites in order to acquire various materials within the Earth. Her explanation sounded rehearsed so I decided not to press her any further.

As the morning dragged on and I waited in vain for Steel, Mark eventually began teleporting as well. From what I could tell, Joy seemed to flash and pop the most often and was gone (presumably on those aforementioned sites), for the longest stints of time. Matt wasn't far behind, traveling almost as frequently and staying gone for almost as long. Mark, however, connected much less often and, when he did zap away, he usually popped back after only a couple minutes. Still, all three of them seemed relaxed and confident in their daily routines.

Hoping to echo that sentiment, I finally removed my coat and slung it onto the back of my chair. I was still cold but, over the last few hours, I had warmed up enough that I could stand separating it from my body and, in doing so, I hoped to squash any musings that I might appear rude or ungrateful.

Before too long, the venting egg, flashing lights and popping sounds lost some of their luster and became almost commonplace, which left me bored with the whole ordeal. Through violent scribbling, I tried several times (all unsuccessfully) to coax some ink out of my three defunct pens; Kidada pecked away at her keyboard; Lulenne and Steel were absent and the rest of the team continued to use those curious devices on their desks to whisk themselves off to places unknown.

It wasn't long before my head was down in my arms, which I used to form a circular pillow, on the top of my desk. I used to sit that way in high school too, as my teachers droned on about various propagandist and overall useless trash, but there, at least, I was able to sleep.

It was then that I first noticed I had been absent-mindedly scratching at my right forearm for some time now. Upon further inspection, I learned it was slightly discolored, as though something had bitten me. I hadn't, however, felt anything to that effect. Intrigued by the mystery, I was just about to ask Kidada her thoughts on the matter, when a certain buzzing above my head caused me to stir and abandon my inquiry.

* * *

Sitting up and looking toward the noise revealed that Steel was hovering above me. As I assumed a proper sitting position, he landed on the empty, broken and dusty letter tray, at the back corner of my desk, about three feet in front of me. "Sorry about the wait, James," he offered. "You doing okay there?"

"Yeah... Thanks," I politely lied. "I was jus—"

"That pen not working?" he scoffed. It would have been clear to anyone who gazed down on those copies in front of me that I had been scribbling on them with an inkless pen. Though there was no trace of the intended stain, the impressions the dry tip carved into the paper were unmistakable.

"Apparently not," I stoically admitted.

"Well, there's more in the drawer, I think."

"Actually, none of them seem to be working."

"Really?" he asked, as though he was more than a little surprised. "I think Mark has some," he then told me, as he flew off towards Mark's cubicle, before disappearing behind its cheaply constructed walls. I could hear him opening drawers and rooting around his desk. Luckily, Mark was off to wherever his teleporter had taken him.

"I can't find any," Steel shouted back, over the wall. After that, in an openly frustrated tone, he let loose a particularly nasty string of expletives.

"It's fine, Steel. Not a big deal."

That didn't deter him though. He explained to me that he was going to teleport himself to wherever Mark was and ask where he kept his extra pens. On Mark's behalf, I quickly interjected, disclosing that I really didn't need any and that I would prefer if he didn't go after Mark to ask.

"Really?" he questioned. "Okay, well, let me know if you change your mind." He then emerged once more, rising above Mark's cubicle walls and hovering somewhere in the space between our desks. He was holding a bright yellow stone of some sort. I was surprised too, for it was nearly as big as he was. He must have been very strong for his size.

"Kidada!" he then called out, under labored breath he had failed to disguise. The helpful bird-girl flew over and, as she did so, Steel groaned a bit and passed the stone over to one of her outstretched hands. "Put this on the mineral furnace," he then commanded. "I want to keep it warm. It's not what we want but it might be the best we can find."

"Was that in Mark's desk?" she asked.

"Yeah. Everything else in there is garbage. I can tell just by looking that it's way too old. Either that or it's not expensive enough. Let him know, will you?"

"Understood and yes," she confirmed and flew back to her desk.

"Was the coffee good?" he then asked me, fluttering over to my area and buzzing softly above me. From his vantage point, he could have clearly seen, should he have cared to look, that my coffee cup was completely full; I had not taken even a single sip.

For a moment, I glanced at the cup and then back at him. I couldn't see his eyes, behind those miniature sunglasses, but his head was tilted in a way that suggested they were focused elsewhere. "Yeah," I told him, as I began scratching my arm once more.

"Yeah. That stuff's great," he attested, keeping his head turned toward Mark's area, as he did so. He then began moving closer to Mark's station until, he was hovering right over where I posited Mark's head would have been, had he been sitting there. "I wonder if those pens fell behind his desk…" he then pondered aloud to himself.

"Steel!" Matt then yelled out, dragging the ape-armed insect out of his contemplative musings about the location of pens. Matt had recently popped back in and had apparently heard some of our exchange.

"Huh? What?" Steel answered back, as if he had just been pulled from a dream.

"James just wants to get out of here. Can you show him how to do that now, please?"

Steel then looked at me, to see if Matt's statement had any truth behind it. I allowed my eyes to show that it did and so the little monkey-armed insect agreed to help and apologized, once more, for the delay. Upon hearing that, Matt began clicking away once more and, before I knew it, he was gone with a flash and a pop.

"Okay," Steel began to lecture, "this is pretty easy, actually. I'm going to enter the coordinates to the dig site, in the Ariestian Desert. No one there will recognize you so I'm sure you'll get through easily."

I was going to experience teleportation! Trying to mask my excitement, for fear he would retract his offer, I fought back a smile and simply nodded my head.

"Okay, now listen up," he said. "This is important. You'll appear at the front gate. With this particular site, that's as close as we can get you. Now, that could certainly change for us, if you're able to get inside, so we're rooting for you as much as you're rooting for yourself!" I didn't understand what he meant but I could see he was in no mood for questions so I remained silent. "When you get there," he continued, "just walk in boldly, like you own the place. Don't ask permission to be there. Demand it!" he shouted.

"I don't know if I can—" I started to say, though I wasn't able to finish.

"You have to demand it!" Steel interjected, with abounding conviction. With imposing irritation in his voice, he began roleplaying with himself and said, "As soon as someone asks you what you're doing there, get curt and ask, 'Where are the bloodstones buried?'" He sounded angry, as he spoke the words. "'Yeah? How do I find them?'" Then, in a tone I would have thought exclusive for reprimanding poorly-behaved dogs, he screamed, "'Well, what else are you mining here?!? Really? Where's *that* found?!?'" I could tell he was very pleased with himself, as he demonstrated this faux conversation aloud, for Kidada and myself to hear.

"It's hard for me to treat peop—" I began to softly protest, before Steel cut me off once more.

"You're too friggin' nice!" he accused. "I can tell already! Cut it out. Be mean! Also, don't give 'em your real name. Tell them you're an expert digger and get offended if they ask any questions. Just say, 'Just point me toward the bloodstones!' If they still want to know who you are after that, give 'em a fake name. Tell 'em: 'It's Shawn; where are they?' If they *still* want to know what you're doing there, make something up and then immediately demand she point you in the right direction."

"Really?" I asked incredulously. "Are you su—"

"I'm the friggin' King of Bristles!" he screeched back. "Just do it. And make sure you find ones that are under fifty thousand years old."

"How would I even begi—"

"Just bring back as many as you can. I'll be able to tell, just by looking at them. The more you can bring me, the better our chances." After affirming as much, Steel flew behind the metallic egg in front of me and began tinkering with something beyond my visual scope.

"Okaaay…" I projected toward the area where I believed him to be hovering but I was beginning to lose faith. My arm was itching again but I barely noticed. My thoughts were elsewhere. I was no expert and I didn't want to allege to be one either—especially if I would be claiming it to someone who was likely to be one him or herself.

I hated deception; besides, I lacked the ability to determine the age of *any* rocks—bloodstone or other. Had Lulenne told me I needed those skills to succeed, I would have never agreed to follow her in the first place. True: Steel had offered to tell me which ones were too old but that just meant I would have to bring him multiple stones. Taking one was bad enough but he wanted as many as I could carry.

When he reappeared in front of me, holding a black, egg-shaped object not much bigger than a golf ball, he said, "Once you have them, all you need to do is hold this device and say the word 'hornswoggle.'" Upon uttering this, he dropped the object into my hand and explained, "Once you do that, you'll be teleported back here. You can say it at any time, actually, to return here. The machine's been specifically calibrated to respond to that phrase."

The miniature egg was heavier than it looked. It seemed solid and not easily breakable. Unlike the larger one across from me, this one was vent-less and smooth too. It was also cool to the touch. I studied it for a moment, before dropping it into my pocket—all while Steel was finishing his instructions. In a more somber voice, when he was done, he told me that he had something that required his attention but that Kidada knew the transmission code. She could punch it in, when I was ready.

With that, he used his wings to retreat toward the sliding glass doors behind us. He must have been too small to set them off on his own though. Without having to even request her assistance, Kidada immediately flew over and hovered in front of them, until they opened for him and he flew out into the sunlight.

Almost immediately, I felt a palpable levity in the room. I can't well describe it but it was clear—almost like a drop in barometric pressure that sailors can feel in their bones. It felt as though the censorship of an authoritative regime had just crumbled and its people were suddenly allowed to speak freely, for the first time. Seizing that feeling, I addressed Mark, my froggy friend who had just popped back into the room. I had hoped he might be able to clear something up for me.

"Hey, Mark," I called out, in the direction of his makeshift cell. "Yeah?"

"He keeps saying he's the King of Bristles. Does he mean 'Brussels,' like 'Brussels, Belgium?'"

Before he could answer, though, Kidada flew in, between our two stations, and, hovering there, she asserted, "No; it's Bristles." At this, I furrowed my brow and Kidada said, "How do I explain this? Um, Okay! You remember how we're sort of… archeologists, right?"

"Yeah; that's what you said."

"Welllll, Steel formed his archeological career around helping coprolite excavators. Coprolites, by the way, are ancient, fossilized poopies, heavy in calcium phosphate, silicates and other various minerals—in case you didn't know." I didn't. "Anyway, that's his specialty. Coprolite sites are obviously rich in coprolite but they're deficient in most other areas, which means they need other commodities, like Tanzarillium and bloodstones, in order to keep the Earth's defenses at bay. You with me so far?" Before I even finished nodding, she excitedly added, "Well, Steel has a knack for getting those coprolite excavators to purchase Tanzarillium, bloodstones and lots of other rare stones—so they can excavate their sites without having to worry about crystal barriers and other various defense mechanisms."

Mark must have taken my silence as a cue that I wanted further clarification and so he began to give it to me, before I had the chance to verbally request it. "So," he then began, "You know the bristles on those plastic toilet bowl scrubbers?" I responded that I did.

Unable to contain her excitement, Kidada then waved several of her arms about and exclaimed, before Matt could continue, "We call him The King of Bristles because he's always digging out new opportunities in coprolites—the way the bristles on a brush dig out hardened excrement in a dirty toilet bowl."

I was flabbergasted by all of this—to the point that I didn't even know where to begin deconstructing it—and so, for a moment, I said nothing. Kidada then filled the silence, explaining, "It's because he and the brush both dig out—"

"No; I get it," I assured her, before she had a chance to finish her repugnant analogy. "What does—" But, my question, too, would face an interruption, for, at that moment, we all heard Lulenne call for Kidada, through her office door, two stories above us.

Without any hesitation, the nimble little bird-lady darted toward my teleporter, input a sequence of keys and then flew off toward Lulenne's. Before I could even ask what she had done, the screen flashed a bright light that consumed everything else in the room. Seconds later, when it faded and I was finally able to see again, I found myself standing amidst a sandy desert, which I presumed to be the Ariestian dig site.

CHAPTER NINETEEN

As I came to my senses, I found that I was standing on a dirt road, which led directly into a well-fortified, gargantuan excavation site. The site itself was protected by an encircling crystal wall—much like the one that had absorbed my truck. Upon closer inspection, however, I could see that the crystal was not one piece but many and, since the crystals were not all connected, in the places where they were absent, they left natural gaps in the wall.

I didn't know if the crystals had been destroyed in those places, or if they had never been present at all, but, in those sparse sections, a man-made wall had been built to fill in the gaps and form one congruent wall that connected everything together as one solid barrier surrounding the site. From what was available to my eye, however, those "filler" chunks seemed to comprise only a small percentage of the wall.

Behind me, there was only a trampled-upon path, mountains of sand and a white-hot sun, perched high above my head. Immediately, it began to relentlessly beat down upon my newly coatless, exposed neck and head. I did not much mind though. Truth be told, I actually welcomed its gentle assault, for it served as an ever-present, physical reminder of my escape—albeit a temporary escape—from The Hive.

The site itself was on a massive, dusty hill that seemed to stretch for miles—well beyond the walled-off facade at the bottom. Far above that partially-crystalized barrier, at the crest of the hill—where the site likely originated, before spreading downward—two giant cylindrical shapes towered well beyond any other structures within the city. At the top of each of them, a bright red flame danced in the wind, for all to see. I wondered, as I watched the fires burn, if they were there for decorative or pragmatic purposes that had eluded me.

Entrance into the site, from what I could tell, was controlled by an enormous wooden gate, at the bottom of the hill. Two large brown doors that swung outward, into the desert, delivered access to those wishing to either come or go. At this particular moment, the doors were open and being guarded by a slender, human-looking woman. But for her black wings, black, furry ears and yellow, cat-like eyes, she would have seemed completely human. She had long, straight black hair and dark makeup around her eyes. She was dark-skinned, well-toned and somewhere in her mid-twenties, I guessed.

With no other options on which to fall, I began walking toward her, as confidently as I could. As I got closer, I was able to note some of the aforementioned features I used to describe her but, even from a distance, anyone would have been able to tell she was stunning.

She was holding something in her hand. I thought, at first, that perhaps it might be a flag of some sort but, as I drew closer, I discovered it was a long, golden spear. During my approach, the tip of the steel blade caught the sun just right and flashed a momentary glare of brilliance I couldn't help but notice.

Despite her forbidding weapon and authoritative leather armor, I did not fear physical violence from her. What I feared more was deceiving her—not because of any repercussions but simply because it was the wrong thing to do. I could see, as I drew ever nearer, that she was greeting a caravan of would-be visitors with a large smile and that only further humanized her in my mind. It's hard, after all, to simply label someone as an obstacle when they're friendly and well-intentioned. As the saying goes, "You catch more flies with honey than with vinegar."

I was nervous when I finally reached her. What would I say when she began her line of questioning? Would I lie, as Steel had instructed? Something told me I would end up fumbling all over myself if I did. What about telling her the truth? What good would that do? I doubted very much that this guard, or any other, would be so inclined to help a complete stranger abscond with any treasure she was sworn to protect. Panic began to set in, as I considered my limited and somewhat dismal options.

To my much welcomed surprise, however, this desert beauty never bothered to ask me my name, business or any other questions. She simply flashed me a trusting smile and allowed me to walk right by her. I gathered there could be only two reasons for this: (1) she found me to be so inconsequential that I lacked any real threat to her or this organization or (2) she assumed that, in one way or another, I actually belonged here. Neither one of those scenarios was particularly complimentary—a thought that was not lost to me, as I moved beyond the threshold she guarded—for one assumed I was incompetent and the other that I was skilled at deception.

I was, of course, relieved to have gained entrance to the site but my camouflaged intentions actually made me feel worse about what I planned to do. If only she knew I was there to rob her. Would she be somehow punished if it was later discovered that she aided in the transgression I was about to commit? I doubted that I would ever forget the way I was feeling at that moment but I tried not to dwell on it, for I knew I would have plenty of time to torture myself with guilt later.

The inside of the walled-off site had an interesting design. The middle pathway offered a straightforward journey up the hill—high in foot traffic but devoid of commerce or equipment of any kind—while the side alleys, on each side of the main road, formed a twisted labyrinth. Scaffolding and ancient-looking digging equipment abounded all around the numerous twists and turns but, much to my surprise, merchants and various street vendors were also generously littered throughout. The intoxicating aroma of their sizzling meats permeated the air, with a temping intrigue I was begrudgingly forced to ignore.

Though my exploration of the side streets sometimes dumped me back out into the main square, it was only by accident. I did my best to stay tucked away from the bustle of the main road.

Contained inside the protective walls of this metropolis, I witnessed a plethora of bipedal beings, all exemplifying predominantly human-like characteristics mixed with varying degrees of cat and/or bird-like features, like the young guard I encountered at the gate. Some of those animalistic features were subtle, while some were much more pronounced. Some of the people wore armor and others, tattered rags. I caught an even smaller number of them dressed in expensive, well-put-together outfits that seemed to denote status and influence. I took them to be the ones in charge and so I avoided my part in anything that might catch their attention.

In addition to the denizens, street vendors and digging implements, I also saw no shortage of small one person-sized clay huts, stacked on top of each other, providing temporary lodging for those who were able to pay for it. For a moment, I considered sitting down in one to remove the sand and small rocks gathering inside my boots but I knew that doing so would cause unwanted attention from the owner, advertising these miniature sleep spaces to anyone within shouting distance.

It all made me feel like a tourist—one with a fake passport who was only one conversation away from being discovered. I had no idea where I was going but, as of yet, no one seemed to suspect me of anything untoward (despite the insecurities I was doing my best to mask).

For some time, I trudged forward like this. The sun was quickly sapping me of my energy and my parched lips and bone-dry throat persisted in their cries for hydration. I paid them little heed and persevered in my quest, despite their nagging. Sticking to the alleyways provided some alleviation because the shadows spawned from some of the larger structures within them were thicker, more plentiful and secretive in nature.

One of those alleys was uncommonly sparse in foot traffic and, for the first time since entering this fortress, I found myself wandering its muddy streets alone. It was then that I came upon an ossuary, piled high with humanoid remains. This death-soaked scene, however, is not what originally caught my eye and caused me to stop.

Before I even noticed the insides of the tiny hut—insides crammed full of bones and discarded clothing—I saw the sign above the entranceway. As was the case back at The Hive, I wasn't able to read the text; however, in this place, I had found that crude drawings often accompanied the written words on signs and this particular sign, hanging above the ossuary, was no different. Instead of the skull and crossbones pictorial one might have expected to see, there was a crude drawing of a metallic, vented egg with a giant red "X" through it. It was that drawing that caused me further examine the building and to peek inside while nervously clutching the smaller egg in my pocket.

I could avoid neither the figurative nor the quite literal signs any longer. Despite having been told otherwise, I abandoned any trust in Steel and Lulenne's claim that I was in no real danger—here or, for that matter, back at The Hive. Staring intently, at the people piled before me, I began to wonder: To whom did these bones belong and what befell them that they ended up here? Did they know Lulenne?

Did they perhaps know people *like* Lulenne? Would this place be *my* tomb as well?

No one inside these walls had given me reason to conclude anyone here harbored ill intent—not any of the people I passed on my way here and certainly not the guard at the gates. The mysterious and ominous room before me, however, made me want to utter the word "hornswoggle," in order to engage the extradimensional tether back to The Hive. I didn't, though, for I was equally concerned about what might happen if I returned there without any bloodstones.

Now, I truly had no choice. Facing a hopeless dilemma, I decided the only way to get out of it was to forego my own ethical code, locate the stone, steal it and leave. There was simply no other choice. I was, at the same time, both as disgusted with myself as I was determined to succeed.

Leaving the shadows and the alleys, I strode into the bustling center of the site. I walked with purpose—pompously even, as Steel would have wanted—to sell the effect. The sun's attack on my head fueled my determination. Thankfully, I eventually found my quarry.

I reached my destination in a seemingly innocuous corner of town, as if it were hidden in plain sight or perhaps altogether forgotten. There, I came across a giant tent—the largest I had seen yet. Feeling inexplicably drawn to it, I cautiously stepped inside and saw that it was covering an equally enormous, deep, man-made hole in the Earth. I was in luck: both the ground level, where I stood now, and the subterranean basement below me, appeared unguarded and altogether vacant. Overlooking one of the dusty and gnarled ladders before me, I peered down into the hole and confirmed that assessment. Even better, my inspection had revealed piles upon piles of various stones, sorted by similarity, at the bottom of the hole.

It was a long climb down but, with such a golden opportunity before me, I quickly overcame any hesitancy that still festered within me and began my descent down the ladder. My arm was once again itching as I carefully made my way down the dusty rungs. Though I wanted to scratch it terribly, I thought it safer to wait until I reached the bottom and so I tried, unsuccessfully, to ignore its mocking and persistent irritation.

Eventually, I reached the bottom. I was standing in a very dark, damp, circular room that was illuminated—quite poorly, I might add—by haphazardly placed torches, scattered sparingly throughout the room. As I alleviated the itch in my arm, I perused the many piles of colorful stones, looking for the bloodstone Lulenne required to free my truck, my dog and my home from the geological anomaly she had inadvertently caused.

It was only then, as I began to scan all the piles of colorful rocks before me, that I realized I didn't even know what a bloodstone actually looked like. Why didn't they tell me?? Why didn't I ask?? Did they assume I already knew? Was this some sort of test? Under my breath, I cursed myself for not raising the question earlier, when I had the chance.

In the corner, there was a pile of red, smooth-looking rocks. They varied in size but, in hue, they could all have easily been said to resemble the color of blood. I didn't have time to dillydally and I figured that choosing the stones in this pile gave me as good a chance as any to be correct.

Finally, I was on the precipice of escape. I could almost feel my truck's shifter in my hands once more. Leaving that memory behind, I focused on the task before me; I couldn't help but wonder which of these stones were older and which were younger. They all looked equally sufficient. I couldn't tell so, as Steel suggested, I reached out my hand to fill my pockets with as many as I could. It was only inches away from the pile when I heard a familiar yet panicked voice from above. "Stop!" it screamed.

The character above had adorned himself with a mysterious brown cloak, which concealed his face from me. We looked to be similar in size, though it was hard to tell, as I stared up at him, from deep within the hole. For a moment, I deliberated on grabbing as many stones as I could and escaping, before this intruder could advance toward me.

Knowing it would take him no short amount of time to climb down to where I was, however, gave me a bit of security and allowed me to pause and better assess the potential threat before reacting blindly. I decided to try and engage in a conversation, knowing I could literally disappear at any time. Naturally, my first verbal response was to demand that the cloaked being identify himself.

"It's me: Matt." I recognized the old dog's voice from our interactions back at The Hive but he offered further confirmation of his identity when he threw off his secretive garment and instructed that I stay still and not touch anything—that I was in danger. I don't know why but I believed he was telling the truth and so I simply waited, scratching my arm, in confusion, as he climbed down toward me.

* * *

It wasn't long before Matt eventually reached me, at the bottom of that man-made hole. I could hear the relief in his voice, as he approached me and thanked me for waiting.

"Don't come any closer," I warned, when the distance between us was almost negligible. I partially trusted him but not completely so I held tight to the egg I had removed from my pocket. Matt's motives were unclear and, as such, I wanted to ensure I had enough distance between us—enough distance that I could grab a stone and speak that magic phrase, for extraction, before he reached me. He seemed to understand my concerns without me having to voice them and so he halted his advance; in fact, he even backed up a bit, until he had left a comfortable fifteen yards between us.

"What are you doing here?" I asked before he had a chance to offer an explanation. "How did you find me?"

"I know this is strange but I swear: I'm here only to help. You were about to make one of the biggest mistakes of your life." As he spoke his words, he subtly adjusted his conventional, dog-like eye so that it left me and focused itself more on the assortment of stones next to me.

He said nothing else after that; he just continued to stay fixated on that pile of stones (almost obstinately so). The way he was so blatantly staring—it was as if he was insinuating that I follow his lead and do the same. Eventually, I relented and did just that, cautiously following his gaze to the that pile, all the while readying myself to grab a stone and disappear, should he lunge for me.

I studied the pile for a moment and then looked back on him. When I returned to his countenance, he was nodding, for he knew he had silently shared his concerns with me.

"What other choice do I have?" I asked.

"Looks like it's starting with your arm," he then remarked.

I had been unconsciously scratching it but hadn't thought much of it until he uttered those words. Wanting to keep him in my line of sight I raised my arm to my eyeline. I noticed, upon inspecting it, that the little irritation, at which I had been absentmindedly scratching, had grown to the size of a penny.

"It usually starts small," he started, before I had a chance to impose any questions upon him. "Like a little spike protruding from your arm or leg or something. It's not always that though. Sometimes it's antennae. Sometimes tiny wings. You never really know for sure." Then, pointing to his giant fly eye, he concluded with, "Something like this? That takes a little more time, of course."

"What are you talking about?" I asked, in horror. Was I fated to undergo a similar metamorphosis?

"The Hive… their mining operation… it changes you," he told me bluntly. "Only a little at first but, if you let it… well, it'll consume you. It's how they trap you and how they start to control you."

"What are you talking about?" I demanded.

"It's all just a sham," he said with a twinge of misanthropy.

"What do you mean?"

"This whole thing—it's all a scam."

I could hear the disgust in his voice but I didn't understand its origins so I urged him again to explain.

"They *want* you to take that," he said, pointing toward the pile of stones next to me. "They *need* you to."

"Why?"

"You see, right now, it's a lot easier for you to slip into places like this—for you to give *them* access to slip into places like this. You're still fresh. You're still… unchanged. Someone like me? That's another story. Someone here takes one look at my eye and it's over. They know who I am *without* even knowing who I am. You know what I mean?" I didn't and I told him as much.

"I can't just waltz right in but I still look normal enough to at least *sneak* in, with a little help," he then added. Next, he nodded toward the top of the ladder where he threw off his coat and continued: "I followed your trail. I kept my head down and here I am. I had to stop you before you left with that stone and started to slowly become one of them.

"You pull that stone and head back to Steel and it's over. You'll turn into something no one wants but what's worse: you'll give them a path to follow. New coordinates. A way into this room. And, before you know it, they'll take everything here and soon after this place will crumble."

"What other choice do I have?" I accusatorily asked, still not fully grasping what the upright dog before me had just explained. "Just wait? Wait for that crystal to release everything in weeks… maybe months from now?!?"

"The crystals are a defense mechanism against The Hive and others like them—not you. You can still walk right through it," he solemnly explained.

"But I saw Lulenne chopping at it wit—"

"The land there recognizes *her* as a threat. It doesn't want to let *her* in. You? You're no threat at all. Not yet anyway. Did you actually try to get to your truck? Did you actually see the state of your home?"

I thought for a moment and then realized I hadn't. I had just taken Lulenne's word for it.

"Try it," he confidently told me, before I could answer him.

"So, all this time I could have just… left?"

"They love to make it look like you don't have any other options but yes. It's as simple as recognizing the truth and taking action."

"So why tell me this?" I asked, as if I expected to somehow catch him in a lie. "Won't they be upset you're helping me?"

"It doesn't matter. I'm done with that place. I just came here to tell you the truth before I disappeared. I'll worry about the aftermath later. Right now, I just need out."

"I see…"

"I tried to warn Mark too," he told me, "but he just doesn't get it. He will, of course, but then it'll be too late. Right now, he thinks the monetary compensation is worth the dissonance. I used to think that too. Anyway, I told him what I was doing and, after he declined to join me, I dialed my final coordinates and arrived here. I covered my face, snuck past the guards, followed your scent and now here I am."

"So what's the plan then? Assuming I believe you, how do we get out of here?" I changed my tone and tried to sound more pragmatic, as I asked my question. As I waited for a response, I put my hands on my hips and looked around the room, as if the answer was hidden there somewhere.

"Break the cycle," the sly old dog finally replied, when my eyes returned to him.

"But how exactly do I…" But I stopped myself when I noticed that Matt was deliberately directing his gaze toward my left hand—where I was nervously clutching the smooth black egg that served as my ticket back to The Hive. I watched, with a confused look on my face, as he then pantomimed a motion that looked like he was snapping a branch in half.

"But won't that… won't that… strand me here?" I asked with unrestrained concern.

"Everyone's path is different but there *are* other ways to get out of here. You'll have to find them on your own, of course, but I promise they're here." As he casually licked his arm, he then said, "I think the question you need to be asking is if you'd rather be stranded for a bit, with a clear conscience, or if you'd rather be back home with a guilty one. Uncertainty or serfdom—which do you prefer?"

While I was considering his query, Matt had produced a small black egg of his own. He'd been rolling it around in his hand, while he studied me. After he apparently finished his silent deliberations, he grasped the object with purpose and hurled it high into the air. I held my breath and watched its trajectory, as it quickly returned to the Earth and shattered there on the ground. When a strange green substance oozed out, onto the dirty floor, Matt tilted his neck, raised his head toward the heavens, closed his somewhat normal eye, breathed in deeply and smiled.

He looked calm and at peace standing there—as if he had somehow absolved himself from some unspoken guilt. Feeling encouraged from his demonstration, I watched him for a few moments before letting go of the egg in my own hand. It thudded into the dirt below me but it didn't break—not until I drove my weight into it and squashed it under my boot.

PART VI

SATURDAY EVENING

CHAPTER TWENTY

With a flurry of violent coughing spasms collapsing my lungs, I hastily awoke inside of my tub. As I clutched the outside wall, I felt as though something inside of my chest had wrapped itself around those two mirrored organs and was constricting them to the point of imminent implosion. Such was my consternation, in all of this, that I had been forced to bypass the brief moment of reverie, which I frequently found between the dreamworld and what I reluctantly perceived to be the real one.

To say the least, this departure from a more naturalistic transition was as unexpected as it was unwelcomed. Since the introduction of chemical sleeping aids into my sleeping regimen, I had found solace in those fleeting moments of twilight but not this time. This time, I immediately launched myself into a position where I was helplessly kneeling on all fours, with my back arched, like a sick dog. As I held that posture, my lungs involuntarily convulsed and threw me into an asthmatic state.

This was the type of cough that expelled itself with such brute force that it evacuated every last trace of oxygen from within my lungs. Worse yet, my inability to keep from flushing all of that oxygen out into the atmosphere left me desperately failing to inhale, through a constricted diaphragm that was unable to do anything but push outward.

And so, in this way, the game, for which I gave no consent to play, was played nonetheless: all of the air was forced out of my lungs, through a thunderous evacuation, leaving me only microseconds to suck back in enough to keep from asphyxiating before the process repeated itself. I couldn't see my face, as I suffered through all of this, but I was sure it had adopted a darkened shade of blue.

After the longest thirty seconds on Earth, my wheezing eventually subsided and I was left, still kneeling, gasping for air in my bathtub. I hadn't smoked tobacco in over twenty years but my throat felt as if I had spent an entire evening chain-smoking cheap cigarettes, in a noisy, dimly-lit bar somewhere.

As my senses began to return to me, I noticed I was once again back in the same pair of comfortably tattered jeans, with that same ripped shirt and those same black high-top shoes. Somewhat defeated, but unexpectedly optimistic, I assumed a position that had me resting on my rear end, with my right knee spilling over the side of the tub, in a space-constrained, half lotus position. For a moment, as I replenished my breath, I sat there, trying to glean some sort of meaning from Lulenne and my escape from her world.

While wiping sweat from my brow and attempting to recount the details of an adventure that was still fresh in my head, I suddenly grew distracted by the gun lying at the bottom of the tub. As if I'd never seen the instrument before, I picked it up to examine it. It was heavy—not to the point that holding it was strenuous but its weight was always something on which people commented, when they first gripped it for themselves. I decided, then, to have a look inside. Still empty. Still clean. Still ominous yet oddly alluring. As I was holding it and admiring the engineering and craftsmanship that went into producing the weapon, I couldn't help but wonder if it held the power to rid me of my tormentor.

Without really noticing it, my breathing had begun to stabilize while I handled the firearm. So entrenched was I in my own head that I had almost forgotten that it was ever strained at all. Feeling thusly revived once more, I rose from the tub and ventured out into the world outside my bathroom.

Blue, as expected, was there to meet me. He was scared but also curious and I couldn't tell which emotion, of the two, was actually dominating him. As I knelt down to pet his head, I could see the digital clock, through the hallway, in the living room beyond. It was well into the late afternoon, which I recognized as the time of the week when, up until recently, my phone would typically begin to fill with various requests to join with friends at obscure watering holes throughout the city.

I was glad those calls had tapered off, though. From a physical sense, I was much more isolated now but, mentally, I felt no worse sitting alone in my trailer than I did when I was surrounded by people who couldn't actually see me. At least here, I could be myself. At least here, I didn't feel invisible or (worse) inconsequential.

With a desire to clear my head, I trudged down the hallway, with Blue happily in tow. I didn't even utter a word of my intentions but the beast somehow knew I was planning on taking us both for a much-needed, head-clearing walk. It was obvious in the way he was prancing and wagging his tail. I wondered: was that because he was especially intuitive or was I just that predictable?

Regardless of the reasons, Blue was oftentimes more perceptive than I gave him credit but, on this particular day, I needed more than he could offer. I needed *human* perception and understanding. I was both concerned and dismayed at how quickly my mental faculties seemed to be deteriorating but who could handle, or even understand, the insanity of my life? Certainly not my dog! Chris, of course, would listen if I engaged him but I wasn't ready for that. My doctor would listen too but I wanted to practice on someone else first. Unfortunately for me, Fisky was the only person with whom I felt comfortable enough to try.

Just before I committed to reaching into the closet to fetch the animal's leash and walking collar, I braced myself, took a deep breath and brought my phone to life. Within an instant, its vibrant shine was dancing across my eyes. Instinctively, they darted toward the top notification bar, scanning for any icon indicating I had a missed call or an unread message of some kind but I received no such confirmation. Just to be sure, I opened up my text messaging app and there, at the top of my conversation list, sitting alone, was Chris.

Despite the palpable warning emanating from my heart, I then logged into my social media account, made my way into the "settings" tab and clicked on "blocked users." There was only one. For a second, I hesitated, with my thumb hovering above the "unblock" icon, before I engaged it and reopened access to Fisky's account. The first thing I saw, after I clicked on her profile, was a picture of her left hand, adorned with an expensive-looking diamond on her ring finger and an endless stream of comments congratulating her on her betrothal.

For a moment, I was dumbfounded but, after the initial shock wore off, I decided I was actually happy for her. In a strange twist, I felt more than a little relieved as well. That ring on her finger represented the undisputed finality of our relationship and, in that way, it also meant that I no longer had to worry about her—at least not in the way I had been. With that door now completely closed, I no longer had to wait outside of it so I closed my phone and finished accessorizing Blue for his walk.

Upon stepping outside, I immediately noticed that it was uncommonly warm for an Ohio December; although, asserting that *any* type of weather is uncommon during *any* portion of the calendar, in Ohio, is itself actually quite common, I suppose. With that in mind, I guess I really shouldn't have been surprised by the fact that just this morning it was snowing and now the sun was shining so brightly that I was actually considering turning back and leaving my coat inside. After a moment of deliberation, however, I resolved to keep it.

On the ground, next to my truck, there was a pool of water, from where all the snow and ice had melted off of it. A mild inspection proved that the doors were still secured tightly to the frame; what's more, the stereo and the rearview mirror were pristine and undamaged. I stared at the vehicle for a moment or two and, once I was satisfied it was real, I stepped out of my driveway and onto the street.

Without any further assistance from the owners of the park, the snow on the streets had begun to recede as well. Their lack of effort in removing it did not stymie Mother Nature from implementing her own pavement-thawing process. About 70 percent of the street was still caked in white powder and hardened ice but the other thirty was full of pockets of black asphalt, peeking out, under the sun's indulgence.

Those sloppy, slushy pockets of unencumbered street made for excellent—albeit messy—footholds and so, whenever I could, I made sure my boots found them. Once again I'd chosen them over my high-top sneakers and, as I splashed along, I knew I'd made the right choice. Blue, on the other hand, wasn't stricken with the responsibilities of making such fashion choices. To him, it had always been "bare paws or bust." As I watched him happily strut along, stopping every four seconds to sniff something new, I couldn't help but envy the simplicity of his life.

Toward the end of our street was a wooded, undeveloped area where, on many occasions, I'd seen deer and other wildlife gather and sometimes peep out of the tree line. I usually avoided that area because, during my only expedition there, Blue came back with ticks—an inconvenience that disgusted me far more than it did him.

Though the day was beginning to warm up, I recognized that it was still the dead of winter. To my point, the natural ground—unlike the paved roads inside the park—was still completely covered in snow and most of the ankle-high vegetation beneath it, where those parasitic blighters lived, was presumably inhospitable. Because of that, I decided that there was little risk in contracting more ticks and so, with Blue enthusiastically walking beside me, we made our way toward the edge of the forest entrance.

After about fifteen minutes of stepping over downed trees and guiding Blue around the various obstacles of the forest, we arrived at the edge of a cliff I never knew was there. This region was historically known for being rich in a multitude of desirable rock quarries and, through no direct intention, it seemed that I had just stumbled upon the remnants of one of them.

As I peered over the edge, there was no doubt that a fall from this height would be not only fatal but gruesome as well. For some reason, I felt compelled to fixate on this fact, much to the chagrin of my dog. He was pulling in the opposite direction. He wanted to sniff something I was sure.

Blue had never been the type of dog that wanted to escape and he usually came when I called him so I knelt down and unhitched his leash, after which he stared up at me for permission to explore. With a friendly gesture of my arm, I granted it to him and he sauntered off behind me only to stop and pour all his attention into sniffing a bush, not twenty feet from where I released him.

I trusted him enough to be unconcerned and so I allowed my attention to be recaptured by the summit of the rock edifice on which I now stood. It was obvious that I stood on the top of a wall that was clearly man-made because the sheer angle of the cut, into the giant rock, was completely vertical. To even a child's eye, the precision would have been unmistakably mathematical. Based on my admittedly limited experience in skydiving, I posited that a leap from where I stood would have me splattering against the jagged rocks below in no less than three seconds.

Free-falling through the heavens… The feeling it had elicited in me was unexpectedly calming, to say the least. Fisky and I only tried it once and, in that solitary experience, I felt more like I was floating or hovering—not like I was falling at all. It was quite peaceful, actually.

For a moment, I closed my eyes, spread open my arms, as if they were wings, and imagined simply letting go. Could I recreate that serenity in this very different set of circumstances? Would I panic for that three-second-free fall or would I fall free, as I did before?

And what about Blue? Would he try and find a way down to me? Would he wait there, at the top of the cliff and, if so, for how long? Surely he'd eventually find his way back into someone's yard, wouldn't he? Although he was frightened of nearly everyone and everything, hunger's a powerful motivator and I imagined it would, at some point, overtake his trepidation.

While deep in contemplation, I had unknowingly removed an Alcoholics Anonymous "sobriety chip" from my coat pocket to unconsciously fiddle with it. In my unfortunate clumsiness, however, I inadvertently dropped the coin, which landed safely next to my boot, at the edge of the cliff wall. Seconds later, when I carefully squatted down to grab the keepsake, I felt the slug inside my head begin to squirm.

Simultaneously, the snow and the trees around me turned gray and, from within my skull, I heard the familiar demand to "DO IT!" That's when a feeling of vertigo began to make its way through me and, in my suddenly dizzied state, I felt as though I might inadvertently tumble over the side. Using as much concentration as I could muster, I kept control over my swaying, carefully reacquired the chip, transferred my weight behind me and then let myself go. I landed on my back, next to a snowy log, just as the voice inside my head disappeared and the natural colors of the sky, trees and snow returned in full.

Bewildered by the fact that I had somehow repelled the demon in my head, I slowly sat up and looked around the snowy forest. It was as if I was viewing it for the first time. Its beauty was affecting me and so, in what I hoped would be perceived as an act of gratitude, I decided to stay a bit longer. After clearing some ledge snow that had already mostly melted, I plopped myself down, at the edge of that cold, wet cliff and let my legs dangle off the side.

For several hours, I sat and ruminated over all of my recent experiences and tried to derive some meaning from them all. Was I simply going crazy? I wondered what my psychiatrist would think after hearing all my stories and reading the doomsday note inside my back pocket.

As I pondered a plethora of unanswerable questions, a solitary tree unexpectedly caught my eye and pulled my consciousness back into the forest we both inhabited. I hadn't noticed the leafless, dead-looking husk before but—with its winding trunk and flaky gray bark—it looked strikingly similar to the tree into which Fisky and I had once carved our names. Just to be sure, I pulled my phone from my pocket, located the photo and compared it, side by side, with the tree before me.

Unfortunately, the tree on my phone wasn't as prominent as the one in front of me. Although Fisky had intended for it to be the focal point of the photo when she captured it, it was sandwiched between our two smiling faces. Still, it was undeniable that the two trees were nearly identical—save for the carved letters that distinguished them.

So, in a symbolic gesture, I half scooted/half crawled over to the new tree, sat with my back propped up against it, faked a smile and raised my phone above my head, in an effort to recapture the same angle as before—this time sans Fisky, of course. Several times, throughout the process, I compared what I was doing to the photo on my phone—in order to make sure I reproduced the image, to the best of my ability.

When I'd finally created a likeness that satisfied me, I deleted all the attempts that didn't. After that, I began clearing out the older, original pictures as well. When I got to that final one—the one I had used as a template for this new picture—I stared at the label Fisky had attached to the bottom of it. It said, "That Island next to The Docks." The Docks was the name of a bar located on the same lake where we had ice-skated and took the original picture. I thought about the bar, the lake and the tree for a moment before I took a deep breath, closed my eyes and deleted that last photo.

Blue was happy when I finished and finally stood up to re-leash him. For hours he'd been interrupting my meditation, nuzzling me to let me know he was still in the area, before disappearing once more to investigate whatever it is that dogs feel so compelled to investigate.

By the time we'd returned home, the sun was already beginning to set. I was glad. I figured the darkness would only aid me in my newly-formed, destructive plan and so I grabbed my axe, activated the GPS on my phone and set the destination for The Docks.

* * *

It was well into the evening, by the time I parked my truck outside The Docks. As I opened my door to step outside, the last gaseous remnants of an extinguished heater evacuated the cab and escaped into the air. For a moment, I apathetically left the door ajar and found myself in a moment of indecision and inaction.

Within seconds, most of the heat had already dissipated out of the truck cabin but I silently soaked in what was left over. As I stared out of my quickly-fogging windshield, I could see The Docks, to my left. It was a popular bar that catered to a multitude of different tastes—one such example being the boating crew who preferred anchoring their various nautical vessels, at the end of the titular pier. Though, on this particular night, they no doubt consisted of a significant portion of the crowd, the frozen lake had made them harder to detect. It insisted that their arrival, like mine, had been dictated by land-based vehicles only.

Their vehicles of choice, however, when available, were usually captained by older, upper-class businessmen and aging divorcees who had talked themselves into a reality where they were much younger and less encumbered. I always smiled and let them continue to believe that narrative, without my reproach, but it was a version of reality that was much different than the one to which the rest of us were beholden.

There was also the younger crowd, who pretended to be much older and more sophisticated than their years would have suggested—a charade that usually broke down after they'd imbibed a few cocktails. There were those who danced to popular dance songs the DJ was playing, on the indoor dance floor, while others preferred the local band, playing underneath a hanging row of outdoor heaters, on one of the many-tiered, massive decks outside.

They were covering "oldies" that many of my peers thought were edgy when they first came out, in the mid-'90s. Those closer to my age seemed to enjoy it, while the older folks tolerated it and most of the younger ones avoided it altogether, preferring the DJ inside instead. A lot of the older folks preferred him too—that, or they preferred the indoor heat, along with the attention they received when they danced to the songs he selected from his playlist.

There was more than just music though. Billiard tables inside attracted both the serious and the obnoxious competitor, as well as spectators of varying levels of sobriety; so too did the cornhole boards, in the corner of one of the outside decks.

There was a giant rectangular bar outside, with outdoor heaters burning brightly around it, and a smaller counterpart bar on the inside. All the stools surrounding both of them were filled and, unless one was lucky enough to have a friend that could hold one for him, he'd lose it the second he left it for a trip to the bathroom.

Above both bars, a sea of televisions were broadcasting various sporting events—some live and some long since passed. Some of the patrons focused on their captivating, glowing flashes exclusively, while others directed their attention to the attractive bartenders struggling to keep up below them. All in all, the backgrounds were diverse but the goal was unified: liberation of some sort. Some were there to eat; most were there to drink but, in one way or another, everyone there wanted to escape something.

Sitting there in my truck, I supposed I was no different. I wanted to escape too but, for me, this bar (and others like it) were no longer the place to do it. There was nothing I wanted in there anymore—nothing I couldn't at least get an improved version of elsewhere anyway. Camaraderie, respectable discourse, enlightenment, music, participating and spectating in various games—alcohol only impaired my enjoyment of all these things.

For most of my life, I thought quite the contrary—that it enhanced those experiences. The reality in which I now lived was very different though. The friendships I thought I was forging when I was drinking were illusions; most of the times, the people I met either didn't remember me or vice versa, or both! Discussions usually devolved into shouting and I rarely learned anything of consequence.

I struggled to see the bigger picture in most things but the smaller, background details eluded me as well. Even my motor skills suffered and so too did my retention of the topics I discussed and the events I witnessed. In the end, it was all just a mirage—an expensive, poisonous mirage.

I used to think I was so outgoing; I was even proud of it. Most of that was the alcohol though. I wasn't outgoing; I was a drunken buffoon. Since quitting, I'd actually become quite a bit more reserved. As sad as it was to admit, I was able to see that people used to view me as more of a party favor than a friend.

That realization, when it first came to me, was gut-wrenching but also necessary. To change that perception is hard too—especially when it's been true for the majority of my life. Still, the process had slowly begun and for that I was grateful.

If there was any downside to my sobriety, I guess it would have been that not drinking had made it so much more difficult for me to engage with people who were. I'd smile and nod, while I listened to their drunken delusions, but so many of them never even give me a chance to respond. As a drunk, I probably would have simply yelled over them but I no longer felt the ease in doing that. That said, I had effectively gone from a human party favor to a free, mute therapist.

I often felt it would have been better to leave a life-size cutout of myself at the table and then simply go somewhere else. I doubted they would even know the difference and, even if they did, they'd forget about it the next day anyway. That's the thing: they'd always forget what they talked about and that meant they were just going to tell me again the next time I'd see them.

I enjoy listening. I enjoy helping. I really, truly do. Down in my heart, I do. There comes a point, though, when I'm just listening to the same stories and the same delusions over and over. It's an endless cycle and the drunker my counterparts became, the more detached they'd become; that means, the drunker they became, the less likely I was to actually help them. Still, in most cases, it was either that or sit at home with Blue. Too bad man is a social animal.

While thinking about all this, I stared out into the barely visible bar to my left. My breath had been sticking to the windshield—specifically, to the driver's side portion of the glass. It was thickest and most prevalent there but I knew it wouldn't be long before it covered the entire surface area of the glass and obstructed my view completely.

Even so, I could still *hear* perfectly well, at least. The laughter… the music… it was all very inviting but, for reasons I've already stated, I knew it was a mirage. Through the passenger's side of the windshield, I could also see the frozen lake and the aforementioned island about two hundred yards from the icy shore. It was much colder than it had been when the sun was still out; besides, I knew the ice was likely thick and, while I didn't *want* to fall in, I also didn't much care if I did.

So, with a sudden surge of determination, I took one final look at my newest photograph, grabbed hold of the axe behind my seat, exited the truck and began walking toward that island, in the middle of the lake. On my way there, I had to pass by The Docks, on my left. I could hear a few drunk women hollering at me but I pretended otherwise. With the loud wind and louder music, I convinced myself that it would be an easy lie to maintain.

I could see, out of the corner of my eye, that one of the women was wearing a tiara and a white sash with writing I wouldn't have been able to read unless I purposefully looked her way. It probably said "Bride to Be" or something of that nature. She was probably part of a bachelorette party.

Her friends continued to yell and I continued to walk, as though I hadn't noticed. It didn't seem to matter how believable my performance was though. They weren't buying it. I couldn't deny that I was lonely but I doubted the woman I needed was, at that moment, drunk, and catcalling at me from an outdoor deck of a bar.

So I continued to walk. Alone. As I half walked/half slipped across the ice, I thought about my situation. All this depression, change and uncertainty that I was going through—it wasn't stemming from failing to achieve the life I wanted. Some of the punishments/ailments I'd incurred were, to be fair, unforeseen but, for the most part, I was unhappy/unfulfilled because I had *exactly* the life I wanted and, as I tried to separate from it, I was being forced to rebuild myself from nothing.

Up until very recently, I thought the dream life was working Monday through Friday, at a job I didn't *completely* hate so that I could enjoy my weekends getting wasted somewhere. Sure: I traveled. Yes: I went to a lot of different events but, at the focal point of all of it was a desire to be inebriated. It wasn't just a baseball game; it was getting drunk at a baseball game. It wasn't just Europe; it was getting drunk in Europe. It wasn't just bowling; it was getting drunk at a bowling alley. It wasn't just a concert; it was getting drunk at a concert.

And that's how I lived… for twenty years! Then, one day after quitting, as my alcohol-soaked brain began to rewire itself, I realized that I had changed and that I didn't want that life anymore. I used to think that something had gone terribly wrong in my life but, in actuality, the problem was that it had gone, for the most part, according to plan. I had gotten exactly what I wanted: just spending my time getting hammered, with like-minded companions, until I eventually die. It's tough to admit but the truth of the matter is that I was in crisis because I got exactly what I wanted.

As I walked, I was thinking about all of this and that obnoxiously loud bridal party. I wondered if they would ever look back and think similar thoughts about their own lives. I hoped not. That is to say, I hoped this night of debauchery was special for them and not simply as "run-of-the-mill" as it would have been for me.

Though I didn't realize it in real time, I could see, after the fact, that alcohol helped me to normalize the abhorrent. Blacking out, forgetting entire conversations, saying things I shouldn't have said, embarrassing myself, waking up sick… I used to sort of laugh it off. It was "normal."

Needing extra time in the morning because I knew I was going to be sick was normal. Having to try to piece together my night, through the accounts of others, was normal. Passing out, facedown in my dog's bed was normal. It wasn't until very recently that I started to see these things for the abnormal behaviors they were. I hoped those girls on that dock would never have to sink as low as I did and that none of them would end up wasting twenty years, or maybe even more, before they realized the lives we think we want are often exactly the ones we get.

With my axe in hand, I had traversed halfway across the lake, on my way toward that carved tree, when I began to take note of the lights in the parking lot across from me. They were bringing everything into better focus. They'd helped me to see an auspiciously-placed billboard, in a drugstore parking lot, across the lake I was crossing. Quite simply, it said, "Cabinets by Chris. I can help." It also listed a phone number I recognized, as belonging to the same Chris that had been invading my own life.

Despite my efforts to avoid him, he seemed to be pursuing me in a relentless fashion. Thinking about that sign, in that manner, caused me to laugh at the absurdity of such a notion and it conjured up a couple well-intentioned curses under my breath. What a spectacular coincidence! This was the kind of situational humor for which comedians lived!

The ice was both solid and slippery, at the same time. At least that's what I was thinking about when one of the light bulbs surrounding Chris's sign suddenly popped. As soon as the glass bulb shattered, the remnants of the now-defunct bulb began behaving like a black hole, sucking in all the color from the otherwise white, snow-covered lake and leaving it as a dull shade of gray.

It was so unexpected that I barely noticed when the ice broke under my boot and it suddenly filled with frigid lake water. Before the water reached my knee, however, my attention abruptly shifted from the lightbulb to drowning and hypothermia. Perhaps, I wasn't as prepared for death as I had assumed I was.

CHAPTER TWENTY-ONE

I don't know exactly how accurate he was when he relayed the following information but my dad had always told me that if one were ever to fall through the ice, into a frozen lake, that person would only have a few seconds to get out before the cold would overtake him—paralyzing his muscles and drowning him. Needless to say, that was the foremost thought on my mind, when my head followed after my feet and I found myself fully submerged, staring up at the broken ice above me.

Determined to resurface before hypothermia claimed me, I held my breath tight and began to swim upward. My heavy boots and bulky coat made it much more difficult than I could have imagined. I had always been a decent swimmer but navigating back toward the top, at that moment, was like trying to swim through molasses. Oddly enough, it was not, however, cold. Even through my coat and gloves, it felt as if the lake was heating up, specifically for me. That's not to suggest that fate was conspiring in my favor though. I found quite the opposite to be true.

The physics and composition of everything I thought I knew about the world had changed by the time I reached the top—where there should have been a hole, out of which I could have surfaced.

Instead, what I found was that my gloved hands were pressing up against something quite solid. This wasn't ice at all; the jagged contours made it feel more like a collection of various-sized rocks.

In a desperate attempt to gain my bearings before my breath ran out and I was forced to drink, I kept my hands on the rocky ceiling and bent my head backwards, in order to ascertain my surroundings and, more importantly, my escape route.

In the blackness of the lake, I expected to see very little. I was, therefore, surprised when the liquid surrounding me (I don't know if I'd even call it water) all at once changed into an orangish, brownish color. It was, as I said, warmer than I had expected too. It was also riddled with little bubbles everywhere, though they were descending (rather than floating upward) all around me.

It burned my eyes horribly—much more than water (even heavily-chlorinated water) ever should. Regardless, I fought through the pain and kept them open, for if I were to drown they'd be of no use to me anyway.

In that moment, one of the anomalies they showed me was a collection of numerous pockets of green, lake vegetation, sporadically growing above my strained neck and head. Desperate to gain under-standing, before I was completely deprived of oxygen, I whipped my head forward and saw silt trickling downward. My gloves had somehow kicked it free. It traveled a few inches, toward my face, and then fell upward and landed back onto the hard surface around my hands.

It was at that moment that I realized I was upside down. Somehow my body had been turned and my gloves had found the ground, at the bottom of the rapidly warming, brown water lake. Instinctively, I flipped myself around so that my boots were touching where my gloves had just been. I crouched down and, as Lulenne had done back at The Hive, I used all the power I could muster in my legs to rocket myself toward where I now believed the surface to be.

I was trusting in the logical deductions I had made (that I was traveling in the right direction); however, I still felt upside down—like I was somehow sinking deeper into the abyss. I was not afforded time to ponder my decision though. In that moment of truth, I had to rely on the upside-down plant life, ascending silt and falling—rather than rising—bubble as evidence that my presupposition was correct. All of those oddities, in my mind, were strong enough logical indicators that I needed to quickly travel in the direction that still felt so wrong to my soul.

I hadn't much breath left in me. I was kicking my boots as best I could but their awkward shape, size and weight made treading water difficult. Fisky always hated these boots. I wonder what she'd think if she ever learned that they aided in my own demise.

My lungs were on fire, begging me to draw air into them. I had just about reached my limit and could stymie their violent insistence on oxygen no longer. Just as I was about to give in and inhale, I suddenly and quite unexpectedly somehow emerged.

Like so many other impossible affairs as of late, here too I found myself enveloped in circumstances I couldn't understand. Below me was the lake I had just escaped but it was above me as well. Looking up, I could see that it still went on, seemingly indefinitely. Such was the case in every direction I looked. To the right; to the left; down; up… it just went on and on in perpetuity. It was as if I was treading water inside a watertight rectangular box, with invisible borders.

Still, even being invisible, I could see where the borders were; the juxtaposition of the encased night sky around me pushed against the brown liquid that surrounded it, making it easy to tell where sky ended and lake began.

As I treaded water, baffled by this development, I spied a small, solitary island, not far off in the distance. Inside the enclosed pocket of absurdity that had imprisoned me, it was the only land available to me. On it, I could see a fire burning and the outlines of several characters camped around it, which, along with the obvious presence of an atmosphere, led me to postulate that the same physical laws I had always been forced to obey in my own world had manifested themselves here too.

The characters on the island didn't seem to have noticed my appearance. They were laughing and talking loudly amongst themselves, over the sounds of some melodic, oddly beautiful music I recognized but was unable to place. Although my boots would have preferred to pull me back down into the saltless brine, I pushed them against the liquid around me and propelled myself toward the island. When I finally reached it, I pulled myself onto the beach, lay on my side and breathed a heavy sigh of relief.

For about thirty seconds, I laid there, sucking in air, as if I had never done so before. I was, therefore, surprised when none of the group came to greet me, or even inquired about me amongst themselves. I was only a few feet away from them, after all.

Taking the initiative myself, I stood up, removed my coat, placed it on the dry sand in front of me, wrung my shirt as best I could and began my soggy march toward them. My socks were squishing inside my boots and I wanted to take them off but I didn't, for fear I might need them to defend myself. Their steel toes had come in handy more than once—most recently when a neighbor's dog ran into my yard to attack Blue.

A swift kick in its ribs had humbled the beast and sent it scampering away, back to its own residence. I wondered if I would have to employ any similar actions here. I hoped not, for I was far outnumbered.

There wouldn't have been much room to run either. The island was small—maybe half of a city block, at most. From what I could see, the small group in front of me comprised its only inhabitants. Sand was its only ground, brown, bubbly water, its only surrounding and palm trees its only vegetation. In addition to the strangers there, there were also the chairs, on which all but one of them sat a small stereo and a tattered, decrepit shack off in the corner. It was behind the aforementioned individuals, who were burning palm tree wood and dried leaves.

* * *

I would have been tempted, in most instances, to try and describe the group in front of me as "strange"; however, as the paradigm of reality itself continued to shift, I couldn't help but recognize a contrarily inconvenient truth—that encountering "strange and peculiar" beings, such as the ones inhabiting this particular island, was actually becoming quite a "normal" occurrence for me. Perhaps, with that in mind, it was actually *I* who was the "strange" one. Perhaps, then, I should stop using my own axioms as the gauge for which to measure normalcy—especially when I was, in the eyes of this world, so clearly abnormal.

Besides their apparent indifference to me, the first thing to strike me as what I'll call "traditionally unnatural," as I approached the group, was the fact that I could see through everyone in it (and I mean that in a quite literal sense). They were visible but, as with the unseen borders protecting this pocket of reality, I could look at them and see through to the other side—as though I was looking through clear, human-sized vessels, full of extremely murky water.

From the choices they had made with their attire—attire that was also somewhat translucent—I got the sense that they were close to me in age. I could not say for certain, though, because not a single one of them had a face! Instead, that particular part of their heads was completely smooth! That part of their heads, to use an earthly example, more closely resembled the sleek, plastic mannequin faces that one might have expected to encounter in the department stores of old. Their heads turned; their bodies gestured but their faces were devoid of any hair or facial components whatsoever.

They were all drowning out their music with their laughter, as I approached. Three of them were sitting on folding chairs that had been strategically placed around a medium-sized fire. The fourth was wearing cargo shorts and a V-neck T-shirt; he was sitting on the sand, in front of his chair. I wasn't sure if he had fallen off of it or slid down to the ground on purpose; regardless, he seemed quite content wallowing in laughter, on the sandy beach that surrounded us.

Just before I reached the group, I heard the fat one, on the ground, exclaim passionately, as if he were arguing a very important case, "Because they're amazing! That's why!"

"Excuse me," I said, breaking the ambiance. When they all stopped laughing, I added an apology and inquired as to whether they knew where I was.

"Eh, where is anyone, right?" answered the chubby male on the ground. I wasn't sure if he meant to be philosophical, comical or confrontational. His voice and mannerisms were somewhere between arrogant and insightful; however, everyone laughed in a way that indicated it was probably a mixture of all three.

"Right," I told him, "but, I mean, how did I... I mean, how did *you*... How did you all get here?"

"We always come here!" the faceless gentleman on his right happily exclaimed from his chair. I was standing behind and a bit to the right of him so he turned and showed his un-face to me, as he spoke. While his expression was lost to me, I did get a good sense of his attire. He was clothed in a T-shirt that tightly hugged his muscular arms. Through the ripped, mesh backing of his chair, I could see his boxer shorts and his jeans, which began to gather around the bottom of his butt—instead of around his waist, where the manufacturer had intended.

"Okay, well, how do I... leave?" I asked him.

"You have somewhere you have to be?" his companion on the ground asked.

To his left, the only one wearing a skirt, flip-flops and a girl-cut T-shirt mumbled an invitation that would have probably been accompanied by a smile, if she was given to possess one. "Hang out for a little bit," she said. The implication in her tone was not overtly sexual but I did detect a trace amount of veiled flirtation. It insinuated that I would enjoy my time getting to know her and the others, should I decide to linger.

Behind her right, flip-flopped foot, I saw, for the first time, a collection of unused, red plastic cups, a half-consumed package of hamburger buns and container full of ground-up, rancid meat. Though, from where I stood, I could not smell its stink, the maggots infesting it made it easy for me to tell that it had long since spoiled. I was just about to warn the group about the condition of the meat, when I suddenly thought better of asserting myself into their lives and possibly offending them.

Answering his own question, the hefty one whose cargo shorts-covered-bottom was resting on the sand then posited, "Yeah; he's got somewhere to be, I think." He did so just as I arrived at my decision to keep quiet about the meat.

"Do you?" the one in front of me, with the saggy pants, asked.

"Well, I don't really know," I told him honestly. "I don't know what happened. I was walking across the lake whe—"

"Dude!" screamed the one to my right—the only one, as of yet, who had not spoken. He was wearing a jean jacket, littered with various patches and pins. Most of them related to '70s rock bands but I recognized a small number of them as skateboard companies. There were a few of them, however, that vexed me completely, for I had never seen them before. "Do you know who I saw last week?" he anxiously asked the group.

Cargo Shorts and Saggy Pants both asked "Who?" at the same time. Flip-Flops had her head hanging low. She didn't seem to show much interest in the question; in fact, I wasn't sure she even heard it at all.

Turning to me, Patches said, "Sorry, dude, but I just thought of this and I don't want to forget." He seemed to be as sincere as he was excited so I told him that there was no need to apologize. He then blurted out "Katie!" as if it was a revelation of some sort.

"She's crazy!" Saggy Pants vehemently testified.

"I always thought she was kind of nice," Cargo Shorts said, emotionlessly defending this Katie person.

"Well, you're crazy too!" Saggy Pants pronounced, which produced another round of laughter from three-fourths of the group. I didn't hear any coming from Flip-Flops but her shoulders shrugged once, which indicated she had at least heard the comment.

Suddenly, she raised her faceless face and asked, "Wanna know who *I* saw last *summer*?"

It was becoming clear, at this point, that I wasn't a priority in this group but I didn't want to be rude so I continued to let them speak in hopes they would acknowledge me when the guilt from ignoring me finally confronted them.

"We already know!" Saggy Pants answered, laughing as he did so.

"Nuh-uh," she denied.

"Then who?" he challenged.

Patches then ventured a guess: "Mike Ditka."

"Mike, Ditka," she proudly affirmed.

"We know!" Saggy Pants declared, in a way that suggested he had heard this revelation before.

"I didn't tell you everything though," the woman teased but Saggy Pants insisted that she had. He seemed to be laughing both out of frustration and a cognizance over the absurdity of the situation. That put he and I, at least momentarily, on a similar level and I took the opportunity to interject on my own behalf.

"Hey, everybody," I started. "Sorry to interrupt again. I'm James, by the way. Again, I'm really sorry but I don't really know what's going on here. I think that I'm probably dreaming again—or maybe I'm finally awake—but I have a strong suspicion that, at some point, I'm going to come to, lying in my bathtub. I'm just… I'm just wondering how to expedite that process."

By now, I was experienced in the preposterousness of my subconscious but I hadn't yet learned how to control or even avoid it. I had little faith any of these folks would be able to tell me how to achieve that goal; nonetheless, I held out hope that at least one of them would be able to offer some small fragment of a clue.

Cargo Shorts was the first to speak. He told me he didn't know what I was talking about but that his name was Blake. He looked over to his right and told me his companion—the one with the saggy pants—was named Boom. Boom told me it was nice to meet me, at which point Blake told me that the person to Boom's right (Patches) was named Ace.

"What's up, dude?" Ace offered, along with his hand. I shook it. He had a firm grip. I know it's shallow of me but, for some reason, that made me respect him a little more. A firm handshake always made me respect people a little more. At that moment, I wondered why. I wondered if that sentiment was one that was created by the culture around me or if it was more widely spread across the globe, in other places where handshakes are common.

"And that of course," Blake informed me, "is Star."

Flip-Flops said nothing but nodded slightly upward at her introduction. Even without a face, I could tell she was getting ready to say something she deemed to be important. As if on cue, she then stumbled out of her chair, into a half standing, staggered position, raised her pointer finger to the air and said, as profoundly as she could, "He didn't look the same, ya know? He's a lot older now. When I think of him, it's how I remember him from back in the day. He's still the coach, in my head."

Blatantly ignoring her attempt at changing the conversation, Boom then asked of Blake, his friend on the ground, "You know who she reminds me of?"

"I don't know," Ace answered in his place, "but I want to finish our conversation about this band first!" He seemed annoyed but still jovial, as he pointed to the speaker on the ground and criticized his friend's interruptions.

"Yes!" Blake fervently agreed.

At this point, I began to try and speak again but all I got out was an "Um," before I was overpowered by the group. No one even heard my "Um." All they heard was Boom telling Blake, "She reminds me of you, ya wank."

"What are you talking about?!?" Blake demanded to know, as Star plopped back into her seat. He was puzzled (or at least he was pretending to be).

"You know what I'm talking about," Boom insisted.

"Hey!" Star then called out, before the interrogation could proceed any further.

"What?!?" Boom demanded, trying to pretend he was angry, despite the glee I detected in his voice.

"He's a lot older now..." she started to say.

"Anyway," Ace began, raising his voice over Star's until she gave up, which didn't take very long at all. "I'm not saying I don't like them or anything. I just don't understand your obsession." As he spoke, he was directing his body language toward the ground, where Blake sat. "You think they're, like, gods or something! You've been listening to pretty much nothing else for three years, right?!? Don't you realize how insane that is?!?"

"Ace," Boom then called out, before Blake could answer. "This guy," he said, with his thumb pointing toward Blake, "is all sorts of insane! He tells groups of random senior citizens at Applebee's about that band, when he's drunk, aaaand…" He paused to make sure he had the room. When he was sure he did, he continued: "And the same night he did that, he tried to pick up this gross hussy behind the bar by telling her he met Billy Mays, at a charity auction."

Ace seemed intrigued. "Yeah? Did it work?" he asked.

"I wasn't trying to pick her up," Blake insisted, in a way that suggested he had given this defense more than once.

"No!" Boom yelled out joyously. "Cuz he's Mumbles MacGoo, like this one over here!" He was pointing at Star, as he made his statement.

"Not every one of my conversations is a pickup attempt," Blake tried to explain. "Geez."

"Nooooo!" Boom replied. He was chortling as he said it and I expected he probably wanted to wag his finger but he opted not to do so. "She was gross too. Seriously." He seemed to punctuate his statement with that last part.

"Billy Mays! Psshh!" Star scoffed. "I saw Mike Ditka!"

"It was the same night we got thrown out of that hillbilly bar you like too." Boom claimed, while looking in Blake's direction.

"Penny's?" his cargo shorts-wearing buddy guessed.

"No."

"Suzie Q's?" Ace speculated.

"No!"

"He was at this restaurant in Chicago," Star began to explain. "A really fancy one. That makes sense… for him to be there, I mean, right?"

"No," said Boom, placing his facelessness in his hands.

"Guys!" I was quickly reaching my limit and so I very nearly screamed the word. I certainly hadn't intended on seeming so brash and I was a bit ashamed in my lack of decorum; however, upon hearing that call, everyone stopped and looked at me, as if they had only just then remembered I was ever there in the first place.

With everyone's focus now solely on me, I asked, "What's in that shack over there? Is it a way out maybe?" Other than getting back into the "water," which I had very much resolved not to do, it seemed like the only other plausible place for an exit of some kind.

"I wouldn't go in there," Blake cautioned. I asked him why not and he told me that, "It's better out here."

My interest was fully piqued, at this point. Somehow I knew I had to face that shack but I was, at the same time, terrified to do so. In some strange way, I could almost feel it calling to me—beckoning me to explore its insides.

"What do you mean it's better out here?" I asked Blake, hoping he would enlighten me and possibly quell some of my trepidation. "I feel like I'm supposed to go in there, for some reason I can't quite figure out." I admitted, as the song on the stereo ended and another one, by the same group, immediately took its place.

"What I'm trying to figure out," Ace said assertively to Blake, "is your deal with this band!"

"Dude, *he* doesn't even know!" Boom exclaimed. "He was trying to tell these old people about it once, while he was falling-down drunk!" Boom tried to stifle a snort but was unable. He was now openly guffawing at the memory he must have been reliving in his head.

That's when I turned my attention to Star. I was content to let the group reminisce over whatever nonsense they wanted, so long as at least one of them could recognize me. "Star," I began softly, "I'm sorry to bother you but do you know what's in that shack?"

As I waited for a response, I could hear Boom in the background. He was addressing Blake and Ace, regaling them with some story about how he and Blake almost got thrown out of an Applebee's once. I wasn't really listening though. I was more concerned with getting out of there—not with making myself comfortable for story time.

"All I really know is you're not supposed to go in there yet," Star half mumbled, half slurred, as though she was surprised I didn't already realize what she was telling me.

"But why not? Who told you that?" I sounded more demanding and more desperate that I would have preferred. I was never good at concealing emotions.

"Listen," she told me, in a near whisper. I leaned in closer to better hear what she was about to say. "I want to tell you something, okay?"

"Yeah. Of course. What?"

Star then inhaled deeply. Before she spoke, she looked over toward where Boom was seated. He was speaking loudly and laughing heavily. She then turned her attention my way and was silent for several seconds. Finally, she spoke: "Mike Ditka does not look the same as he used to. My boyfriend didn't even realize it was him, when I pointed him out, but it was!"

I closed my eyes and sighed heavily, with my fingers interlocking behind my head, in a sign of defeat. She didn't seem to notice and so she proceeded to tell me, "At the end of the night, he did a double take and goes, 'I think that *IS* Mike Ditka!'"

* * *

Upon hearing Star's revelation, I turned from her and told the middle of the circle, in a voice that would have been audible in most settings, that I was going to just go over to the shack and see what happens. In this setting, however, my voice was not heard. That, or it was ignored.

I was hoping that my threat would illicit more information about the shack but Ace was talking much louder than I was. He and the rest of the group seemed to be debating a medley of topics including bartenders, indie rock bands, retired football coaches and failed pickup attempts. I let the two of them carry on for a few moments and then declared, in a more commanding but also amenable tone, "I'm sorry

I crashed your party, everyone. I really didn't mean to. I'm just trying to find my way out of here." I then looked over my shoulder, at the shack, and said, "Do any of you want to come with me to that shack over there—to see if there's a way out?"

Without seeing any of their faces, I wasn't sure what to think of the silence that followed. Eventually, Ace took the floor and reasonably said, "I don't know about any of that. I just want to hear his reasoning for why *this* is 'the greatest band in the last twenty years.'" He made air quotes when he said that, which I assumed denoted he was quoting Blake.

"Listen," Blake began, eager to explain himself. "Have any of you ever seen the movie *Amadeus*?"

"No. Sounds dumb," Boom insisted.

"I saw it; I liked it," Ace confirmed.

"Who's in it?" Boom asked.

"Uh," Blake said, struggling. "I don't know the guy's name."

"Is it Mike Ditka?" Boom offered, causing the room to erupt in laughter.

"Listen to me!" Star spat in frustration. "It's not funny. I noticed him. And it made sense. We were in a fancy Chicago restaurant."

"Uh-huh," Boom groaned.

"Even my boyfriend didn't know who he was, at first—"

As if Star wasn't speaking at all, Boom then turned toward Blake who, at this point, was beginning to crawl off the ground and back into his chair, and asked, snickering to himself, "Hey, what was the name of that movie we were watching that night you got sick and threw beefy tacos up all over the table?"

"*Love and Death*. Woody Allen," he answered, without hesitation.

"Yes!" Boom shouted in jubilation.

"Anyway," Blake began, "*Amadeus* is about Wolfgang Amadeus Mozart. In the movie—this wasn't true in his real life but, in the movie—this guy named Salieri is doing his best to secretly kill Mozart. Salieri is another composer who comes to hate Mozart because he's consumed by jealousy over Mozart's unquestionable genius. He just can't believe the gift that Mozart's been given. He doesn't think that Mozart deserves, or even appreciates, it the way he should. It all just comes so naturally for him."

"Does anyone know of a gifted NFL coach like that?" Boom sheepishly inquired.

"Yes!" Star shouted.

Boom was beside himself laughing, when Ace threw his hands into the air and cried, "Duuuuude!"

Without giving credence to Ace's outburst, Blake continued his synopsis, as if he had never been interrupted in the first place: "So, there's this scene where Salieri comes upon a sheet of Mozart's music. I don't remember if he stole it or if it was just sitting there or what… I think it was just sitting there. Regardless, he picks it up and starts reading it and, as he's studying it, it's clear almost immediately that it's divinely beautiful—that it's art, in its purest form.

"He's flabbergasted by how perfect it is. Every single note is perfectly placed. There are exactly the right amount of them; they're played for the exact right amount of time and they're played in the exact perfect sequence. It's as though God himself wrote it for Mozart and Salieri admits as much. Despite his personal feelings toward Mozart, he cannot help but stand in awe of his genius. This half-finished doodle of Mozart's is so beautiful, that Salieri almost cries!"

"Okaay…" Ace said, as if he was impatiently waiting for the conclusion.

"Well," Blake explained, "THAT is how I feel when I listen to this band."

Everyone at the table laughed heartedly at this—everyone except Blake. I could tell he was serious. So much so that he didn't even have to answer when Ace and Boom asked him if he was. With everyone in the group laughing hardily, I silently absconded away, toward the shack.

CHAPTER TWENTY-TWO

Once under its leaky roof, the island's solitary shack appeared even less inviting than I had imagined. The old, rotted-out planks on which I stood had already begun to deteriorate—as evidenced by the two-foot hole in the far corner of the room. Off to my right, the frame of the only window held just a few shards of glass still in place. The rest of it laid in various-sized chunks, scattered on the sandy, dusty floor below.

The room's only furnishing was an old wooden casket, lying on the floor, in the center of the room. A liberal coating of dust and debris had settled on the lid and that delicate layer of waxy grime helped, in a way, to decorate the otherwise austere, human-sized box in front of me. From what I could tell, it was cheaply constructed, from low-grade wood, and it had no markings of any kind. It looked flimsy too—like I could put my fist through it if I felt so inclined.

It gave off no aroma, which told me it was either empty or that it was very old and the body inside had already decomposed. I deduced that it was likely the former, for the crypt showed no signs of tampering from grave-pilfering scavengers nor did it display any signs of forced entry from rodents or insects. That was, of course, assuming the island *had* rodents and/or insects.

Cautiously, I approached the coffin, as the laughter outside continued on, unabated behind me. My grasp on why a pall would be placed in such a manner was tenuous at best. Still, I felt a compulsion to investigate so I walked around it, studying the floor, ceiling and walls, as I did so. Nothing else seemed out of the ordinary—a detail that, once realized, allowed my body to release some of the tension it had been unconsciously storing. Feeling a bit more assured, I relaxed my shoulders and exhaled in relief but before I could even draw in my next breath, the situation changed completely.

In an instant, the room grew dramatically bright—so much so that everything except the casket in front of me became utterly indiscernible. The light wasn't blinding in any way though; it just sort of filtered everything else out. Everything was gone: the commotion outside, the island, even the shack itself, it seemed.

In this new and utterly eerie silence, I called out to anyone who could hear but I received no response. There was nothing—only me and the wooden box before me. Not sure of what else to do, I reluctantly placed my fingers underneath the unhinged lid and lifted. Without having to exert much force at all, the lid slid off and I watched as it dematerialized into the ether.

I tried to tell myself I was dreaming but I knew I wasn't. Everything was too cogent. If I knew I was dreaming, I should have been able to control the experience, right? *This* experience felt more supernatural, though, and, despite trying, I certainly wasn't controlling it, in even the slightest capacity.

Upon timidly peering inside the coffin, I found a stack of hand-written pages, with a blue pen resting on top of them. Cautiously, I set the pen aside and picked up the pages to examine them in greater detail. Almost immediately, I recognized the writing as my own. Just like before, the pages in my hand looked like exact copies of the doomsday confession I had recently finished.

The pages weren't in any order but, as I skimmed over them feverishly, I suddenly stopped and patted my back pocket to try and assess if my note was still there. No sooner did I learn that it was absent than I felt the presence of something insidious enter the room. I can't well describe it, for it had no visible form, emitted no smells and made no sounds but I perceived it, nonetheless. A sense of dread came over me at that moment, for I knew I was no longer alone.

Without warning, a darkness then began pulsating from within the casket, spilling into the light in which I had been standing. It emerged as a gaseous-like cloud and began walling us into a rectangular-shaped room it was systematically creating. Panic began to take me. I could feel my lungs expanding and contrasting at a rapid rate, while my heart threatened to burst out of my chest altogether.

Consternation set in and, at that moment, when I felt the most helpless, my stalker appeared. There, inside of the casket, that dark silhouette that once tried to strangle me in my own bed revealed himself. I don't know how else to say it except that he was suddenly… "there," as if he always had been but I was just now noticing him.

I tried to take a step back but I couldn't. When I turned my head to learn why, I saw that the gassy darkness had already created a wall behind me and my back was stuck to it, like a strand of meat caught between two teeth. As I struggled, it was spreading throughout the whole of this reality and suffocating all of the light inside of the room it was diligently creating.

When I drew my head forward again, I found that sadistic, shadowy devil hovering only inches from my face. Both his terrible odor and his sudden closeness shocked me so thoroughly that I nearly dropped the pages I forgot I was still holding. Before I could react in any way, however, his arm quickly lost its shape and, in a flash, reconstituted itself in the form of a thick, smoky black snake that began to wrap itself around my arm and my wrist—just above the pages I was gripping.

It seemed this new, serpent-like appendage was both constricting and tugging at my wrist, in order to try and separate me from the pages in my hand. I don't know why but something inside of me was telling me not to let go—that I needed to keep him from those pages. I could tell my resistance angered him because, when I tightened my grip, he let out a screech unlike any I've ever heard in the animal kingdom.

His howling and his blank face terrified me so deeply that I purposefully averted my gaze back toward the documents I was trying to protect. To my surprise, I saw no traces of blue ink or written words of any kind. The pages were all blank! I knew that to be true because all at once they flew out of my hands, through some unseen force, and began flying at my face, cutting me repeatedly as they scraped across my skin.

When I raised my free arm to cover my face from the assault of the possessed, flying pages, I could feel the slug inside of me growing restless. As if it was heeding some inaudible command from its master, it then ripped through the skin of my forehead and began emerging into the world. It didn't seem to be in any hurry to completely vacate its nest though. I could feel its bottom half casually tickling my brain, while its top half was thrashing about and slapping itself against the skin of my forehead.

I was going to try and grab it but, before I could, a sticky, stinky, black tentacle wrapped itself around my other wrist. Once my attacker seemed satisfied that my biogenic restraints were sufficient, he silently abandoned his influence over the possessed pages flying about the room and sent them fluttering lifelessly downward, toward the floor. He then drew his head near to mine, in order to absorb a multicolored beam of light that the slug sticking halfway out of my head had begun to involuntarily emit. With his own head just a few feet above mine, I watched in terror as he greedily inhaled that colorful beam into the part of his face where a nose should have been.

Just as I began to wonder how much longer this ritual would last, my tormentor disengaged from the creature in my head and lifted me off the ground, as though I weighed no more than an empty trash receptacle. He then slammed me down into the empty coffin from whence he originally materialized. I was struggling to get up but his left, snake-like arm, which had moved up my body and wrapped itself around my neck, was holding me down with ease.

While it continued to restrict the air to my lungs, most of his form began to dismantle itself and return to the coffin, filling it the way water would fill a tub. Ironically enough, it felt warm, as it filled in the empty spaces around my legs. It was, in fact, unnaturally warm—like something from another dimension altogether.

Through sheer effort and determination, I was able to raise myself up a bit but the remaining smoke that was still in human form effortlessly threw me back down, submerging my head under the darkness. I was helpless—as helpless as I had ever been. I believed that death was imminent and, while I didn't want it, I knew no way of avoiding it and so I simply closed my eyes and waited for it to take me.

PART VII

SUNDAY MORNING

CHAPTER TWENTY-THREE

Without warning, my body lunged forward and I discovered I was dripping wet from a tub that had been slowly filling with water. During heavy gasps of both relief and a lingering horror, I could see that the water level rose only a few inches during my slumber—not enough to completely drench me but enough to soak most of the left side of my clothing. My behind, too, was wet but it was that "new wet" that comes from suddenly sitting up in a small pool, instead slowly marinating in one.

It was then that I came to realize my foot must have just barely dislodged the warm faucet handle from the closed position where I had intended it to stay. I theorized, as I watched the catalyst for my subconscious torment slowly circle and eventually deposit itself down inside my drain, that my other foot must have been blocking that drain.

The gun wasn't able to elude the intrusive penetration of the water either. A mixture of water and gun oil poured out of it, as I raised it up to examine it, alerting me that every crevice of the weapon had been defiled by the damp remnants left behind. I assumed the instrument's functionality had been compromised—at least until it dried out—but I didn't much care anymore.

Not wanting to drip all over my floors, I stripped naked inside of the tub, grabbed hold of the gun and walked into my bedroom. Blue was there; he was wagging his tail and waiting to greet me. After slipping on a pair of boxer shorts, I bent down to give him a hug and scratch behind his floppy ears. I then placed the gun on top of a towel and set that on top of my bed, to dry.

Though my curtains were drawn, a beam of warming sunlight found a gap between the independently-hanging pieces of fabric so that it could gently warm my chest. I didn't need a clock to tell me this was morning sunlight. For a moment, I basked in its embrace and let it rejuvenate me.

Blue allowed this reprieve to last about ten seconds—until his half whimper, half growl reminded me he was waiting below me. I apologized, in language he couldn't understand but a tone that he could, and strolled down the hall, to the patio door. Once there, I let him out so that he could take care of his morning business.

Instinctively, I began to check my phone, as I waited for him. Another message from Chris. He wanted to know if I could call him later. Of course he did. Trying my best to ignore him, as the sun invigorated me, I opened the weather app on my phone and was pleasantly surprised to learn that, by noon, it was going to be sixty-five and sunny.

There's a saying in Ohio. I've mentioned it already but it bears repeating: if you don't like the weather, wait a minute. By that same token, however, one could assert: if you *do* like the weather, take advantage of it quickly, before it changes. I definitely planned on it too—riding, in a euphoric state, on my motorcycle. Like last night, I knew the temperature would drop dramatically by the time the sun went down, which made my riding window—my "escape" window, as it were—small.

From the bay-style window in my kitchen, I peeked outside and confirmed that the snow had completely melted off of all of the side streets inside my trailer park. It was still plentiful in all of the yards around me but that didn't matter. If the streets are clear, I'm changing gears.

With today's blueprint now in place, I called my mother, as I was pouring Blue's food into his dish. After a few hollow rings, I was connected to her voicemail, where I left her a brief message. I finished the call by stating, "I'll be on the bike so I won't be able to talk today but I'll try you again tomorrow." No need to tell her anything that could tip her off about my ever-declining, muddled perceptions of reality.

Though the troubling and somewhat dystopic events from the last few days were fresh in my mind, they didn't seem to matter as much today. Somehow, things were looking up. Was it the anticipation of my ride, I wondered? Perhaps it was the fact that tomorrow I'd finally receive the psychiatrist's judgement on my situation. Maybe it was a culmination of those things. I wasn't sure exactly but I could feel that something was changing inside of me.

After I hung up, I let Blue back inside, served him his breakfast and began to bide my time, anxiously awaiting noon and the rare, seasonal gift Mother Nature had promised me.

* * *

Before I knew it, noon had arrived and I was outside, sitting on my front step, ready to embark on my journey. My memory of the hours between my phone call and this moment was hazy but I suppose I must have dressed myself at some point: a long-sleeve T-shirt displaying the logo from an obscure video game I won't bother mentioning, a gray, riding jacket with crash padding sewn inside, blue jeans, a backwards ball cap on my head, and two mismatched cotton socks. Looking down, I noticed that one was red and gray, while the other had struck a black and red medley.

In my hand, that same abused pair of black Doc Martens boots, which I'd owned for nearly half of my life, was ready to envelop my feet. The brown, incongruent, replacement shoelaces seemed out of place and only served to bolster the "indestructible" nature of the boots that I had been prattling on about for years. The helmet next to me, as well as the gloves inside of it, constituted the rest of ensemble. I was also bringing an unopened water bottle, in case I got thirsty.

Then, from out of my shed, I produced my prize: a European, midnight black, two-wheeled piece of modern engineering that brought me joy every time I saw it. It wasn't the fastest bike I'd ever owned, nor was it the largest—far from it actually. As my life crumbled around me, however, it was one of the only material things I'd been able to retain and I loved it as much as any non-deranged human being can love an inanimate object.

For the duration of the winter, thus far, it had been on a trickle charge so that the cold couldn't drain the life out of its battery. I undid the connection, inserted the key, held in the clutch and hit the starter. First try and that fuel-injected piece of art was humming inside of my shed.

After a moment, I backed it down the ramp and let it sit, in the sun, in my driveway, giving it time to warm up both internally and externally. As it did so, I checked the tire pressure. It had lost a couple pounds but not enough to warrant any concern. I then found and affixed a pair of sunglasses, banished my hat and water bottle to the tail bag, tightened my helmet, threw on my gloves, zipped up my coat and shamelessly gawked at one of the last remaining idols in my life.

There was comfort in knowing this would be my literal and figurative vehicle for escape today. I'd been riding for nearly two decades but I very rarely rode for the sake of transportation. I rode specifically to escape.

I had a couple hours to dispatch before the temperature would begin to wane so I considered the routes I might take. How far away could I get within the time that had been given to me? Where should I go? South? South. The answer was almost always south.

Going south meant getting away from traffic, from buildings, from life in general. There was the occasional motorist or horse and buggy to dodge, when traveling south, but doing so was easy. Double yellow lines were more of a suggestion where I was going—at least to me they were. I suppose speed limit signs were as well. But that's the way I'd always ridden—as if I had a kilo of cocaine in my tail bag and there was an officer in pursuit. I liked to push myself. Hit that gear quicker. Cut that corner tighter. Give me a thrill. Give me some sense of life.

When I was alone (and I usually was), I rode like tomorrow was a foreign concept. Other riders couldn't, or more likely *wouldn't*, keep up with me and most of my potential passengers usually seemed to have something better to do. That's okay, though. I liked riding alone. I felt as though I was less obligated when I was alone.

I was much more reserved; in fact, I was a completely different rider when my pillion was occupied by Fisky or, for that matter, by anyone of the opposite sex. For some reason, I valued their lives much more than my own. They calmed me; they unknowingly coerced me into obeying traffic laws I would otherwise ignore.

Dying on a bike was a risk I was willing to accept for myself but I couldn't bear it if I was somehow culpable for ending the life of a fellow voyager, gently hugging my hips behind me. If I was doing anything reckless when that happened, I wouldn't be able to live with myself (regardless of how I myself fared in my hypothetical accident).

Today, though, wasn't the time for those thoughts. As was the case most days, I didn't have to worry about that distraction. Today, I only concerned myself with my own life, which I have already admitted was much less valuable than others'. That's not necessarily a bad thing though. When something isn't as valuable—that's when it's sometimes easier to have a lot more fun with it.

When I'm romping around in the muddy woods, for example, I don't wear my good shoes—the new ones I just got and still haven't even paid for yet. I wear the old, tattered pair of boots that I don't mind getting muddy, scuffed or otherwise destroyed. I wear the Docs that I love and I have more fun doing so because I'm not worried about what happens to them.

This isn't to suggest I'm completely careless though; after all, I've been doing this for a long time and I've never had a single accident. And so, despite my sterling and blemish-free history, I still took moderate care to somewhat dress appropriately, as I've already begun to explain.

Because I don't want my toes ripped off, you won't catch me wearing flip-flops, like some of those dude-bros I see around town (boots are always a must) but I'm not decked head to toe in leather either. That leather-heavy "Mad Max" look, however, seems to be the pinnacle of fashion for most of those "American Pride" riders who I whiz by, while they pretend it's Halloween and they're on their way to some secret pirate-themed party somewhere.

It's somewhat ironic to me how so many of those leather-clad fashionistas fancy themselves as rebellious, or at least "unique," all while taking such special care to make sure they conform to a very particular type of look. It's by donning some variation of the "biker uniform," as it were, that these individuals self-affirm their member-ships to this very stylistic group—a group they so ferociously and passionately venerate.

This isn't an issued uniform, though—like the kind distributed by sports teams, businesses or the armed forces. It's not "required" by any higher-ups, that is. In the biker club, the members *choose* to wear their uniforms.

Despite any collective delusions inherent within this community, however, an outfit alone won't liberate someone from the clutches of modern society (no matter how much leather that outfit might contain); moreover, those who allow fashion to dictate their lives, are actually conforming, on a much higher level, than even the average non-bikers, from whom they try so desperately to separate themselves.

Bikers do it; frat boys do it and, in high school, I did it too. During my teenage years, I did it throughout my "punk rock" phase—complete with its own attire requirements—but, at least for me, a desperate need to show I fit in only lasted throughout puberty.

I've known a lot of these folks and, at least in my own experiences, the majority of them are most concerned with finding the closest bar, sitting on one of its stools and immersing themselves in a sea of similarly-dressed peers. That's not to suggest these are bad people though. Quite to the contrary, I typically find this group to be helpful and polite, as long as I don't admit that less expensive and vastly superior, foreign-made bike outside is mine.

It's just that they're almost always more concerned with how they present themselves at the fashion shows they throw for themselves, at their local pubs, than they are with actually riding. I'd even go as far as to assert, at least from what I've seen, that the harder an individual tries to prove he belongs—via his outfit—the less two-wheeled miles he typically logs each year.

Many of them, if questioned about their fashionable attire, would try and make the excuse that their orange and black leather vests are for safety. I find that explanation comical, however, when the person giving it chooses to wear a cloth bandanna over a DOT-approved helmet.

While I'm on the subject of helmets, I can say, without question, I've always preferred a three-quarter helmet with a flip-up visor in front. It's much more comprehensive than a half-shell but it's not as stifling as a full-face because my jaw and my chin are not encumbered behind a fiberglass shell. The helmet will protect my head in a wreck, yes, but its true and more pragmatic purpose is to keep the wind out of my eyes and to prevent golf ball-sized welts from the bugs that slam against it, at 100 miles an hour.

That's one nod of respect I'll definitely give to a very small group of folks I see who don't wear helmets. I would say that 90 percent of the time, they're not going very fast, for the reasons I just mentioned, but every now and then, I'll see someone on the highway, no helmet, getting after it. It's rare but I can respect it, when I see it. "Get it, son!" I'll yell out to no one but myself, as we give each other the wave, from across the divided highway.

Because I don't want bugs finding their way into my underwear, I'll also never wear shorts. Always jeans. Always fingerless gloves too (full-fingered gloves when it's colder, like today), though they're more of a crutch than a safety precaution; I learned to ride with them and I simply don't feel comfortable without them. In summer months, my dark brown forearms, juxtaposed against the vampiric white of my wrists and hands, can provide all the visual evidence one would require to prove I never ride without them.

My normal preference is to avoid the highway and there are three main reasons: (1) it's boring (2) most people don't seem to understand the concept of a passing lane and (3) there are too many distracted drivers. Whether they're millennials on their phones or blue-haired boomers who can't see over the steering wheel, I've lost count of how many times someone has come unabated right into my lane and nearly crashed into me.

Today was an exception, though, and the highway beckoned. Most of the side streets still had too much gravel, which the snow had carried and deposited there, in the middle of the road. The highway would be much safer, in that regard. With that in mind, I straddled my ride, kicked the stand back behind me, pulled in the clutch, knocked it down into first and pulled out onto the street.

The weather was accommodating and I was thankful for the momentary reprieve it had granted me; however, I was far from comfortable, as I sped down the interstate. Sixty-five degrees, on a windshield-less bike, feels more like forty-five—especially when moving at a good clip and I was virtually always moving at a good clip. Still, the gloves, jacket, helmet and sun provide just enough warmth to keep my expedition enjoyable.

The speed limit, like the temperature, was sixty-five but the semi-truck in front of me, in the passing lane, didn't seem to feel the urgency to do more than fifty-five. Nonetheless, the left lane was where he'd decided he belonged. Without being too overtly obnoxious or unsafe, I tried to make my presence known, in his side mirrors, emphasizing, as best I could, that I'd prefer he speed up or get over.

He couldn't get over though. On the right was a motorcade of American-made, cruiser-style bikes, riding two bikes to a lane, stretching at least twenty rows deep. Unfortunately, the two lead bikes, as well as everyone who had fell in behind them, seemed unbothered and completely content to also maintain an eye rolling pace of fifty-five.

Most of these vehicles were piloted by leather-clad pirates with beards that would have made Santa Claus jealous. Throughout their massive crew, I didn't see a single one of them wearing a helmet, which suggested, to me anyway, that they were likely resolved to maintain this slow pace indefinitely. Again, it's difficult to ride—not just to putt around but to really ride—without a helmet.

A lot of them were wearing various facial coverings, to protect themselves from the cold, which I found comical due to the fact that a helmet would also satisfy this concern. Additionally, it would protect their heads from a crash and keep the wind out of their eyes so they could actually do the speed limit, which, in turn, would also make them safer on the highway. As with most biker gangs, though, fashion almost always triumphs over reason and, as such, they had succumbed to wearing bandannas around their faces instead of helmets on their heads.

Helmets didn't seem to be a concern of theirs, just as the truck driver didn't seem concerned with the responsibilities inherent with occupying the passing lane. The bikes and the truck had thereby trapped me. Together, they had created a sort of moving wall, slowly trudging forward, two car lengths in front of me.

The truck was blocking my view so, as I pressed him, I instinctively followed the same path as his left back tires—concerned that if I were to ride in between them (in the middle of my own lane) an animal carcass might just suddenly appear in my path.

As the journey progressed, it was becoming more and more clear that the truck operator didn't seem to care that he was in the passing lane. He was content moving at the same speed as the procession of bikers to our right. Eventually, I backed off a bit more and gave the truck a wider berth so that I could safely swing over and get behind his right tires. Nothing was in the road and I made the transition without incident.

As my impatience festered, I drifted even further out so that I was occupying the empty lane between the truck and the closest motorcycle. I knew that, in a flash, I could zip through it and continue my ride without having to consent to the will of the inconsiderate motorist in the truck who stunted my progression and hindered my vision. In parts of Europe, people use that lane between lanes all the time. Driving through Rome was nerve-wracking, it happened so often. I didn't want to elicit similar feelings in the slow-moving gang next to me but the lack of vision—the lack of an escape route—was weighing too heavily on me.

Because I'd traveled this stretch of highway many times before, I furthermore knew that, in only a few miles, the road would cease to function as a four-lane highway; with nowhere else to go, all of the traffic would be forced off an exit ramp and we'd all be subject to a double yellow, two-lane road. I'd have my lane on the right and oncoming traffic would have its lane on the left. That's it.

At that point, I decided that I had two choices: slow down to a crawl and fall way back, behind the procession of bikers, thus relegating myself to a painfully slow pilgrimage across the plains—one which could last for twenty miles—or zip past them recklessly, for a moment only, and then be on my way. To the surprise of no one who has ever seen me ride, I chose speed.

I was in fifth gear but that was only so as not to overstress my motor. At this speed, fifth was more of a comfort for the bike than a necessity for travel. For the maneuver I was planning, however, it's better to have some pop. My uncle taught me that: "You always want to have something left in the tank—you want to be able to shift into a higher gear—if you're going to be passing someone. You never know what could happen," he wisely instructed.

I remembered his sage words, as my full-fingered, gloved hand pulled in the clutch and ordered my transmission to be alert for my upcoming command. Less than a second later, I gave it when my left boot kicked my shifter downward into fourth, where it belonged. The sudden change caused my RPMs to spike and my bike lurched forward. That's what I wanted though; it gave me that redline-worthy pop I desired. Without hesitation, I ripped the throttle back and my bike screamed forward between the congregation of leather-clad, helmetless pirates and the clueless truck driver on my left.

I was already beyond the lead bikes in the motorcade when everything around me instantly faded to gray. The sky, the truck, the bikes, the road, the trees—all of it. It all lost its luster. Inside of my helmet, I heard a familiar voice tell me to "DO IT!" but, in an attempt to outrun it, I nudged the bike back into fifth and laid on the throttle. The tachometer breathed a sigh of relief and the sudden abundance of newly available, unused power propelled out of the gray world and back into the more familiar one.

As if I had rocketed past an invisible line of demarcation, everything around me instantly filled back up with color; what's more, the voice inside my head fell silent. All of this happened at the same time that I was whooshing by the biker gang, which only made my usurping of their position all the more pronounced. It was in that brief moment that something sounding like a baseball crashed against my face shield.

As my eyes readjusted themselves to the colorful world around me, they showed me the splattered carcass of a wasp, pasted across my face shield, just above my left eye. Its head was still intact and the wind was animating some of its legs but the gooey stain in the middle of my visor, where it first made contact with me, told me it wasn't not long for this world, if it was even still a part of it at all.

Little did I know that, for the next several minutes, my fate was about to become inexorably interlocked with his.

CHAPTER TWENTY-FOUR

The distance between myself and the motorcycles in my rear was already substantial when I sent my own ride into sixth gear, several seconds later, for an even greater boost of speed. With the congestion of the road behind me, the open stretch of asphalt in front of me offered an optimistic invitation to dig my tires in and carve my presence into its endless embrace.

Ahead of me, I could see the exit ramp drawing closer. It was the solitary option of all the travelers using this stretch of road. I'd be there soon... alone and unencumbered by the moving wall behind me. At that moment, as I was basking in the freedom that is synonymous with riding a motorcycle, I heard a peculiar voice that almost seemed to have emanated from within my head. This one, however, was much more familiar and seemingly concerned with my well-being. "Watch out!" I heard it warn. "They're coming."

It's hard to hear much of anything on a bike—especially when tearing down the highway at breakneck speeds. At motorcycle shows, I've seen various telecommunication devices, which can be sewn into helmet padding and used to enhance communication between a rider and a passenger. I had never used one before, though, so all my experiences with talking to someone, while riding, meant I had to kill the motor, angle my head back and listen to the instructions my companion was yelling into my helmet.

In this particular scenario, however, I had no such passenger on board; what's more, the blustering wind was crashing against the outside of my helmet and reverberating off the walls inside of it with such ferocity that it was, at that moment, just as deafening as it ever was.

From whence did this strange voice emanate then? I wasn't even concerned with its message but rather with its location. Looking down, I saw only a massive, aerodynamically-shaped, black gas tank. That and my jeans; they were wrapped around it, hugging it like a snake.

To the left, the northbound side of the highway made itself present, although I knew it would soon disappear, when I got on that quickly approaching exit ramp. To the right, there was only farmland. Above me, as always, were the heavens. I already knew what was behind me... didn't I?

Though I had perfectly suitable mirrors, I opted not to use them. Instead, I engaged the clutch, which momentarily disabled the engine. While my left glove continued to hold the instrument flush against the hand grip, I dipped my right shoulder back behind me and let it create a balance-friendly path for my head to follow. Staring back behind me, I saw five of the bikes I had just passed streaking toward my position. I didn't think much of it though—only that they too must have wanted to go faster than the pack from which they had just broken free.

"Don't slow down!" the agitated voice for which I had been searching screamed once more. The timing of that demand was particularly auspicious because this was where I usually sped up. The circular, winding exit ramp was the perfect place to lay into the corner and let it rip. Going into a corner too fast has claimed the lives of many riders but accelerating inside of them while pushing myself down, into the turn, was the best way I knew to gain a speed advantage.

It was only then that I began to envision a scenario where the bikes behind me were actually pursuing me. Something inside me suddenly validated that concern and so I leaned into the turn and took the ramp at nearly three times the recommended speed. The adversaries behind me chose to be far more conservative in their approach and that was enough to put me well out in front again.

For about a mile, mine was the only lane on the road. After that, another lane, to my left, opened up and began to fill with traffic moving in the opposite direction. There weren't many places for motorists to disperse though—just the occasional side street or business (empty fruit stands and garages mostly). Nevertheless, I was now committed to the two-lane state route, winding throughout the Ohio countryside.

Upon checking my mirrors, I could see I had a good bit of distance between myself and the bikers behind me but I knew it wouldn't hold. In front of me, slower-moving vehicles threatened to impede the flow of anyone approaching from behind them. As I considered this, that voice spoke once again: "There are five of them and one of you." I began scanning my surroundings once more, trying to find it. "Actually," it continued, "when their friends catch up, there are about fifty of them and one of you."

To my stupefaction, I then realized the voice was coming from the tiny insect splattered against my face-shield. I didn't see his mouth moving but it was definitely the point from which the sound had originated. I didn't know how he was talking—especially in a tone I could actually hear—but he was talking nonetheless.

"What am I supposed to do?!?" I yelled into my helmet. "There's too much traffic ahead."

"Don't pull over. Look for an opening," he then responded. "If you pull over, they're going to beat you half to death—maybe even all the way."

No sooner had my unapproved new passenger given his warning than I was forced to apply my brakes and downshift into a lower gear. In front of me was a blue sedan of some sort and in front of him was another semi-truck. My bike wasn't the quickest but it was quick enough to take them both if I could find an opening.

I swung close to the double yellow and tried to peer around the two vehicles to judge my probability of success in attempting such a maneuver. The road had turned into a moderate incline and, although I could see around the truck, I could not see beyond the crest of the hill in front of us. Too risky. Another car could hit me head-on and splatter me like my insectoid friend. I had to stay put.

Within seconds, the bikers I had passed were upon me. The first one had long blond hair. The top of it was tucked behind an American flag bandanna but the back of it was flowing freely in the wind. He also wore a black leather vest, adorned with some large stitchwork patch I had never seen before.

I never got a look at the front of Blondie because he came right into my lane, forcing me to drift aside, to the right, and let him pass. He continued on ahead of me and claimed the space between the blue sedan and myself. Once there, he took over the middle portion of the lane and slammed on his brakes. I engaged mine as well but not before veering back to the left-hand side of the lane so that he wasn't directly in front of me.

Though I didn't recognize the stereotypical insignia on the back of his vest, I don't believe it was the branding piece for any group of organized criminal activity. It was far more likely that he and his friends were simply just another group of fashionistas who had, as their outfits suggested, lost their own individuality, along with the ability to reason for themselves.

I felt confident that these were aged-out frat boys who traded in their Sigma Alpha Sigma T-shirts for sleeveless leather jackets and various trendy, black and orange accessories. I've been witness to both drunken frat boys and fashionable biker groups quickly devolving into collective-thinking mobs, though, so I decided to keep my thoughts to myself.

By the time we reached the top of the hill, another rider had claimed the right side of my lane and was now "sharing" it with me. He was fat—really fat. He wore a tight-fitting vest—not unlike the one the biker in front of me had donned—and his gut was spilling out over his pants, which was smudging up his yellow gas tank. His gray hair was short so he didn't seem to have any need for a bandanna. Just above his flapping chins, a pair of steampunk goggles clung tightly to his face and saved his eyes from passing debris.

To my left, oncoming traffic had ceased and the former hill became flat but I wasn't able to make my move because another gang member—this one too with long blond hair—swung out, over the double yellow, and took up a position to my left, thereby blocking any attempt I might have taken to make the lane my escape route. He was much younger—late twenties or early thirties, I'd say.

Behind me, two more of them were following closely. I was completely boxed in. Nowhere to turn that they too couldn't turn. I felt a sinking feeling in my gut. Fighting was one thing but this could easily turn into a murder scene if I didn't play everything correctly.

"Pull over!" I heard the fat one to my right bellow. We were moving much slower now and he was almost close enough to touch so I could hear his shouting.

"Don't pull over!" my dying coach then advised. I wondered if they could hear him too. For that matter, I wondered if they would hear me, under this helmet.

I flipped my face-shield up, sending the dying bug upward so that the sun shone down on him directly, and tried to explain myself to the rotund husk of a man on my right. "I'm sorry!" I started. "I just wanted to get around you guys." I knew I was wrong—that I shouldn't have passed them the way that I did but their response seemed just as inappropriate. It was about to get even more so.

Chins said nothing but instead tried to reach out and actually engage my front brakes. Instinctively, I swerved over a few inches so that he missed. His stubby arm hadn't made it onto my bike but just thinking about the devastation he could have inflicted by grabbing hold of my bike, while traveling down the highway, was enough to cause my adrenaline to surge in a way it never had before.

At that moment, I realized that this group was far more homicidal than I had originally assumed. I could have easily dropped my bike. I could have easily caused a pileup that would have likely included Chins himself as one of its victims. Over the last few months, I had been thinking that I didn't hold my life in a very high regard but, when I was confronted with someone like this—someone who clearly cared far less than me—I saw what true nihilism looked like and realized that I wasn't as empty as I thought I was.

The bike to the left of me would have kept me pinned there but he suddenly engaged his brakes and drifted back to a position behind me. He did so in order to allow an oncoming truck to pass by without smearing him. I hadn't even noticed the truck was coming because I had been so focused on Chins. After it had passed, the lead bike in front of me went left of center and swung out to block me, as if he was anticipating I would try and accelerate past him. He stayed there until his companion, who looked like he belonged to an '80s hair band, retook his position next to me. "Pull over!" he too then demanded.

"You're going to have to make a move," the wasp above me then yelled out. "Wait for the right opportunity." My heart was beating a million beats per second but I knew he was right. Apologizing and explaining away my brashness wasn't going to guarantee my safety with this crew. This wasn't fight or flight. It was flight or death.

I dropped my face-shield back down and my focus tightened immensely; I began to see the road almost as if it were a grid. The pieces around me, the gaps between them, the timing of the oncoming vehicles. My mind was making split-second calculation after calculation, trying to find the right move and the right time to commit to it. I said a quick prayer and waited for my moment.

By the time I had finished, Chins had produced a small whip from somewhere on his enormous person. When I say whip, I don't mean Indiana Jones. I mean more of a fetish-type whip—one with multiple tassels across it. He was swinging it and connecting with my wrist. The wind had pushed my jacket up over my wrists, as it usually does, and exposed my flesh to his attacks.

After the third lashing, I was actually tempted to laugh at him. It caused only the slightest discomfort—an annoyance more than anything—and I felt the urge to tell him so. I fought back that urge, though, because I didn't want to enrage him any more so than he already was. I write this because, while the tiny sex whip didn't hurt, there still existed a chance that it might catch on something and bring us all down in a gruesome vehicular death.

By now, the rest of the gang had caught up with us so a wreck would have surely meant multiple deaths—not just my own. If there was any doubt about the lengths my pursuers would go, it vanished at that point. I knew I had to get away.

My bike's design made it much nimbler than the cruisers that were surrounding me but, as I've already asserted, it certainly wasn't the fastest. It was ample, to be sure, and I knew it would smoke most standard American-made bikes but a lot of the bikes in the pack behind me were rat bikes—i.e., they were constructed from various pieces and parts so I had no idea what any of their capabilities actually were.

Regardless, I knew one thing to be undeniably true: beating someone in a street race is very rarely about how fast a bike is or how well it performs; those things certainly help, of course, but beating someone in a street race is about being able to ride better than your opponent and, more specifically, being willing and able to take risks your opponent won't or can't. When we began descending down the next hill, I got the chance to prove my theory.

Being on the top of a hill allowed me to better see the board and that gave me an advantage on which I knew I had to capitalize. I could see that in front of the blue sedan and the truck who were blocking me, there was a large stretch of open road before I would ever encounter anyone else's taillights. I could also see that the white oncoming van left an approximate seven-second gap between it and the next vehicle following it. At our current rates of speed, I also knew that van would be upon me in about five seconds.

The eighties singer must have known it too because he pulled back, content to get behind me and let the van pass, as he had already showed he was able to do. That's where he made a mistake; that's where he created an opening. I knew that after the van passed, the biker in front of me would swing out to thwart my attempt to pass. This would give Eighties enough time to resume his position to my left. I didn't give them the chance though. As soon as Eighties decelerated, I cracked the throttle back and went screaming into the redline, as I swerved left and squared myself with the impending van.

The move was insane but, in my mind, less so than remaining boxed in until I eventually ran out of road and out of opportunities. "Go! Go! Go!" the bug screamed and I heeded its words. Within an instant, I was ahead of the blue sedan and closer to a head-on collision with the van. With far less of a berth than what was reasonable, I darted in front of the sedan, placing myself between him and the semi-truck. I'm sure it must have scared him but he had six metal walls to protect him. I had none.

One second later, an irate driver in a white conversion van whipped past me and the instant he was clear, I immediately shot back out, across the yellow lines and prepared to pass the semi in front of me. I was so close to the back of the truck that I couldn't see out around it but I had logged the board before I took this position so I knew I had time to clear the pass attempt. And I did. Switching gears, as if it was as natural as blinking, I shot past him and claimed the open road in front of me as my own.

In my rearview mirror, I could see that two of the bikes behind me had eventually found their own opportunities to pass the sedan and the truck, as well. By the time they did, however, I already had a good lead on them and it got even better around the curves ahead of us. "Lean into it!" the bug instructed and I did, carving up corner after twisty corner. Eventually, I caught back up with more traffic but I timed each passing maneuver perfectly, so that I never had to slow down completely. In and out of cars and bikes I went.

I saw my stalkers do the same to a few vehicles but they were far, far behind me at this point. They weren't far enough that I felt safe, though, and so I continued to attack the traffic, as if my life depended on it, for it almost certainly did. Eventually, I could see no bikes behind me at all.

When I had the option to take a new state route, the splattered bug told me to take it and so I did. Back and forth I went, zigzagging between various state routes until I came to a better developed area with a giant Walmart beckoning me. "Pull in there," my fellow voyager commanded and I obeyed. Once in the parking lot, I followed a side road around the back of the building, back where the loading docks were, and parked next to some trees, once I was sure I was out of view from anything on the road.

At that point, I killed the ignition, removed my helmet and held it close to my face, to better examine my tiny, splattered riding coach.

CHAPTER TWENTY-FIVE

"Where'd you learn to ride like that?" the dying wasp on my helmet asked me, after I unbuckled my strap and removed the device from my head. I was uncomfortable with the little fellow's interest in my life but I did appreciate the supportive coaching he had just provided me. As I stared down at him and he waited eagerly for my response, I couldn't help but pity him, for I knew he couldn't survive much longer. The fact that he was still alive at all was a miracle in and of itself.

As I stared down at him, I flipped my visor to the "up" position and turned my helmet sideways, so I could see his face, through the inside portion of my visor, without having to put the helmet on my head. Had I not done so—had I viewed the helmet straight on—all I would have seen was his splattered body, pasted to the outside of my visor.

"Who… Who are you?" I finally managed to ask. "And how did you know those bikes were going to come after me? Come to think of it, how did you even see anything at all, other than my face?" I knew it was rude to answer a question with more questions but, in this particular case, I felt it prudent.

"Thomazzz," he buzzed. Then, with a bit more clarity, "Thomas. Thomas izzz my name."

Thomas's broken body was barely moving. His eyes seemed to be staring off into nothing, rather than focusing on me. I wasn't even sure how he was communicating at all. I wanted to ask him but I decided against it.

After coughing weakly and subsequently clearing his throat, he then cryptically explained, "I can see much in your eyezzz. I can see the confusion. You think I'm juzzzt some strange wasp but I know much more than what you give me credit for, Jamezzz Zzzinger."

"You know my name?"

"I do."

"How is that possible?" I asked the mangled insect, as it clung to life on the surface of my face-shield.

"When it'zzz time… When it's time, you'll know." Then, trying to sound a bit more upbeat, he sighed and said, "I can't seem to pry myself off your helmet. Could you give me a hand?"

I didn't want to deliver any dismal forecast concerning the remainder of his life but I also thought it was incumbent on me to not lead his hopes astray. In truth, I really didn't know *what* to say so I simply let, "You might want to stay put for now, Thomas. You don't look so good," spill out of my mouth.

Instantly, I regretted my phrasing. In such a delicate moment, however, I tried not to let him see that regret. I figured that would only make the situation worse.

Though he tried to hide it, I heard a faint tremble in his voice when he then asked, "Is it bad? Is this… Is this the end?"

As I considered how to best answer his question, I placed the helmet inside of my tail bag, on its side, with the visor still flipped up, so that Thomas's face remained pointed toward my own, in a stable position. I purposefully pretended that achieving this goal was more difficult than it actually was because, in doing so, I was able to stall my response a bit. I continued this tactic when I slowly and deliberately took a seat on the curb that formed a barrier between the parking lot and the empty field behind us—so that he and the helmet that contained his body were close to my eye level.

I could stall no longer and I still didn't know how to answer him. I didn't want to give him false hope but I didn't want to crush what little spirit he had left either. His eyes... His eyes were so fragile; they were so desperate. They made me wonder: is he asking about his life because he has something he needs to say—something he's been purposefully putting off until the last moment?

I've heard it said that people often know when they're close to death. They can feel it—just like a sick animal who purposefully wanders off, to secure its final resting place. Surely, then, he must feel it too, right? Why is he asking for my confirmation? Is it because he wants me to lie and, if that's the case, should I? Would doing so keep him from speaking whatever words I assume he wants to speak? Is impending death less obvious to him because of how sudden all of this was? Would he better accept the situation if he had been given more time to prepare for it?

I've always wondered what that would be like—to know one's natural expiration date. Would I want the stress of knowing (and all the emotions, thoughts and responsibilities that come along with knowing) or would something more sudden—something more like this—be better? In a sudden, unplanned death, people are robbed of closure but, in my own experiences, a longer, more drawn-out sentence doesn't typically yield it either.

In the movies, when people are on their hospital deathbeds, they usually get that closure. They're always imparting some kind of last wisdom to their family and/or friends and their "words to live by" are often accompanied by some sad but uplifting melody.

In my own experiences, though, that's rarely the way it goes; quite to the contrary, we don't usually get those moments at all because we're constantly pretending that it's *not* over—that there will be another day and so our loved ones' words don't have to come out now; in fact, if we do actually admit that they need to come out then, at that moment, we are subsequently admitting that the end is here. Now. Right now. And we no more want to face that terrifying truth than we want to be responsible for admitting it and (we assume) burdening the one we love with the consequences inherent within that knowledge.

For many of us, honesty like that is just too terrifying so we ignore it altogether. We pretend—we pretend not only to our loved ones but to ourselves as well. We talk instead about the mundane because we prefer to delude ourselves into the belief that there exists more time. I, therefore, always find those deathbed TV scenes to be so unnatural.

To be truthful in those situations requires no small amount of bravery so it caused me great shame when I told Thomas, "You don't know if this is the end. No one knows when his time will truly come."

Anyone looking at him could see that wasn't true though. I thought that virtually every uneasy breath, which somehow found its way out of his lungs, would be his last and that piercing truth sliced deeply into my heart. I didn't know why but this tiny being who, in most respects was a stranger to me, had touched me deeply. I began to become overwhelmed with remorse for his situation and, were I able to barter with God, I would have gladly given some of my own life force to him.

As I was thinking that thought, Thomas broke the silence and asked, once more, "So where'd you learn to ride like that?"

"Well," I began, trying to hide the fact that I was still a bit shaken but also grateful that he had moved the conversation over to something less ominous, "nobody taught me to ride like *that* but my dad is the one who taught me the basics."

"Do you two ride often?"

"No. He passed away some time ago."

"Oh." he said but then stopped. I could tell he didn't know what to say. People never know what to say. "Well, I'm zzzorry… I'm sorry to hear that," he then offered as sympathetically as he could.

"It's okay," I tried to assure him, touched that he was somehow more concerned with my own well-being than his own impending fate. "It was a long time ago."

It wasn't okay though. It would never be okay and it didn't matter how much time had elapsed. I just gave people that standard response in order to let them off the hook—so that they wouldn't feel anywhere near as uncomfortable as I did, in those situations.

What can one truly tell someone who's lost a father, a husband, a son, a mother, a wife, a daughter? I've heard it all and it's never made any difference. I've said it all, to others in that position, and I doubt it ever made any difference to them either.

"Were you close?" he then asked.

I didn't want to answer but I could see that talking about something other than himself was bringing him comfort and so, for his benefit, I provided the information. "Not really," I said honestly. "I mean, he was my dad. He was always there; he didn't desert the family or anything. He always provided. He was certainly a good and fair father but… we just kind of… butted heads for most of my life.

"The truth of the matter," I continued to explain, "is that motorcycle riding was really the first thing we ever had in common. He taught me the basics, in a parking lot, and he even went on a couple short runs with me too—illegally, of course," I chuckled to myself, "but that was it. He was too sick to do any more and, in all honesty, he was probably too sick to have even done that.

"He died shortly after that—just as we were finally starting to connect in a different dynamic. We were no longer rebellious son and stubborn, authoritative father; we were just father and son—the way he probably dreamed it up before he ever had me. It felt nice. It just… It didn't last."

"Well, it's good that you had that time together, short as it may have been," he explained. "I'm sure he wazzz grateful for it too."

"I'm sure he was…" I trailed off.

"What?" the perceptive insect asked.

"It's nothing. But don't you think we should be tr—" Before I could finish my sentence, though, he cut in and told me he wanted me to finish my thought so, reluctantly, I obliged him.

"I… I was just going to say that I feel like I didn't get a chance to ever meet his expectations—that he never got to see me 'succeed.' At the time of his death, I was an unmarried, recent college graduate, with a license to teach high school art that I hadn't' turned into a related job yet.

"Though I couldn't admit it, or even realize it, at the time, getting drunk with my friends was the only thing that was important to me. Knowing that, I think he must have been worried about me and that, of course, makes me feel guilty." I paused for a moment and then said, "I guess he probably felt unfulfilled, in that part of his life. If he could have lived only a little longer, he could have seen me 'make it'—whatever that means." Using my index and middle fingers, I made quotation marks in the air, as I was finishing my statement.

"What do you mean by that?" he coughed.

"Are you sure you want to talk about this?" I sheepishly asked, feeling guilty for speaking about myself, in a time like this.

"Yezzz… Yes. It's helping," he then affirmed. "What do you mean by him not seeing you 'make it'?"

"Honestly," I cautiously began, "it doesn't even mean the same thing to me anymore so I don't really even know why I keep saying it. I used to think that I wanted him to see I had secured a good job, purchased a house, got engaged. Just… you know: for him to have peace and security in knowing I wasn't going to starve to death, alone in an alley somewhere. It'd probably be more succinct to simply say that I wanted him to know I was going to be okay.

"Funny thing is: I know now that everything is temporary. Regardless of what happens to me—to any of us—starving alone in an alley somewhere is *always* a possibility. We're probably never 'okay,' despite what we might think about our circumstances at any given time. Everything is fluid. Careers are lost, empires fall, attitudes and priorities shift and our love for one and other diminishes but also expands—all at the same time. Even the Earth and the stars above are in constant flux. Over time, everything changes. Stability is a mirage."

"With kids, all you can do is raise them, to the bezzzt… to the best of your ability, and trust that they'll make the right choices—that they'll make the best choices available to them, when those changes come."

"You have kids?" I asked, hoping to change the subject.

"I do," he said proudly. "I have many zzzons and daughters alike and I don't feel that way about any of them. Once I'm gone, if I could, I would tell any of them who feel as you do now that regrets are pointless. They don't move anything forward. Follow your instinctzzz. They're often God's way of guiding us."

"You're surprisingly positive, Thomas," I told him bluntly. "I have a lot of respect for that."

"If you find comfort or meaning in my words, repeat them to others. Repeat them to your studentzzz… to your students, Mr. Art Teacher. The world seems more content than ever at crushing their souls."

"The kids don't stand a chance," I mumbled to myself as I looked down at my boots.

"What?" the confused bug asked.

"I… I don't have students anymore," I then corrected, in a much more confident tone. "I wasn't an art teacher for more than a couple years."

"Oh. Well, that's probably for the best. You know what they say: 'Those who can, do; those who can't, teach.'" He was quoting George Bernard Shaw and, as he was doing it, it seemed like some intangible weight had been lifted off of him. Repeating that famous line almost seemed to energize him, despite his dismal state.

* * *

"Those who can, do; those who can't, teach.'"

During my senior year of my college, I remember one of my professors reading us that quote and asking us to write a paper that would essentially stand as a defense against perceptions such as these. The funny thing is, I don't even remember what I wrote. Being that becoming a teacher was, at that time, my only real goal in life, I would think I would have some recollection as to how I defended my career choice but the fact that I don't probably points to a good move in distancing myself from that profession.

I'm sure I wrote something; I'm sure I argued passionately and I probably received an "A" but whatever it was, it was probably hollow as well.

"You don't care for teachers?" I quizzically asked Thomas.

"Never found much of a uzzze for 'em, personally," he answered.

I then thought carefully before saying, "I think there are a lot of great teachers; it's the educational process that's broken—especially in high school."

That statement was only a half-truth though. That wasn't the true reason I left education and became a cog in the corporate world. I had always had a great respect for everything teachers had to endure (especially in this modern age); after all, I had studied hard to eventually attain a piece of paper that stated I belonged amongst them and I knew—better than anyone outside of the education field—what the job truly entailed.

Still, I didn't want to pontificate on the subject, for I knew this creature was dying. Experience told me he was probably satisfied in discussing the mundane but, for reasons I can't explain, I tried to convince myself that he was holding onto some sage, movie-like final words that he would utter at just the right time. With that in mind, I decided to try and keep my responses short. I hoped that doing so would coax him to speak those words I only half-expected to hear.

Should I have decided to tell him the truth, though, it would have gone something like this: some people truly dream of teaching kids. I don't. If I'm being honest with myself, I never really did, actually. I tried to convince myself otherwise and, to a degree, I did but it was all just an elaborate deception—a ruse designed for my own detriment. I see that now.

An inner-city high school teacher, whether he likes it or not, has to be more than someone who disseminates subject matter to his students. He has to *live* for his students. He has to advocate for their success and become obsessed with helping them unlock their potential. He has to develop into an agent of change in his community—to show his students there is a way out of the cycle of crime and poverty that plagues most of their lives. He has to open their eyes to the fact that education could be their way out of the only life they've known. *That* is the job of an inner-city school teacher—at least it should be.

It took me a long time to realize it but, if I'm being truthful, to the point of self-deprecation, I have to admit that I wasn't willing to sacrifice for any of that—not for any amount of money, let alone my actual, laughable salary. I wanted my job to exist in a vacuum—one that didn't go beyond the classroom and into my students' real lives. I just loved art and I wanted a job where I could create and talk about it all day, with other like-minded individuals. That's the reason I naively and selfishly became an art teacher and that's the reason I didn't last in that profession.

My real dream… my "true" dream—the one I was too afraid to admit because admitting it meant facing the possibility of failing in it—was and always has been art itself. I didn't want to teach it; I wanted to create it.

But those voices… the voices in our heads—the ones that are so critical of us and all that we do—they would say things like, "Painting isn't about how talented you are; it's about who you know and you don't know anyone," or "Sketch artists are a dime a dozen," or "No one is going to care about anything you would have to say through art."

Eventually, I started to believe those voices. I internalized their message and let it guide my future. So, teaching kids art for themselves and teaching them about the works of other famous artists was simply a more realistic backup plan—one that I knew I could achieve without having to risk much or worry about actual failure in that well-traveled career path. Better to succeed as a teacher than to fail as an artist, I thought. Now, I'm not so sure.

"You're quite a bit more forgiving than I am," the little insect croaked, as he pulled me away from my own thoughts, "but you're actually thinking along the same linezzz as me, in criticizing the high school itself." He then coughed, took a deep, raspy wheeze of a breath and continued. "High school's more of a socializing agent than anything, izzzn't it? It'zzz… it's full of adults with broken spirits—people who have just given up and are waiting for retirement. The more time that goezzz by, the more disconnected from reality they become."

"That's a pretty generalized statement," I told him.

"Do you dizzzagree… disagree with it?" he moaned.

"A teacher's job is to inspire," I told him, after a moment of reflection. "'Teaching' is more like a side effect of that process."

"Then why don't they call them inzzzpirers?" he proudly mocked. He seemed to revel in the possibility that he had stumped me and, for his sake, I wanted to give him a credible answer, as his life was only moments from ending and this conversation seemed to be prolonging it.

At that moment, I suddenly remembered my defense of George Bernard Shaw. It basically said that there are plenty of teachers who are lacking in real-world experience and, when we encounter them, we think thoughts like "Those who can't, teach," but there are also plenty of highly successfully "real-world" professionals working in schools—especially in colleges—that haven't the foggiest idea how to teach. In their own way, those individuals can be just as detrimental to a student's growth.

With that in mind, I believe that teaching is an art form—one that not everyone can do well—and that it would be more cogent to say, "It's difficult to learn from good teachers with a poor grasp on real-life experiences but it's equally challenging to learn from experts who don't understand the art of teaching; however, when one encounters a teacher who excels in both pedagogical practices as well as proven success outside of education, one ought to pay attention."

Of course, I don't remember if I wrote that *verbatim* but I'm sure it must have been some derivation of the argument I just laid out. The only difference between now and then is the fact that I had convinced myself I was going to be that rare teacher who had mastered both sides of the coin (teaching ability and real-life knowledge) and I now know I never was.

That's not the argument I articulated though. Instead, I simply said, "You're right: schools are full of terrible teachers who care more about their tenure than they do about helping students. They've given up and they're just holding on for retirement. You've also got the teachers who just want to talk about their subject matter and try to ignore the world outside the school. They want an eight-hour day with no curveballs. I myself am guilty of being one of those.

"Then there's those who aren't masters in their subject matter. I used to think, 'Why would I listen to the English teacher who has never published anything or to the economics teacher who can't afford a new car?' I took everything too literally and I think you are too.

"Teachers shouldn't be expected to show you the way to success in every single individual facet of life. If that's your barometer then, yes: a lot of them are substandard. If, on the other hand, they imbue their students with the confidence and the basic skills to achieve their own individual goals, so they can figure out their paths for themselves, then I'd say they're succeeding as teachers."

I then waited for a moment but Thomas said nothing. After more silence ensued, I said, "Thomas, you said that, when the time was right, I would know—I would know how you knew me. I don't… I don't know how to say this; in fact, I've been avoiding it but I think that now is the time for you to say what you need to say.

"The truth is: I don't think you have much time left. I'm sorry it took me so long to be honest with you but you deserve to know. Is there anything… Is there anything at all I can do for you? Is there anything you need to say?"

After a few more seconds of silence passed, I softly called his name but I already knew he was gone—that he wouldn't answer. Ashamed of the way I handled the last moments of my disfigured friend's existence, I silently lamented his death, in the abandoned parking lot.

From out of my tail bag, I removed a bottle of water I had packed for the journey. Holding my helmet out over the somewhat verdant but still mostly white field behind me, I solemnly let the water run out, over Thomas's body, until he slid off of my helmet and disappeared into the snowy weeds below me. By the time I capped the bottle, only a few small, caked-on spots remained on my helmet. I didn't mind their presence though; in fact, I actually experienced a sense of relief that I had not removed him completely.

Though the chaos of our short relationship didn't grant me the opportunity to know him in a way I would have preferred, I could already perceive that, for the rest of my life, I would always be extremely grateful for his tutelage—for his instructions that got me here, away from the danger that had nearly engulfed me. I didn't know exactly where he had taken me but I knew I wasn't lost. I knew that simply retracing my steps and following the route he had just created would eventually get me to a point where I would recognize my surroundings and safely forge my own way home.

PART VIII

SUNDAY EVENING

CHAPTER TWENTY-SIX

It was nearly dusk by the time I awoke from the tub and opened the frosty bathroom window, in order to peer outside. There, across the horizon, I marveled at the brilliance of the heavens—how they churned together with the ever-darkening sky, to create a crimson and mauve medley of fleeting assurance. That is to say that, while the opulence of these Ohio skies presented a momentary, picturesque calmness, I lamented the unescapable truth that, within minutes, the absconding sun would surely drain them of even the most remote remnants of color.

Much in that same vein, the day's unexpected warmth had already vanished—an observation made all the more clear by the involuntary shiver that was shooting down my back. I found the sun's fading influence unmistakable, as I pulled the window shut with remorse and watched my gathering breath disappear before my eyes. With the window once again locked into a position designed to prevent the invasive cold from completely infiltrating the thin-walled room, I shut my eyes and tried to center myself in the moment.

It was then that I realized I had been absentmindedly clutching my wrist. It was throbbing in a moderately annoying way. Upon closer inspection, I recognized that the outline of my belt had been carved into the affected area I was grasping. While I tried to massage the discomfort of another night in the tub away, I told myself that at least I hadn't woken up wet this time.

While the state of my wrist had caught me slightly off guard, I was not at all surprised to see Blue waiting for me, when I opened the door, to emerge from the bathroom. He was happy to see me and the feeling was mutual. After a proper hug and kiss on the head, I let him out and prepared his bland and unimaginative dinner.

Once he was back inside and happily munching away—blissfully unaware of my impending doom—I decided that I could stomach my own filth no longer. Determined to cleanse myself, I stepped into the shower to wash away the grime I must have accumulated, while stewing in my own discontentment.

My tangled hair was greasy and painful to move. Once I smothered it with shampoo and conditioner, however, it relented in its stubbornness to remain in a stationary position. I could once again run my fingers through it effortlessly and it felt wonderful.

After I toweled off and dressed, I decided to help myself to some cold cereal. Blue watched me eat it from across the room, as he always did. Though he tried to feign indifference, I knew he was very much invested in our ritual because it frequently culminated with me allowing him to lap up the remaining milk, from out of my bowl; in fact, when handing it over to him, I almost always poured in a little extra because of how much he seemed to love it.

Before I reached that point, though, the ringing/vibrating device in my pocket rudely interrupted my meal. As I was chewing, I lifted it closer to my face and read the name on the screen. It was Chris. Again. In that moment, my guilt got the better of me so I decided to answer him. I knew he'd just keep calling until I finally did anyway. Frustratedly, I exhaled out of my nose, finished chewing, and hit the green "connect" button.

"Hey, man. How's it going?" I initially asked, before he had a chance to introduce himself.

"Good, brother! Good" he answered back enthusiastically. "How are you?!?"

"Not too bad. Just working on some cereal." I hoped to use my dinner as a precursor that would set up a respectable time boundary and, to my delight, he picked up on the cue.

"Oh!" he started. "I'm sorry, bro. I didn't realize you were eating. You want to call me back when you're done?"

"No; I've got a quick minute," I told him, trying to keep the situational time impediment intact. "What's up?" It was always like this with him—a verbal form of chess, almost. I frequently wondered if he felt it on his end too, or if it was just me.

"Oh. Okay. Hey, real quick: I wanted to run something by you, if that's okay."

"Shoot."

"Okay, so, I actually have to be down in your neck of the woods tomorrow morning. There's somebody I have to meet up with kind of early—a client. Really nice woman. You'd like her, I think. She does a lot with arts and crafts. It's really... actually... well, it's very neat what she can do. It's amazing."

He wanted me to ask him to go into more detail but I didn't take the bait. Instead, all I muttered was, "Cool."

"Anyway," he happily continued, apparently able to shrug off my deflection, "I thought maybe you might want to grab a bite to eat after I'm done."

"What time would that be?" I asked, knowing that I'd respond to whatever time he gave by stating I had something else planned that conflicted with his proposition.

"Eh, I have to be there by eight but I'll probably be done by nineish. So... maybe nine fifteen, nine thirty?"

I didn't even have to lie! I *did* have something planned at that time—or at least close enough to it. I didn't let my voice show it but I was ecstatic about being able to avoid him with honesty instead of deception. "Oh. Yeah; that's not going to work. Sorry. I actually have a doctor's appointment then," I explained. In having done so, I felt like I'd taken control of the game and I was closing in on his conversational king piece.

"Oh, okay!" he exclaimed in an over-exuberance that didn't match the situation. "Well, you could always just call me when you're done and we could do something then." And just like that, his king escaped.

"Honestly, I have no idea how long it's going to take. Don't worry about it."

"It's really not a problem," he insisted.

"I know but I'll feel bad if I'm in there for a long time. Let's just try for some other time, okay?"

"Yeah. That works. What are you doing next Friday?" And, with that statement, he'd flipped the board. If I didn't act quickly, it would be me who was checkmated.

"Crap!" I announced in staged frustration. "I've got another call coming in, Chris," I lied. "Can I just take a look at my schedule and get back to you later?"

"Of course! That's fine with me. You know you're a bro."

"Right. Okay, well, I'll talk to you soon," I attested impatiently, trying to sell the idea that my nonexistent caller was an important one.

"Okay. Good luck tomorrow. Let me know if I can help with anything."

"Will do."

I felt ashamed for lying, as I hung up the phone—so much so that I didn't even want the rest of my dinner. Blue, if he had the chance, would probably encourage my deceptive side more often because, in this instance, it had caused me to lose my appetite and subsequently present him with the rest of my cereal. Although he happily accepted my offering, he seemed confused as to whether he should eat it or drink it; however, with a bit of experimentation, he eventually found a way to drive it all into his gullet.

Not long after that exchange, I found myself in the bathroom once more, holding my bottle of sleeping pills and contemplating whether or not I was ready to submit and take a couple. Turning the bottle over in my fingers, in order to read the warning on the back that I'd already read a thousand times before, I lost my grip and reacted too slowly to recapture the plummeting collection of narcotics. The bottle then slid down, into the small gap that existed between where my wall ended and the vanity began. On my knees, I tried to reach for it but it was no use. The gap was too small and the bottle was too far back.

A moment later, Blue timidly watched me return with an industrial-grade work light, a yardstick and no shortage of determination. Whether it was the physical presence of those foreign objects, my confident strut or a combination of both, I'll never know but, for whatever reason, Blue undoubtedly felt compelled to scamper off and hide.

After taking a seat on the floor and fumbling about with the yardstick I had hoped would assist me in digging out my captured pills, I switched on the work light and pointed it at the dark crevice. Instead of proceeding with my plan to retrieve that all-important plastic bottle, however, I was unexpectedly distracted by a series of concentrated and systematic vibrations against my leg. When I paused from my task and opened up my beckoning phone, I saw that my doctor's office was on the other end. My "Hello; this is James" fell on automated ears though. The prerecorded message talking over me was just a reminder of my in person appointment tomorrow.

After I disconnected the call, I set a corresponding alarm on my phone and then sat on the floor for several minutes without moving.

I was thinking about my life—about all the recent experiences I had endured, as well as the one that was still looming over tomorrow morning. I realized, then, that this could very well be my last night in this world I'd created for myself. Whether by death from the slug in my head or by tomorrow's imprisonment, I knew nothing would ever be the same. With that in mind, I rose to my feet, propped the yardstick against the wall, used my foot to nudge the industrial light up against the tub, left the bathroom and plopped down in front of my computer.

After a few minutes, I had composed the following paragraph:

Dear _____,

For some time now, I've been trying to escape a pernicious and relentless force that's been trying to destroy me. Tomorrow, in some form or another, it's going to succeed but, before it does, there are a few things I'd like to say to you, in the form of this letter.

I then duplicated the document many times over and saved each iteration as a separately-named file. The first one I named "Aunt Angie." I then personalized the proud kinswoman's letter, after which I began writing a note where I apologized for minimizing her mental condition for so many years. I told her I finally understood, at least to some degree, some of the issues that ailed her throughout the years and that I wished I had been a little more supportive of her struggles; moreover, I told her I was sorry, that I loved her and that I wished I had been a better listener.

Once I finished, I wrote a note to Beth's parents apologizing for my antisocial behavior at the funeral and for the way I disassociated from them after it was over. I admitted I loved their daughter very much and that, even now, I still thought fondly of her.

I wrote letters to disassociated friends, my old boss and to Fisky as well. After that, I wrote a letter to Tina, where I apologized for my awful advice and, when I reached the end, I included some suggestions to improve her resume. I even wrote a letter to Officer Walcott, which served both as an apology and also as a thank-you. I told him I appreciated the fact that he treated me with the respect I didn't deserve on that fateful day six months ago.

Once the letters were completed, I stared at the blinking cursor for several moments before I printed the pages, tucked them into individual, personalized envelopes and left them on my desk, where they could easily be found. After that, I walked into the living room, removed my framed high school art teaching license, from off of the wall, and drove to the cemetery.

With all the writing I had been doing, it was nearly three in the morning by the time I arrived at the place where both my father and my wife were interred. Although it was close to home, this was the first time, since their corresponding funerals, that I'd ever visited either of their graves. Something about doing so just didn't seem right. I think, in my heart, I knew that visiting this place meant confirming several truths I didn't want to accept—truths I would have preferred to forget.

It had already begun to snow when I finally located my father's headstone. In silence, I stood there for a few minutes, while the snow gathered, like cold dandruff, on the shoulders of my heavy coat. I then knelt down and placed my framed license next to his grave. For a few moments, I watched as the falling flurries commenced in their efforts to bury the cheaply-constructed frame. When I was satisfied, I rose back up and started making tracks in the freshly fallen snow.

Ultimately, those tracks would find their way to Beth's grave. Once there, I stood silently and thought about the part I had played in all of her unhappiness. I considered, as I'd done many times before, all of the things I could have done differently—all of the things that would have kept her from leaving and subsequently getting into that car. Deep down, however, I had finally come to accept that the past was unalterable and, as such, I had to let go. So, in a cathartic moment, I placed my hand on her headstone, whispered an apology and closed my eyes.

I held them shut for a long time, while the wet snow and the frigid, early morning air blasted the back of my neck. Undeterred by the elements, I remained in a calm, meditative state. When I finally reopened my eyes, however, I found myself quite dry, warm and kneeling in my tub, with my hand placed firmly on the lightly-corroded silver spigot.

* * *

My bathroom looked the same as it did when I had left it except for that oppressive, gray blandness that now permeated the room. Accepting the situation without question, I rose from the tub, walked toward the hallway door, prepared to face whatever terror was on the other side and then swung it open. The empty hallway that appeared when I did so was much longer than the one I was expecting to find. It was so long, in fact, that I could barely see where it ended. At the edge of my vision, I could just scarcely make out a tiny, rectangular light, which indicated an illuminated room beyond the closed door at the cusp of the absurdly long hallway.

Before I proceeded down it, though, I opened the bathroom's other door—the one that should have led to my bedroom. When the door squeaked open, I was surprised to learn that, from what I could tell, it contained the exact same unusually long hallway. Like its counterpart, this hallway also had a single door at the end, which, from where I stood, looked no taller than a few centimeters. Without much deliberation, I then casually strode into the corridor and began walking toward the door at the end.

In silence, I walked for several minutes—all the while stealing glances over my shoulder—as the door at the end grew larger and larger. When I finally reached it, I cautiously gripped the handle and waited. After a moment of complete silence, I put my ear to the door and strained to hear anything at all. There was nothing. When I finally twisted the knob, however, my ears detected that same clicking I heard six months ago, when that ghastly wraith first appeared in my bedroom.

Though I was afraid, I was also tired—tired of everything—and so, with a determination to see my situation through, I slowly pushed the door open and, as soon as I did, the room fell deathly silent. In that abrupt silence, from across the threshold where I was standing, I found myself staring at the same gray version of my bathroom that I had just left! Well... the same, with one key exception. In this version, my gun was resting on the counter, in plain view.

The only other discrepancy I could detect—a minor one—was in the dirty window blinds in front of me. They were flittering about as though someone had left the window behind them open and the wind was having its way with them. When I pulled them up toward the ceiling, I looked out and saw a grayed out version of my yard. Even without color, I could tell it was eerily dark outside and that, mixed with the pin drop silence surrounding me, was beginning to make me tense.

As I dropped the blinds back down and turned away from the plain and uninteresting window, I began to focus on the gun, sitting on top of the counter. It was prominently displayed right in front of me, with the barrel facing toward me, and it almost beckoned me to take hold of it. I could feel it pulling me somehow—not literally, of course, but my curiosity was raging around it and, for some reason, I could not quell my compulsion to hold it.

When I extended my arm to reach for it, however, I quickly drew back and turned my attention to a new sound I hadn't expected to hear. At first, I thought it was an animal because the noise I was picking up sounded like the tiny nails of a raccoon or a squirrel tink-tinking across the aging metal roof above me. As I turned back toward the window to investigate, the sound became more pronounced, more frequent and much more menacing.

When I finally extended the space between two of the window slats, with my thumb and index finger, to try and inconspicuously ascertain what was happening outside, the noise had grown to a full-blown roar. Instead of an animal's claws, it began to sound more like rocks, violently pelting the roof. Seconds later, my eyes confirmed my hypothesis, when, from the safety of my window, they showed me golf ball-sized chunks of hail smashing into the yard outside.

Suddenly, one of those rocks came crashing through the roof above us, like a meteor rocketing toward the Earth, and slammed into the floor, across from me, at the back of the room. As I looked up toward the newly-formed, four-inch circular hole it had carved out of the ceiling above me, I could see a dark gas seeping through, from the outside air. It moved as if it were alive, splitting off in various directions and making its way toward all four corners of the room—eating its way through them, as it passed over them, on its descent toward the floor.

In place of the ceiling and the walls it passed over, it left only a black, endless void—similar to the one I had accidentally discovered below my trailer, when fleeing from Purple. When I stared into it, I could see for miles, although there was absolutely nothing to see.

Instinctively, I spun around to exit but there was no longer any door there—just an endless sea of nothing. When I twisted back around, toward the gun, I noticed the floor was no longer present either. The nothingness had taken it. My feet were in the same position as they were when the floor ceased to exist but I no longer felt like they were supporting the weight of my body. It was more like I was floating there somehow.

The last remaining semblance of what the room was before the darkness invaded could only be found in the floating counter and the gun (and those two objects were mere seconds away from being claimed as well). Already, the growing evil had begun to make its way up the sides of the vanity, effectively erasing it, as it progressed. Out of a desperation to protect myself, I reached, with my left hand, to snag the gun before the darkness dissolved it.

In what certainly appeared to be a weightless environment, the momentum behind my frantic, erratic lunge sent my body into a slow but manageable quarter spin, which brought me horizontal with where the floor should have been. My feet shot out from under me and propelled me forward, putting my hand in front of the weapon with just enough time to grasp it. Another second and it too would have been consumed by the shapeless disease spreading throughout eternity.

* * *

Though my efforts had left me equipped with a tool I hoped was capable of saving me, I was now surrounded by total darkness. Concepts like up and down no longer held any meaning, as I floated in the seemingly endless abyss. In this situation, I hadn't much faith that the weapon in my hand would do me any good but I was nevertheless glad I possessed it, for it seemed to be my only means of protecting myself.

At that juncture, I reached into my pocket and invoked the small light on my keychain, as I had done the last time I was in a place like this. Like last time, it provided some relief against the darkness but not much. It did, however, lend me enough light to at least better inspect the pistol in my hand.

Upon closer examination, I could see the gun was similar to my own—a six-shot revolver, black, with a brown handle. It was heavy like mine too. That meant, at the very least, I would be able to use it as a blunt object.

Wanting to see if I could also use it to fire bullets, I relocated and then held the light between my teeth, in order to free both of my hands, which I would need to better check the weapon. I then released the lock that held the gun's six-chambered cylinder in place and, in doing so, it fell open and allowed me to peer inside the innards of the device.

Due to the apparent dearth in gravitational pull, the ease in which the cylinder dropped open surprised me, though I tried not to think too deeply on it. I knew I had to keep myself spry and ready to repel any potential attack.

With a conscious focus on self-preservation, I hurried to take inventory of my assets and, in doing so, learned the weapon contained five chambers primed with ammo and one that appeared, at first glance, to be empty. As I looked closer, however, into the perfectly circular space that I had hoped would have held another round nestled within it, I saw that, while it was indeed missing a bullet, it was not completely empty.

There was something small, stuck to the inside of the chamber. At first, I took the unknown object to be a piece of pocket lint but, as I looked a little more closely, I noticed that its shape was probably too smooth and well-defined for that. Its refined, geometrical shape looked man-made.

For some reason, my mind became obsessed with that small fleck of matter. I had to know what it was and so I tried sticking my smallest finger inside the chamber to fish it out. Alas, even the smallest of my digits was still too fat to scoop anything out of that minuscule space.

I had no worthwhile tools on my person and tapping on the cylinder did not release the object so I brought it up close to my face and peered inside. When it was right up to my head, it dawned on me what was inside. It was a miniature bathtub; more specifically, it was MY miniaturized bathtub!

For the next minute or so, as I floated in silence, in what (save for my light) would have been perpetual darkness, I studied the bathtub as best I could, peering at it with my giant-sized eye, from beyond the cylindrical walls that kept it out of my reach. Eventually, I accepted the oddity before me as an unexplained anomaly and pushed the cylinder back into place. Before nudging it into its locked position, however, I made sure to rotate the barrel forward so that I would skip the chamber containing my bathtub—so that an actual .357 round was in position and ready to be discharged.

As my mind raced to and fro, dissecting the improbability of my current situation, along with everything else that had befallen me over the last few days, my body hovered calmly in stasis—an inconsequential speck of matter, floating in a sea of nothingness. I felt helpless. I felt lost—physically, mentally and even spiritually. Staring down at the gun, I realized that it might be my only way out and I began to consider turning it on myself.

Just then, off in the distance, bright light began pouring out from behind what I can only describe as a crack in the empty space around me. Within seconds, it was spilling into the room, dissolving the darkness around it. It was far away at first but, as I continued to stare at it, it seemed as though I was somehow getting closer to it.

I was only about twenty feet away from reaching it when I came to an abrupt and unexpected stop. Just then, between myself and the four-foot crack, a shadowy cloud unexpectedly crept up from within the darkness below and manifested itself into the apparition that had been haunting me.

Without the presence of the white, penetrating light in between he and I, I would have never even been able to see him nor the cloud from whence he came. It made me wonder if he had always been down there, waiting for me in the dark, choosing this very moment to reveal himself.

We were face-to-faceless-face now—about fifteen feet apart—and so, out of desperation, I raised the gun and brought it level with his head. With my thumb, I tried to pull the hammer back but, before I could, the cylinder fell open, as though it had never been locked into place. This mechanical failure would have given the form before me more than enough time to advance and get his hands on me but, for some reason, he didn't approach. Instead, he just floated there, upright, blocking my way through the crack in his reality, with his presence and his self-assured, intimidating aplomb.

Not wanting to give him the chance to reconsider his decision to remain motionless, I slammed the cylinder back into place, aimed the gun at his head and, once again, the cylinder tumbled open, neutralizing the effectiveness of the weapon. Two more times, I frantically tried to get the revolver in working order and two more times, I experienced the same results, all while my nemesis took no action. He was letting me flounder and was no doubt enjoying witnessing my ineptitude in repelling him.

Just as I was about to give up, the wraith-like creature raised his arm toward me and wrapped his hand around nothing, in order to mimic my own posture, as though I was looking in a mirror. When he did this, the gun flew out of my hand and came to rest in his. My mouth was agape and, though I had just witnessed the telekinetic event with my own eyes, I struggled to believe it.

Regardless, the gun was now in his hand but the six-chambered cylinder was still hanging open, in a manner that kept it only partially attached to the rest of the weapon and, more importantly, kept it in a state where it was unable to fire. I thought that he would try and shut it, as I too had tried, but instead he just let it hang open. Before I could ask myself why he was doing this, I felt the gun begin to very slowly pull me toward it, as if I was stuck on a conveyor belt.

I tried to scream for help but, in doing so, managed only to lose the tiny flashlight that had been held in place by my teeth. Out of my peripheral, I saw it spin off into the distance, as I pleaded for the being across from me to release his invisible grasp on my life.

I had no footing and nothing onto which I could grab and so, I was unable to halt my advance toward the weapon. What's more, the closer I got, the more I began to shrink in size. By the time I reached the gun, I was small enough to fit inside one of the chambers and that's where the invisible force pulling me deposited me—inside the chamber with the bathtub.

Just as I came to rest on the floor of a room that looked like my bathroom, I could feel the entire room rising and turning slightly to the right, as if I was a passenger on some twisted carnival ride. Then the light from the crack outside was somehow rendered moot and everything went dark. That's when I heard a thunderous click, which told me the gun, with me inside of it, was now locked and loaded.

Everything inside the gun chamber was now pitch-black. On my hands and knees, I grasped for anything, in the abounding darkness, and it didn't take me long to find the familiar contours of my tub. In a panicked distress, I quickly put my hands where I believed a light switch should have been and was thrilled when my fingers actually landed on a plastic nub, in a downward position. Without a moment of delay, I flicked it upward and was overjoyed when light filled the room, revealing my bathroom.

It wasn't exactly like my bathroom though. Two major differences stuck out almost immediately—the first of which being that the switch I had just thrown wasn't a light switch at all. The plastic rectangular backing plate of the switch—the part that covered the hole in the wall and the electrical wires behind it—was still the same but the actual switch itself (the nub that I had just flicked upward) appeared to be a blue pen cap. It seemed to function the same as a regular switch; it's just that its appearance was so odd.

Aside from the switch, the only another anomaly came from the space where the doors should have been—both the one that would have led into the bedroom and the other, which opened up to the hall. The doors themselves were missing and in their places were solid walls that had been covered with lined notebook paper. It was almost as if someone had dipped them in glue and then pasted them to the walls to let them dry, like a child's paper-mache project.

The papers covering the space where my bedroom door should have been contained only one page with any handwriting on it. The rest of the many pages were blank. The space where the hallway door should have been, however, was overflowing with handwritten pages—to the point that no blank pages could be seen at all.

As much as I wanted to stay and read those enticing pages, my desire to escape my current plight was much greater and so I stepped back and examined the room more closely, looking for a way out. Solid walls with no entrance or exit, of course, meant that I was a prisoner to this strange yet familiar room. Feeling suddenly claustrophobic in that tiny space, I began running my hands against all of the walls, looking for an opening somewhere but it was to no avail.

After I had exhausted myself searching for an escape route, I sat down, on the edge of the tub, and put my head in hands. I felt like crying but my body had other plans. Instead, it began to shake violently, alerting me that another panic attack was on its way.

I stood up and grabbed the shower curtain, in hopes that standing might calm me but my involuntary convulsions caused me to rip it from the plastic rings that held it in place above my head. When I let go in disgrace, I could see that, like my own sanity, it was only half hanging there and ready to fall.

Before I could react any further, a slight glimmer caught the corner of my eye and I turned to face it. It was coming from the bathroom mirror. At first glance, it looked like my very ordinary vanity mirror; however, it quickly ceased displaying any true reflection and turned itself, instead, into a gateway—one that was showing me the world outside of the gun that I was unwillingly inhabiting. It showed me that evil, shadowy figure, in that same boundless void, floating in front of the illuminated crack. In his hand, he held the gun that had somehow imprisoned me.

Then, as if he could see me, he pointed it at me, in a manner that suggested he was planning on shooting me through the mirror. Terrified, I tried to sidestep but I had misjudged my proximity to the ledge of the tub and it caused me to fall backwards, inside of it.

The mirror then detached itself from the wall and floated over toward my face. In a pathetic effort to defend myself, I raised my arms in a defensive position and buried my head inside. Undeterred, the possessed luxury item then began to move around, toward the back of my head; I could see it doing so through the natural cracks in my folded arms.

Before it could get completely behind me, I scrambled to my knees and started to scamper over the lip of the tub, through that half-dismantled shower curtain, when a dark, lifeless hand protruded through the mirror that had been encircling me. Before I could escape over the side, it grabbed the collar of my shirt and pulled me backwards, so that my back thudded against the tub floor.

While one of the shadow being's hands was still grasping the collar of my shirt, through the mirror, the other took the gun and pressed it up against his own gassy head. Without a word, he then pulled the trigger and, in that moment, everything went black but I could feel myself—feel the entire tub—moving at an incredible speed as we no doubt passed through his head. As I clung to the side of the speeding tub, I felt like I was on a roller coaster whose track was nothing but a perpetual downward lunge (as if the engineers had never built any turns, loops or hills—just the initial maddening descent).

For what I guessed was about thirty seconds, I endured this breakneck pace until it finally began to gradually slow. Everything was as dark as it had ever been but I could tell I was still inside the tub. I couldn't see it and I couldn't see outside of it but I didn't care. I just wanted out.

When we slowed enough that I dared attempting it, I finally gathered the courage to stagger back to my knees, at which point I catapulted myself over the side of the tub, into the unfamiliar and mysterious blackness around me.

PART IX

MONDAY MORNING

CHAPTER TWENTY-SEVEN

The impact of my face smashing hard against the firm, unforgiving tile floor of my bathroom left not one shred of discomfort within me; in fact, I awoke, instead, to a joyous gratitude, emanating from deep within my soul. Though I could taste blood trickling out, from the corner of my mouth, I didn't even bother to wipe it away. Instead, I began to laugh uncontrollably.

Whether I was laughing because of the elation of having escaped back into this more familiar reality or because I simply knew no other recourse for internalizing the bizarre circumstances that led me here, I was not sure. Whatever the reason, though, laughing seemed somehow appropriate, as I lay there, bleeding on the floor.

In front of my prostrate body, I discovered the yardstick and the cumbersome work light lying right where I had left them. Peering through the space between the vanity and the wall, I could also spy the familiar bottle of sleeping pills, as if they were patiently awaiting my next attempt to retrieve them.

While staring at that bottle, as I tried to piece together the events that led to me lying there, I deliberated with myself about whether or not that potent collection of prescribed narcotics was even worth retrieving anymore. As I reached into my back pocket and felt the doomsday letter resting there, I decided that they weren't and so I put them out of my mind and staggered to my feet, in the sluggish manner one might expect from someone in his early forties.

Once upright, I waited for my mind to fully adjust to my new set of circumstances and, as soon as it did, I realized that the fateful day had finally arrived. At that moment, the alarm on my phone began calling to me and didn't stop until I fished it out of my pocket and switched the reminder off.

Feeling relieved but still more hurried than I would have preferred, I threw open my bedroom door and rushed inside, scaring Blue as I darted past him to look out my window. Half expecting to see a black nothingness enveloping everything, I was greeted, instead, by lightly falling snow. As it aimlessly drifted through the sky, on its descent toward my backyard, the faintest hint of invisible sunlight had already begun diluting the once pronounced blackness of night, giving it the look of an old shirt—one that had lost its crispness through repeated washings. No: the sun itself was not yet visible but I could nonetheless feel its presence, ebbing away at the potency of the surrounding night.

As for the snow, it was sparse and it wasn't sticking to the ground but seeing it fall was enough to remind me that the chill of winter was far from relenting and loosening its grasp on the lifeless Ohio wastelands. As I had thought it might, yesterday's heatwave proved itself to be an anomaly and that knowledge convinced me—even from behind the glass barrier of my window—that there would be no motorcycle riding for me today, or anytime soon.

With no time to spare, I had gotten myself ready to go. I'd taken care of Blue, washed myself clean and changed my clothes. In doing so, I'd tried to enhance my appearance, for the sole benefit of the doctor I was bound to visit. I knew he didn't require such sacrifices but, for some reason, I felt compelled to try and impress him.

After kissing Blue's head goodbye and instructing that he be a good boy while I'm gone, I strolled outside, jumped into my truck and turned the key. The touch screen in the center console illuminated itself and began trying to connect my Bluetooth, as it always did, but, as before, the engine didn't turn over. Knowing I'd always been able to overcome this slight impediment with a little persistence, I was only mildly concerned. With that in mind, I turned the key back to the "off" position and tried again, making sure that I pushed the clutch pedal all the way to the floor this time.

When the next several attempts produced the same outcome, I grew increasingly alarmed. I didn't know much about automobiles and what little I did know wasn't applicable here. Finally, I accepted that the truck wouldn't get me to where I needed to be and so I pulled out my phone and opened up one of my two ride-sharing apps. The first one told me the closest car was twenty-five minutes away! The other one provided no cars at all and that's when I began to panic. I had friends but, given their proximity to me, even if they were awake, ready to go and patiently awaiting my call—like a starting pistol to a race—they wouldn't arrive in time.

Racking my brain for a solution, I suddenly remembered Chris. I remembered that he said he was going to be in the area. I felt guilty calling and asking for his help, after the way I'd taken him for granted, but my desperation overtook my desire to be autonomous and so I dialed him up.

As my phone attempted to connect with his, I paced back in forth, in the cold air surrounding my driveway. Were it not for the sight of my own breath, I might have thought myself dead and already in Hell.

After he answered with a "What's up, brother? I'm glad you decided to call," I explained my situation to him. I apologized for coming to him in such a desperate manner but tried to make him sympathize with the fact that I had nowhere else to turn. Chris seemed calm and understanding, which helped to alleviate some of the guilt behind my request for his assistance.

During our conversation, as I began to feel a bit more relieved, I noticed that the sun had finally begun to peek over the horizon. The orange and purplish hues surrounding it stood out against the otherwise depressingly dead and altogether barren Ohio winter landscape.

At that moment, while I was basking in the beauty of the sunrise, I suddenly become cognizant of a dip in the conversation—the kind that signaled I'd allowed myself to become distracted and, as such, the person on the other end was silently waiting for an answer of some kind (my address, to be more specific). I then composed myself, gave him the information he'd requested and also relayed to him the general vicinity of my doctor's office. He told me he knew the place well and that he was happy to help.

It's strange but I actually believed him too—that he was *happy* to help. Just before hanging up, he explained that he was only a few minutes away, which alleviated the dread that had been building in my heart. Thanks to Chris, it seemed like I'd make it after all.

* * *

Chris's had his music cranked so I heard him approaching, from down the street, as I nervously sat on my front step, huddled inside of my coat while awaiting his imminent arrival. Seconds later, when his Jeep Wrangler slowly came to rest right behind my truck, I saw that it had icy, muddy, salty slop caked all over it. That seemingly insignificant detail was funny to me, for this was not at all the type of vehicle I would have assumed he would have driven. Looking at it made me fondly remember my own Wrangler—the most fun I'd ever had on four wheels.

When I stood up, Chris shouted, "Great to see you, brother!" from behind his rolled-down window. He wasn't even trying to contain the massive grin that had spread across his face, as he stuck his head out and proudly displayed it to me. He wanted to help me so badly that it didn't even seem natural so, as I made my way toward his ride, I told myself: I guess I'll let him.

The rising sun was steadily dissolving the night, at a rate that made me take notice and question whether or not I was perceiving the star's beautiful, yet commonplace ascendance correctly. While making my way toward Chris's Jeep, I marveled in its glory, as if I was seeing it for the first time. Eventually, I accepted what my eyes were showing me and I took solace in the fact that the darkness lingering around me was fading rapidly.

In this critical moment, when the scales of night and day finally began to tip toward the latter, Chris probably didn't need his headlights but he had them on anyway and they were all I could see, when I stepped in front of his vehicle and approached the passenger side door. Once there, I opened it, took a seat, shut the door and locked it, as I always did, with a perfunctory indifference.

Chris's headlights were bright but it was bright inside the vehicle too. The sun had already begun to poke over the tree line and, in doing so, it had risen enough to penetrate the glass, in a near blinding fashion. It was coming through brightly, from Chris's driver's side window—so much so that I had to lower my head and cover my eyes just to see him.

Despite fully believing what my eyes were showing me, I found the expedited manner of this celestial body's ascension odd (almost unnatural), for it was not long ago it was barely visible. Now, however, it was rising toward the heavens and radiating its brilliance through the prism of Chris's window. It was quite a sight to behold.

I hadn't seen Chris face-to-face in some time; in fact, I'd almost forgotten what he looked like. His olive complexion accented his dark beard well. As I said before, the man was at least ten years my junior but he gave off an aura that made him appear much wiser than his age suggested. He was wearing sunglasses, a white leather coat and a style of jeans I'd not seen before, though he was certainly pulling them off. All in all, his outfit was well-suited to complement his hair, which he had stylishly pulled up into a fashionable bun, on top of his head.

Through the vehicle's speakers, he played foreign music, sung in a language I didn't understand. He must have sensed my discomfort with it because he shut it off the second it started to make me feel stupid for not comprehending it. I began to explain that he didn't have to turn it off and that I was enjoying the music but he somehow knew I was lying and told me it was okay—that he was tired of listening to it and that he'd rather chat anyway.

Chris must have noticed me squinting because, at this juncture, before we'd even ventured out of the trailer park, he offered me his sunglasses. "Uh, sure, if you've got another pair," I told him.

"Here you go." And with that, he removed the sunglasses he was wearing and offered them to me.

"Oh!" I embarrassedly shot back. "I didn't realize you meant *your* pair. No. You keep them. I'm fine."

"I don't need them," he insisted, as we slowly crested over one of the speed bumps, which had been strategically placed there to keep hooligans from speeding through the park. "The light doesn't bother me. Here you go, brother."

"You're driving. You need them more than me," I argued.

"No. Really. I don't need them. Trust my word. I'm fine. Take them."

At this point, I would have felt even more rude refusing his sacrifice and I could see he was determined that I accept his gift and so, reluctantly, I did.

"Thanks for calling me, brother," he then gushed, as he turned out of my neighborhood and toward the familiar highway that ran alongside of it. "I've been wanting to connect with you for a while now."

Why was *he* thanking *me*? What a strange position to take. He was the one doing me a favor and after I had treated him so badly too. Though his words were completely sincere, I couldn't help but feel guilt welling up inside of my soul.

"Hey, man, you're doing *me* a favor," I eventually told him. "*I* should be thanking *you*. And I am. Thank you. Seriously: thank you."

"Not a problem, bro!"

His accent was slight but, to the trained ear, it was still detectable. I was able to key in on it more when he uttered certain phrases, like the one he just exclaimed. It made me want to ask him more about where he was from; I wanted to suddenly hear more about his life but I was afraid to ask. I was afraid that, at this point, it would be rude to ask; it would have been rude to admit that, after all this time, I still barely knew him.

Wallowing in my own guilt, I let the moment pass and, in doing so, he took the opportunity to fill the dead air with words of his own. "The doctor you're going to see—I actually know him pretty well," he said with a smile.

"Really?"

"Yes indeed."

"You go there?"

"I suppose you might say that," he answered. I thought about his cryptic answer for a bit but that only served to further confuse me. I was afraid of feeling stupid, though, so I didn't ask him to explain. There was something intimidating about him and I was only then beginning to realize it.

Perhaps that's why I'd been avoiding him so—not because he was annoying me but because he was, in many ways, beyond me. I often didn't understand his words or why he acted the way he did and that made me feel inferior. Someone less prideful would have probably asked for an explanation but, alas, I was not gifted with a dearth in hubris.

After I let another opportunity to question him pass, he asked me about my current situation: how I was doing, what I planned to do moving forward and if he could help in any way. I knew our ride would be a short one and, for that reason, I didn't want to get into a lot of details but I felt he deserved something more genuine than what I had currently offered him and so I told him that I was unsure with life—how to live it, what I wanted from it and why anyone even bothered with any of it.

I didn't admit that I was on the brink of ending it and, oddly enough, in that moment, I no longer felt like I wanted to either. As I briefly explained the trials and tribulations that led to my depression, I actually felt optimistic for the first time, in quite a while. He was listening… actually "listening" and, though I didn't deserve his compassion, I was glad to have it.

By the time I finished talking, we found ourselves pulling into the doctor's office. What a selfish thing to do—to monopolize the conversation like that. I barely gave him a chance to get a word in. I realized then that he was far more patient that I, for I wouldn't have been able to listen that long without interjecting my own opinions, quips or questions. I actually envied that patience of his and so I decided that I should strive to attain a similar disposition in my own life—if, that is, my life was able to continue on after I turned over the note in my back pocket.

In as humble a manner as I could muster, I thanked Chris for the ride and then added, "I would have never made it here without you."

"I know," he answered. "That's what I'm here for." Then, as he pulled up to the front door of the small office building, he said, "We'll have plenty of time to talk later. Just do me a favor, bro, and listen to what the doctor tells you, okay?" I nodded my head with conviction because I actually meant it. After having done so, he asked, "Do you want me to pick you up after your appointment?"

"No. I'll be fine. I'm going to text my other buddy. He'll be able to grab me and, if not, I can always get an Uber."

"Well, it's no problem if you change your mind, brother. I'm always just a phone call away!" he excitedly proclaimed.

"All right. Bye. Thanks for the ride!" And with that, I stepped out of the Jeep and watched as he drove off, into the distance.

* * *

As I walked toward the entrance of my psychiatrist's building, I reached to remove my sunglasses and suddenly remembered they weren't mine. I further realized that Chris must have seen me wearing them when he said goodbye and, despite that fact, he didn't bother asking me to return them. That guy—there was something... "off" about him. But in a good way, I posited.

The door to the doctor's office was unlocked—offering me no resistance, as I pried it open and stepped inside the quaint little reception area. At first glance, I guessed there were around twelve chairs, scattered about the room—all of them empty.

As I approached the reception window, I discovered that it too was vacant. Obeying the laminated "Please Sign In" memorandum taped to the glass divider, I bowed my head and located the clipboard, resting on the counter space below. In the middle of that clipboard was a bright yellow sticky note, with a handwritten message that read, "Mr. Singer, please sign in and head to room #1. Sorry! We're short on staff☺"

The writing on the note, unlike the signature on any of my prescriptions, was actually legible so I knew my doctor hadn't produced it. I assumed it came from the grumpy receptionist with whom I had spoken several days ago. Strange how someone with such a pessimistic outlook could wield such beautiful handwriting.

Judging by the whimsical and artistically flowing nature of her penmanship—complete with her exaggerated loops and her playfully placed smiley face at the end—I couldn't help but wonder if she, in some way, had recently adopted a more optimistic outlook than the one she had exhibited on the phone a few days earlier. A small part of me hoped I'd get the chance to ask her before I left.

Shrugging off the perceived anomaly, I signed my name to the sheet, noted the time and opened the heavy oak door, which I presumed led back to Room #1. As I progressed toward it, down the narrow, white-walled hallway, I didn't see any patients or staff milling about.

Had I not been left the personalized instructions at the front desk, I would have begun to worry but, while irregular, I could still understand the strange situation in which I found myself. I reasoned that there was no use in worrying about it and so, upon reaching Room #1, I opened the door and stepped inside.

The room wasn't very large and its furnishings were sparse: just two brown, comfortable-looking chairs, a small brown couch, in the corner, and a coffee table, with a box of tissues resting on top of it. It was a small but intimate little room with brown carpeting, beige walls and a lone window hidden behind dark brown blinds. It also had a large, rectangular, industrial-type light fixture on the ceiling.

After I plopped down, into one of the two chairs, I spent a few disinterested minutes perusing some inconsequential news story on my phone. It was not long, however, before I started to grow impatient. In my growing annoyance, I raised myself off of the surprisingly comfortable seat and strolled out into the hallway so that I was hanging half into it and half into the room.

"Hello?" I called out, as I scanned the room for life. No audible response. No movement either. I waited for about thirty seconds and then tried again. Nothing. No response at all.

Letting out an overly dramatic sigh, I walked dejectedly back into the room and began pacing back and forth—a nervous habit of mine that I sometimes exhibited when my anxiety was on the rise. I walked toward the wall, then toward the door. Wall. Door. Wall. Door. This pattern continued for a minute or so. It ceased when I reached the wall, turned and then saw that the door had completely vanished. In the place where it should have been, there was just more wall.

Cautiously, I approached the newly-discovered surface and placed my hand on it. It was solid and it showed no trace of any door ever having been there. Then, before my fear could begin to manifest itself, I suddenly felt a strange but comforting warmth that I cannot accurately describe. All I can try to explain is that it felt like I was standing under a waterfall of pure, concentrated love.

It was so intense I couldn't help but weep tears of joy. In that moment, the light above began to glow and it quickly grew brighter and brighter until it reached an intensity that wouldn't have been mechanically possible. The whole room was enveloped in a magnificent, purifying white light that overtook everything else so that nothing but its radiance was visible. It existed as perfected, glorious, positive energy and it was wrapping me in a love I had never felt before.

Basking in its glow, I fell to my knees and my crying quickly progressed into uncontrollable sobbing—the kind of sobbing in which my father always told me men should never partake. I couldn't help it though. The energy... the light... it was penetrating my very soul and it was both encouraging and terrifying at the same time.

It's terrifying for I knew, without a doubt, that I didn't deserve the love it was relentlessly casting onto me but it was also encouraging because I received it anyway and I knew I'd do anything to stay there, letting it fill me up.

My face was buried in my hands when I felt the creature inside of my head push up against my fingers. Instinctively, I pulled my head back, away from my cupped hands, and, as soon as I did so, the slug that had been living inside of me fell out of my head and onto a floor I couldn't even see. For a few seconds, it was pathetically writhing there, in agony, until it suddenly burst into flames and then completely disappeared into the light.

With my body trembling, from the amount of love coursing through it, the light then spoke to me. It didn't use language though. It didn't use traditional communication of *any* sort. It simply… "opened me" and, in doing so, it bestowed on me a clarity that I had never before experienced.

It didn't say "Do this" or "Do that" or "I think this" or "Have you tried that?" It simply imparted everything I had ever needed to know, without uttering a single word.

It "showed" me more than it "told" me but even that explanation is lacking in clarity, for it didn't "show" me any images, objects or anything tangible at all, for that matter. With complete transparency, however, I was able to ascertain its message—despite the fact that the whole experience felt as if the light surrounding me had some sort of supernatural bond with my soul and my body was only catching the basic gist of their conversation.

Since no words, pictures, gestures or any other communication forms I've ever known were used, it would be impossible for me to recount, in my own comparatively primitive language, exactly what, in particular, was relayed but, with that disclaimer in mind, I'll try my best to explain, given my limited capabilities.

Still, I can't overstate that any explanation I give will be infantile, at best, and that makes me not even want to try and divulge what I'd discovered in that light; however, I think it's important that the world learns what I have and so I'll try to reproduce the message, in the same way that a toddler with a box of broken crayons might try to reproduce the *Mona Lisa*.

In the most succinct terms, it showed me that my life was worth living, that the past did not need to define my future and that being true to myself and following my passions are the best ways of achieving the worthwhile life I thought was impossible. To my surprise, this message wasn't hidden behind some grandiose, complicated set of instructions; neither was it disguised behind an intricate set of cryptic symbols and omens that would take years to decipher. I just simply understood—as if some unexplored area of my brain had just been set free.

And, in that way, the light had educated and refocused me; it gave me "permission" to try and live the life that felt most natural and fulfilling to me. Not only that, it assured me that, with perseverance, I'd eventually be successful and that no other path I could ever take would be as fulfilling or emotionally rewarding as the one that had always been intended for me.

Then the light disappeared and I was left weeping, on my knees, in that very regular-looking doctor's office. I knew, in that moment, that something inside of me had instantly changed and, for the first time in many, many years—since the poor choices of my youth first began to obscure my path from me—I was filled with hope.

From a pragmatic or "tangible" point of view, my situation was no different than it was when I walked into that office but somehow it just doesn't seem as terminal anymore.

* * *

After the light had left me, the internal debate inside of my mind had ended and every cell in my body had come to the same unanimous decision: that I would become an agent of change—rather than stay a slave to what is. It was as if I had been reprogrammed and, in an instant, all of the doubt, depression, insecurity, pride, distrust and unease that filled my heart had been washed away. Those emotions had been replaced with a feeling of security, a sense of purpose, a calming serenity and, above all, love.

My knees were trembling, as I awkwardly rose back up to a standing position. For a moment, I stared ahead at nothing until I remembered the doomsday note in my pocket. When I fished it out and unfolded it, I watched as all of the letters slid off the pages and spilled onto the carpet below. The blank pages in my hand then turned to dust and broke apart right before my eyes. I was still reeling from the entire experience when I tentatively swung the door open. When I finally decided to walk through it, the halls were still completely silent and devoid of any activity whatsoever.

In a euphoric-like stagger, I made my way out of the office, down the empty hall, past the vacant reception room and out the front door. I encountered no one and said nothing. When the cold air entered my lungs, I felt as though it was the first time they had ever been filled with it before. I breathed deeply, savoring every moment of the experience and, after I'd had my fill, I started walking toward the direction of my trailer.

What was a relatively short drive took several hours on foot but I didn't much mind. The walk gave me time to think. Over and over, I replayed the scene in the doctor's office and pondered the life-changing ramifications of that interaction.

Somehow that light had made it evident that everything that had ever happened to me, happened so that I could be there in that moment to receive that message and that was a potent thought I couldn't ignore. The declaration I had received was inspiring and instantly transformative. During my walk home, I could think of nothing else.

PART X

FINALE

CHAPTER TWENTY-EIGHT

It was early afternoon by the time I finally reached my driveway. It was still cold but the sun was high and shining brightly, which, in some strange way, seemed to make everything much more manageable. Blue was eager to greet me when I pushed through my front door but I was deep in thought and, as such, I barely acknowledged him. Undeterred by my rude behavior, he followed the snowy, muddy tracks my boots were making all the way into the bedroom.

Once we were both there, I tossed my soggy coat onto the bed, took a seat next to it and then kicked off my sloppy, disgusting boots. For the next several minutes, I just stared at the wall in front of me, revering that magical white light I had just encountered. When Blue finally worked up the nerve to approach me and nudge his snout against my leg, it pulled my attention back to the room we both occupied. As I once again became present in the moment, I smiled at my friend and acknowledged him with a few gentle pats on his eagerly awaiting head.

While looking down at him, I suddenly noticed the slush I had drug in with me and so I leapt off of the bed, in order to address it with haste. Muttering under my breath, as I did so, I hurried into the kitchen, obtained a roll of paper towels and then briskly made my way back into the bedroom, while being careful to avoid all of the wet spots my boots had made. When I got back to my bed, I dropped to my knees and began sopping up the mess I had made but I stopped when something caught my eye.

Blue was watching with an obvious curiosity when I crawled a few inches forward, to the base of my nightstand, and shined my keychain light in between the legs of the cheaply-constructed piece of furniture. There, I found my missing ammunition: one, two, three, four, five... five bullets were scattered about, underneath the nightstand—next to a crack in the floor, which I assumed had swallowed the sixth. I hadn't lost them in the move! I lost them six months ago, when I frantically knocked them off the tiny, two-drawered stand, while fumbling around for them in the dark. Reaching out in front of me, I grabbed the bullet closest to me and then rose to my feet.

Still clutching the silver shafted, gold-tipped, hollow-point round, I discarded the rest of my soggy outfit, in order to change into a white T-shirt, with gray sweatpants and fresh scarlet socks. Once adorned in the forbidden outfit, I deposited the solitary round into my new pants pocket, crawled into bed and then pulled the covers up to my neck. The new clothes and the soft bed felt like heaven—especially when compared to my tub—so, much to the befuddlement of my dog, I closed my eyes, in the middle of the afternoon, and tried to force myself to sleep. I was much too amped-up to be tired though. Instead I just lay there, waiting for my spiritual stalker to show himself.

Luckily, it didn't take him long. Before sensing anything else, I caught wind of his unmistakable rotten stink. Within seconds of noticing it, I was nearly gagging on it but I pretended otherwise. I ignored it and lay still, in order to give the impression I was asleep. Next, I heard that same clicking sound from before. It was coming from above my head, which told me that faceless wraith was hovering there, waiting for me to open my eyes and, in that moment, I happily obliged him.

As soon as my eyes beheld him, his hand shot out and grasped my throat but this time—no matter how hard he squeezed—he couldn't constrict my breathing in even the slightest manner. It felt like I was being attacked by a toddler so, without any worry for my own safety, I let him struggle for a moment before I reached my right hand out and grabbed hold of his own throat. Immediately, he began thrashing and wailing, in an attempt to break free, but it did little to affect or deter me.

Blue, as before, stayed curled up in his bed, in the corner of the room. His face was buried under a pillow but part of me was hoping it wasn't. I wanted him to witness my moment of glory but I was too intensely focused on my plan to be distracted by my undiscerning dog.

From out of the ceiling and the bedroom walls, his darkness began to manifest itself and, as I rose to a seated position, it lashed out at me. Unlike any of our previous encounters, however, this time it evaporated, in puffs of black smoke, the second it touched any part of my body. Feeling my confidence grow, as I witnessed all of this, I threw off the covers and began dragging my nemesis toward the bathroom.

He felt like a lifeless rag doll, while he howled and tried desperately to escape. In what I perceived as an act of desperation, black tentacles jettisoned themselves from his body and wrapped around my bedpost, as a means of anchoring the wraith and making it impossible for me to drag him away. It did him no good. I just kept walking and, as I did, his numerous appendages continued to stretch out further and further, in order to compensate for the increasing distance between the bedpost to which they clung and the bathroom where I was heading.

When I strode forward a few more feet, beyond the archway that separated the two rooms, I reached the tub and, once there, I halted my advance. With my free hand, I ripped open the shower curtain, stepped inside of the tub and then slammed my enemy's lifeless body down, into the porcelainly bane of my existence. His anchoring tentacles broke apart and wafted into the air, as I did so.

Finally, for the first time since encountering this wraith-like creature, I felt like I had the upper hand. He must have come to the same realization, as I pressed his neck into the floor of the tub. As I held him there, he clawed at my arm, in an effort to separate my hand from his throat. The room then began to pulsate back and forth, between the reality I knew and a grayed out version where black tentacles shot out from every direction and turned to smoke the moment they touched me. The two of us remained present as the two realties flashed around us—him howling and thrashing violently and me calmly holding him in place.

While the room continued to flash like a strobe light in a holiday-themed haunted house, I stared down at him and came to a realization—that we were two halves of the same coin but that coin was teetering, coming to the end of its spin, on the edge of a table, and only one side could land faceup. I knew it had to be me but, for the first time since he began haunting me, I actually felt sorry for him. I pitied him, for I finally knew him. I finally understood him and with that understanding came the realization that he was more lost than he'd ever know.

With the pulsating lights terrorizing my eyes, his shrieks reverberating inside my ears and his stench burning my nostrils, I reached into my pocket and removed the newly reacquired bullet. Gripping it tightly, between my thumb and my index finger, I placed the golden tip of the hollow-point round against the phantasm's forehead and began sliding it in. His shrieking intensified and the room began flashing so fast that the two realities began to look the same.

Sliding that bullet into his head was as easy as pushing a toothpick through butter. Still, I took my time. Once it was all the way in, courtesy of my thumb, I drew my hand back, let go of the monster and rose to my feet. He, on the other hand, curled into a fetal position and began to twitch. His convulsions seemed to be parallel with the strobing lights that had begun to slow their pace since I released my grasp on the demon below me. Slower… slower… slower. After each change, a new twisted position and a new agonized, tortured cry.

At that juncture, as he raised his left arm toward me, in a gesture that suggested he wanted me to grab hold of it, I knew he was utterly and thoroughly defeated. In truth, there was a part of me that wanted to help him but, as I considered doing so, it suddenly dawned on me that the only way to truly help him was to leave him to his fate and so I stepped as far back as I could—until the back of my head bumped into the shower head jutting out of the wall behind me.

Given the spatial limitations of the tub, I was still close enough for him to try and grab my leg but, when he attempted it, his arm broke apart, like waves crashing against a rock. It reformed, when he repositioned his shoulder, and it was then that he buried his head in between it, his other arm and his knees.

Seconds later, a solitary beam of light shot out of his back. Then another from his arm. Then his head. Then another out of his back.

Again and again they kept piercing his body from the inside out, until I could barely see him any longer. As I watched, in awe, I recognized that my decision to refrain from interceding on his behalf made me culpable for his impending demise; nevertheless, I felt justified in the knowledge that my future held no place for him.

Finally, he let out one more guttural scream and, with it, his entire body burst into light and he was gone and I knew, in my heart, that he was dead.

Feeling both remorse and inspiration, I looked down at the black tar he left lying there on the floor of the tub. After a few seconds, it burst into smoke and blew away to reveal my gun. Out of my peripheral vision, I could see my bedroom returning to normal but it didn't interest me as much as the abandoned weapon and so I stayed focused on the firearm at my feet.

Squatting down, I reacquired it, while thinking about the irony surrounding the instrument. I had always thought that it was my only hope—that it was the only thing that would ultimately bring me peace but, as it turns out, it was actually quite useless. It didn't help me defeat my enemy or end my suffering. In the end, to accomplish that goal, all I needed was love, forgiveness, acceptance and purpose.

There, inside that bathtub, I had let myself die and yet I was alive. For, while the old me had indeed died, the new me now lives in his place.

NOTE FROM THE AUTHOR

Dear Reader,

If you enjoyed *Compunction,* please consider leaving a review on Amazon, Goodreads or on any one of your favorite online book sellers.

In most cases, reviews are the lifeblood of an author's career so, even if yours is only a few sentences, it would still help me immensely.

Thank you in advance and, if you're so inclined, please also feel free to connect with me online:

Website: www.ehmbeeway.com
Instagram: @ehmbee_way
Facebook: Ehmbee Way
YouTube: @ehmbeeway
Tiktok: @ehmbee_way

All the best,

Ehmbee

P.S. Visit ehmbeeway.com/thankyou to download a free chapbook of poetry and join my mailing list for occasional updates and news.

ABOUT THE AUTHOR

Ehmbee Way is a former corporate success who earned his undergraduate degree in the field of education. For many years, he battled internal feelings of nihilism, alcoholism and depression. He wrote Compunction with the hope that it would help others affected by similar issues.